22

98

THE SILENT CONVERSATION

THE SILENT CONVERSATION

Caro Ramsay

SEVERN HOUSE

First world edition published in Great Britain and the USA in 2021
by Severn House, an imprint of Canongate Books Ltd,
14 High Street, Edinburgh EH1 1TE.

Trade paperback edition first published in Great Britain and the USA in 2022
by Severn House, an imprint of Canongate Books Ltd.

severnhouse.com

British Library Cataloguing-in-Publication Data
A CIP catalogue record for this title is available from the British Library.

ISBN-13: 978-0-7278-9076-4 (cased)
ISBN-13: 978-1-4483-0596-4 (trade paper)
ISBN-13: 978-1-4483-0595-7 (e-book)

This is a work of fiction. Names, characters, places and incidents
are either the product of the author's imagination or are used fictitiously.
Except where actual historical events and characters are being described
for the storyline of this novel, all situations in this publication are
fictitious and any resemblance to actual persons, living or dead,
business establishments, events or locales is purely coincidental.

All Severn House titles are printed on acid-free paper.

MIX
Paper from
responsible sources
FSC   FSC® C013056
www.fsc.org

Typeset by Palimpsest Book Production Ltd.,
Falkirk, Stirlingshire, Scotland.
Printed and bound in Great Britain by
TJ Books, Padstow, Cornwall.

PROLOGUE

The spinning wheels of his new bike splashed into the puddles, winding through the trees in the early-winter dawn on a day when it would hardly get light. He was peddling as fast as he could; he was late for school.

Again.

Maroon 5 blasting in his ears, listening to 'Moves Like Jagger' as he raced up and over the hill, the mud splattering his trousers. He stuck his legs out, lifting his feet clear of the filthy water, feeling the rush of air against his face.

He was going fast on the downhill path, then up out of the saddle for the sharp incline, his rucksack lumping from side to side, the straps digging into his shoulders as he crested the hill, huffing and puffing. Ignoring the rain in his eyes, his red, frozen fingers gripped the handlebars tightly, keeping control on the slippery, twisting path.

He was going dangerously fast now, the wind in his ears drowning out the noise of Maroon 5 from his ear buds.

He zigzagged around the metal fence, left then right.

Moving like Jagger.

By the time he saw the tarmac of the road glistening in the headlights, it was too late.

THURSDAY 24TH JUNE

The small hand, balloons of puffy skin the colour of putty, trembled as it reached up, trying to pull back the curtain to allow some light in the room. But it was too far.

It was always too far.

They had put the film on again, the one about Nemo. But right now he wanted to look out of the window to see what was going on in the garden below. He liked to know what they were up to, because, let's face it, nobody ever told him anything.

Today, they had left a doll, a soft cuddly thing, but not his Bob Bear. They left him something to eat but it was not his food.

Yesterday – or was it this morning? – they had left him cornflakes and milk. This time it was an egg sandwich and an Abernethy biscuit. And some orange juice. There was a routine, a pattern to the way the food came up on a tray and the row he would get if he hadn't eaten it all by the time they came back.

Today the sandwich and the juice would lie untouched; he wasn't in the mood. Hunger was becoming a habit.

He tried to see out of the window again, moving from one side to the other, peeking behind the curtain, holding on to the window ledge to keep steady on his feet. He could see better now. His friend wasn't there – no silent conversation across the darkness tonight. There was something he should remember. He had forgotten. There was a memory, another idea that was cloaked by the clouds in his head, a memory that slept and dissolved with the tick-tock of the clock, the daffodil clock on the wall where the hands never moved because time stood still.

ONE

The temperature in the Maltman Green had eased down to the high seventies during the evening and Carol Holman was enjoying the gentle heat of the shadows on her balcony after another blistering hot day that had bred exhaustion and short tempers. But not here, not in the paradise of the Green. Carol sat in her favourite easy chair, an unread book on her knee, pretending to work while she spied on her neighbours in the quadrangle below – the Green as they liked to call it. It was quiet now, the slow strains of 'Stranger on the Shore' floating across the grass. This afternoon, the children had been celebrating the start of the school holidays. The four Jonsson girls, of course, looking like the von Trapp family. Then the sulky, lanky boy from the duplex opposite joined them, plus some other teenagers and three younger kids Carol had never seen before. They had lain around in the sun, played on the trampoline, dipped in the hot tub, eaten the sausage rolls, the garlic bread and the pizza delivered from the Quarterhouse Deli as they discussed their plans for the long, hot summer ahead. At one point, they started dancing, supple-limbed jerking, stick-thin arms waving in the air before the sudden laughter and screaming filled the Green as Sven Jonsson put the sprinklers on. The girls got their revenge on their dad by dragging him into the shower, ignoring his comedic pleas for mercy. Then they fell silent, the older girls sitting on the stones at the wildlife pond at the far side of the Green, watching the dragonflies hover over the long grasses, the younger ones basking on the garden chairs, drying off.

Then they had disappeared like changelings in the forest, back to their own homes. The Wallaces from the Grainhouse came out to help themselves to the leftover food that was now lying covered on the long table on the Jonssons' decking. The husband, a bearded silver fox whose name sounded like Murder, was as well dressed as always in suit trousers and a white short-sleeved shirt, still cool in the heat that had everyone else frazzled. Pauline

Wallace had a wine cooler in her hand, rattling the ice inside, signalling to Sabina Jonsson that she could come out now. She placed it on the table, then arranged the wicker chairs to face the late-afternoon sun before sitting down, gathering the folds in her floaty dress, pulling the pink and purple flowers together. Carol thought it a lovely dress, but it matched the bruise on Pauline's shoulder a little too well. Carol watched as Pauline poured the wine for her husband, herself, and a third glass as the Swedish mum, Sabina, appeared from the Maltman House with her own bottle of chilled white. She strolled out in her long blue shirt and white jeans, her blonde hair fluffily dancing as she flopped on to one of the loungers, kicking the clogs off her bare feet, exhausted by the company of so many teenagers. The three of them chatted, quietly content in each other's company, too far away for Carol to eavesdrop. The Swedish dad, Sven, had retreated to his house to dry after his soaking and would join later, after having popped into his home office, settling for an espresso rather than wine.

Carol enjoyed the ever-changing tableau. She was a voyeuse on these young lives with their endless legs and bright futures. She had been watching them for four weeks now, mostly from her bedroom balcony, but sometimes from the living-room one, through her binoculars; knowledge was power and power was security. She lifted her *Daily Record* to fan herself against the suffocating heat. The Green below was airless; weather like this sucked every ounce of energy from her. She may have dozed off, startled by a cheer from her neighbours when Joshua from the deli appeared with a cool bag of Maisy Daisy ice cream. Pauline, his mum, hugged him. His dad dived for the cool box. Just for a minute, Carol wished that Joshua would look up and see her, give her a wave, or even invite her down to join them.

But he didn't. He handed over the ice cream. He kissed Sabina on the cheek and said something that made them laugh, then he was gone through the shutters, probably back to work.

Pauline put her bare feet up on the table, the floral dress draping from her legs like a curtain as she licked her cone, listening to Sabina. Wallace sat with his hand on his wife's knee, eyes closed, listening to gentle jazz drifting from a solo piano somewhere. Carol wondered what Louise, or Eloise, and her silent son were doing. Maybe they were up on their own balcony looking across at her, or maybe observing the Green, too, watching their landlords living their best life, listening to 'Summertime'.

Carol turned back to her book. She was supposed to be translating an academic paper about the ecosystems in different layers of the ocean, and at the moment she was tackling a section about the microenvironment within the carcass of a blue whale. It was very depressing, not exactly what she had intended to do with her degree, fluent in three languages, passable in another two. Ten years ago she had set off round the world, working as a language teacher during the winter, travelling in the summer. She had arrived in London, stayed there for a few months, then come north to Glasgow to walk the West Highland Way and admire the spectacular scenery of the west coast, where every turn in the path reminded her so much of home that she could walk round a corner, her eyes misting with tears. She had decided to stay on in Glasgow, doing some more work to finance a tour of the islands, so she taught Norwegian to British adults and conversational French to teenagers hoping to go Interrailing.

And that was when it had all gone wrong.

Carol closed her eyes, forcing out the memory, enjoying the chatter and the music from below, the company without the stress. The teenagers in the Green that afternoon had reminded her of the girl she used to be, the rainbow girl who swam naked in the Fjords during the summer, skinny-dipped in the winter. That girl had been stolen.

The Swedish girls would become rainbow girls in their time: they'd do well at school, stay on at university and pursue fulfilling lives; they'd visit on Mother's Day and not forget birthdays. Carol's life had been easy until that day she went out running, leaving her a husk like winter, cold and broken.

She had loved that freedom so much. Now she struggled to get through the front door. She couldn't even stand out on the balcony, thirty feet above the Green; it was too big, too wide, too high.

Carol sunk lower in her chair to protect her eyes from the glare of the evening sun, now perfectly angled to sparkle against the solar panels of the Halfhouse and the glass on the roof garden. The patio door of the Maltman House door slid open, Sven coming out with his coffee, the golden retriever Jussi trotting out after him, and the soothing tones of 'Summertime' rolled slightly louder over the Green.

The conversation fell quiet.

Carol had lived in the Quarterhouse at Maltman Green for exactly a month, and while she did not feel at home yet, she felt she was in control. There was the sense of being protected; the four houses formed a barricade between her and the outside world. Less help than she had hoped because her demons came from within.

Carol glanced at the newspaper she was fanning herself with, open at the TV listings; it was the only reason Bobby from the deli brought her the paper. She couldn't bear to read the news these days. The top of the folded page was a picture of Naomi Clearwater; she was making an appeal on the *BBC Scotland 24 Hours: Eyes and Ears* programme at nine p.m. tonight. Carol glanced at her phone: ten past eight. The caption underneath said it was the fourth anniversary today, 24th June, of four-year-old Johnny Clearwater going missing.

She couldn't imagine losing a child, with no idea what had become of them. The residents of the Green had such blissful lives, hermetically sealed within these walls from such horrors. Carol suddenly felt exhausted; but for the sound of the company below, she might have drifted off to sleep for a moment, curling up in her big chair. Maybe she did. Maybe she didn't, but she was awake again now. The sun was slowly dropping; warm air was wafting up from the Green, making the curtains billow, a sinuous wave the full length of the balcony window.

She reached down and picked the paper up, looking at Naomi Clearwater more closely. A normal woman who had lived through a terrible tragedy. Opening the newspaper, she saw the small black-and-white picture: a very familiar picture.

Eric Manson.

For a moment she stopped breathing, then she dropped the newspaper and lifted her bare foot. She stamped on his face before closing her eyes, concentrating on the sun and the music. It was summertime, and the living was easy.

Except it wasn't.

TWO

C olin Anderson rubbed a towel through his wet hair and glanced at his phone. It was nearly time to call in the order for the curry. Brenda was going to eat hers upstairs with their daughter, Claire, while he watched the programme *BBC Scotland 24 Hours: Eyes and Ears* with the guys. The programme was supposed to be about public awareness, appealing for witnesses to crimes, but it had a very popular pre-recorded filler section where an older Scottish crime was put under the spotlight, looking at how it was solved – or not, as the case may be. In the previous few weeks, the programme had covered the classic Glasgow Square Mile of Murder: Madeleine Smith, Oscar Slater, Jessie McLachlan and Dr Pritchard. Then in future weeks the more modern atrocities of Peter Tobin, Angus Sinclair and Dennis Nilsen were to be placed under the spotlight. This week was a case where DCI Colin Anderson himself had been the senior investigating officer.

The case of the Night Hunter.

Eric Manson.

Anderson had foreknowledge of the filming involved, mostly because of Elizabeth Davies from Police Scotland Media Liaison. The production company had contacted her, wanting details of any police officer who had been involved in the apprehension of Manson. After trawling through Human Resource files, requesting audition tapes, performing screen tests and then having a few sessions in the studio to check the on-screen chemistry with BBC Scotland's 'voice of the moral majority', the lovely Miss Lamont, Detective Sergeant Wilkie MacDonald had been chosen from the ranks to deliver a five-minute segment on each episode while wearing a reassuringly shiny uniform. Within three weeks, Wilkie's unsavoury past had been uncovered by a tabloid journalist, and he was bounced back to his desk in Helen Street. The general consensus of opinion was that shit happens and couldn't have happened to a nastier bloke. But with three days to go, *Eyes and Ears* and therefore Elizabeth Davies were back on the hunt for an intelligent and telegenic replacement. When the memo came round, DI Costello was overheard saying, 'So basically any cop who could read out loud and not fall off the seat.' She had considered that a high bar.

But then, in the style of fairy tales, DCI Colin Anderson had been invited into Davies' office where she explained that they wanted a voice that could add some gravitas. In these days of chronic underfunding, Police Scotland needed some good PR. He had the choice of being interviewed or doing the voiceover himself. He was well spoken and intelligent, and she liked the fact that he had a 'long-lost disabled son whom he adored'. That was how she had actually phrased it, running the tip of her pen along the words on some document she was reading. At that point Anderson had sighed and looked out at the trees behind her head. It had been very hot that day, the third day in a heatwave that was still rolling.

He had looked at her round face, her warm office, her nice comfortable life, and thought about the victims, the faces that he saw in his sleep, their emaciated limbs, the girl who had been chained to the wall, the one who had been contained in a box and left to die, the dead girl buried in the heather at the top of the Rest and Be Thankful, having run across the open hills until she could run no more. They had found her where she fell. And then the paper-thin skin of a girl who fell from the sky on to the bonnet of a Toyota Prius; the poor man who had been driving had suffered a nervous breakdown.

Another silent victim of Eric Manson.

Elizabeth Davies had then shrugged at his silence and closed her file. She asked about the blonde detective he worked with, DI Costello. 'That might be interesting,' she said. 'Two women fronting the programme.'

'She'd be a nightmare,' warned Anderson with such conviction that Davies looked alarmed. He wrote a name down on a bit of paper and slid it over to her. 'That's the officer you want to speak to.'

It was quarter past eight; he needed to get a move on. After getting dressed, he walked across the quiet hall to his son's room. The house was peaceful, an unusual interlude in what Costello called 'The Andersons' before humming the theme tune to *The Waltons*.

He could hear Claire upstairs talking, her boyfriend answering back, Skyping each other. Downstairs, Brenda was in the kitchen putting glasses, plates, cutlery on a tray, turning the oven on to warm up the serving dishes. He still felt vaguely uneasy about viewing the programme – it didn't seem right to beam the tragedy into everybody's front room. Watching it might trigger forgotten details, regrets, mistakes, things they should have seen, things they could have done to get there sooner, to save those women their terror.

Or save them, full stop.

Standing in the beam of sunlight coming in the window, he looked at Moses, snuffling in his cot, the mobile dancing in the draught. Anderson walked over and was hit in the face by one of the brightly coloured balsa wood balloons. The room was still unbearably hot, and he was concerned about Moses' chest; the wee guy didn't do too well in extreme heat and extreme cold. Norma the wiry mongrel had settled in her usual position across the doorway, ears up, tail thudding on the carpet, keeping one eye on the stairs, one eye on the cot. Anderson smiled at her before turning to look at his son sleeping, checking the ease of his breath.

Snuggling down in his favourite chair, enjoying the draught, he closed his eyes, listening to the gentle creak and whirl of the mobile as it danced and drifted. The TV programme was on soon. Wyngate was coming round to watch it, and Costello was going to try to make it. It'd be good to see them again.

'Did he fall asleep eventually?' asked Brenda, closing the oven door, wafting the heat away from her face. They had the back door open and the midge screen down. Norma had already left the guests in the front room where they waited for the TV programme to start, and trotted down the hall to the kitchen as soon as she had scented the naan bread.

'Yes. Well, I think so – every time I got up to walk away, his eyes were wide open before I got to the door. I swear he's bloody at it sometimes.'

'Oh, behave! Take that tray through. I'll be there in a minute with some drinks. Do you want a beer?'

'Non-alcoholic, yes.'

By the time Anderson had entered the front room, Costello had taken her boots off and was sitting with her feet up on the coffee table. She had a hole in the toe of her left sock.

'Oh, this is going to be good. I bet he makes a right arse of himself!' Costello snuggled down in her boss's big white sofa, took a piece of pakora and dipped it in sauce, taking care not to drip any on the fine brocade. She felt a wave of nostalgia for when Colin Anderson was a DS and his living-room floor was covered by Lego and the air scented by nappies drying on the radiators.

She even missed her boss's wife being in a foul mood. Brenda was almost civil to her these days, still scowling but agreeable with it.

'When's it on?' asked Gordon Wyngate, peering at the muted TV screen, feeling slightly sick with nerves.

'It's on this channel so we won't miss it – in fact, it should be starting any minute . . .' Anderson glanced at his phone, wondering where the evening went. Brenda appeared with a small plate of naan breads which Costello dived on as if she hadn't seen food for a fortnight, despite the fact she had to jam the pakora down her throat to make way for the starters.

'So why did they offer him the job?' asked Wyngate.

'Because he has been blessed with cheekbones that most guys would die for, and . . .' said Anderson.

'And he can read.' Costello munched her naan, licking off onion relish. 'And that's about it.'

'It's a wee bit more than that, Costello,' said Anderson, handing Wyngate a Bud Light and Costello a Coke before bumping the other settee round, so he could get a better view.

'That's right – it was more than that,' agreed Costello. 'They wanted somebody with dark hair so they looked better on screen with the wholesome Kathy.'

'That's rubbish,' said Anderson, settling in.

'It's not, you know – I read that bloody email. I think he's dyed his hair. Last time I saw him, he was going a bit grey – looked like a startled pigeon was perched on top of his napper.'

'He has that thing,' said Wyngate wistfully, 'that he'll be even more attractive with a hint of grey. I bet he's . . .'

'Shh, they're doing a bit about Johnny Clearwater,' muttered Anderson.

'So the four books, the three documentaries haven't been enough? Why are they going through it again?' moaned Costello.

'I think it's the anniversary,' suggested Wyngate.

'And there's nobody better to talk us through one of our most enduring and troubling, cold cases than the mother of the boy who went missing that hot summer afternoon.' The voice of Kathy Lamont. 'Now, Naomi Clearwater appeals for your help in finding out what really happened to little Johnny exactly four years ago today. It's rarely been out of the headlines, but please, each and every one of you, pay attention. You may have a vital piece of information, you may hold the key to his disappearance in June 2017. Here's Naomi. Please help get the wee boy back to his family where he belongs. This was recorded in Cellardyke, ten miles from St Andrews, at the Stewart Hotel, the very place where she last saw her only child.'

The screen changed to a soft green landscape, then focused on the lone figure of Naomi, talking as she strolled over the lawn of the Stewart Hotel. Her lined and troubled face, red-eyed, looked straight at the camera as she repeated the words that her son was and that somebody out there knew him, knew of him; he was the boy next door or the new boy at school. The camera caught a tear gathering slowly in her eye before tumbling down her cheek. The scene pulled back to show the lawn full of children playing. Then, slowly, the children faded and all that was left was the empty stretch of grass running down to the stream.

Wyngate and Anderson, the two dads, let out a long sigh.

'They're looking for a body,' said Costello. 'Somebody should tell her that. Anything else's cruel.'

'But no body has ever been found. There's hope.'

'No proof of life has been found,' snapped Costello. 'Johnny Clearwater's dead and hidden under a patio somewhere. They keep flinging money at it, especially trying to appease the media. It's emotional nonsense.'

The others had to accept that Costello had a point. It was Naomi Clearwater, the force of her personality, her fragility and, it had to be said, her social connections, and those of her husband, that had kept Johnny very much the focus of the media.

'She's made a career out of being the distraught mother,' said Costello. 'I think her man would rather move on. It's been four years.'

'That's a horrible thing to say,' said Wyngate, then apologized as technically he had disrespected a senior officer. Costello didn't notice.

'Well, honestly, how long are they going to spend on it? How much heartache do you want that family to go through? The future is in front of you. Operation Aries spent too much money, far too much money – and why? Because she's middle class and pretty, and because her man is a jumped-up lawyer with God on his side. And it's not often God is on the side of a lawyer, let's face it.'

'I think if God was on his side, then his son would still be with him. Oh, here we go, the bit we've been waiting for. I'll put the sound up a bit.' Anderson sat back, pressing the volume on the remote. He, too, was feeling nervous; he wanted to see what the BBC had done with the investigation he had worked so hard on.

The camera started on the road through Glen Croe, filmed at dusk, or maybe at dawn. The view was low to show the height of the rock wall towering above the road, the famous road known as the Rest and Be Thankful. The panning shot rolled along the tarmac to the one vehicle stuck at the red signal on the temporary traffic light. The camera tracked up the boot of the Toyota Prius to the back of the head of the driver, then to his hand reaching out to the car radio, his fingers turning down the volume of Deacon Blue, 'Queen of the New Year'. The engine quietened as it idled, then cut out.

The only sound now the gentle rhythmic thud of the windscreen wipers. Through the front window, the tarmac strip rolled down the glen, into the darkness, only a faint green light showing on the road from the single pole of the other traffic light.

There was a dull thud.

The screen went black.

Against the metronome of the windscreen wipers, the screen lifted from darkness. Anderson felt himself drawn in as he tried to ignore the changing views of the moor above the road, looking down upon the car, the amber lights flaring and dying in the darkness, pulsing over the naked body lying on the bonnet.

A familiar voice: 'I was sitting there waiting for the light to change. I don't think I'll ever forget that sound. She fell from the sky. I couldn't do anything . . .' And so the voice faded again, drifting behind the soundtrack of the car, the wind and the rain. The screen filled with the ascension of the rock wall.

Anderson remembered. It hadn't been raining the night Lorna Lennox fell to her death. A brave young woman, she had taken her chances and run away from Manson after he had kept her alive for what, weeks? Months? Long enough for her to be emaciated, so much that she managed to slip her manacles, removing the skin on her thumbs and wrists, and found her way out of the tunnels to the water clock, and into the black night, on to the top of the moor with no way of knowing where safety was, in what direction she should go.

So she ran.

Maybe she had spotted a light and ran towards it – the headlight of a car over in the far glen – but was so crazy with fear she misjudged it. Or maybe she just ran as any direction was away from what she was leaving behind. She ran off the top of the rock wall and fell to her death.

On the TV, Kathy Lamont was talking again. The trailer clip had passed. They had changed the subject and now words scrolled across the bottom of the screen highlighting dates and times, email addresses, confidential phone line numbers. She spoke about some Bernepoo puppies that had been stolen from a breeder in Lothian. Kathy went through each pup, pointing out the markings with the notion of making them too hot to handle, ramping up her loveliness by holding a similar puppy to her ample chest.

Anderson muttered something about that being the best way to get them drowned, but at four grand a pop, they could be dyed and moved to Ireland or south of the border. The item finished, a close-up on puppy and cleavage. Then there was a pause, and the lighting in the studio altered slightly, becoming more subdued. In the background were the ghosts of civilians manning the phones, a few uniformed cops wandering back and forth, looking busy and giving an air of authenticity. Kathy turned in her seat, looking directly to the camera, and started reading the autocue.

'And now, to talk about what it was actually like to solve one of the worst cases in Scottish criminal history, we'd like to welcome to our team Detective Sergeant Viktor Mulholland . . .'

Anderson, Costello and Wyngate cheered.

Brenda rushed into the room, leaning on the back of the settee. 'Is that him on?'

'Listen . . .' muttered Anderson.

'As part of one of our most successful cold case squads . . .'

'Who's that, then? Successful cold case squad?' asked Costello, genuinely confused.

'Us,' snapped Anderson. 'Be quiet.'

The camera angle changed and panned on to Mulholland, looking incredibly relaxed and handsome, with the right degree of concern and approachability. He said good evening and his three old colleagues started to clap. Wyngate nudged Costello's shoulder, causing her to jerk her hand. The sauce on the half-eaten pakora dripped and slid down the white brocade of the sofa, leaving a dubious-looking skid mark.

THREE

Costello stretched out on her settee, thinking about going to bed, but she had eaten too much korma at Colin's while watching Vik on TV. She was dog-tired but too wired to sleep. And it was bloody hot. The big windows that looked down to the river were wide open, but the draught was cold; the minute she closed the windows, the room was like an oven again. The time for sleep had passed, but she didn't want to spend another long night staring at the ceiling or flicking through Netflix. She yawned.

She could rewatch *Eyes and Ears*. She wasn't that interested in Naomi Clearwater's continuing search for her son, but she had been genuinely engaged by the segment they had filmed about Eric Manson and the Night Hunter – those spooky night scenes up on the moor, the creepy water clock slowly turning, passing the time for nobody. She could watch it on catch-up so she could fast-forward through the missing fishing boats and stolen designer dogs, items included so that they ticked the box for community service TV. She didn't need to watch it to know what the Night Hunter case had been about; she had lived and worked every minute of it. But she was curious to see what the programme had made of it – that fine line between sensationalism and fact. From what she had seen, even with Wyngate's excited mutterings and Anderson slurping his non-alcoholic beer, the director had been careful, getting a forensic pathologist who had not worked on the case to talk about it with medical precision. The victims had been represented by the photographs that had been released to the press at the time they had been abducted. There had been no heightened dramatic reconstructions of the horrific injuries these women had suffered, the starvation, lying in their own filth for week after week. They'd gloss over that in case the *Daily Mail* readers got upset. Those poor women, one taken after another, then another, until the investigation team had made the connection. It was Elvie McCulloch, the sister of a missing woman, who had put the case together, with one great irony: her sister was not one of Manson's victims.

Costello pressed play, thinking how enthusiastic she was in those days. Now she was tired of her work, tired of the lack of reward, tired of the police service being the public whipping boy. Even this programme was, in its own way, a celebration of the killer. It had ended with a still of Manson, a few years younger than he had been when his mother died, his wife left him and he went insane. The feature didn't fade out to an 'in memory of' followed by a slow procession of photographs and the dates of the incredibly short lives of his victims. Costello tried to remember the exact sequence of events, but her one overriding memory was of those dark tunnels, as cold and black and frightening as they had been when the prisoners of war had tunnelled them out of the hillside.

Those poor women – and right now, somewhere in the world, there would be women, kids and men, still held captive, still being tortured and exploited. Costello sighed. Human beings were a load of sick fucks and the good guys did not seem to be winning the war.

Her colleagues – younger, cleverer, smarter colleagues – were being promoted over her, when she still thought of herself as the young smart one. She was tired of them and they were tired of her. Probably, if she was honest, she was slightly more than a little pissed off with herself, a constant feeling of unease with the way the world was going and the way she was struggling to find her place in it. Maybe it was genetic; her mother had taken refuge in a bottle, taking a step sideways when she was the age Costello was now. Was that ahead of her? Her eyes looked at the television and then along at the digital display of the clock.

The date.

She was still contemplating the fact that the year was nearly half over when she heard a noise out in the hall and lifted the remote to reduce the TV volume: the lift coming up, the door opening, then quiet chatter. She silenced the TV altogether and sprang to her feet with more energy than she thought she was capable of. Going out to the hall, she walked towards the front of the flat, then stopped and listened hard.

She could hear Vik Mulholland, coming out of the lift, fresh from the success of the programme. Peering through the spyhole, she could see Vik and Elvie on the landing; they'd been an item for years now. She didn't know the other man, the one complaining that the pizza was burning his fingers. Costello did recognize the voice: a new constable – John somebody – who had been drafted in as a babysitter for Mulholland, although the rumour was that he was redundant already because Elvie McCulloch was ever present.

Vik made a comment about not being able to get the key in the lock. The younger man said something that Costello couldn't hear but it made Vik laugh. Then Elvie took the key and opened the door.

Vik Mulholland had sipped from the poisoned chalice of fame; he was on his way to becoming a public figure. Costello couldn't blame him, the dreadful year he had suffered.

It crossed her mind, only for a moment, to open the door and say hello, turning into that praying mantis of a neighbour that she detested. The thought was dead as soon as it had been born.

She had wondered if they might become friends, living across the landing; it had been a good solution to the problem of what to do with the flat.

After the shock of Mrs Craig, her neighbour, dying and leaving the flat, and most of her possessions, to Costello, she'd heard that Vik needed a ground-floor flat as he couldn't manage the stairs of his mother's flat where he was staying. Costello had suggested, not entirely seriously, that they move into the empty flat in the meantime. It was a big apartment, three bedrooms with the same view of the river. And it had a car park and a lift.

They hadn't exactly jumped at the offer, but after consideration they agreed, and had hardly spoken to Costello since. They had been grateful, though not grateful enough to invite her in. Indeed, it was too much effort to say hello to her.

So she had become a spy, not a confidante.

She watched as Elvie opened the door – this dark figure who had come into their lives during the Manson case. Elvie and her sister had lived next door to Manson; they had been the wee girls who had played in his garden.

Costello thought Dr Elvira McCulloch was unafraid of murder; in fact, she was perfectly capable of it. Just as she had that thought,

Elvie held the door open for the two men and looked back at Costello's flat with that weird thousand-yard stare she had.

Costello stood up, shame flooding through her as she thought how she had been snooping on them from behind her front door, friends and colleagues she had known for many years.

She slunk back to her sofa, bashed her head into a cushion and glared at the ceiling again.

Vik was different. His illness had changed him, and as he had faded from the team, so Wyngate had morphed into the vacancy. Not so daft, after all, young Gordon with the big ears. Maybe he had been kept back by Mulholland, assuming the role of subordinate, but now that his immediate boss had gone, he was more confident being centre stage.

Even Anderson was different, softer. He seemed incapable of thought without consulting the family about something or another. Moses had melted his heart, and she thought that if there were ever anything that could melt a man's heart, an unknown grandchild with Down's syndrome would about do it. Throw in Norma, the orphaned old dog with flatulence and a bad limp, and the Anderson family was complete.

Even Wyngate was happy at home, always making phone calls, always keen to get out of the door because there was a picnic or a trip to the cinema or a family bike ride to the park.

There was a lack of cohesion in the unit, she could feel it. The ice was breaking under her feet. She had to get out of there before she went right through and disappeared for ever.

Carol lifted her cup of green tea and walked across the kitchen, still uneasy that her translation wasn't going well; she was allowing herself to be distracted by everything. Even the rather beautiful poster on her wall, showing the different depths, the pressure and the darkness of the zones of the ocean, could be a magnet for her attention. More people had walked on the moon than had travelled to the hadal zone. It was darker than hell down there, and Carol found that rather an attractive proposition. She often had her bedtime cup of tea looking at it, using it as a barometer of her mood for the day that was drawing to a close. It had usually been down at the darker end in more recent times.

She climbed the stairs, holding her tea steady as she passed the boxes she was still unpacking, the suitcases and three bin bags on the top landing – she was sure she had stacked them up, one on top of the other two, but now they lay side by side like rotting jellyfish. Once she'd found her laptop, the carved stone pony – a present from her grandmother – her scarlet dressing gown, enough clothes to get by, and the toaster, she lost interest.

In her bedroom, she sat on her favourite chair, at the balcony, in the cover of the three large conifers that shrouded her corner of the Maltman Green. Looking over the garden, she noted with some dismay that nobody was there – it was still hot, and it looked glorious, quiet. The wild pond with the riot of colour and the stepping stones, the formal Japanese pond with the koi and the arched bridge, the twisting path, the fire pits and the chiminea. She was tempted to go down and walk around, experience the place for herself.

Carol had enjoyed watching the body language of her neighbours over the last four weeks. Sven Jonsson, with the Volvo and the ponytail, was definitely the alpha male; he protected his property, his possessions and his tenants well. His wife looked after the four girls. Pauline and the man with a name like Murder seemed very much in love still. Louise or Eloise from across the Green seemed to keep out of their way.

Carol sat back, placing her book in her lap and switched her reading light on, angling it carefully so the brightness spilled on to the Green below. She watched the other lights going off and on in the houses, imagining what the inhabitants were doing, where they were going, making up their conversations. The lights in the Halfhouse went out first: the living room, then the ground-floor hall, then the upper landing, then the bedroom. After twenty minutes the whole house fell to darkness. That duplex was a mirror of her own, a quarter, maybe an eighth of the size of the other two residences. Louise and Carol had the top two floors of a building three storeys high, narrow from front to back but wide. She loved it the minute she saw it on the internet – all that wall space. Neighbours but no neighbours. They were all on a different street.

And she lived above a fantastic deli. In the morning she'd phone down her breakfast order and then Joshua or Bobby would come up with her salmon and cheese bagel or maybe some fresh croissants. She looked down at her translation for tomorrow – pollution and algae – skim-reading it, looking for words she might need further reference on.

Something caught her eye, somebody coming down the path outside the Grainhouse, running. A female police officer. Carol put her work down to watch, then saw a man in a baseball hat follow her. The woman ducked into the shadow of the folded trampoline; her head jammed tight against the wall of the hut, her hands out, trying to disappear into its walls, the folds of plastic fanning out over her. She was doing her best to hide. Carol held her breath as the man closed in on the policewoman, walking slowly but directly. He knew exactly where she was.

Carol started to shake. Opening the balcony doors wider, she picked up her mobile and stood up, watching the horror unfold as the man turned the corner, lifting his hand and knocking the woman's hat off. The woman moved as if to get something out of her belt. He raised his hand as if to strike her. As Carol watched, the woman seemed to slump down; the man dropped her on the ground and ran back the way he had come in. Carol tried to shout down at him, warning him there was a witness, but no words would come out. She reached for her phone, clumsy, panicking fingers pressing the wrong digits for her PIN, the phone slipping through her hands. Then more movement below. Another man, moving quickly, going to the victim's aid. Trying to concentrate, Carol pressed 999, then her knees buckled and the wrought-iron base of the balcony came up to meet her.

FRIDAY 25TH JUNE
BEFORE DAWN

He sat at the window, as close as he could get to the glass. They hadn't closed the curtain properly and he could see out. He balanced Bob Bear on the window ledge beside him so he could see as well, see the lights – red and white and orange and blue – dancing around the garden, throwing a kaleidoscope of shadows on the walls. He pulled off his glasses, spat on them and cleaned them on his jumper, and looked again, cupping his hand to the darkened glass of the window, trying to see. It was dark out there, but the fairies were back in the garden.

He couldn't see much. It was out of his view, on the corner where the trampoline normally was, but he could see the fancy-dress people in brightly coloured suits walking over the Green. The whole area had been lit up now as bright as it had been at midday, and the fairies were dancing. Over the heads of the people, he looked out for his friend, but he must have been distracted, maybe by the party below. Maybe he had even been invited. The men and women had gathered in the middle of the night. He tried putting his ear to the glass – he heard nothing.

He left a mark, so he huffed on it and wiped it with his cuff. He listened more carefully – a bit of background noise, doors opening, closing, two voices shouting. He thought they sounded happy. He watched their mouths moving, silent conversations that he wanted to hear, so he stood as close to the window as he could, bracing himself. His little bony fingers under the catch, he tried to lift it.

It didn't move. It never did.

FOUR

Anderson knew that Costello had been talking ever since she had picked him up from his house, merely three hours after she had left it. He had been listening to the 'Could they not have phoned when I was still awake?' speech and the 'You can't tell me there was nobody else available' rant, before he began to drift away with the movement of the car through the hot, dark city streets. He leaned his head against the window, some instinct telling him that there was a reason why *they* had been called out.

There would always be a reason.

Costello bumped the Fiat on to the pavement, behind two squad cars, two private cars and a wall of uniformed officers standing behind the incident tape. The jerk rattled his skull against the glass, then he was aware of lights, noise, footsteps, voices on the other side of the window. He was still opening his eyes when he heard Costello snap.

'Eh?'

'Eh, what?'

'It's this place – do you remember? I've been here before, when it was a bloody bombsite. I recognize that pattern of yellow bricks.' Costello looked up at the tall walls of the building, high windows looking down on to the street. 'The Maltman Green? What a load of pretentious shit. This used to be a marmalade factory. The whole street stank of oranges.'

'Who died?' asked Anderson.

'Reputed to be a police officer, died at the scene, so they called it in immediately. Surprised the ambulance didn't take her, but they must have their reasons.'

'Bloody hell, one of our own.' He was still sighing in shock when his inspector continued as if he had not spoken.

'I came here as a rookie. The back yard was full of junkies and alkies. Stank of pish, covered in old mattresses. It had a name. What did we call it, now? Paddy Mac's Corner or something.'

'Reputed?'

'What?'

'You said she's reputed to be a police officer, or do you mean reported to be a police officer?'

'It was reported that she's reputed to be a police officer. There's no staff unaccounted for, but she's in uniform.'

Anderson looked at the huddle of police officers concentrated at the corner. 'Do we have a name?'

'Well, not that I've been told. Any officer who'd be in this area is accounted for. Still, we need to get on, give her our best game.' She paused, looking out of the rear-view mirror. 'You forget how dangerous this job can be, don't you?'

Neither of them moved. They looked at the scene, at the two high walls that met at a corner, the lower floor missing right at the angle of the corner to allow a wide steel shutter for vehicle access to the rear of the property.

'Is that why the vultures of the press are already gathering?'

'I think so. Better put our good face on and our best foot forward. We're heading over there. This building's rectangular with a huge grassy lawn on the inside, and it's gated at two of the four corners. There's a doorway in the bigger garage shutters for easy access. Once we're in, the door can be closed and we'll be free of any press intrusion.'

'So it should be an easy site to contain, then?' asked Anderson. 'Makes a pleasant change.'

'Easy to lure somebody off the street and murder them at your own convenience. Think of those two female officers who attended that false call-out only to be gunned down. One of them was only nineteen.'

'God, that's the same age as Claire. You hope you'll get through it without it ever happening in your lifetime. I hope to God it hasn't happened now. I hope it wasn't somebody we know.'

'Does it matter if we knew her or not?'

'It would to me, but not to her.'

'There's no record of any units being dispatched to this address, but two emergency calls were received from here. She was discovered by an off-duty cop, a PC from Maryhill – Callaghan or Gallagher or something. Come on, we'd better go.' Costello got out of the car, slamming the door shut with frustration, or anger, before she went striding across the pavement. Anderson followed, his heart sinking at the thought of telling yet another happy soul that their partner had died while in service – somebody who had eaten an early lunch, driven into work, sat in on their briefing with no idea it would be their last. Modern policing should be safer than this; as Costello had reminded him, it wasn't.

But a police officer shouldn't have been on her own. There should be a partner somewhere. Maybe the message had been mangled and it was the partner, Callaghan or Gallagher, who had found her.

Costello was walking ahead, muttering out of the side of her mouth, 'We need to go through this gate to get to the Green.'

Anderson muttered back, 'So if we know she's a cop, how can we not know who she is? Don't we keep track of our own people these days, for fuck's sake?'

'I just got the intel that there's a deceased female police officer on the scene, but that she'd no ID on her. From the ambulances and paramedics here, I guess the deceased was still alive when they arrived, but died despite their attentions. But they didn't think she had a chance if they got her to hospital? How quick would they have got there? Ten minutes?'

'Sounds like she bled out or something.'

Costello halted slightly at the start of the driveway into the Green, a short path of access for a vehicle, blocked by a large steel shutter the full height of the passage, a doorway cut in it, a complicated keypad at the side. The door was held open by a couple of bricks, closely guarded by one uniformed officer. Beyond that, there was another world. In the bright lights, they could see the crime scene officers crouching in the grass, the flash of the photographer, the ballet-like movement of the video camera operator in a beautiful garden of ponds, maple trees and fire pits.

Anderson nodded at the young female officer on duty at the door, showing her his ID. Costello watched him disappear through the door and along the side of the garage, as she paused to speak to her, a black girl she hadn't met previously.

'What's your name?'

'Redding?'

'Just Redding?'

'Ruby, ma'am.'

'Forget the ma'am. So what do we have?'

'One female, pronounced dead at the scene. One of the witnesses, that guy there.' Constable Redding nodded towards a man slowly walking up and down, pacing each step, backwards and forwards, dressed in a baggy white T-shirt and jeans, crumpled and dishevelled, but then, if he had been doing CPR on a colleague, keeping it going until the paramedics could attend, he had every reason to look tense. In the harsh lights of the crime scene, the distress was apparent on his pale, tear-stained face. 'He's Constable Martin Callaghan, from Maryhill. He didn't see the attack, but he caught a glimpse of the guy who chased the victim in here. By the time he got to her, she was already unconscious, struggling to breathe. He did CPR, and two residents, Mr Sven Jonsson and Mr Murdoch Wallace, came out. They kept going with the CPR while Callaghan called it in. He admits that he was panicking, though he did everything he could. But she died.' She looked at her notebook, 'Oh, and they thought there was no ID on her body, but the doctor has already been, pronounced life extinct, and he found one credit card she had tucked into the mobile phone case clipped on to her belt. The name on it is Rachel Sinclair, so I called it in while I was waiting. We don't have a Rachel Sinclair as a serving officer, according to our HR. She might have changed her name due to marriage or divorce. But – well, you'll see for yourself.'

'OK. Do you suspect that she might not be one of us?' Costello was aware her tone had come out as hopeful, as if that might make it better. It would make it simpler, but just as tragic.

'I think you should see for yourself.'

Costello nodded. There was something the young constable didn't want to say. 'OK, that's good work, Ruby. Nice and succinct. Stay on the door until relief arrives, then grab a coffee when you can. You look like you could do with it.'

'Yes, ma'am. Thank you, ma'am.'

'Like I said, forget the ma'am.' Costello lifted her leg to climb through the door, taking a quick look at the locking mechanism.

Ruby peered round the side of the door. 'She had no handbag, no mobile phone, and she had no utility belt on. So she could be ceremonial rather than operational, you know. She had a normal belt with an empty mobile phone holder, neckerchief, epaulettes like they had in the old days,' she said, talking about the uniform Costello had worn as a new recruit.

'Or was she mugged – hence no personal goods?'

'She had a skirt on.'

'A skirt?'

'Yes. Like the start of *The Bill*. And Callaghan said that he was at the top of Plantation when he noticed her, because she was a cop. We're first on the scene, so yes, maybe she was mugged and it all went wrong.'

Costello frowned, her eyes darting through the gap, watching the paramedics pack up, the machinery lying around. She stood slightly to the side to stop any onlookers seeing through the gap. Ruby Redding closed the door over slightly.

A smile passed between them.

'OK. Did you get a close look at her? Any obvious cause of death?'

'Not that I could see, but to be honest, by the time I got here, they were working on her, then she was covered in tubes, her jacket cut open, her blouse ripped. I let them get on with it. Callaghan was in a bit of a state.' She nodded in the direction of the young man, still pacing up and down. 'I think one of the neighbours has given him a cup of tea.'

'OK. Thanks. And well done.'

Anderson ignored the sideshow around the body of the deceased for the moment, walking over to Callaghan, a young man, a friendly face creased by deep wrinkles round his blue eyes. On closer inspection, he may have been a little older than the late twenties Anderson had first thought. Or maybe he was stressed and over-worked like every other cop in the force. He smelled vaguely of beer. His baggy T-shirt was creased at the bottom as if he had previously tucked it into his ill-fitting belt and now hung unevenly outside his jeans; his face was streaked with sweat, hands relent-lessly running through his short, sparse hair. Anderson introduced himself. Callaghan wiped his face with the back of his hand, as if ashamed of showing emotion.

'Are you OK?' asked Anderson, gently leading the younger man away from the dead body. 'DCI Colin Anderson. It looks like I'll be leading on this one with DI Costello, so can you tell me what happened, from the start.'

'Sorry, I'm a bit rattled, that's all. Shouldn't be really – I should be used to it.' Callaghan looked back over his shoulder to the deceased, then turned back, walking with Anderson towards wooden decking with two sofas and a central fire pit.

'I don't think you ever get used to it. And it's not often that you witness the actual passing of another human being. You never want to harden yourself to that.' He patted the younger man on the shoulder, thinking of himself at that age and how shocking it was to feel helpless while watching life ebb away.

'When on duty, I guess you feel a bit protected by the uniform.' He turned back to look at the deceased once again, his eyes starting to well up. 'You'll get the recordings from the camera, won't you?'

'Already requested. He won't get away,' Anderson reassured him, then prompted, 'So you saw her . . .?'

'Yes, I was leaving the Drunken Monkey, walking down Plantation.'

'The Drunken Monkey?'

'Yes, the Drunken Monkey, the pub on the corner there, having a drink, and I had walked out on Brewer Street, heading home, and I saw this cop in front of me. It was the cap, it kind of struck me, you know. Then there's a guy that I thought might have been giving her a bit of aggro. He was walking after her, quickly; I got a sense of something. There was a fair few folk about, but it struck me, her rushing, and then she was gone, and I saw him juke up this side alley here. When I got here, the door in the shutter was open – swinging open, I mean. This place's like Fort Knox. So I walked up, popped my head through, and there she was. No, sorry, that's wrong. I had turned into the alley when this guy comes running out and pushes me out of the way. The speed he's going at, I guessed that something had happened, so it was at that point I looked in the door, and I saw her legs – she was already on the ground, but not dead. She was gasping, choking, jerking. I called it in. She was in real trouble. I tried CPR and then the woman came out and the two guys from that house there.' He pointed to the large glass doors, open on to decking, the open-plan living room beyond low-lit in greys and creams, a blonde woman pacing behind, carrying a young child in her arms, no doubt woken by the circus. 'That's the tall guy with the ponytail; his wife's holding the kid. That wee girl came out, God knows what she saw.'

'And the other bloke?' Anderson nodded at the bearded man, still neatly dressed, looking calm in the chaos.

'He lives here – she died in his back garden. Look, I need to sit down.' He nodded to a large wooden garden table, the parasol above it closed up, neatly tied.

'Of course, wait for forensics and give a detailed statement to DC Wyngate.'

'Yes, fine. Just feel a bit shaky.'

Anderson saw Costello walk into the Green, her handbag slung across her chest like a Glasgow Corporation bus conductor, a notebook in her hand – she had probably broken her iPad again. At that moment, the two paramedics backed away, continuing their little chat, and Anderson saw the victim for the first time. On an initial glance, she did have a uniform of some kind on: short jacket, white blouse, neckerchief, one epaulette showing. Her hat was lying tilted on its peak beside her. Her skirt was crumpled but still down to her knees. The white blouse was open down the front, her neckerchief pulled down to one side where the paramedics had tried to get a line in, in an effort to get a heartbeat. A small rose pendant sat between her breasts, the red of the flower lost in the blood and bruising, but her blonde hair was still nipped neatly in the back of her neck, a few strands loose, sticking out. Her eyes stared at the sky, looking mildly surprised. He couldn't see any mass of blood, any obvious cause of death. Not that that meant anything.

He looked back at Costello who was walking quietly around the victim, keeping her distance, her eyes scanning the whole scene, dipping down every now and again to get a better look at something nearer ground level, working from the outside in, occasionally making notes or maybe doing a sketch of something. Her own plain clothes uniform was not unlike the victim's – a plain white blouse, plain black flat shoes – but Costello had on her usual navy-blue trousers which made the victim's skirt even more incongruous.

He closed his own notebook, walking over to her, disturbing her thoughts. 'What kind of uniform is that?'

'Well, I have two ideas,' said Costello.

'Two more than me,' he admitted.

'Either fancy dress or a sex worker, or a sex worker in fancy dress – so three options, actually.'

'Oh, really?' He grimaced. 'I thought you were going to say she was from another force, a bigwig here for some ceremonial dinner that nobody told us about.'

'She's wearing stockings. Believe me, she's not a cop if she's wearing stockings.'

Anderson walked up the brick lane between the two buildings, a tunnel blocked by the high steel shutter that rose the full height. The tunnel led to a garage. Once the shuttered door was closed, this place, the Maltman Green, was a fortress. He looked round at the garden to end all gardens: trees, curved paths in soft cream stone, flowerbeds, two ponds, a fountain, connected by a lawn that wouldn't have looked out of place at Lords, a summer house and a play area for the children. The two houses that opened on to the Green had huge areas of decking with patio heaters, soft garden furniture, dining tables, coffee tables lit up with fairy lights. He looked up. The buildings were three storeys high. Some windows bore a resemblance to those of the old factory; some had been converted to doors on to balconies. The two buildings on the longer sides were luxurious. Anderson could smell the money.

'It's paradise, isn't it?' he said, walking back to Costello.

'Somewhat marred by the dead body lying in the corner,' said Costello. She had checked the door again, testing the locking mechanism, the keypad. 'So what do you think has gone on here? The rest of the troops are doing door-to-door, and the CCTV is being gathered.'

'Constable Callaghan found her. He lives in the flats on Rowan Way and was walking home from the Drunken Monkey.' He repeated the police officer's story, watching Costello run it through her mind.

'Really?'

'He wasn't on duty.' He nodded at the young man, sitting talking to Wyngate, his hands tightly wrapped round a mug. From the gesticulations and pointing, Wyngate was working out who lived where around the perimeter of the Maltman Green.

'The white-shirt guy with the beard is Murdoch Wallace. This is his house – they're the owners of the folded-up trampoline. It's his wife, Pauline, who's making the tea.'

'There's a lot of people hanging around.'

'You should see the media gathering at the gate, but Jonsson says we can go in and out of the door at his garage that's two streets away.'

'O'Hare is on his way. He was held up.'

'Any ideas about the victim?'

Costello shrugged. 'No obvious wounds. She could have clonked her head, but she doesn't appear to have been strangled or stabbed, no signs of violence on her apart from those from the resus. I hope the paramedics did the right thing – so little time between her being alive and being worked on to there being no hope. Seems odd to me.' She looked around. 'O'Hare will give us the answer to that one.' Costello looked at her watch. 'Where did Callaghan bump into the attacker?'

'He rushed past him quickly on the other side of the shutter,' said Anderson. 'I think just as the passageway opens out on to the street. Our perp nearly knocked Callaghan down as he exited the scene.'

'I've checked the gate – the lock is OK, the keypad is working – so how did they get in? I have the feeling that this place is kept pretty secure and away from the grubby little fingers of the average Glaswegian punter. And what were they doing round here? Planning a sneak in? A break-in? Was she actually pretending to be a cop? Or was she a sex worker and had found this nice little place that she thought was private.'

'I doubt it. The folk who live here are pretty smart, as you would imagine. They have security cameras up there.' He pointed up to the wall of the building, the camera focused on the steel shutter. 'We'll get footage soon.' Anderson took a final look at the woman on the ground – mid-thirties, he reckoned, thick blonde hair, and too much make-up for a uniformed officer. Costello could be right; she might have been going to a fancy-dress night out somewhere, but it had gone wrong. She didn't look like a strip-pergram; the clothes were too difficult to get off. She looked more like a school mum ready to have a night out with the girls, maybe a fancy-dress hen night. That shouldn't be too difficult to trace if she had been with a group.

'So, did you get anything useful from them?' asked Anderson once DC Wyngate was in earshot. 'Were they aware of anything before?'

'Murdoch Wallace says he thought he heard a noise; he muted his TV but there was nothing after that until he heard Callaghan shout for help. He went out and took over the CPR while Callaghan called an ambulance. They have a Great Dane but it was asleep, and the big house has a dopey retriever. Neither dog reacted.'

'Norma would bark the place down,' said Anderson, paternally proud of the wiry wee mongrel. 'How's Callaghan?'

'In shock. Keeps thinking that if he'd been a bit quicker, he might've been able to do something.'

Anderson nodded. 'He'll think that for the rest of his life. Nothing prepares you for somebody dying right in front of you. It's always awful. You think you should've done something better or done something different.' He saw a flashing image pushing through his head: Sally falling from the roof of the Blue Neptune to her death. Did she fall or did she jump? It wouldn't have happened at all if he had refused to go up on the roof with her in the first place.

Hindsight was an accurate science.

'So talk me through it. What did he say?'

Wyngate topped and tailed the story that Callaghan had told him: a young cop out having a quiet drink after being in the house with the kids all day. 'He thought she might have been a high rank or something. He clocked the uniform wasn't quite right.' Wyngate checked his notes. 'Interestingly, the call handler took a call from this area, but nobody spoke. She was concerned that the person making the call didn't have the breath to speak. It might have been the victim, dying, then the phone was taken off her. The call from Callaghan came in about seven minutes later. To keep ourselves right, I'm going to put Ruby Redding on to the geography of this place. That's the Halfhouse – the big duplex over there. It's above a very expensive ladies' boutique. This one behind us is the Quarterhouse, above the deli.'

Anderson looked up, thinking how still and warm the air was in this enclosed quadrangle, slightly oppressive. He pointed to the balcony three storeys up. 'Those doors are open; they'd have a good view from up there. Give them a knock before you leave, get their statement.' He looked back at the victim. 'Did Callaghan know her?'

'Never seen her before in his life,' Wyngate said, 'but when I asked him that, his eyes drifted past me to her. Like it meant something. But I might be reading too much into it.'

'You and Mulholland are spending too much time together.'

Anderson looked over to Callaghan who was standing in the dull shadow of the Quarterhouse balcony. He was still looking over to where Rachel was lying; his eyes seemed to be searching for her soul.

FIVE

C arol slowly regained consciousness, her nightmares interrupted by the persistent noise of the entry system buzzing. Her cheek hurt, red and swollen from being jammed against the wrought iron of the balcony floor, each breath agony as she had fallen on the metal threshold of the door. She decided to stay asleep, dreaming that she was out running; the day was sunny with a cool breeze, and she was keeping a good pace round the head of the reservoir. In her dream, the run was endless and effortless. Then, as expected, the nightmare started; she heard the thudding behind her, felt teeth in her calf. Then she was face down in the grass, a sharp stone biting deep into her cheek, feet walking towards her.

She thought he was going to help.

She wasn't on the ground now. It had been ten years. She had survived.

The buzzer sounded again. They were getting impatient.

This flat was safe. They couldn't get in. The entry system enabled her to identify the caller without alerting them. Crawling over to her bed, she looked at the screen on the bedside table, guessing that it was either police or a journalist. She was not keen to speak to either of them.

'Carol Holman? Carol? It's PC Redding here. I'd like to ask you a few questions about an incident in the Green.' An ID was held up to the small screen of the security camera.

Carol remained still and silent, hiding.

The heat was building, and the Green steamed with the lack of breeze. All the activity was focused near the folded trampoline. A small team was searching the ponds and the decorative grasses, the fire pits and the chiminea, trying to locate the mobile phone, the handbag and the car keys. Costello walked round with her notebook, nodding at various people she knew, incubating a vague feeling that the crime scene might be getting out of control: too many people talking to each other, chatting out of turn.

She looked up at the high walls. This place was a fortress.

Costello had noticed how long it took Wyngate, using subtle persuasion, to separate Murdoch Wallace and Sven Jonsson, but now they had settled, she could tell by the inclinations of the head, the nodding and the finger pointing that they were talking through the incident. Pity that Jonsson and Wallace had already chatted, maybe getting their stories straight, maybe denying that they knew the girl. Costello strolled to the wild garden, stepping over the stones in the pond, glancing down at the goldfish mouthing the surface, searching for food. A scene of crime officer was kneeling, shining his torch into the water. She stood on the central stone looking up at the balconies of one of the apartments. All the doors were closed, but as she stepped off the last stone, the back door on the ground floor opened and a woman came out, looking as if she had just got out of bed and pulled on a pair of leggings and a big jumper.

Costello walked along the decking to the two steps and held out her warrant card.

'Is it OK to come out? What's happened?' the woman asked, looking over her shoulder.

'I'm DI Costello. There's been an incident and somebody's been injured, I'm afraid.'

The woman's eyes drifted past Costello to the gathering of crime scene officials, the police officers, the other residents down at the corner near the trampoline.

'I could see a little from upstairs. I hope she's OK.' Her hands lifted to the neck of her jumper. She shivered a little.

And Costello noticed. 'And you are?'

'Louise. Louise Dawson.'

'And you live here?'

'Yes, this is the Halfhouse. That's the Quarterhouse, the Grainhouse and the Maltman House itself.' She pointed as she spoke. 'But you'll already know that.'

'And do you live here on your own, Ms Dawson?'

'Mrs, but I'm divorced. I live here with my son, Joe. He's still upstairs in bed. He sleeps the sleep of the dead – teenage boys, you know.' She was nervous, words tumbling out, a slight lick of the lips.

'Did he see anything?'

'No.'

'Can you ask him?'

'He's asleep.' The gentle voice was definite.

Costello changed tack. 'Did you see or hear anything tonight, anything out of the ordinary?'

'I don't think so. I'd gone to bed early, but something woke me. I think I heard Sven shout. There's often noises in the Green – I didn't think much of it until I looked out of the bedroom window and realized that something had happened. I thought it might be one of the children. There seemed to be enough people around, helping' – she shook her head – 'so I didn't come out. Didn't want to be one of those people who hang around looking at accidents.'

'Did you call nine-nine-nine?'

'Me? No.' Louise glanced over to the pond, to the crime scene guy and his torch. 'Is she OK?'

'We're waiting to hear the outcome. Will you be around tomorrow so we can take a formal statement?'

'Yes, I'll phone work, tell them I'll be late in. I'm the office manager; we're short-staffed at the moment. Bailey and Gordon accountants.'

'Here's my card. If it's an issue, leave a message on that number.' She saw Wyngate out of the corner of her eye. 'I'll let you go in now.'

Louise paused at the door. 'Was she anybody we know?'

'No, I don't think so, but we're working on it.' Costello nodded her dismissal as Louise slowly retreated behind her door.

Costello sensed deceit. The four houses occupied the same space. The families must know each other well – the four women; the Swede, the tea maker, the one with the open balcony and Louise. Sabina Jonsson was looking after her children. Pauline had made the tea. The balcony woman had still not been contacted. And nobody admitted to making that first 999 call. And why did Louise refer to the victim as 'she' if she had seen nothing? The body was at the other end of the Green behind the loggia.

A fifty-fifty guess? Or did she know?

*   *   *

Carol lay on her stomach in her dark bedroom. She had inched towards the edge of the balcony as far as she could, so she could see without being seen, too scared of the big space. There was a small blonde woman in a suit, talking to Louise at the Halfhouse; she was something official, probably a police officer. Louise had then pointed at the four houses, including up at the Quarterhouse. Carol didn't think she had been seen, so why were they pointing her out? The door entry system buzzed again. Carol reversed enough to be out of sight. She heard her laptop ping. Furtively, she crawled over to it, seeking out the new message.

Hi Carol,

I hope you don't mind me emailing but I didn't want to come and chap your door cold, so to speak. I wanted to reach out to you after the incident tonight.

I live in the Halfhouse, so I'm watching the aftermath. The police have just been in to see me, drinking cups of tea and talking to me and Joe (my son – he's the tall lanky one you might see out in the Green as if he's taking the lawn-mower for a walk. That's him attempting to cut the grass with no enthusiasm at all). The police were with us for some time and they were asking us about you. Joe saw more than I did, I was really only aware of it when the Jonssons came out and Jussi started barking.

I heard that the young woman has died, and that couldn't have been pleasant to witness. Was she a police officer? Joe said she was, but the police wouldn't say one way or the other. I know you've only lived in that house for a month, so you might not know many folk around here yet. It took me a long time to be . . . well, not accepted, that's too strong, but the Jonssons are so lovely, so welcoming and so perfect that they are a bit intimidating. I bet Sabina came round with some home baking – a blueberry pie or an apple crumble – the minute she heard you had moved in. They're such nice people but her house is immaculate, she homeschools, she makes her own bread. She does everything – sickening really.

You do sit looking out from your balcony sometimes, don't you? Wave to me, if I'm in my living room, I'll see you. If it's a nice night – I think we're going to have more sunshine for a week at least – I might meet you in the Green for a glass of wine. We can sit anywhere, they don't mind. There's no fences. Wallace and Jonsson – or Gromit as I call him for obvious reasons – work really late one night a week, so that's when I go out, knowing they won't come and be nice to me. Sometimes they are away for a few days building something or walking a mountain, kayaking round some island, generally being exhausting. Going to Morrisons for a coffee is enough for me.

I do see you sometimes, sitting behind your balcony reading into the small hours; I'm often up at that time myself.

Josh from the deli said you were a book translator so I traced your website, hence me having your email address. I'm not a stalker, I'm a concerned neighbour because you were on your own. Hope you don't mind. Wave next time you see me,

a fellow insomniac

Lulu (the Halfhouse with the white curtains)

Carol read the email again, rolling on the floor before snapping the laptop shut. She started biting her nails, pulling and tugging at the surrounding skin with her teeth. She kept going until they were bleeding. She crawled back to her bed, so nobody looking up from the Green would see her. Trying to ignore the tremors in her body, she sat on the side of the mattress, opened the drawer and checked the dolls were wrapped up in their comfort blankets before replacing them, making sure they were neatly in the corner of the drawer. She closed the drawer slowly, then pressed two Sertraline tablets from their blister strip and washed them down with a few mouthfuls of water. Exhausted, she slid on to the carpet and rolled under the bed, pulling her duvet with her, safe at last.

Costello had checked the streets outside for Mr Baseball's path of entrance as witnessed by Callaghan, and his options of exit, which would have been witnessed by many as yet unknown and untraced persons. There had been a few folk about – pubs closing, late-night coffee culture. There were restaurants among the insurance and legal offices that surely would have security footage. Her heart sank when she noticed that Brewer Street and Plantation, the two obvious avenues of exit, had many service lanes behind them. He could also have taken off across the park at the front of the Maltman House. If Mr Baseball was a local, he'd have scooted down one of the alleys and disappeared into the night. Redding was out requesting CCTV recordings and gathering information about the neighbourhood. She had already reported back to Costello that their internal cameras were not operational at the time of the incident; they had been switched off. Costello had smiled: Redding had good instincts.

Looking over the Green, she saw Anderson was marshalling the troops, getting more out of them than she'd ever get. Professor O'Hare, the pathologist, and his assistant were starting their initial examination and were already deep in discussion, as if the pathologist's expert eye had already spotted something. Costello hoped they weren't talking about how Rachel might have lived if she had been taken to A&E. That could make the case very complex. Her stomach flipped, thinking of the internecine conflicts that would ensue, instead of getting after the man who started the chain of events: Mr Baseball. But paramedics knew what they were doing; when there was no hope of life, they'd stand back to preserve a potential crime scene.

The victim herself was keeping quiet as if it suited her to die in this beautiful place. Rachel had left her house tonight, on her way to a fancy-dress party if Costello's theory was correct. A hot summer night in a stream of hot summer nights, there was a lot of midsummer madness around. Dressed for a good time, Rachel had been murdered. She'd had five strangers fighting to save her life, and, still, life had slipped from her. That was a one-way street. If she had turned a different corner, she would still be alive. She might never have run across the man with the baseball cap. Maybe Callaghan would never have found her and she would have died there alone in the Maltman Green among the flowers and the fairy lights.

Life was like that.

She looked around the Green of the Maltman quadrangle: a communal garden. It looked like the neatly manicured lawn of a posh hotel. There was a lack of fencing, no boundaries indicating what belonged to whom, which meant they got on very well, or one of them owned all of it. Everything was perfect, expensive, in the best of taste, but there was a sense of it being the same, designed by the same hand. It looked like a little piece of heaven, until somebody was killed in their private paradise.

It wasn't always like this. She could remember, very early in her own first days in uniform, chasing somebody and rugby-tackling him in the weeds and old tyres of the no-man's land here in the middle. There were no steel shutters then; it was a dump, bonfire city, a home for those with no home, the walled buildings offering shelter from a cold Glasgow winter. She couldn't locate the alley she had run through when she followed that suspect; it was almost unrecognizable now.

But here she was, back where she started.

Costello turned to see that Rachel was still being photographed. O'Hare was taking a long, long time, which meant either that he was making totally certain of something or that he had no real idea what had happened and was making doubly sure he was not missing a single item of evidentiary value.

She looked up at the buildings, thinking how lucky people must be to live in a place like this, how privileged they were. What ego had developed this? And who was paying for its upkeep? She couldn't imagine how Louise, a single parent, earned enough to live here. But she obviously did.

The team would already have a list of residents and their families, plus any others who were living at that address. Then the door-to-door where statements could be checked and cross-checked. All that could wait until they had the contact details of those in the street who had witnessed the woman come in and seen who followed her. Of all the places Rachel could have gone, why did she decide to turn up this little alley with the closed steel shutters. Within that shutter was a door, and she seemed to possess knowledge of its presence and how to open it. Did she have the code to unlock it? Had the door been left open? This place was built like a fortress. Costello wondered if anybody would dare to leave the access unlocked. There were kids here – the four that belonged to the Swede and the one that belonged to Louise. Where there were kids, there would be a door or two left open; most kids lived as though they had been born in a cave. But it was the sort of thing that worried her as a detective; it was a question that insisted on having an answer. Maybe she was reading too much into it. Did they get a pizza delivery and leave the door open for them, locking it later when they took the dogs for their evening constitutional?

She walked back. The night was moonlit and quiet beyond the noises they were making in the Green itself.

The one property that had its own part of the enclosed courtyard cordoned was the Quarterhouse Deli. They had a very narrow concrete strip surrounded by a trellis fence, covered in ivy so that it was impossible to see unless viewed with a careful eye. Looking closely, she saw it was camouflage for the bins. The two garages, at opposite corners of the Green, were similarly concealed. The two floors above had balconies; that flat had no outdoor space to call its own. That resident had still not opened her door to them.

The first floor and floors above ran unbroken along the four walls of the quadrangle. The ground floor was broken on two opposite corners where the steel doors were, allowing access to their respective garages. Costello stood back and had a good look. Bigger than it seemed on first inspection, still magical despite the reason for being here. Lights were on inside the houses, curtains and blinds were opening and closing. Costello could imagine children being kept back from the windows, wanting to see what the excitement outside was about, being sent back to bed. Word would have got round that there had been a fatality, and they would be kept in, away from the news. The horror of it would be brought home to them soon enough.

It was about four a.m. when Costello finally lay down, back on her sofa, having the same internal argument between the intense heat in the flat and the cold draught from the river; there was no easy medium: it was one or the other. Wondering if she was ever going to get any sleep, she closed her eyes, trying to push the thoughts of the case from her mind. The killer had been unlucky; they hadn't had the clear opportunity they thought they would get. Callaghan had seen them and noticed Rachel running and then the man she was running from.

Costello had many questions. Why did Rachel not shout for help? Did she run up the lane and step through the door thinking that the killer would not know where she had gone? Once she was in the Green, she was trapped. Her only way out was the way she came in, unless she also had the foreknowledge to run across the diagonal of the Green with certainty that the other gate would allow her an exit. Costello thought the man who was chasing her might not have been that easy to get past or get away from, depending on what exit strategy Rachel had decided on. Was she familiar with the place?

There might be witnesses, as yet uninterviewed, to exactly what had happened. The four houses of the Green had their big windows and living spaces facing the Green – at least one balcony had been open, maybe two. The night was hot. Somebody would have seen something, heard a noise and looked out.

Leaving the gate open didn't fit well with the sense of intense privacy, the small but numerous windows out to the street, the huge windows into the Green itself.

She shouldn't be in her flat thinking about it alone; she should be with Wyngate, Mulholland and Anderson in an incident room throwing around ideas, four brains being better than one, eating stale sandwiches and drinking lukewarm coffee. But no, Anderson went home as soon as he could, desperate to get back to Moses, Wyngate had left to put his kids to bed, and then Mulholland, with Elvie McCulloch in tow, had put the tin lid on it by turning up with Kathy Lamont and a film crew. He'd spent ages sorting his hair so that he'd be ready for his close-up. They started filming on site for the next episode of *Eyes and Ears*, catching an exclusive on the death of Rachel Sinclair.

The team were going their separate ways. She was being left behind.

This was a terrible day in what she knew would be a shite week. She thought about Rachel, getting ready for her night out. Her day wasn't going so well either.

Carol couldn't sleep. The buzzer for the door entry system sounded off a few times. She might be wrong about that: her head was woolly and cloudy.

What had she seen really? The girl struggling? She had thrown her head back, he had raised his hand, then brought it down. The woman had crumpled to the ground.

What could she have done? Could she have stopped it happening? Then he might have come after Carol. He would know exactly where she lived.

Maybe he was out there, waiting for her. That could have been him ringing at her doorbell, trying to prise her out of her sanctuary.

That was nonsense. She took a deep breath and leaned forward so her forehead was on the floor, her arms lying along the cool tiles, forcing out the panic and trying to take control.

Ten minutes later, feeling more settled, she eased herself forward to the balcony until she could see the police and the crime scene specialists in their protective outfits. One of them, kneeling beside the body, might be a doctor working on her, but the ambulances had left, and there was a black van sitting within the gate. She knew what that meant.

She could remember being stretchered out, past the water clock, the body bags and the black vans. The kind man who had opened the lid of her coffin, lifting her clear and wrapping her naked, insect-ridden body in a blanket; he had a kind voice, saying her name over and over as he carried her out of the tunnel. And then there was sunshine on her face for the first time in months.

She could still sob with the relief of that.

And the other face, the face that had opened the lid and closed it again. Carol had thought she would die from despair. That face was etched in her memory.

And here was another dead woman, a pathetic figure in such a beautiful place. Carol looked down at the hive of people, wondering if the woman had a husband at home waiting for her, maybe kids. A life lost, others changed for ever.

She heard the noise of the shuttered door to the Jonssons' garage opening. Three or four people walked in the Green, one of them carrying a camera on their shoulder. A uniformed officer approached them; there was a conversation. Carol recognized the blonde woman from the TV; she was the one who had appeared on the programme about the Night Hunter she had watched – that evening? Yesterday evening? What time was it now?

The air in the Green was still very warm. From behind the balcony doors, she watched as the little group of people got the camera into position, moving around to include some of the crime scene activity in the shot but not so much that it might cause offence or intrude on the investigation. The man – she recognized him as the man who had also been on *Eyes and Ears* – was the handsome detective who had worked on the Night Hunter case.

He had been one of the team who had saved her life, and here he was right in front of her; if she called out, he would hear her. She crawled forward to get a better view, watching him carefully, wondering why he was walking the way he was, limping badly, seeking out a chair to lean on as if he couldn't quite support himself unless he was moving. The fourth figure was dressed in black trousers; short black hair, spikey, two earlocks, gave her the appearance of an elf. That figure got hold of another chair, pulling it over to where the detective needed it to be for him to do his piece to camera. They spent a moment or two adjusting a light, the camera taking a view of the blonde presenter in her summer coat talking to the detective about the case unfolding behind him. While they were fine-tuning this, or moving that, two steps to the right, three steps back, the figure in black looked bored, walked over to the garage and leaned back against the wall. Clasping her hands behind her, she turned her face upwards to stare at the moon.

Carol let out a squeal, an involuntary little shriek, recoiling to the floor, keeping her eyes on the face that had haunted her for so long. Watching in horror, she saw the figure in black drop her eyes from the sky to look up at Carol's balcony. For one heart-sickening moment, they looked at each other.

The last time they met, she had closed the coffin lid over, leaving Carol to die.

FRIDAY 25TH JUNE
AFTER DAWN

He stayed under his blanket with Bob Bear, Hamlet lying on the side of the bed beside him so his fingers could stroke the long silky ears. Last night's milk was still in the glass beside his bed, and it had curdled in the heat. He didn't feel like getting up today. His knees were sore from sitting at the window all night, watching. They had come in and given him his breakfast, two of them this time, short-tempered, telling him to get out of bed and eat his breakfast at the table properly.
He stayed under his duvet, and in the end they gave up and went away. If they annoyed him any more, he'd pee the bed. That would sort them out.

SIX

Carol was lying on top of her quilt, wrapped in her favourite scarlet housecoat, worrying that something awful had followed her to this strange and enchanting place. Her delight in finding a home so protected from the outside world was turning to fear that it was a prison. She was sure she had recognized that face out on the Green, or was some synapse in her brain firing erroneously with the mix of emotions?

She could see the top windows of the duplex opposite, home to her new friend, Lulu. Carol thought that the two of them might have much in common, both keeping themselves to themselves, not like the Swedes and the Wallaces who were in and out of each other's houses every day. Lulu would occasionally sit on her balcony, holding a cup of tea or coffee with both hands, her jacket over the rail. The way she sat down and slowly peeled her shoes from her feet suggested she was weary. Sometimes her son would appear, handing her a plate of something, and he'd lean on the rail with his back to the Green talking to his mum. They'd hug, a simple gesture that made Carol feel very lonely, the way the woman would reach forward and ruffle the boy's hair, envious of the touch of a human hand.

They seemed close.

Since moving into the duplex, Carol had slipped into the habit of sleeping late into the day after working into the small hours on the translation about the oceanic layers. For breakfast, she'd phone down to the deli and the boys would bring up her food order and an Americano. Her hands had been shaking the first time she tapped out their number, preparing for a conversation to justify why she couldn't come down a flight of stairs to collect a coffee and bagel. She had been so nervous she had actually reverted to thinking in Norwegian. But Joshua Wallace had said it wasn't a problem and asked if she wanted milk on the side. He had handed the delivery in through a door she could hardly bring herself to unlock, trying to release the three deadbolts and two Yales quietly so that he wouldn't hear from the other side and think that she was a psychotic bitch.

Then, as she sat on the inside of the window at the balcony, hidden by the shade of the lower branches of the huge pine tree, sipping the coffee and nibbling the goat's cheese and spinach pizza, she had felt at home. That first weekend, dusty and tired, boxes everywhere, she had woken up and felt contented.

Her view then was the same as it was now. She'd wanted outside light, without going outside; it was one of the reasons she had rented the flat, this duplex – the glorious light. The view didn't go on forever, bordered by her neighbours; within the Green was an ever-moving tapestry of life. The beautiful Swedes, the Wallaces who were always wrapped up in each other's arms. Lulu's duplex sat above the clothes boutique, which was for, as Joshua once described it, the more mature woman.

That first day she had noticed Sven first – a tall man, hair in a ponytail, flip-flops on his feet, messing about with the barbecue. He had been joined by the man whose name sounded like Murder – always well dressed, with his neatly trimmed beard – who carried a tray of burgers or sausages. They were joined by Sabina with a platter of bread that was placed on the long table, now covered with a red-and-white checked cloth. They appeared one by one, her new neighbours, all bringing something to the party. The girls appeared – the four beautiful, leggy daughters in floating smock dresses, each a mini-me of their mother, walking around the lush grass of the Green, passing around the drinks and canapés. There was a teenager, who she knew now was Lulu's son, who spent the evening talking to the older two girls. Carol had been intrigued by it all, the comings and goings, in the cooling evening sun that turned everything the colour of rose gold, fading to purple in the darkening corners.

Had they known she was watching them? They must have known. A casual glance across the grass may have missed her, but anybody looking up would easily have seen the outline, behind the greenery, of her figure, sitting on her big chair behind the full-length glass of the balcony doors. She was content that they had not invited her yet as it would have been awkward to refuse when they seemed so nice with their respectful chatter and tidy garden. She had no intention of going. She had no intention of ever going out again – her weekly shopping was delivered, she bought her clothes online, her translation work arrived by email, and the deli would send orders up to her: a tub of their Maisy Daisy ice cream, a bespoke sandwich. She had asked for combinations that had proved very popular with their office-based lunchtime patrons; the relationship was becoming symbiotic. They had sent up a whole loaf last week – a new sourdough they were trying. Bobby and Joshua, two nice guys making a good go of their small business, an artisan café and deli on the outskirts of artisan café and deli land.

She never asked them about the Swedes, or the man whose name sounded like Murder, or Lulu. She never asked them anything; it would have seemed rude.

Anderson had called a meeting for the four of them for nine a.m., so they could confirm ideas and the results of their interviews before the bigger briefing. O'Hare was going to start on the post-mortem as soon as possible, but as far as gathering evidence was concerned, they were treating it as a murder until it was proven otherwise. Investigation rule one: no second chances.

Anderson himself had come in earlier to see how the intelligence was doing, the gathering of the overnight information from the door-to-door teams. As it was, he wasn't the only one who had had the idea of coming in early to get ahead of the game.

Kathy Lamont from *Eyes and Ears* had already been on to Media Liaison, wanting an exclusive to do an appeal for informa-tion on the Rachel Sinclair case. Anderson had misgivings about the lines of duty becoming faded, blurred or maybe obliterated altogether, and those fears were confirmed as he saw the flicker of excitement in Vik's eyes when he had been asked to do the filming with Kathy. It was still there when Anderson saw the BMW in the car park and Viktor Mulholland being dropped off by Elvie McCulloch in her role of driver and personal assistant. Anderson went over and exchanged a few words, promising that Vik would get to the incident room safely. There was a lift, and Mulholland was doing well on his prosthesis, but it was early days. His girl-friend, the dark-eyed Elvie, glared at Anderson, that stare that he recalled so well from the time they had worked on the Night Hunter case. Elvie had been looking for her sister, Sophie. Anderson had been searching for the other missing women, and for the man who had abducted them. That steady, expressionless, disconcerting stare was part and parcel of Elvie being on the spectrum. He still found it unnerving.

He wondered how the representation of Eric Manson on the TV programme had gone down with her last night. Of them all, she had been the one most affected; she had lived next door to the killer for her entire life, and then her sister had gone missing.

As Anderson and Mulholland walked through the main doors of the station, Anderson thought he could feel Elvie's eyes boring into the back of his head as he listened to Vik enthuse about the TV programme. When he turned to open the door for his colleague, sure enough, there she was, looking straight at him.

They walked along the upper floor to the meeting room, Anderson strolling slowly so that Mulholland, his prosthesis clumping on the tiles, didn't feel the need to hurry. Mulholland was upbeat and chatty. The *Eyes and Ears* producers were pleased with the piece he had done to camera, and for the first time a mobile unit had been dispatched to the scene of the crime, beating the other TV crews, because Sven Jonsson had given them permission to go in. As he owned the Green, it was up to him who was there. The search had been completed by then, so as long as they didn't disrupt the crime scene area behind the blue tape, Jonsson could do as he wished. Anderson smiled as Mulholland chatted, happy as a bat in a sandbox, the trials and issues of the last year left behind. He had risen to his new challenge, but sometime soon he'd need to be reminded of the fine line he was walking. Not that Costello would allow Mulholland to stray into the land of celebrity, but Anderson had no doubt that Kathy Lamont could be very persuasive, and being caught between Kathy and Costello was nowhere for any sane man to be.

As Mulholland settled into his chair, Anderson grabbed them both a coffee and had a quick look at how the newspapers had dealt with the broadcast the previous night. They were full of the public's response to the Johnny Clearwater appeal. It was too early for any real intelligence to be released to the press, but they had gone ahead with lots of pictures of the blonde mop-headed boy with the gap in his teeth, the terrible eczema that raged on his skin. There was, of course, a recent picture of Naomi, and one of her and Richard, her husband, a man who liked his grief to be less public. Anderson flicked through the pictures and the major features; much of the copy had been written in advance, he thought. Images of Naomi headed up every article. The police said they hoped that promising leads would bear fruit. Among how many by absolute nutters? And who would come forward now if they had held back four years ago? And what would their reasoning be?

He read the usual trite statement of DCI Bob Allison who had headed up the original case, hoping for new leads and assuring the public that the case would not be closed until there was some kind of resolution. Anderson knew the background of Johnny Clearwater's disappearance by heart; every police officer in Scotland knew. But here it was again in black and white. As a father, he hoped the appeal would do some good; as a cop, he doubted it. They were looking for a body; too much time had passed.

To fill the page, there was the usual information of the circumstances of the boy's disappearance. Anderson read it through to see if there was anything different from the common perception of the situation, but it was the same old, same old.

That was a cold case going nowhere; he had Rachel to deal with.

They heard Wyngate's hurried footsteps along the corridor, and he walked in the door, looking very tired. Uncharacteristically, he was drinking a black coffee from Costa. The constable collapsed into the nearest chair, explaining that he was exhausted. When he got home last night, he had tripped over something that his wife had left at the door for him to take out to the bin. The noise had woken the whole house up. He had then spent the next hour sitting on the settee with his three kids, eating toast and drinking milk, until they had calmed down enough to go back to bed and get some sleep. Then they had decided it was too hot to sleep. The kids wanted to sleep with the windows open, but Wyngate was reluctant to do that – too many times, he had seen an open window being used as an access point, perps gaining entry for theft of property or worse. There had been cases of very young children being taken through open windows – rare, but tell that to the parents it had happened to. Wyngate chattered on, slightly nervous ahead of his presentation of the intelligence that had been collated overnight by the uniformed team in the office. Colin recalled, as they opened the windows in the room and pulled chairs around the table, that he had closed the windows tight and locked them when he had left wee Moses' bedroom the night before. It was habit. It was a state of mind.

Anderson pulled out a chair for Mulholland, as Wyngate beamed a drawing of the Maltman Green on to the wall, already talking about the day ahead, passing around ideas and their difficulty in getting hold of the resident who had their balcony doors open. Every other resident of the Green had been forthcoming, but not the resident of the Quarterhouse.

'Should we start or wait for the boss?' asked Wyngate.

'I'm here,' joked Anderson. 'But if you mean our DI, then, yes, I think we should wait. She has signed in, and her car is out there, so she's in the building somewhere.'

'Hear that? That quietness is the sound of good men not offering their opinions on anything in case she disagrees,' said Mulholland.

'She's major-league grumpy at the moment – much worse than usual.'

'I guess we all have our off days,' said Anderson mildly, while recognizing the truth of the situation. Costello's attitude was starting to affect the working of the team as a whole, and he, being the one nominally in charge, had to sort it out. The human management of a team was always a difficult task, and not one he relished.

Then they heard footsteps along the hall: fast walking, not a heavy step but a determined one. They casually assumed more formal positions. Wyngate moved to the board, testing marker pens for the one that worked best. Mulholland was looking intently at a file. Anderson pretended to make some notes so that when she walked in, they looked as if they had been there for ages, industrious.

'Sorry, I'm late,' she snapped, needlessly, since she was not late, 'but I've been downstairs for a couple of hours doing some background on Rachel Elizabeth Sinclair.' She continued, glaring at Mulholland, 'Were you really there last night filming when the body had just been removed?'

Anderson didn't know that she had clocked that. 'It was decided at a level higher than us that the publicity would be good. It was an act of violence metres away from a very busy thoroughfare, so the benefits outweighed any implied lack of respect.'

His DI looked at him, a long, slow glare out of those cold, grey eyes. He felt like a slow old stag that had spotted a hungry wolf lying in wait in the trees.

'Don't lie to me. You don't know any of that. You're predicting what you think they would say upstairs, despite the affront to common decency. Is everything about being on the telly now?'

The atmosphere in the room dropped by several degrees as she sat down, scowling at each of them in turn. Then she folded her arms before snapping a smile on to her face. 'So, I've the background on the deceased. Were you going to look at the scene, Wyngate?'

'Yes, we were waiting for you.'

'I wasn't late.'

'You weren't here,' said Mulholland.

'No, I was downstairs working while you were getting a run in from your chauffeur and a help up the stairs from your manservant here. So, Rachel Elizabeth Sinclair, the victim, pronounced dead at the scene, no visible cause of death that O'Hare is willing to take a stab at, if you pardon the turn of phrase. There was nothing obvious on the examination at the scene. Rachel was thirty-seven, ex-cabin crew. She left British Airways two years ago to set up her own business designing and making jewellery. I'm going to visit her flat in Hardgate when we finish here and then on to the fancy-dress shop who supplied her with the cop's outfit – it's a place in town called Lookin' Good – to see if Rachel said what she wanted it for. She has one brother that we have traced so far; parents deceased. She has a Nokia phone registered to her – as yet we cannot find it. It's turned off and has been since the incident. Ruby Redding got on to her Facebook page, printed out this picture from it. She advertises herself as a bespoke jeweller and her relationship status as "complicated" so that might be worth looking into. On the Green, there were no personal effects on her, apart from the credit card which was in the mobile phone pouch on her belt.'

'So Mr Baseball took the phone but left the credit card? Sounds personal.'

'The fingertip search of the Green came up with nothing. We're

waiting on the CCTV to find out where and maybe why Mr
Baseball started following her, as there's no footage from the
internal system. Most of the eyewitnesses to the chase had walked
away, or were too drunk. Callaghan is the best we have – he was
aware that Baseball was following Rachel from the Rosserman
Street/Brewer Street corner as he came along Plantation. I noted
that Rachel didn't scream or shout, which I find odd. The residents
heard Callaghan shout, so I'm presuming that either Rachel didn't
or couldn't.'

'And the location where she died?' asked Anderson, nodding at
Wyngate. 'Redding's tracking the deceased's movements that day.'

Wyngate coughed before he continued. 'Yes, so the Maltman
Green – it would appear that although folk think it has been there
for many years and that it's old and lovely, in fact it was a—'

'Marmalade factory,' interrupted Costello.

'Yes, it was. Then it fell into disrepair and was bought for very
little money by Trappa Property which is owned by Sven Jonsson
and Murdoch Wallace. They, or somebody, has actually rewritten
the history of the place – hence the village feel of it. There're
four dwelling houses – the Maltman House, the Grainhouse,
the Halfhouse and the Quarterhouse, homes to the Jonssons, the
Wallaces, Louise Dawson and Carol Holman respectively. And
there's the Quarterhouse Deli under the Quarterhouse duplex, and
the Looking Glass dress shop under the Halfhouse. The Maltman
Green itself forms a block on the street; there are roads on four
sides – Brewer Street, Park Lane, Plantation and Rosserman Street.
Rachel entered the Green through a door in a shutter that few
folk would notice. I've looked at the plans and they seem to be
still developing the upper floor.

'The houses, all four, have a lot of high-tech energy-saving kit
– geothermal heating, photovoltaic panels, grey water collection,
triple-glazed windows. There's a garden on the roof of the entire
quad to offset . . .'

'Can we get on to Rachel, please? She wasn't there studying
the architecture, was she? She was there being murdered,' snapped
Costello, refolding her arms. 'The Maltman is only interesting
because that was where she was chased. We need to know how
she knew to get in and who Mr Baseball is.'

Wyngate glanced at Anderson, looking for permission to go on.

'The characters that live there are important, Costello; the whole Green is important,' said Anderson. 'It is an interesting building – it's been in its present incarnation for about ten years now. That clothes shop is very exclusive. I think you need to make an appointment.'

'It is indeed appointment-only for the mother-of-the-bride type of thing. Everything in there costs a fortune,' said Mulholland.

'And you know this how? Are you thinking of getting married?' asked Anderson, genuinely surprised.

'Nope, but so many friends have, you get to know. Who are the Jonssons? Was that the guy who let us through his garage to film?'

Wyngate nodded. 'Tall guy, ponytail, blue sunglasses on the top of his head? That's Sven Jonsson. The set-up's still owned by the company that Jonsson and Wallace own. I have their bios here.' He held up sheets of A4 paper. 'The witness who hasn't come forward is a Carol Holman – only been there a month, and the others don't seem to know her at all. She's the one with the open balcony doors.'

'We need to speak to her sooner rather than later,' said Anderson.

'They tried but she wouldn't open up, won't answer her phone. She gets her meals from the deli downstairs, so they seem to know her best.'

'So she's not short of a bob or two – a cheese bagel out of there is a fiver,' said Wyngate.

'The two owners, Bobby Connaught and Joshua Wallace, say she's quiet – a little odd maybe.'

'Why're we looking at the locus? What about the victim?' asked Costello.

'I told him to. Rachel seemed to know where she was going. A woman being pursued by a man is not going to risk somewhere that she doesn't think she can get out of,' said Anderson slowly.

'She could have been blind drunk for all we know. She could have run off with that guy's wallet, he followed her into the Green, got it back, and then she fell over and hit her head on the side of the trampoline,' argued Mulholland.

'For whatever reason, she ran in there hoping to find sanctuary. Did either Wallace or Jonsson say that they knew her? They both did CPR, so they both must have seen her up close,' Anderson reasoned.

'They didn't recognize her,' said Wyngate.

'So who owns the steel shutter at the corner, the one she ran through?'

'There's only two, both owned by the company – the Wallace family have one and the Jonssons have the other. It was the Wallace one that Rachel ran through. The duplex tenants are not expected to have a car so they don't have vehicular access to the Green. There's a garage attached to each of the shutters. And neither of the women, Sabina or Pauline, has a vehicle registered to them.'

'Green living, one car.'

'Or control.'

'We need to look at the CCTV, see if she looks round and sees the doorway open and takes a chance of getting through it before Mr Baseball knows where she has gone, or if she ran down there knowing that she could open it. It's a six-digit code to get in,' said Costello.

'Really?'

'The place is well protected, yet Rachel got in quickly while under stress.'

'So what does that mean?'

'That she knew exactly where she was going,' snapped Costello.

The flat was a lower-quarter conversion of a grand villa, blonde and white chuckies raked in the long driveway, and there was no sign of the red Mini Clubman registered to Rachel Sinclair at this address. Neatly cut laurel bordered the garden, and over the door a small slated roof was held up by two Roman pillars the colour of sundried maze. The stone steps beneath were worn with footfall over the years.

Wyngate whistled appreciatively when he saw the house; living in half of it, or even a quarter, was impressive and not manageable on his salary.

The property factor, a thin anaemic-looking man with transparent skin, was waiting with a key to Rachel's flat; her own keys, her phone and her car had still not been located. He was suffering badly in the sun, but Costello ignored him, taking her time, standing in the baking heat, trying to square the woman lying in the Maltman Green dressed as a cop with the woman who had lived in this fine house. Rachel had taken a package from BA, but Costello wanted to look into her financials. What did she do to earn enough money to live here? Costello didn't know much about jewellery, but she couldn't see Rachel making enough to keep up a place like this. So where was the money coming from? Sex work? There was a market for high-class call girls – with Rachel's height and build, Costello could see that might be a possibility. But whatever it was, Her Majesty's Revenue and Customs knew about it. Her PAYE had ended with her time at British Airways but she now submitted self-assessment tax returns. Or had she got herself involved in drugs? Maybe Mr Baseball was carrying out a punishment? Did Rachel know the code for that gate because she used to deliver there? The residents looked like the kind that might enjoy a snort of coke recreationally. Rachel turning up as a cop. Was it a joke that had gone wrong? BA cabin crew were intelligent, well-read people. Costello had always found that staff of Rachel's vintage were the cream of the crop.

Somebody was paying her way; there was a man, or a woman, that they had yet to identify. The 'complicated' of her Facebook relationship status? Is that where Mr Baseball came into the picture? The underwear Rachel was wearing pointed more to that kind of liaison.

The factor coughed. He was sweating profusely in the morning heat – an obsequious little man with rivulets like tears running down each cheek, only to be ineffectually daubed away with a neatly folded white handkerchief. He was muttering something about anything they wanted, that he'd be waiting in the driveway, then added that it might be useful if they got a move on as he couldn't be two places at one time.

Costello looked up into the cloudless blue sky, and then motioned to Wyngate that they should go in and that she'd like them to stay together. If they found anything of interest, they were to film it and then remove themselves before securing the scene. Once Wyngate was behind her, and the factor out of sight, Costello pushed the door open into the square hall, enough so she could slip through it sideways and look behind. The floor was good-quality oak, covered in an expensive thick rug. The shower room and toilet were straight ahead. Although the hall was little more than space for the four doors that led off it, the ceiling was high and corniced, curling as it rose, taking a corner out the room.

'Nice gaff,' muttered Wyngate. 'I bet it took somebody ages to sand these floorboards down, and then they realize how bloody cold it is and spend a fortune on rugs to cover it up.' He pulled some gloves on and bent down to pick up the mail.

'Leave that where it is and photograph it. Anything that looks important?'

He put his hand down.

'Without touching it, is there anything important?'

Wyngate knew not to ask. 'It looks run of the mill.' He tilted his head round to get a better look. 'Bills and junk mail.'

'What are the bills?' she asked, walking round the hall, peering into each room one after the other.

'Credit card and a letter from HMRC.'

'OK, come on, let's see what else we can find.' Costello turned round, heading for the bedroom, smiling to herself. She trusted him implicitly; he had a kind heart and was honest as the day was long, but sometimes he thought like a nice guy and that would be the reason he might never get to the top. She looked round the bedroom, which was not what she had been expecting from the décor in the hall, the all-natural colours and quiet good taste. The bedroom was a riot of colour: bright red walls and the duvet cover was cream with bright red flowers that matched the wallpaper.

The living room had a desk, and she noted the obvious space where a laptop should go. She looked round. There was a flex. A mobile phone charger but no phone. A car parking space with no car. And no car keys. If her car wasn't here, then she may have driven to wherever she had been before she ended up at the Maltman. They had the CCTV under review: a striking woman dressed like that would be noticed and would be noticeable on film.

Wyngate spotted what she was looking at and drew the same conclusion. 'Be good to find that laptop. Do you think it might be in her car with her phone? I suppose there's no sign of the Mini?'

'Nothing yet. I was hoping it would be here. Mr Baseball might have lifted the keys, used the car to get away.'

'So he knew where she'd parked it. He could have been watching her, I suppose. Oh, look here.'

The spare bedroom was obviously her craft room. A table, a collection of tools that resembled surgical instruments, two powerful adjustable lamps and a small blow torch. It looked tidy and carefully stored. Rachel was a neat and fastidious person – she would have lived her life within certain parameters. There was a stack of little pictures, beautifully drawn, of a horse galloping over a bridge, the rider hanging on for grim death. She looked more closely. Ghosts? They were repeated, and then she saw the italic writing on another design. Then drawings of attachments for fastenings and chains, loops and clips. Rachel was doing a range of silver jewellery based on the poem that every Scots kid learned at school.

'"Tam o' Shanter",' she said out loud.

'And "My Love is Like a Red, Red Rose", here?'

'What?'

Wyngate pointed at the wall – a frieze of beautifully drawn pictures, the same image again and again from different angles. They were the two-dimensional designs of the three-dimensional pieces she'd later craft out of silver. Then she saw what Wyngate was pointing at. The Burns Rose. The lovers' rose.

'She had that round her neck?' asked Wyngate.

'No.' She looked again. 'But nearly – see, she's designed it so the two roses entwine, but they are on two chains. There?' She pointed with her gloved forefinger. 'The Burns Rose is two entwined roses, one for each lover. And Rachel had one.'

'So who has the other?'

'That is the big question. Take a photograph of it.' Costello stood back and looked. It was indeed the double-headed version of the necklace that Rachel wore. 'Would you wear that, Gordon? If your wife bought you it?'

'She'd know better.'

In the living room, there were a few photographs on top of the bookcase, mostly of her and friends, work colleagues maybe, in various parts of the world. There was one of her with an older man and another woman; the distance between the two figures spoke volumes. The next photograph was Rachel with two kids, a boy about ten and a girl about fifteen. The children bore a close semblance to the woman in the previous picture. Could this be the half-brother?

'Do you have pictures of yourself in your house?' asked Wyngate.

'Nope.'

'Me neither. I'm going to look at her bathroom.'

Costello was looking through the selection of books on the bookcase – Jojo Moyes, Nora Roberts – when she heard Wyngate shout. She found him kneeling in front of the cupboard under the bathroom sink, holding the top of a small container patterned with blue whales and seashells. He pointed into it, his gloved hand tilting it to one side so Costello could see the small packets of white powder lying at the bottom.

'OK, bag that up. Somebody has been in here since she died; the door has been opened, after the post was delivered and before we got here. Which is more than interesting. And they must have had a key – maybe the same person that she had the code for? The person with the other half of the pendant?'

Wyngate nodded.

'She left this flat at some point yesterday early evening and has been in the mortuary all night, so somebody opened the front door and pushed this morning's mail back. It was off the mat away to the side, yet in her kitchen was a rack of important bills and things. She was a woman who picked up mail and opened it when it arrived.'

'So who's been here? Mr Baseball?' Wyngate held up the bag of cocaine.

'I think so. There's something in here that would have identified him, so he came back to retrieve it. Maybe that's why the handbag was taken. There's no forced entry. We need to get a door-to-door round the neighbours here, see if they spotted anything, anybody unusual. Can I leave you to action that?'

'Yes, of course. Did Callaghan say that there was a handbag in the possession of Mr Baseball as he ran away?'

'No, I think he'd have noticed, but if it was a small clutch bag, Mr Baseball might have stuffed it up his jumper as he legged it.' She looked round. 'Let's lock this place up, put somebody on the door, and we'll talk to Colin, see if it warrants a full forensic investigation – sorry, I mean if it warrants the expense of a full forensic investigation.'

As they were walking to the car, Costello checked her phone. 'I'll try to get hold of Carol Holman. She's our best bet at getting an eyewitness account. You manage this location, I'll take Redding with me. I'm just concerned that if Holman has an issue about opening her front door to us, she might be more comfortable with two women.'

'No problem. Where did the factor go?'

'Probably melted in the heat.'

SEVEN

Carol heard the buzzer and crept over to the door at the landing, switched on the discreet camera and saw the two women standing outside: an older one at the front and a younger black woman in uniform. They had finished their activity on the Green, but had not finished, or started, with her. She took her finger off the button that worked the camera. She had no wish to speak to them, not now, not ever.

Carol moved along to the kitchen window, catching sight of the bruise on her face in the mirror, then she looked down on to the street. It was lunchtime on a Friday but the scene below was like a summer resort: women strolling in sundresses, kids enjoying the first day of the school holidays, nagging their mums for a Maisy Daisy ice cream, everybody in sunglasses. From behind the curtain, she saw the two police officers, deep in conversation, walking towards a red Fiat, making their way carefully through the small crowd that was permanently outside, looking at the menu in the deli window.

She thought about making a coffee, or even calling down for a really strong Americano, but she was jittery already, so maybe not.

Then she heard her laptop ping.

She was expecting an email from her editor, and she still had to respond to Lulu, so she picked up the laptop and went back upstairs to her bed.

> Hi Lulu,
>
> Thank you for your email but I am OK, really I am. I feel a wee bit foolish for being the only witness to a crime, a murder at that, and then fainting at the wrong moment. I hope the police are understanding when they catch up with me and don't ask me too many questions that I can't answer.
>
> I'm slowly getting unpacked in the duplex. I didn't notice

when I looked round it just how high up it is over the Green. Being two floors and the high ceilings, it gave me quite a fright first time I stepped out on the balcony; there's a great sense of height and lots of fresh air. I was watching Pauline and . . . Oh, can I ask you what her husband's first name is? I hear him being called something that sounds like Murder? I'm sure he can't be called that, though with the way things are going in the Green after last night . . . I wonder if the police will tell us to be careful until they catch that man. I hope they don't ask me to describe him as I didn't really see him.

You seem to know a bit about this place. I don't believe in ghosts but I was wondering if this building was haunted. I hear all kinds of weird noises in the night, footsteps, and then not so weird noises. Like the toilet flushing!

Kind regards,

Carol

She pressed send and scrolled through the contents of her inbox for the new message. Her mother asking if she was OK. Her editor again, asking her how the translation was going and whether there was a problem with a reference on page sixty-seven. Carol was finding it difficult to work in the heat. She lay back, enjoying the breeze drifting in from the open balcony doors. It wasn't the weather. It was her; the anxiety was coming back, her mental health was relapsing. She hadn't been able to find her scarlet dressing gown this morning; she normally left it on the floor at the end of the bed. It had been hanging on the back of the bathroom door, the loop at the neck neatly over the hook. She opened the drawer of the bedside table, checking that her dolls were wrapped up in their beds and safe. The sleepwalking had started after her ordeal at the hands of Eric Manson. Then that sight of him in the newspaper and watching the TV programme had triggered her anxiety.

For a moment, she considered flinging everything into a case and booking the first flight back to Oslo, sleeping in her own bed, chatting with her mum and dad over breakfast. That idea was starting to appeal to her when the laptop pinged again.

Hi Carol,

It's Murdo. That's Pauline's husband's name, short for Murdoch, but when I think of it, it does sound like Murder. Has he been annoying you, Mr Wallace? Do you notice that he never sweats? I typed he 'never swears' there by accident, but I bet he doesn't do that either! Do they ever give you any hassle?

I hope Sabina is OK. She went out last night and saw the dead body. She was really upset. Do you ever see her without a glass in her hand? It worries me a bit that Sven has got these security cameras on the Green but it seems they weren't working when they were most needed. What's the point of that?

Anyway, noises in the night, yes. But as for the ghost, nope. But there was a lot of belief around that there is one who wanders the old passages at night. Alas, it's only the heating, that geothermal system.

So no fun there!

Have you ever been into your loft? I think your house will have one, as we do. Joe uses it as a third floor – he almost lives up there with his computer games and his mouldy toast. I think the other two houses have really old storage areas in the attic with wooden sections and some chains – I am kidding you not – it's not just an attic. Mine retains some of the old features that they had when it was still working as a brewery.

Hope you are settling down OK. Have the police been round to see you yet? I think the pseudo Swedes will be summoning us for drinks on the Green soon. You have realized that Sven is as Swedish as a deep-fried Mars bar? Please say you noticed! He's Swedish because it helps his business. If they do, you know, summon us, you will be there, won't you? If you're too nervous to walk into the Green on your own, you can walk round to us and we can walk in together. The secret is to be early so you arrive while they are still setting up – that way you'll get a job to do instead of plenty of chat that makes you feel you are totally inadequate as a parent, a woman and a human being. They don't mean it, but they really are totally lovely, so totally lovely that it would make me vomit if I didn't like them.

And, of course, if you ever feel like popping down for a coffee, just say so. We can invite Joe if you wish. He'd like to meet you – well, I'd like him to meet you. School's off and his circle of friends is small, so anybody else offering to distract him to get him out of his room is good by me. Meeting a real Scandinavian might be good for him. In fact, shame you weren't Swedish instead of Norwegian, but then Sven would never have given you the lease as he can't speak Swedish and I think you might have noticed!

So hope to see you soon, but I get it if you only want to face us one at a time.

Don't be afraid of anything that goes bump in the night.

Lulu

While eating a tuna sandwich and a packet of salt and vinegar crisps, with the windows of his office fully open and a floor-standing fan oscillating with an annoying noise, Anderson sat at his desk and considered the notes he was ready to type up about Martin Callaghan. The cop was being lauded by social media as a hero, the Good Samaritan who had been concerned enough about a citizen to check on her welfare, even though he was off duty. The minute that comment had been published, the strange adversarial nature of social media kicked off with speculation that Callaghan wouldn't have bothered if she wasn't an attractive blonde and/or a police officer. Anderson understood that Davies at Media Liaison had dragged Callaghan off normal duty for some media coaching.

Anderson was burdened by the fact that this was a young police officer, a man with a partner and three young children. What he wrote down now could influence Callaghan's career and he didn't want to burst the positivity bubble around his actions. Callaghan had acted, as he himself had often acted, as a police officer when he was off duty. After a few years in the force, it was an instinct when things were not quite as they should be, and that was what PC Martin Callaghan had responded to. A perfectly normal thirty-year-old cop had gone out for a quiet pint at the Drunken Monkey. He had been in the house all day with his kids while his wife, Rebecca, known as Becs, had been at work. It was his Thursday night routine. He was leaving the Drunken Monkey, crossing

Plantation, when he saw a female police officer, as he thought, and the rest of the story was exactly as he told it at the scene.

When he found the woman lying against the folded trampoline, it was obvious that she was in trouble. He then realized that the uniform was not correct, but at a first glance, it was an understandable mistake to make. In his first version, Callaghan had acted like a police officer; he phoned it in straightaway. But he had actually attempted CPR initially, only requesting help when Jonsson and Wallace came out. Any serving officer would call it in first. It was drummed into them from day one. Yet Callaghan had not done that.

Understandable, but not professional.

Anderson's fingers halted over the keyboard again. Just write it as his colleague had reported it. Callaghan was a hero.

But his own copper's instinct, twenty years of it, was telling him that there was more to this situation than Martin Callaghan was telling him.

He dropped his pen and started typing, looking for the video files of the CCTV. The possibility of doing a reconstruction to time the events correctly was floating around in his head. Just to see if anybody could identify Mr Baseball.

Kathy Lamont, the presenter from the *Eyes and Ears* programme, had offered to do the voiceover for the TV production of the appeal for witnesses, giving out the phone number of the incident room at the studios in exchange for an exclusive.

Anderson would let somebody else fight that battle. The tech guys had done a good job of picking out images from the CCTV. Anderson always preferred to look at a sequence of stills, with variations in movement. It was easier for the eye to catch detail, something that might help identification.

At 23:23:20, a side view of Rachel Sinclair could be seen against the glass of the ladies' boutique, easily recognizable by the bride and groom in the window, dressed mannequins resembling a family wedding. As the camera caught Rachel moving across the shop front, she was looking straight ahead, then her head in a half turn and then to the front again. She seemed to be smiling as if she had caught a glimpse of something pleasing when she looked back. She didn't appear in any distress.

He would have been convinced by her appearance – at a quick

glance, she did look like a serving police officer. As she turned left to go down Brewer Street, she moved out of vision of that camera and into the range of the one mounted high on an insurance office on the opposite side of the street. At this point, Rachel still appeared to be relaxed, not fleeing for her life, yet there was a little look backward that hinted she may have seen who was behind her, and that she knew them. She was certainly not alarmed at this point.

That was the last time that she was caught on the recording. Anderson checked the timings for Mr Baseball who was not that far behind her, visible by his light-green skipped cap: 23:23:28. Anderson took a mouthful of crisps and looked closely at the image, knowing that the lab boys would have looked for a logo, blowing the image up much more than he could on his monitor, but he looked anyway. Light-green skip cap, a light-coloured shirt, open-necked, long-sleeved – long, very long, he thought, giving the impression that the man was short. They might be able to gauge a height from the red bricks of the wall of the Maltman, calculate in the angle of the camera. And he had on jeans, perfectly common jeans. The boys would be looking into the make, the size; maybe they were designer and traceable, but he knew they'd never have that kind of luck. They'd be Asda, something far too common to be of any evidential value. His trainers had a pattern down the side, a Nike flash or Reebok maybe. Again, the pictures showed that he wasn't running. There was no sense of urgency about his motion; he was just catching up with her. That put the idea of a 'chase' into question.

He looked back to see if Callaghan was caught anywhere on these stills. But as expected, he had crossed at Plantation out of CCTV range. If needed, Anderson could request further footage, but it was Mr Baseball they were interested in.

He put the stills down, trying to think what Carol Holman might have seen from her balcony thirty feet up, over to the right side, but on checking the system, he noticed that she was still proving elusive. Anderson made a mental note to review the interaction between Rachel, Mr Baseball and Callaghan. Maybe re-enact it – Callaghan could be himself and a female colleague could wear the same mock police outfit. They'd ask Carol to help: what she saw, what she heard. The appeal might bring in more information.

Rachel was a very tall woman in a uniform, and people, mostly men, would have noticed her no matter how politically correct they believed themselves to be.

Some people drew attention.

He was now viewing footage from a camera that swung a ninety-degree arc. By the time it got to the steel shutters, it picked up Callaghan, looking podgy in his T-shirt, his balding head clearly visible, looking down the street. So Mr Baseball had already pushed past him. Callaghan seemed to be staring after him, then he looked to the left and moved quickly, obviously now able to see Rachel on the ground and wanting to offer assistance.

And that was that.

That was the moment he should have lifted his mobile.

Anderson turned back to the still of Mr Baseball and studied it for a long time, looking carefully, scanning the pictures, searching for any identifiable marks. Mr Baseball had a watch on, a watch with a light-coloured traditional face, not the dark, digital face of a Fitbit. Looking even closer, he thought he saw a wedding ring. Which might explain why he legged it when he did.

But for identification, it was no bloody use at all.

Anderson stood up and went out of the office. 'Wyngate, do you fancy a wee jaunt? Go and visit Martin's missus while he's over at Media Liaison. Get some background on him, casual chit-chat, nothing more.'

'Should we see the deceased's brother now?' asked Ruby, finishing off her Maisy Daisy raspberry ripple cone.

'Maybe, but we do need to see Carol Holman. Why is she hiding from us? Too freaked out? Can't be bothered? If she thinks that we're going to go away, then she's very wrong. She might have had the best view of the incident.' Costello wiped her hands on a tissue. Her chocolate mint chip had been melting in the heat of the car as fast as she was eating it. She scrunched up the paper wrapper, looked out of the window for a bin and, not seeing one, chucked it into her handbag.

'Well, we've put a card through her door – that's all we can do if she doesn't physically answer her buzzer – but if we keep waiting outside the deli, we're going to put weight on.'

'That ice cream was delish.'

'We'll be back here later so we can review the menu then.'

'Caramel crunch next time.'

'OK, for now, let's go round the back and see what the Green is like once the circus has left. Come on.'

They walked past the deli again, winding their way through people standing in line at the ice-cream window. The air was stifling hot. It was difficult to concentrate. At the steel shutter where Ruby had stood on duty that night, they paused to let Costello test the security of the door. It was closed tight. They walked further round to the crimson front door of the Grainhouse, which opened on to Brewer Street, home to the Wallaces.

It was Pauline who came to the door in response to them ringing the bell. She was hanging on to the collar of a panting and dribbling Great Dane. Costello felt Ruby recoil.

'Oh, hello.' Pauline took a step back. 'Hang on while I put this idiot in the Green.' The door closed over and they heard the scrambling of claws. They waited quietly until it opened again. Pauline rubbed her bare arms, pulling down the short blue sleeves of her T-shirt. 'He's young and excitable.'

'Useless guard dog?' asked Costello, smiling.

'Sven trains them not to bark; it annoys him. But Hamlet is as thick as mince. Do come through.' Then Pauline turned to Ruby. 'He won't touch you.'

'We were wanting another look round the Green, if that's OK. The door at the side is locked at the moment,' Costello added pointedly, holding out her warrant card.

'Yes, that should always be locked. We can't explain why it was left open last night. Sven was furious when he found out. He's so security conscious.' She rolled her eyes as she opened the door wider. 'That side gate should always be locked.' She showed them into the house, a small hall wider than it was deep, then through a broad archway into the huge living room. The patio doors straight in front of them framed the grass of the Green beyond. It was, as a designer would say, a beautiful open space in grey and cream and taupe, airy and the full three storeys of the building. Weight-bearing steel beams held lights in place, high over the light-grey tiled flooring. It could have been a cover for a modern lifestyle magazine.

Ruby gave Costello a look; even standing here, they made it look untidy.

Pauline, wiping her hands on her linen trousers, guided them through the Nordic-style kitchen and out of the patio doors on to the decking and then on to the Green itself.

Costello was aware how quiet it was the minute they walked on to the grass. She took in the beauty of it, the serenity of the surroundings. Hamlet was lying in the sun, chewing a bone. Both cops stood admiring the Japanese pond, the small trees, the mosaic of colours of the wild garden flowers, the dragonflies and the white curtains still flowing out of the balcony doors above. Costello turned, looking up at the roof garden, the hanging vines; she turned round 360 degrees, the film *Rear Window* coming to mind.

'Do you want to see exactly where it happened?' asked Pauline, pointing to the end of her decking. 'The kids had been playing with the trampoline so it was stacked against the loggia' – Pauline pointed, then dropped her arm – 'but you know that. You were here, weren't you?'

'Yes, but it looks different in the daylight. What do you do for a living, Pauline?'

'I'm the secretary for the company. I have a small office of my own in the house.'

'The company?'

'Trappa. It's owned by Sven and Murdo. The offices are at the end of the Maltman House – they have three floors. The girls have a den up there, Murdo has a collection of historic artefacts, and they want to build a small cinema, when they have time.'

'Does Sven's wife work? Sabina, is it?'

'Oh, good God, yes. She homeschools the girls until they get to secondary school age, but official paid work for Trappa, no. Do you want to talk to her? Shall I give her a call? I know she's in. She's really upset about last night. She got a real shock.' Pauline pulled out her mobile and tapped twice.

Costello walked over and stood next to the trampoline legs and looked up. Thinking about what she could see of the balcony and what the resident of that flat might have seen from there. She strolled back to where Ruby and Pauline had taken a seat on the padded wicker chairs, Ruby pretending to chat but doing a subtle interview.

'Do you know her, the woman who lives up there?' Costello pointed to the small balcony above them.

'In the Quarterhouse? No, I've never met her. Sven and Murdo did the interviews for the rental. They say she's very nice, a Norwegian translator. The boys know her better than us.'

'The boys?'

'Joshua and Bobby, my son and his partner. They run the deli.'

'Yes, we've been sampling the ice cream. Is it a family concern?'

'Two families. Award-winning ice cream and award-winning architecture – it's a strange mixture.' She laughed, her brown hair falling loose. She had slightly over-large teeth that gave her a broad grin when she smiled. 'We never meant it to happen – more like it evolved, which is often the best way.'

Ruby had turned her face to the sun, her car keys lying on top of the table. The small Tigger was lying on his back so he was facing the sun as well. 'How did that come about?'

'Bobby had a place in St Andrews, a small ice-cream and pancake place, so when they got together, it was a good fit. They used to . . . oh, here's Sabina.'

A blonde woman, smaller in height and a good ten years younger than Pauline – which made her, by Costello's calculation, twenty years younger than Sven – had stepped out on to the decking, followed by a dopey golden retriever, exhausted by the heat. The dog looked at Hamlet, looked at the bone, then went back to the cool of the kitchen.

Costello empathized; even Ruby was beginning to wilt in the heat.

Sabina looked like a woman who coped well with everything. Her clothes were scruffy chic: Crocs on her feet, long dirndl skirt, a white cotton vest top that flattered her finely muscled shoulders.

Costello let Pauline do the introductions. It was obvious the women were mutually supportive of each other, the business and the children. As Ruby spoke to them both, they voiced concerns for the girl, asked about the young man who had come in to help. 'Have you been OK?' she asked. 'We do have counselling services we can offer.'

'I'm OK, but it's a big shock,' said Sabina. 'I got a fright. You never think it'll happen in your place.' Her accent was much stronger than her husband's. She was a very pretty woman, blue-eyed and lightly tanned. She looked around the Green, squinted slightly in the sun. 'We're very happy here. It's a terrible thing.'

'Neither of you knew the girl? Here's a recent picture.' Ruby handed it over.

Both women looked at it for a long time. Pauline shook her head, saying that the victim looked so young. Sabina started to cry, asking if they knew what had happened to her.

'Not yet, but we will.'

'If there's anything we can do to help. So sad.'

They had no idea why the woman would have arrived in their back garden, and they had never seen Martin Callaghan before either. Pauline was very sure, as she had spoken to him during the evening, offered him a cup of tea.

'He didn't look like anybody I know,' said Sabina, 'but I only saw him through the patio doors. Still, I think I would have recognized him.'

'Do you have any idea why she came in here?'

'No, not really, but it's a little puzzling that she knew the code,' said Sabina, looking at Pauline.

'Or the gate was left open. The vehicle shutter has a buzzer if it's left unlocked, but the small door doesn't. Maybe one of the kids left it open. Joe uses that door, doesn't he? He's always rushing around.'

Costello caught an implied criticism there. Maybe the child of a mere tenant should have more respect for the sanctuary of the Green.

Pauline might have caught the quizzical look on Costello's face, so she added, with a trace of apology, 'Teenagers will always be teenagers. One of the constants of life.'

'What about the rented flats? Louise and Carol? You must be very careful with the tenants, make sure they aren't going to have raves or take up playing the bagpipes?'

'Sven does many interviews to get the right person. So far, touch wood, we've never had the wrong individual.' Sabina laughed, wiping her tears away. She had a very light, tinkling kind of laugh. Ruby joined in, while Costello pondered about Sven, wondering if he was a design genius who was fussy about who lived in his property, or if he was a control freak who wanted to surround himself with women who thought he was wonderful.

'Are the girls at home? Maybe Ruby can have a chat with them, but she'd need you to be there, Sabina. It was the young one who ran out, wasn't it? Sophie?' Costello noticed a delay, slightly longer than the usual maternal concerns. 'Just a wee chat to see if they saw anything. I'm sure they'd want to help. Sometimes it's reassuring for the young mind to know that the authorities are taking control over a traumatic situation.'

Sabina looked at Pauline, something said without being spoken.

'She's right, the girls might sleep better with some reassurance that the situation is being dealt with,' suggested Pauline.

Sabina nodded, then asked Ruby to follow her.

Nice people, thought Costello, hearing them chatter: the four Jonsson girls, their mum and Ruby sitting round the kitchen island as she fanned herself, trying to keep cool. Costello let her eyes wander over their kitchen/diner that ran the full width of the house, the windows that must look on to the street simply known as Plantation, tall slim windows left over from the days of the factory, the ones they couldn't change because of the planning regulations about the street-facing aspect of the building. The kitchen opened out by the big patio doors that Costello knew had been closed on the night of the incident when Sabina had been pacing behind them, holding her youngest child, tears in her eyes.

Pauline chatted on about how wonderful life was here, Costello half listening and adding the odd non-confrontational question. How long have you lived here? How do you keep the grass so green?

'Is there any chance we can talk to Sven and Murdo?' asked Costello. 'So we can complete our interviews and not disrupt you again.'

'Of course,' said Pauline. 'If Sven's not too busy working, you know. "Oh, you must never interrupt me when I am busy" – this is what he says, then sits down to talk about football with Murdo. Men!' She looked at her watch. 'They'll be out soon – their meeting's over. I'll get some fresh Danish. Do you want coffee or tea?' And off she trotted to her kitchen, returning with a tray of coffee, tea and a plate of mixed Danish pastries.

They came out, Sven and Murdo, bringing Sabina and Ruby

with them. Ruby was pocketing her notepad; the four girls had
disappeared back into the house. Costello felt restricted in what
she could ask, so she asked them again if they knew Rachel. They
looked at the picture, but they sipped their coffee, ate their pastries
and denied any knowledge of her. Sven enquired how the investigation was going. Murdo adjusted his cuffs as he asked how the
young policeman was. They chatted, drank good coffee, according
to Ruby. Costello had a cup of tea and munched an apricot Danish,
watching how judiciously Pauline served her husband and Sven.
Ruby talked and Costello listened, paying much closer attention
than it would appear. It was interesting to watch the four of them
interact. Ruby asked a few questions that might be relevant to the
case, but didn't pursue it when the question was batted away and
replaced with some titbit about life on the Green and how lovely
it was, the same wording used when Costello had been alone with
Pauline. They were good, these four; they really knew the script.
    She scrutinized them: Pauline talked nervously, Sabina was sad,
Murdo was the well-dressed charmer. Costello could paint him as
the ladies' man as he dusted the flakes of pastry from his fingertips
with the napkin; his shirt was free of sweat, the fine creases down
the length of the sleeve still visible. It was Sven whom Costello
couldn't fathom. He was polite, amusing, he held Sabina's hand
as they chatted on the quad afterwards, while gently moving the
detectives towards the door in the steel shutter, so they were not
going out through the house. As she walked behind him, Costello
noticed that his grey ponytail was held in place with a narrow
strip of black leather. He was a commanding presence, over six
feet tall, broad-shouldered and slim-hipped. He requested that they
come back later for a more formal interview, if it was needed; it
was the politest dismissal Costello had ever witnessed. He even
recommended the best sandwich to get at the deli – pulled jerk
chicken and salad – if they were still hungry.
    So polite, with good taste in food and garden furniture. Apart
from that, Costello couldn't pin him down at all.

'So what do we think? If Rachel got that key code because she
was having an affair with somebody in this building, who would
it be?' asked Costello, opening the windows of the car which had
turned into a greenhouse in their absence.

'If I was going to have an affair, it would be Murdo. He's more human than Sven somehow,' said Ruby.

'Really? Sven's kind of tall and icy.'

'Too bony. At least Murdo has some beef about him. He looks as if he'd give you a share of the carrot cake.'

'All four of them say that they'd never seen Rachel before. They suspect that Joe Dawson left the shutter door open.'

'They didn't budge when you questioned them. They stayed very firm.'

'They didn't suggest that one of the Jonsson girls left it open, did they? That never crossed their mind. But don't believe them; you learn that in CID. They're lying bastards. Sven's a smooth lying bastard and Murdo's a cake-eating lying bastard, but I can't quite work out what they're actually lying about. But I sense evasion. I'd love to have bugged that place so we can hear what they say the minute our backs are turned.'

'I thought they were lovely,' mused Ruby.

'The men have been friends and business partners for many years, probably closer to each other than they are to their respective wives. Do you know about that case we worked on, the Sideman?'

'I remember hearing about it at the time.'

'Men have the ability to form close relationships with each other that can outlast any relationship they have with a woman,' Costello said. 'Those two spoke for a long time when Rachel had passed away. I'd like to know what they were saying then. Getting their stories straight?'

'Doesn't mean that the two women weren't doing the same thing by phone. Equally devious but cleverer at it,' said Ruby.

'Good point.'

Ruby looked at her watch, then over at the queue at the deli. 'That Danish was good, but it has put me in the mood for another ice cream.'

'Don't lie to me – you were already in the mood for another ice cream.'

EIGHT

Martin Callaghan's house was a small terrace: three bedrooms of bedlam. It reminded Wyngate of his own place a few years before, the problems of too many residents under eight years old. Becs Stewart was a tall, strong-looking woman. Her hair dyed black, light brown showing through at the roots. She didn't seem surprised to see him, or impressed; curious more than anything else, maybe just glad for someone to talk to. He handed her the picture of Rachel, the smiling face framed with blonde hair.

'So is this about that lassie? The one who died?'

'Yes,' said Wyngate. 'We're wondering if you knew her.'

'Do you mean you're wondering if Martin knew her? I don't button up the back, you know. So who's she, anyway?'

'Rachel Sinclair. Do you know anybody of that name?'

She shook her head. 'What happened? They say he's a hero, but that doesn't sound like him.'

'Well, it appears she was in distress and he went to her aid, but unfortunately she passed away,' he explained, thinking that she'd not ask him any more. He was wrong.

She folded her arms and pursed her lips, looking at the picture, a threatening gesture he had seen from his own wife many times when he had said that he might be working late again. 'He'd be more a chat-her-up type. Not surprised if she looked like that. Blonde, pretty, young, great legs?' She rolled her eyes and picked up a cloth, started to wipe a worktop with more aggression than was absolutely necessary, scrubbing away at a lump of something small, brown and hard.

'Do you think he was having an affair?'

'No, not really. Who else would have him? He's such an arse. And why would she look twice at a wee shite of a toerag like him?'

'These your kids?' he asked as he walked over to the front of the fridge, to the photographs of several toothless, red-cheeked wonders pinned up with multicoloured magnets – two girls about six and four, a boy about eight, he'd guess.

'Three – you can tell by the amount of washing. It feels like we've been together for a thousand years.'

'Is it usual for him to go out on a Thursday?'

'Yes, it is.' She stopped scrubbing, her face contemplative. 'But lately, you know, I've thought there might be somebody. He's not been where he's supposed to be, and his phone's turned off. The sad truth is, I'm not sure I care. If it wasn't for the kids, he could go and raffle. So she's welcome to him, except she's dead, so I suppose nobody wins.' She scrunched the cloth into a small ball and threw it into the sink with a strength and accuracy that Wyngate found both impressive and frightening.

'Maybe you should talk to him.'

'I'm bloody fed up talking to him. He never listens. So what else do you want? You obviously came here for something?'

'Just covering all bases. I was looking for the jeans he was wearing on Thursday? Just for DNA?' He looked around at the mountain of washing. The air in the kitchen was stifling hot. There was a smell of unwashed feet drifting around. Out of the window he could see a table and five picnic chairs, their wood sun-bleached and dry.

'You can ask him; I'm not his servant.'

Then he heard a noise and realized that Becs was sobbing. 'Did Martin hurt her?'

'No, no, there's no question of that,' Wyngate said, wondering why she had asked.

A quarter of an hour later, he was outside in the garden playing shops with Emily, drinking tea that he had brewed and having a quiet conversation about Martin Callaghan.

David Sinclair opened the door, wiping his fingers dry with a dish towel; he looked from Costello to Wyngate and then pointed, with a smile, to the sign stuck to the front window that said *No Cold Callers Please.*

Costello, having suffered a fifteen-minute drive trying to calm Wyngate down from the fearsome Becs Stewart, wondered if they really did look like a couple of Jehovah's Witnesses. She was ready with her warrant card and lifted it in synchronicity with

Wyngate, who stood at the bottom of the step, so that Sinclair knew who was in charge.

But at the moment, Costello was smiling her kind and gentle smile which she could switch on and off. Her expression said that she was to be trusted, and she leaned in, inviting the confidence of the man who had opened the door, the man who had heard the front-door bell while he was doing his dinner dishes, and whose life they were about to change forever.

'Mr David Sinclair?'

He nodded.

'Can we have a word, please?'

'Of course.' He opened the door wider, and invited them in.

Costello said something about hoping they had not come at an awkward time, leaving Wyngate to ponder when would be a good time to hear news like this, but then Costello added something about the children being home for the school holidays.

'Rose's having tea with a friend, Jamie's playing football,' said Sinclair, catching something in Costello's tone. 'Only the wife and I in the house.' He gestured that they should both sit down. He went back into the hall and shouted to Doreen, who appeared, still in her dressing gown with her slippers on. Costello hung about in the hall long enough to look out of the kitchen window, at the washing line: shirt, underwear, jeans.

'Sorry, I've been ill,' she explained, glancing at her husband, sensing bad news, and she sat down on the settee. Sinclair sat beside her, holding her hand. Doreen dabbed at her nose with a handkerchief. She looked red-eyed, her voice nasal with congestion. 'Is it the kids? Has something happened to Jamie?' Her voice was quiet. She took a deep breath and looked from one to the other.

'No, don't worry.'

She nodded, relieved; nothing she could hear now was going to be as bad as that.

Costello took a quick look at Wyngate, reading the subtext that there was more than one story here. 'I'm afraid I have some bad news for you, Mr Sinclair.'

'Frank! Has something happened to Frank? Has he had a fall?' asked Doreen, dabbing again.

'It's not about Frank,' Costello said casually.

'Thank God. My uncle, he was in the hospital and they let him out yesterday, and I thought that it was too early . . .'

'No, it's not Frank. It's about Rachel, your sister, Mr Sinclair.'

'Oh?' His voice was totally devoid of expression.

'We believe that she may have been involved in an incident yesterday. Do you have a recent picture of her?'

He nodded slowly, then with hesitation he got up and walked to the small coffee table, where he picked up his mobile phone. 'There's a picture on here of her and the kids at the gala day in the village. She was selling her jewellery.' He flicked through the pictures, swiping them to the side. 'There you go, that's her on the end.'

Costello looked at the picture, definitely Rachel.

'And she's here,' said Doreen, getting up to pick a small framed photograph from a collection above the sideboard. She handed it to Costello, giving the glass a wipe with her sleeve first. Rachel, obviously a bit younger, maybe three or four years ago, with two children, the boy on a bike, the taller girl holding a small white dog. David behind her, smiling for a camera and laughing slightly. 'Rose and Jamie.'

'Rose? It's a pretty name.' Costello took her time studying the girl and then nodded to Wyngate to have a look and confirm her thoughts. The deceased was indeed Rachel Sinclair.

'Rosie's very like her. They're a tag team.'

'I'm not sure an aunt should have favourite . . .' Sinclair seemed to remember who he was talking to.

'We've some bad news for you, I'm afraid. We've reason to believe that Rachel was caught up in a fatal incident very late last night. She passed away at the scene.'

The room went quiet. Costello gave them time to digest the news.

'Will I put the kettle on?' asked Doreen, giving her husband a little pat on his shoulder.

'Yes, please,' he answered.

'Do you know of any reason why she might be going somewhere dressed as a police officer?'

Sinclair laughed sadly. 'Fancy dress or something? She's always getting up to some nonsense or other. So what happened to her? Was it a car accident?'

'We're not really sure what happened to her. That's part of our ongoing enquiries. We don't know how she died, but a body's been found, dressed in uniform. At first it was thought she was a serving officer, and then we found the ID of Rachel Sinclair and she's the woman in the pictures on your phone.'

Sinclair sat back down again, nodding slowly. He didn't seem overly surprised; there was a sense of him accepting the inevitable. His wife had taken the news in a similar way, making Costello think that she would have been much more upset if it had been Uncle Frank.

Doreen entered with a tray with four cups of hot tea. Wyngate balanced his on a side table and pulled his notebook from his pocket.

'So what happened to her, in the end?'

'Were you expecting something to happen to her?'

Sinclair shook his head. 'There've been a few things over the years. She nearly set her flat on fire once – well, she did set it on fire and she was lucky to get out. Before that she smashed her car and was in hospital for a couple of weeks because she banged her head so badly . . . and, well, if there's something to trip up on, she'd be the one who'd trip up on it.'

'She needed surgery on her shoulder after the crash, didn't she, David?'

'Yes, that's right. She couldn't drive for a while.'

'Which shoulder?' asked Wyngate, his pen moving from side to side.

'Can't recall,' said Sinclair.

'I think it was her left; she could still write. What did she do now?' asked Doreen.

For a moment, Costello hesitated, considering how much to say. 'We found her up at the Maltman Green.'

Sinclair shook his head. 'I don't know where that is.'

'Where the Quarterhouse Deli is?' asked Doreen. 'Up there? That's not her normal drinking ground. She's normally more down in the lower end of Byres Road. But she's mentioned it a few times, the deli and the Maltman,' said Doreen.

'Well, I've never heard of it.'

'That's because you never listened to a word she said.' Doreen turned to Costello. 'I got the feeling she was doing a piece of jewellery for somebody there, or was maybe seeing somebody who worked there. We were always hoping she'd meet somebody nice, settle down.'

'She'd be a bloody nightmare. God, she's bad enough when we invite her round for a drink.'

'Did she have an issue with alcohol?' asked Wyngate gently.

'Not with alcohol. She was clumsy, though.' Sinclair's face crumpled. The reality of the news was sinking in: there was no coming back from this one for his wee sister.

'She never looked drunk or intoxicated.'

'Did she have an issue with anything else?' asked Costello, remembering the packets of white powder that were now at the lab.

'No. So what happened?' Doreen's hand was sitting on her husband's shoulder.

'We really don't know.'

'Don't know or you can't say?'

'We genuinely don't know. She was last seen by some witnesses with a man. Do you know if she had a man in her life? Anybody special? Anybody at the Maltman? At the deli?'

Doreen opened her mouth but no words came out, so she shut it again. Her husband glanced at her. It couldn't have been more obvious if he had said, *Don't say anything.*

Costello changed tack. 'Was it usual for her to go out without her mobile phone?'

'No, it was glued to her hand. She had a big hairy cover on it and a few of those dangling things that rattled all the time.'

'And her car is not at her house. Would she drive if she was going out and intending to have a drink?'

'Yes. Even if she had had a drink, she'd always drive and never took a telling, not even after the accident,' her brother said.

'Well, there does need to be a post-mortem examination and we'll need somebody to come down and identify the body if that's OK.'

'I can do it if you don't want to,' Doreen said to her husband, shooting a look at Costello, a silent conversation between the two women, something she didn't want to say while her husband was in the room.

'You can both attend if you wish, and they may want to take

some DNA from you, Mr Sinclair, to make sure. That's very common nowadays.'

'Does it matter that she was only my half-sister?'

'No, as long as we know that.'

'What happened to her?'

'She didn't appear to have suffered any major injuries. She was lying there as if she had collapsed. The emergency services worked on her for some time but they couldn't revive her, I'm afraid.'

They sat in silence for a moment. A dog barked somewhere down the street.

'And she was dressed like a police officer?'

'Yes. Did she say she was going anywhere last night?'

'No, not spoken to her in a while. The last we heard from her was that her new career was doing well.'

'The bespoke jewellery?'

'That's what she said. But there's nothing else. We weren't close, as a family. There's a few years' age difference – same dad, different mums – so we didn't grow up together. I liked her but had no real family feeling for her.'

'She was always good with the kids, though; they were very fond of her. We need to tell them before they read about it online. They get to know everything these days, don't they?'

'Do you think that she might have wanted children herself?'

Doreen paused a little too long before answering. 'I think that might have been something that she wanted.'

Costello nodded. 'OK, can I confirm your contact details? We can arrange a car to come and get you for the identification.'

Anderson looked out of the window of the house in Kirklee Terrace, thinking about Mr Baseball, where he was and how he had managed to leave the scene so effectively. Costello wanted to trace the route he might have taken, moving by foot, thinking about the choices he might have made: left, right, straight on, backtrack, kill or leave to breathe another day. It was one of Costello's hunches that he was finding difficult to resist.

It was unclear in Anderson's mind what Mr Baseball had done. O'Hare the pathologist was being uncharacteristically evasive; he had wanted to consult Rachel's own GP before he reported back with any kind of opinion.

And there was something about Martin Callaghan. Anderson had spent an hour interviewing him that day, trying to reconcile the excellent young police officer that appeared in the early HR reports with the very average, rather listless copper he was now. In his youth he had been tagged as a high flyer, then nothing – no burn-out, no huge stress, just a plateau. Callaghan was a very average man, in a long-term relationship with Rebecca, three children, working hard to pay his mortgage. Anderson knew how difficult that could be, those early years of long hours on the job, when they were hamsters on a wheel.

He was trying to imagine himself in that position, as the cop stumbling upon somebody who had passed away in his arms. He hoped he would have done more; he would have pulled out his mobile and dialled for help. The one thing that Callaghan had not done. But maybe ten years as a constable with no promotion had blunted his sense of responsibility; certainly, being hailed a hero on social media and having a new photograph taken for the press had not removed his anxious demeanour.

Anderson could hear Moses snoring gently behind him, the occasional soft footfall of Claire overhead. She was restless tonight, not settling at all, whereas Moses, normally the restless one, was snoring like a tiny piglet in harmony with Norma who was whimpering in her sleep.

He felt uneasy. Something to do with Rachel lying there, her eyes open, staring at the sky. It was his responsibility to make the situation right. An old man from up the street walked down the mews with his collie, a dog that Norma did not like. The two of them growled every time they caught sight of one another. Anderson watched the man strolling along as if he had all the time in the world, which he probably had – all the time until he died. Anderson could never imagine himself walking that slowly with his own dog, achieving nothing because there was nothing else to achieve. His active life was over. His work was done.

And then there was Rachel. Her death had been quick and far too soon. Yes, he had a duty to do something about that, and if it was arrogant to assume that he and only he could solve the case, then so be it. It was his responsibility.

He turned to sit down on the tub seat. He wouldn't be able to sleep tonight, thoughts of Rachel rolling around in his head. But why? They were trying to trace Mr Baseball. As soon as they spoke to him, a lot would become clear. Despite public appeals, he had not come forward, but as soon as the DNA came back, they'd have a lead and a name, and they could take it from there.

His eyes settled on Moses as his thoughts drifted to Johnny Clearwater. How could a child go missing like that? He had worked on a few cases in the past where it appeared that somebody had vanished into thin air – the case of the Night Hunter was one. But they never did; it was always at somebody's hand and usually at the hand of somebody they knew. He imagined being invited to a party to celebrate a wedding, asked to bring Moses as there would be other children there. He imagined Brenda deep in conversation and him at the bar, each of them thinking that the other had Moses in sight. Then they were called together for a photograph and, in one moment, it would become apparent that Moses had gone. Then it would start, a cascade from slightly annoyed to blind panic.

The manager at the Stewart Hotel had phoned the police immediately but, four years later, there was no sign.

Equally, there was no body.

Nothing.

How did Naomi cope with that? She was relentless at keeping Johnny's memory alive and in the forefront of the media. Richard, her husband, seemed happier to take a back seat. It took all sorts to make the world; it might be Richard who stayed awake at three o'clock in the morning, thinking about his son and replaying the events on the last day he had seen him. Naomi, content that she was doing everything that she possibly could do, might be the one who slept soundly.

But he doubted it.

According to Mulholland, the star of the TV programme, the old investigation team led by Bob Allison was on standby now in case the exposure sparked some more evidence. Something might have crawled out of the woodwork, but after this length of time, there wouldn't be any hope of a good resolution.

Costello was right: they were looking for a body.

He sat for some time, looking out of the window as a weak summer darkness fell, a lessening of the shadows, his feelings of unease growing.

His mobile vibrated in his pocket. It was Mathilda McQueen's personal number. He wondered why the forensic scientist was calling him at this hour, but he answered it and listened to what she had to say. Asked her to repeat it, swore, then he hung up.

He was in the car and away within minutes.

Costello had dropped Wyngate off at the station to collect his car, and was told that Ruby was there, typing up the log for the day – if Costello was heading back out for a chat with Carol Holman, she'd be happy to work on as the deli was open to ten o'clock that night and they did pesto and mozzarella toasties. And there were other ice creams to try, if it was still warm. Which it was.

Costello smiled and wondered what kind of metabolism Ruby possessed. Or was it youth? Maybe a more seasoned detective was used to eating when they could; most of the uniforms these days spent their time in the KFC car park with occasional forays to McDonald's.

She had to admit that the smell from the deli was making her feel hungry as she spoke into the mesh microphone of the duplex flat of the Quarterhouse; it was hard to keep the irritation from her voice as she repeated. 'Yes, they were our uniformed branch who were trying to get in touch with you, but we do need to interview all significant witnesses.' Costello turned to her companion, raising an eyebrow. 'And you're the most significant witness that we have.' Silence from the mesh. 'I really don't want to talk about this out in the street. It's a bit noisy here, so maybe you could let us come up so we could have a chat. The queue from the deli's listening.'

Silence again.

'Did she let the uniforms in?' asked Ruby, looking at her notes.

'No. She wouldn't speak to them, that's why we're here. She's a bit . . .'

The red light buzzed; they heard the electronic lock slide back and Ruby leaned her shoulder against it, keeping it open in case Carol Holman changed her mind.

They entered a small square hall: tiled floor, bare white walls, with a set of narrow concrete steps turning to the right – also brilliant white, cold, no covering underfoot except a few coats of fresh paint that reminded both of the police officers of a multistorey car park. The only difference was the absence of the heady smell of diesel and stale urine. This stairwell smelled of fresh coffee and baking. The white painted concrete stairs looked as if nobody had ever stepped on them, and she noted, as she started up, that there was no mat to wipe her boots on.

'It's very clean,' Costello commented. 'Almost unused.'

'So she doesn't have kids or visitors,' said Ruby, her heavy footfall echoing up the internal stairwell. After a double turn, there was a small square landing with a single pot plant, another exterior door with another camera and another entry door system. Costello pulled her ID from her bag again and showed it to the camera, then stepped aside to let her colleague do the same.

They heard somebody move at the other side of the door. Both their faces were impassive. Neutral. Carol Holman might have other cameras watching, observing them. Costello moved her hand as if to rub her eye and, sure enough, she caught sight of a minute glass lens high in the opposite corner.

Carol Holman either had something to hide or she was scared. Costello decided to give her the benefit of the doubt. The Maltman Green had witnessed a death the night before; this woman may have seen the incident with her own eyes, so it was no wonder she might be scared, except that she seemed to have been scared well in advance.

The space in the flat was impressive; the kitchen, dining and living space ran the whole breadth of the building. Costello noticed, as they walked past the dining table, that they were looking down to the Brewer Street corner. She wondered if Carol had seen anything from the front window. From here, she was more likely to catch sight of somebody fleeing the scene, as their approach to the steel shutter would be out of sight.

Their host seemed much older than they had been led to believe, walking quietly in front of them, like a contemplative nun. She was a pale woman with long frizzy hair, dark eyebrows, washed-out blue eyes that were weary with the simple effort of living. This evening the heat outside was intense. The flat, even with the doors of the living-room balcony open, was still too warm for comfort, yet Carol wore a long fine cardigan over a long-sleeved T-shirt.

'Are you OK, Carol? Do you feel safe here?' Costello asked, thinking about the security on the door.

'Yes, I do, in here.' She sounded relieved. 'I don't feel very safe out there. I don't like being outside.'

'My mum had agoraphobia,' said Ruby, strolling through Carol's lounge, taking a seat on the settee in front of the TV, which was on but muted: dancers were gyrating noiselessly, a singer's mouth opened and closed, silently screaming. 'She'd a terrible time with it – anxiety, panic attacks. She'd break out in a cold sweat, her heart would start thumping, she'd go dizzy, start shaking and twice she actually fainted with it. So I know how bad it can be, Carol, but don't let it rule your life, OK?' Ruby smiled, her lips painted a vivid red. 'There are good medications out there. You should try some.'

Costello, who looked as if she had not gone home for a fortnight, gazed at Ruby, her young relentless energy so apparent in everything she did. Dark ghosts haunted her own eyes; she had been drinking a can of Red Bull in the car on the way over. She felt terrible, whereas Ruby, working a double shift, looked and sounded as fresh as a daisy.

'We're sorry for disturbing you. I presume if you don't like going out, then we'll always find you in if we wish to speak to you at any time. We might come back later with some pictures for you to look at.'

'Yes, I'll always be here.' She smiled and a slightly steely look came into her eyes. 'I'm not going anywhere.'

'So was it you who called the police?' Costello asked as Carol sat opposite her.

It was a striking-looking woman who studied them, her blue eyes examining them for any weakness.

'I think I tried to. Did I get through? I can't remember.'

Costello caught the accent. 'You're not from round here, are you?'

'No, I'm from Norway.'

'Oh, what are you doing over here?'

'I'm a translator – scientific papers. It's very interesting work but it's the sort that can be done anywhere, so I decided to go to London for a few months and then come up to Glasgow.'

Costello smiled and nodded, thinking how off pat that non-answer was. If she could do her work anywhere, then why was she here? But all she said was, 'So you came to Glasgow to be greeted with this. How long have you been here? It looks like you haven't unpacked properly.'

'Four weeks.'

'Have you met any of the neighbours yet?'

'No,' she said, sharp and blunt.

'They seem a friendly bunch.'

Carol smiled, taking years off her. 'They do socialize a lot. But I like to work; I don't like people popping in. And I don't like going out. So what can I help you with? I don't know what I can tell you. I'm not even sure what I saw.'

'Talk us through it. Where were you?'

Carol shrugged. 'I was sitting inside the balcony, not out on it – it's too high up and I get dizzy.'

'This balcony?' Costello pointed across the room, to the wide glass doors that opened out on to the Green.

'No, the one upstairs. It was a hot night. I was sitting inside the door, getting some fresh air. I saw some movement down at my left side and then the woman came in. I thought it was a policewoman. She was running. Then she hid behind the wooden thing. She was hiding, then the man came after her. I couldn't see very well. I was quite high up, but it looked to me as if they were kissing. It didn't look like they were fighting at all. It didn't look as if he was attacking her in any way, but then it kind of changed. I saw him raise his hand to her. I think that's when I panicked. I think he punched her.'

'Can you show us where you were sitting when it happened?'

Carol bit her lip slightly. 'Yes, of course. You will need to excuse the mess.'

They followed her up the stairs to a small landing, a window out to the Green below in the hall and a bedroom to the left and to the right. Carol turned to the right, the room that would have given her the best view.

'Do you mind if I . . .?' Costello went to the balcony, looked out to the loggia, thirty feet below. 'Did you have this curtain up?'

'It was down, then I hung it on the hook.'

Costello looked at her watch. They were ninety minutes away from what the daylight would have been at the time of the incident. 'There's no light on?'

'No, the Green lights only come on when Sven puts them on.

Maybe when there's a noise outside. They keep them off the rest of the time because the windows are so big the light would be disturbing.'

'How long would you say, Carol, from the chap in the baseball hat going out, leaving the blonde lady, and the other guy running in, the one in the white T-shirt?'

Carol looked confused. 'What do you mean? One went out and the other appeared.'

'Instantly?' asked Costello. 'Like this?' She moved her hands quickly out and in.

'No,' Carol shook her head. 'There was a . . .' She looked for the right word, the first time they had an inkling that English was not her first language. 'A delay, a brief time, maybe if I was to count. Yes, that might be good.' She looked out of the window and closed her eyes slowly, recalling. 'Maybe a count of eight – a slow count.'

Costello let her speak about the way the man had followed Rachel as if he knew where she was, and that the other man had been running when he came in.

'Running?' asked Costello.

'Yes. He was running' – Carol nodded – 'faster than the first guy.'

'Was your bedroom light on?'

'Not the main light, but my reading light was. That one there.'

Costello followed Carol's finger to the huge floor-standing light. She switched it on, watching the light filter down on to the grass near where the trampoline was.

'So what did you see of her?'

'The girl looked up.'

'Up at you?'

'No, straight up, over there, to my left. She put her hand to her throat like this' – Carol imitated the action – 'and that was when she passed out, or fell, or died.'

'And the security lights were off.'

'Yes.'

'OK, so what else can you remember?'

Carol was nervous about telling them what she had seen, but Costello felt there was something more to come. 'And you didn't want to look; people never do. Had you seen them before, either of them?'

Carol shook her head. 'No, and it happened very quickly, and I began to feel very uneasy. Then I realized that I was outside.' She went even paler. One hand clasped her dressing table and the other covered her face.

'Are you OK?'

'Sorry, I'm feeling a bit upset by it. I'm not good at being outside on a balcony like that. I don't mind looking out but I can't look down, not when it's so high up. I do recall picking up my mobile, but more than that I can't really remember. I think I woke up lying on the floor of the balcony. I think I fainted.'

'Did you call the police?'

'I'm sure I picked up my phone and dialled.'

'But you didn't speak?'

Carol shook her head. 'I'm sure I just passed out.'

'Are you OK now?'

She pulled her long grey hair round her neck. 'Yes, I am,' she said unconvincingly.

'Can you describe the man who came in the lane with the girl? The one who was kissing her?'

'He was maybe thirty or forty. Average height. He had jeans on. A baseball cap. Slimmish. Not overweight or particularly tall. But he didn't come in with her, so maybe you should not say that. She was there, then he followed her. She was hiding from him. I'm sorry that I didn't do anything more. I could have shouted. I might have been able to . . .'

'I doubt that. I wouldn't let your mind focus on it. Tell me, what did you see of her?'

'Her? Tall, blonde, and I thought she was a uniformed person, but I wasn't sure what – I am not that familiar with what a British female police officer might be wearing. But yes, she was in a uniform.'

Costello nodded.

'And I don't think he was as tall as she was – just an imagined thing in my head.' She shrugged again. 'A shirt – it was flapping, it was blue with a white' – she drew her hand up and down her stomach – 'thing underneath, I think.'

'Could it have been a blue jacket or a blue fleece?'

'Perhaps. Light blue.' She looked out of the window, down on to the Green, then tightened her eyes as if she had seen something unpleasant. Then her eyes opened wide. 'And I think he might have dropped something? Or thrown something.'

'Dropped something?'

'I was quite far away but it looked like he let something slip from his hands.' She brushed her long fingers down her arm, the full length of it from shoulder to elbow to wrist and then off the tips of her fingers.

'But you did not see what?'

She shook her head, biting her lip.

'Do you want a cup of tea, Carol? We can go back downstairs now. You're getting upset.'

Carol nodded, and the three of them went downstairs to the living room where she went to the kitchen to put the kettle on. Costello was staring at the TV screen which showed Naomi Clearwater, hugging her husband, tears of joy rolling down her cheeks. Naomi turned to the camera and started talking. The relief and pleasure was obvious even with the sound turned down.

'What the hell is that about?' Ruby asked Costello quietly.

'No idea, but we'd better find out,' Costello whispered back, then said loudly, 'So thank you, Carol. We'll need to take a rain check on the tea, but we'll be back. We'll see ourselves out. Come on, Constable.'

'It's Johnny Clearwater's DNA.'

Mathilda McQueen swallowed her nervousness and placed the two printouts in front of DCI Colin Anderson. They were sitting in her office at the lab. She had gone down to the front door to make sure he got through security on the way in. It was only when they were in the quiet of her own workspace, with the door closed, that she began to speak. 'There you go. The sample we have on record here. And the questioned sample. The questioned sample was in a multi-profile swab, but one of them is a perfect match. I've run it twice to check.'

'You're sure?' asked Anderson.

'I'm sure. It's Johnny Clearwater's DNA. I'm absolutely sure. It's from a swab taken from Rachel Sinclair's face.' Mathilda McQueen moved some files around her desk, finding a piece of A4 card.

'Yes, you said on the phone, but why're you not singing this from the rooftops?' he asked, guessing the answer; the forensic scientist wasn't as sure as she was pretending to be.

Mathilda sat down at her desk, slumped as if it was only the tension that was keeping her upright, and now that she was among friends, she could let the stress show. Running her fingers through her bright copper fringe, she sighed and started the story. 'Because. Because, at that time, the TV company had been in to film in the lab. Those guys from *Eyes and Ears* wanted some shots of the evidence in the Clearwater case. It was requested that we get it from the store. The Clearwater case was a centrally based investigation, and we had received instructions from on high in a memo that said we had to cooperate with the wishes of the TV company. You can see why – it was an important opportunity to get the case in the public eye again. Not that it had really gone away.' She shook her head.

'So what are you saying Mathilda, exactly?'

'I'm saying that the evidence of one crime, of the Johnny Clearwater case, was on one table, and the evidence from the Rachel Sinclair case was on the other examination table.'

'Shit.'

'I know that there's no cross-contamination – how could there be? We're so careful. It's the way the lab runs. The sample from Rachel's face was my sample, it came from my crime scene, it was my case. It was transported by my technician and tested by me. It's signed for; the evidentiary chain is there and it doesn't lie. Johnny's DNA is on Rachel's face. I don't know who left that transferred trace there – that's your job.' She looked up at Colin Anderson. 'Nobody's going to believe me, are they? They're going to say that it's a matter of cross-contamination. That's what I would think if I was listening to this. There's no connection between the Sinclair case and the Clearwater case. The only connection is where the evidence was lying and maybe one stupid member of staff who moved between the two lots of samples.'

'Shit,' repeated Anderson. 'But your staff are highly trained professionals. They wouldn't risk it.'

'What happened if one of them got carried away, sneaked over to have a look at the evidence they had pulled out of the store? The case has a real fascination for most people. It was only here on the table so it could be filmed. There's a two-man film crew here, things weren't what they should have been. They deny it, of course. I've asked them all, but they say it didn't happen. They say they didn't witness anybody not following the rules.'

'I see your problem. Have you called O'Hare? They'd take more samples at the mortuary, so they cannot be contaminated, can they?'

'I have called him, yes. He's going to run his own tests, but that will take some time. In the circumstances, he's not going to rush it; he's going to use another lab. But that test might come back with only the DNA of some of the others present. It might depend where on the face he swabbed in the lab and where I swabbed at the crime scene. I swab what I think will give the best result. In a case of assault like this, I always swab the cheekbones.'

'Bloody hell.' Anderson rubbed his eyes, trying to see some way through this mess.

'I know, I know,' she said. 'I wanted you to see this because I'm not sure that I have it right.'

'Are you ever wrong?' asked Anderson, scrolling through his own notes on his iPad. 'Who else have you identified?'

'We have PC Callaghan. His DNA was on record. Then we have the paramedics – we took them both for elimination. We've another three samples from her cheek; I think two of them will be the two residents of the Maltman Green who came out to help.'

'Jonsson and Wallace?'

'Probably. We'll get samples from them tomorrow, but the sample's a type of DNA soup. It puts them in the pool of suspects, or at least somebody who has been in close personal contact with the body.'

'To be absolutely clear, are you sure that there's no way there could have been any contamination?' asked Anderson.

'Yes. I'm sure. But no, how can I be sure when I've the evidence that it may have happened? There's always a first time and I hope to God it's not now.

'So can you talk me through who was where on the Green from the statements that you have?' Mathilda looked at Anderson. 'I'd rather embarrass myself in front of you than embarrass the lab in front of the entire service.'

'OK, so I know reasonably well who was there,' argued

Anderson, 'But more importantly, this happened in a very specific time frame. We can't hang around waiting for them to get their stories straight.'

'But they don't know what we know,' said Mathilda quietly. 'Nobody does.'

'It won't stay that way for very long,' said Anderson.

Mathilda looked at him and tapped her finger on top of the diagram again.

'Well, Rachel was lying there. Mr Baseball was there, then Callaghan. He said he gave her CPR as she was already on the ground and not breathing when he got there. Then Wallace came out, then Jonsson.'

'Did they do CPR?' She looked at Anderson who quickly called up a computer file.

'Yes, all three. We're still looking for the man in the hat who ran away, the one we think killed her. Mr Baseball.'

'Yes, do you have anything on him? Fingerprints? Anything I can get DNA from?' asked Mathilda.

Anderson thought for a moment. 'Not yet. But let's be clear, if this is Johnny's DNA, then our first thought is that Rachel has Johnny somewhere. There's no sign of a child at her house. I'll get Redding on that.'

'And it's a small sample for two people in close contact, but then she wasn't wearing her normal clothes, was she? So yes, look at Rachel and you need to consider that Johnny kissed somebody on the cheek, a wee goodnight kiss like Moses would give you. Then that person turned up at the scene and rubbed their cheek against that of the deceased?' Mathilda nodded. 'Or was in contact with Rachel after she last washed her face, and before she died. There was saliva or sweat to help the transfer and help it stick. That's a scenario that fits. So, I've checked and double-checked this sample and, well, I'm sending it away for an independent test. But on her face and only on her face is a small trace of DNA that's already in the system, so we know who it is and . . . The most important thing is that nobody must know about this, not until it has been checked and ratified.'

At that moment, Anderson held his hand up. They could heard the batter of footsteps along the corridor, sounding loudly in a building normally so quiet. Their eyes met. They had no time to speak, a question on their lips unanswered as the sound of fast-advancing feet echoed towards them.

The door banged open. 'OK, so what's this about the DNA?' He was furious, the grey-haired man in a suit and no tie, dripping with sweat, the veins on his temples pulsing as his face reddened. He leaned over the table, hands flat, his face right up against Mathilda McQueen's with such aggression that she recoiled and Anderson instinctively stood up, his arms out, ready to defend her. The man pointed his finger right in her face. 'You'd better be right or your career is over. You'd better be right about this DNA belonging to the Clearwater boy or . . .'

'Or what?' asked Anderson. 'We'll be right back where we started? The more worrying concern is that you have a spy in the camp. Word has got out, but not from us. Mathilda was talking to me about the delicacy of the situation, and the best way to move it forward. We were agreeing to more testing before the results are made public. So I suggest you shut up and calm down, in either order. You should know better at your age. Now Mathilda, what were you saying?'

SATURDAY 26TH JUNE

His knees were sore because he had been on his feet too much, too long standing up, stretching at the window, trying to see out. Then he had woken up with the dog lying on his legs. Earlier, there had been nothing on the Green. It was dark, so maybe it wasn't daytime yet. He had looked for his friend but they weren't there. So he stayed in his bed and did nothing but stare at the sky. That woman had brought juice, with a sandwich that tasted of nothing, so it sat uneaten, missing a single bite, at the side of the bed. Pulling the duvet up over his head, he listened to the tick of the daffodil clock as the minutes passed. That and the occasional banging door. The music and the shouts of children on the swings were all noises he had heard a long time ago.

Or was it now?

So he got up and they were there: the kids playing. The two younger ones from the house across the way, and he yearned to join them, have a wee go on the swings. They had a trampoline out sometimes. Or had he imagined that? The kids went inside, their mother calling them in for their dinner. He wondered what they were going to eat. The Green fell quiet, so he slunk off back to bed. The music went on now. It was supposed to soothe him to sleep, but it meant nobody heard him when he screamed.

NINE

The meeting that morning was unlike anything either Anderson or Costello had witnessed before. For one thing, it was at seven a.m., and for different reasons they had both had sleepless nights: the stifling heat and the random thoughts of the complications and machinations that the discovery of the DNA might mean, the main one being that Johnny Clearwater was still alive and that Rachel, or somebody around Rachel, had been in close contact with him. Having been awake for most of the night, they turned up at the meeting, suited and booted, which was at odds with their superiors, none of whom had a uniform on; the top brass were worried and unprepared. The man who had interrupted Mathilda's speech was looking daggers at Anderson, who smiled politely back. The only friendly face was ACC Warburton. There were two people present who were so high up in the service that dizziness must have been an occupational hazard. With the news of the DNA and the subsequent conclusion that the boy was still alive, careers might be about to unravel. And there was the question of who had leaked the news to the parents.

And who had leaked it to the press.

Police Scotland were now in a very awkward position: a chance break in an investigation that had cost millions and got nowhere. They were nervous, and from the way they greeted the two detectives, Anderson and Costello, they were considered to be the two that might get them out of the hole they had found themselves in. But Mathilda McQueen was nervous, too, her eyes darting around the room, trying to seek out the enemy. She had also been up all night and had been getting a hard time for most of it. Costello stepped closer to Anderson as they were shown in the door, not wanting to be separated from him, and he walked as if to sit close to the forensic scientist until a shiny suit pulled out a chair and asked him to sit down. The suit looked like a civilian; he was not as worried about this development as he would have been if he was a cop. He was here for the ride and to make notes. He then confirmed Anderson's chain of thought by asking who wanted coffee, and that he'd get another pot sent up. Costello asked for tea. The suit asked her which sort. Costello nearly asked what they were doing with taxpayers' money, but simply said, 'Breakfast tea,' which was apposite given the hour of the meeting.

It was a large room, carpeted and painted in several tones of ocean blue. Calming. On the wall at the top of the table was a large screen with Naomi's face, Johnny's face and a brief list of the crucial dates down the side. The large oval table sat twelve, and all seats were taken. Then Anderson counted again – there were thirteen and it looked as though Mathilda McQueen's was the seat that had been added at the last minute.

Anderson wondered what the conversation had been before they had come in. What had been going on through the early hours of the morning as the news had been phoned and texted around the country, while Naomi was sharing her tears of hope with the media?

The air in the room smelled of frantic activity. It was warm, scented with a sense of nervous exhaustion that he knew from so many murder enquiries. Their eyes met but Mathilda remained tight-lipped as she subtly rolled her eyes upwards, frustrated at trying to explain complex DNA to men who spent their lives with spreadsheets and budgets.

'We've been joined by DCI Anderson and DI Costello who have some experience in dealing with this kind of delicate issue,' said the bald man who was sitting at the top of the table. He had not introduced himself; he obviously thought they should know who he was.

'Very good on the Peacock case,' said Warburton, his podgy face smiling at both of them as if he was their great-uncle and they had done very well in the nativity play.

'Thank you, sir,' said Costello.

'And with the confirmation of the DNA at four o'clock this morning, it would seem that Johnny Clearwater is very much alive, near here, and has had close contact with one of those who was present at the scene of Rachel Sinclair's death.'

'Or in contact with somebody who was in contact with them,' said Mathilda. 'To be absolutely clear. So nobody gets this wrong. DNA, in some circumstances, can act a little like glitter. It can be transferred. These were not cells; it was transferred by cells held in saliva, a mixture of saliva. It's not likely but the amount we found was—'

'And now that the Clearwater family have been told,' said Baldy, glaring at a bearded man, 'we're under more pressure.'

'The samples were rechecked at four this morning, as you said. In the meantime, we need to know how to move this situation on. It would seem that DCI Anderson already has a foot in the camp; his sergeant has reported on the case for the television, so we've a public profile that we could capitalize on.'

Costello snorted, realizing too late that the suit had not in fact made a joke, so she changed it into a cough.

'DS Mulholland has already been in contact with Naomi and has formed a bond. Kathy Lamont is keen to help the media angle.'

'You don't say,' muttered Costello under her breath.

'Sorry.'

'Good to hear,' said Costello. 'Vik has a good media presence. He'd be useful, putting a positive spin on it.'

'Do we need to put a positive spin on it? The boy's been found alive.'

'He has not been found. Full stop,' said Costello.

Anderson and McQueen locked eyes. It hadn't dawned on the others that there was the possibility of contamination. They tried to have a silent conversation, while their bosses spoke over the top of them.

But it was Costello's voice, in her most Glaswegian growl. 'They'll ask the question why he wasn't found in the last four years and why have we spent millions of pounds trying to find him when he's been on our doorstep all along. That's only one problem. It could be that—'

Warburton, resplendent in uniform, interrupted. 'It might be worse than that, if I am allowed to speak for a moment. I know this team; let me chat to them in my office. We can't take a decision on this quickly because we're not sure of the provenance of the sample, but the worst decision we can make is to delay. Leave it with me. I'll report back.'

Warburton's office was an oasis of calm and tranquillity until the big man himself arrived, sweating and swearing. 'Well, that bunch of chancers weren't going to take a punt. So we need to think of a strategy to make this work. The search for that wee boy almost crippled that region's entire budget, so don't think that's going to happen here; when we say the investigation's over, then it's over. I've decided to inform the Clearwaters that there's a small possibility of contamination.'

'That'll break her heart,' said Costello.

'The human heart will always cling to the positive, Costello. It's a survival mechanism. Naomi has a right to know, but she must not think that this is a sign that her child is alive and well.'

'But what if it does mean that?'

'We know that Naomi loves her face in every newspaper and she'll be talking on every TV, but we're not her private police service. There's a lot of other work out there that we need to fund and I won't be slow in telling anybody that.'

'You know that she has the public on her side. We'll be crucified, if only for incompetence the first time around.'

'Well, she shouldn't get preferential treatment because she's photogenic when crying. Between you and me, I've never understood that. Why can't folk look after their own kids for God's sake?' snapped Costello.

'That's victim blaming,' said Anderson. 'And it is only relevant if somebody took Johnny. Up until now, anything could have happened to him. Look at that last case: two kids dead, and we thought that one was death by misadventure and the other was missing. Both were murder.'

'So why does Naomi evoke such strong empathy?' Warburton asked.

'No idea,' said Costello airily. 'It escapes me completely.'

'You'll be pilloried in the press if you take this on and get nowhere – again,' warned Anderson.

'No, I won't,' said Warburton almost cheerily.

'No?'

'Nope, because I'm not going to do it. You are, DCI Anderson. Operation Taurus. You have five days. Five days to find out where that DNA came from. Five days to be successful where Operation Aries failed.'

Costello opened her mouth but stopped herself in time. There was a place for this kind of argument and this was not it.

'And that's not because I think that this is going to get you somewhere. It's a PR exercise to show the public that we take Naomi Clearwater seriously; we need to be seen to be caring and sensitive to her needs.' Warburton looked over the top of his steel-rimmed glasses. 'Of course, that is the panacea. But I know what your team are like, Anderson. You'll search out every avenue of investigation that you can and you'll find that boy.

'But you have five days. After that, there's nothing I can do. Anderson, you work the Clearwater case. Costello, you sort out the Sinclair case at the Maltman Green. As far as the press and media are concerned, the investigation will look no different and we'll try to keep it that way. Bob Allison will nominally do a cold case review and take the media attention. Your team has a good track with what I'll term "familial crime" – you seem to understand how dysfunctional families work, so I hope you can bring those skills to bear on this. There's the possibility that one of the family had something to do with what looks now to have been an abduction.

'You need to have a long chat with Bob Allison about the case and how it got away from them. He has a wealth of knowledge about the boy and the family. He's content knowing that we are in doubt as well and that we're not trying to make him look stupid – we are trying to prevent the entire force from looking stupid.'

'That's the second time I've heard that,' said Anderson, thinking that he was the one who was being lined up to look stupid. 'I think I'd like to do a review without Allison's input. Otherwise, I'll end up down the same dead end he did.'

Warburton raised his eyebrows, then nodded. 'So stop wasting time listening to me and get on with it. But I'm going to tell you something that might give you a head start. If you tell anybody that I told you, I will deny it. It's been redacted in the file. Have a seat, both of you.

'You know that when a child goes missing, all the loonies in the world come out of the woodwork – fortune tellers, dog walkers, clairvoyants, mediums – until something happens that we have never been able to explain. A woman, a professional medium or something, called in. Her name is Una Parryman. She told us that the boy was still alive. By that time, the investigation unit had heard everything; they had twenty-three thousand statements and no real leads to follow. But she said a load of stuff and talked about a seahorse. One of the female officers asked Naomi and Richard a whole load of questions, including whether Johnny had a favourite stuffed toy. Did he have a seahorse? Both Naomi and Richard reacted. Naomi walked right up to her and grabbed her by the lapel and demanded, "Why? What do you know?"

'It turns out that Johnny has a small birthmark on the lower back which is shaped like a seahorse. So that might put it into context.'

Costello nodded slowly. 'Shall I go to speak to her?'

'One of you should, and off the record. Yes, see if she can point us in the right direction.'

'Did you make sure that she had nothing to do with the abduction, if she was in on it for the kudos and fame of solving the case?' asked Costello.

Warburton slipped off his glasses and started to rub their lenses on the cuff of his uniform. 'Yes, we did think of that, DI Costello. We're police officers, not idiots. They planted somebody to visit her, and she knew whenever they opened their mouths that they were being duplicitous. In fact, two of them got messages from beyond the grave.'

'Really?'

'Maddie Bridgestoke got a message from her dead father and was in tears all day. Davey Allsop got a message from Bruce.'

'Bruce?'

'The family German Shepherd that had been put down a couple of weeks before. Makes you think there might be more things in heaven, but we need all the help we can get, so I'd make that your first port of call. Time is of the essence here.'

'See if we can get next week's lottery results as well,' said Costello.

The message on the board was simple: Rachel Sinclair's car had been found, parked neatly on Upper Rosserman Street. It was locked. No phone, no keys, no laptop were in the vehicle, and it didn't look as if it had been damaged. The house-to-house around Rachel's flat had come up with nothing except for two dog walkers going past and the cleaner going into the villa.

'So if she walked from there, where her car was found, heading towards the Maltman Green, she'd have walked past the Drunken Monkey where the landlord confirmed that Callaghan was drinking; Ruby spoke to him yesterday. Martin was there, having a quiet pint outside in what passes for a beer garden.'

'If she was on her way to the Maltman Green. And if so, why? To meet whom? And why did she go up the alley?'

'Her phone might help with that, when we find it. I've asked Ruby to take the briefing.'

'Really?'

'She's young. She's got the energy and a really good brain.'

'You like her?'

'I do. Never seen a cop who can eat the way she does, and I used to work with Brian McCallum.'

'Brian the gannet McCallum? That's impressive,' Anderson agreed.

PC Ruby Redding was anxiously standing in front of the rest of the team. Costello was typing. Wyngate was at the board pinning up pictures: one half was Rachel's family and contacts, the other half the residents of the Maltman Green. Mr Baseball was in the centre. Mulholland was reading something that looked like a script, intently.

'Is that police work, Vik?'

'Community Service, sir. Public relations.'

'Really?' said Anderson dryly.

'Well, it's a chance for me. I don't think the service is going to keep me around, but they can't get rid of a disabled officer and I'm not waiting until they give me a job filing. So I'm taking any chances I can get.'

Anderson looked down at the younger man's legs, the stick at his side. He had been to the brink of death with septicaemia; the police wouldn't show him any loyalty. 'Yes, but you're here now, and the more you know, the better you'll be informed when Media Liaison give you permission to talk to Kathy Lamont about the case – what you have permission to reveal and what you need to conceal.' He didn't wait for an answer, but tapped his pen against a cup, summoning the rest to listen. Ruby had written her notes on small cards, and she riffled them between her thumbs and fingers like a card shark. She had already mentioned that she had been up early to do a class at the gym, but looked freshest of them all.

'PC Ruby Redding, as you know, has been digging into the activities of Rachel Sinclair during the day she died. This has extreme significance as it gives us the window of opportunity of the Clearwater DNA transfer. Who left that smear on her cheek? On you go, Ruby,' Anderson said, giving her an encouraging smile.

'On DCI Anderson's orders, I've been through Rachel's life and there's no male child there, apart from her nephew, Jamie.'

'I'm on that,' said Costello. 'Go on.'

'Here's the last picture of Rachel Sinclair found on Facebook. It's the image that most resembles her as she was when she entered the Maltman Green.' Ruby opened a beige file and handed round coloured images of Rachel's face. She was looking at the camera, her hair pulled back as it had been when she died; the open neck of the cream blouse showed the rose necklace, catching the light.

Costello took a closer look. 'It's her own design. It comes in two parts; the roses actually intertwine but are meant to be worn by different individuals.'

'I can't see a man wearing that,' said Anderson.

'The male version is plain silver, not so garish. We need to know who wears the other half. Was that why the laptop and the phone are missing?' asked Costello. 'Is somebody trying to keep a relationship a secret?'

'She makes some lovely stuff and she models it herself – Instagram mostly.' Ruby was on her phone, scrolling. 'The Burns Rose, she called it. I've a silver Tigger on my key ring that my boyfriend had made for me. It's lovely. Here's Rachel.' She held her phone out so her colleagues could see the screen.

The three men in the room looked at the photograph. Costello got up to check that Mr Baseball had nothing round his neck on the screenshot from the CCTV.

It was very quiet.

'And why wouldn't you model it yourself if you looked like her?' said Costello, saving one of the guys from saying it and facing accusations of sexism.

'The most interesting thing her Facebook page says is that her relationship status is "complicated". I've tracked down a couple of her friends, the ones she talks to most on Messenger. They say that' – Ruby looked down at her notes – 'she was definitely happier than they had seen her in a long time, maybe over the last two years or so, but she'd never mentioned his name or anything about him, just that she had met somebody special. Was he married?'

'Mr Baseball? Married Mr Baseball – he wears a wedding ring,' said Anderson. 'What did she do that day?'

'I've double-checked it. I've spoken to Rachel Sinclair's best friend, Gillian Maxwell. They went swimming together on Thursday, the Western Baths at six. They showered when they came out of the pool. Gillian asked her if she wanted to go for a drink. Rachel refused as she was' – Ruby paused to quote exactly – 'going straight home as she was "going out for shenanigans and needed to get changed". Gillian thought that was true. Rachel was wearing joggy bottoms and a T-shirt, but had scraped her wet hair back into the style it was when she was found. She took a phone call on her landline from an ex-work colleague, Alia Hussein, from down south, for thirty minutes at about nine o'clock. Rachel mentioned that she was going out, but could talk for a bit as she was already ready.'

'Shenanigans? Meaning what?' asked Anderson.

'Alia said that was Rachel speak for being up for a laugh. Rachel had a history of having affairs with married men because she wasn't into commitment. She referred to these liaisons as "her shenanigans".'

'Yet she was what, thirty-seven? Her sister-in-law said that she was thinking about having a family, so maybe she was changing her mind about that. Somebody went into her flat and removed her laptop, and her mobile phone has still not been recovered, but nobody living near her flat saw anyone unusual. Are we thinking that Mr Baseball is the man in her life, and maybe she was asking, demanding, more than he was willing to give?' asked Costello. 'But then why the Maltman Green?'

'We'll come to that. Mathilda said there was a lot of her own sweat on the skin of her face at the scene. She took time to die.'

'Do we know how she died?'

Anderson and Costello looked at each other. 'O'Hare still has to get to her, but there's no sign of obvious external injury, so it wasn't a violent, uncontrolled attack. O'Hare got the technician to take more swabs from her body – no other DNA there. It was hands and face; there's Callaghan's on her face and on her right hand.'

'He was there doing CPR, so fair enough.'

'And there's two of the paramedics, but they would be using a Brookes or something like that, surely. And then there were the two men from the Maltman Green. Any more on them? Vik?'

'Sven has an ex-wife, who I can't find yet. He and his second wife, Sabina, have been married for seventeen years. They have four daughters; the oldest is fifteen – Sarah, Sam, Stella and Sophie.'

'Good alliteration there. Hope none of them have a lisp.'

'I'll check out Jamie Sinclair. What age is Callaghan's son?' asked Costello.

'He's about the right age. Action both of them, Costello, please,' said Anderson. 'To be clear, Mr Baseball didn't leave any DNA, or left DNA that we haven't found yet. He's like the man who wasn't there. There should be an unidentifiable sample. Were the paramedics, Callaghan, Wallace or Jonsson involved in the abduction of a four-year-old boy? We know nothing about Mr Baseball except he did something to Rachel Sinclair, probably hit her, and then ran away very quickly.'

'So what was he doing?' asked Wyngate.

'We don't know. I'm not sure about Carol's statement – her reliability,' said Costello.

'So the rest of them? Callaghan was doing CPR, then left her to call the emergency services and the two guys from the Maltman took over. The paramedics kept working on her but her heart would not restart.'

'And?'

'All their DNA is present, and Johnny Clearwater's by transfer from somebody. I've had a quick look into Rachel's past for any connection with the Clearwaters, but nothing obvious jumps out,' said Wyngate. 'I'll keep digging.'

Anderson scratched his head. 'Any connection between Martin Callaghan and the Clearwaters, or Wallace and the Clearwaters, Jonsson and the Clearwaters? Look at the geography, here and Cellardyke, right over on the east coast. Who was over there four years ago and is here now?'

'I want to know how Rachel got through the shutter. It might suggest that she does know somebody in there.'

'No problem if it was left open, but that doesn't sit right with the security and the privacy of the place.'

'It's a quiet spot in a busy city on a hot summer night.'

'But hardly private.'

'So maybe a sideshow for somebody in the Green, maybe all of them getting their kicks from watching Rachel shagging Tom and Dick. That would explain how she got access. I'm speaking to Lookin' Good, the fancy-dress shop this morning.'

'Where did you get that voyeur theory from?' asked Anderson.

'Trying to make sense of it.' Costello pulled a face, turning her pen end over end. 'I'll have a quiet word with her sister-in-law when we go to do the identification. If anyone will talk honestly, she will.'

'Ask her where her son came from, to be clear.'

Mulholland spoke, making the others jump as he had been so quiet they had forgotten he was there. 'Rachel was in receipt of a regular amount of money – five hundred a month paid into her bank account, from another account that the money passes through. I'm trying to track it back. It looks to me like somebody was paying her mortgage for her. And when I say I can't track it, I mean somebody is hiding it. I've been on to the tech boys and they are not finding it easy either. She does pay tax on it, as if it's money earned, but I'm not sure where these earnings are. Or what she does to earn it,' said Mulholland.

'Could it be a regular order of jewellery that she does for a boutique somewhere?'

'Could be, but I chatted to a girl who runs a jewellery stall at the fruit market. I showed her the invoices for the materials that Rachel was buying in and she said there's no way she's making that kind of money selling it. It's not enough raw material. You saw the scale of the operation that she had in her spare room. It's a hobby. The money is coming from somewhere else,' said Mulholland.

'Are we thinking sugar daddy?' said Costello. 'Sugar daddy is Mr Baseball and then things got a little less than perfect? She was thirty-seven, maybe thinking about a longer-term commitment.'

'And he's not thinking along those lines?'

'Or not thinking at all.'

*   *   *

'Well, there are rules and regulations about hiring out uniforms that look too official,' said Mr Adam Leitch, proprietor of Lookin' Good fancy-dress and party hire shop.

'Yes, I know, so what did she borrow, Rachel Sinclair? It would have been around the twenty-fourth of June,' asked Costello.

Leitch looked up from his keyboard. 'Was that the lady who died? On the Green?'

'Yes, indeed. We think she was wearing one of your uniforms at the time.'

'Really? That's terrible. What happened to her?'

'That's what we're trying to find out,' said Costello.

'Let's see.' He scrolled through a few pages on his screen, 'Yes, this will be it. A jacket with epaulettes, neckerchief, hat, and we recommended that the person wears their own shirt and trousers and plain black shoes. There is a mock utility belt and a rubber truncheon.'

He clicked through a few pages. 'That's our most popular policewoman's outfit.' He turned the screen round to show Costello. 'No way that could be thought of as a genuine police officer's uniform, is there?'

Costello looked at the rubberized skin-tight, low-cut outfit, the elbow-length gloves and the handcuffs hanging provocatively from a leather belt swung round her hips. 'Bloody hell.'

Leitch smiled. 'It chafes. So I am told. She didn't buy that, though. She bought the hat, the epaulettes, the plastic handcuffs, the neckerchief and the jacket . . .'

'Can I buy what she bought?' she added quickly.

'We'll donate it, in the circumstances. She bought a size ten. Shall I give you that?'

'Yes, please.'

She took the sizable box, heavier than she thought it would be, and sat in her car.

Rachel could easily have looked like a fancy-dress police officer, with a short skirt that put the suspenders on display, her hair down, high heels; she would have been spotted immediately for a fake. The basic uniform wasn't anything like a Police Scotland one, but she had put her cap under her arm, tied her hair up properly and worn flat shoes. She might have been wearing the stockings but had made sure her skirt was long enough to hide them. They were only for the eyes of the person she was going to take her skirt off for. So a man with a fetish for police uniforms? Mr Baseball? Or had she wanted the outfit to be convincing at a quick glance for some reason?

So Rachel had tried a little to be convincing, but another cop wouldn't have been fooled for long. Was Martin Callaghan? Not by the time he got round the corner; by that time she was on the ground. He had said that he pulled her skirt down over her knees, he had loosened her blouse, and he had tried to breathe some life back into her.

Rachel had spent a few years as cabin crew – she'd know how to wear a uniform. And her years in the force had shown Costello that some women know how to wear a uniform, and others look like an old sack dumped at the side of the motorway.

At Tulliallan police college, they'd been taught they needed confidence. The uniform gave them that; that was how it was supposed to be worn.

Maybe it was the confidence that had convinced Mr Baseball.

And Martin Callaghan.

Anderson pulled down the driver's sun visor of the BMW and looked at his phone. 'It's taken Vik and Gordon two hours to make a timeline wall of the wedding party photos taken at the Stewart Hotel. Two hours?'

'Should have got Redding to do it. She'd have finished it in twenty minutes,' said Costello.

Anderson ignored her. 'Operation Aries requested everybody who took any kind of photograph that day to send over their pictures.'

'Sounds like a total waste of time.'

'So you don't fancy having a look when we get back? There must be a connection between the wedding party and the Maltman.' Anderson flicked the switch and dropped the driver's window in the BMW. He rolled his head and stretched his neck. There were two camera crews parked outside the Clearwaters' house, maintaining a not very discreet distance across the street. Five cars were now parked neatly on the gravel drive of the red sandstone villa in Drymen; the Audi and the Jaguar of the Clearwaters, the VW Polo of the family liaison officer and the Ford that presumably belonged to the detectives who were originally in charge of the case, Bob Allison's team. A nice place, a hundred years old, the garden with neatly tended shrubs in the borders, low-maintenance chic. Richard Clearwater was a lawyer, in a family of wealthy lawyers. The Clearwaters were not short of a bob or two. Richard Clearwater was rumoured to be a rather staid, devoutly religious Church of Scotland man. He looked like it as well: tall, skeletally thin. His skin almost transparent, he'd raise the dead quicker than he'd raise a smile.

'Kathy Lamont and crew are filming the progress of Operation Taurus, from Naomi's point of view. Which might get in our way.'

'Good God. Vik will be preening himself all over the bloody place.' Costello closed her eyes. 'I'm sure I've forgotten something that I should have remembered.' She rubbed her face with her hands. 'But I can't get it into my head.'

'It'll come to you when you're not thinking about it.'

'How long has Johnny been missing?'

'Four years and two days. Not that we're counting. I've no idea what I'm going to say when I get in there.'

Costello snorted and opened the door. 'It'll come to you when you are not thinking about it.'

DI Ferguson, who had been the SIO in the original case, his DS and the family liaison officer were in the Clearwater family home. They had been in there for over forty minutes, probably talking about the TV programme rather than Operation Taurus. Naomi's public persona was very much a double-edged sword, but Bob Allison worked well with her. Anderson was perfectly happy for that relationship to continue. Bob could be the public face of the operation, leaving Anderson free to do the job, but all he could think of at the moment was how to say to Naomi, *It's one thing to say that your son's alive. It's another to actually find him.*

Costello climbed out of the car, almost scorching herself on the metal of the door. 'I have to ask it, Colin: is there no way there could have been a mistake?'

'Mathilda says she's looked at the problem from every angle and she says not, and I believe her. But the fact remains, they were filming that TV programme and evidence from the original case was lying on a different table, sterile and sealed. It looks bloody dodgy, doesn't it?' Anderson sighed.

Costello looked over the roof of the car, shielding her eyes from the glare of the sun with a cupped hand. 'Recall that case down south where the woman and her daughter were killed in a field, in the middle of summer. They found a lot of DNA from the same guy, and they thought they had him.'

'And it was from one of the lab technicians who was suffering from hay fever, doing wee snuffles and sneezes all over the place, over each sample as he was processing them,' Anderson recalled. 'That's why Warburton has engaged that quality processor chap from Edinburgh Uni to do a complete chain-of-evidence map, see if there's any way that it could have become contaminated – on a slide, from a cuff. I know we have to proceed now as if it's valid and the boy is still alive, but the newspapers and the media are full of it. They believe the boy is alive and that we missed something.'

'If he's alive, we did.'

'That's not fair, Costello.'

'Who said life was fair? Death can be a bit of a pisser as well. The press will turn on us as time passes and Johnny's still nowhere to be found. And then he could go the way of the Bernepoos.'

'What?'

'Those wee pups, making them too hot to handle so they can't be sold on. So they get drowned. The same thing might apply to Johnny. They should've kept it quiet; he might have been safe until somebody pulls him into the public eye again.'

'There have already been two hundred sightings of him in the UK alone. Ten of them are of the same boy who happens to bear a close resemblance to Johnny.'

'Better buy that kid a T-shirt saying "I'm not him".' Anderson tried to think how much his own children had changed in those years. 'I wonder if we should get an aged image.'

'Good idea.'

Anderson made no move to go into the house.

'Naomi needs to have it explained to her that it might not mean what she wants it to mean. And Richard – well, he's a lawyer, a sneaky bastard . . .'

'He's an advocate.'

'So an expensive sneaky bastard.'

They stood, looking at each other across the roof of the car, Costello drawing patterns with the tip of her finger in the dust, each of them alone with their thoughts on how to move the situation forward.

'How far did they go into the background of Naomi and Richard?' asked Costello.

Anderson smiled, knowing that their train of thought had been on exactly the same track. 'I presume that idea wasn't at the forefront of the investigation. I mean the wedding party was a closed event – it was for her sister, Natalie. The Wishart girls as they were. The team spent much of their time thinking of an accident in the woods or at the river. But now we know that Johnny is alive and can presume that everybody who was at the wedding party was known to them, and it's logical if he was taken, he was taken by somebody at the party. And somebody there had a reason to take him. He is their biological son, isn't he?'

'The DNA says so.'

'So we look again at Naomi, Richard, Natalie and Niles.'

'Niles?'

'The American that Natalie married. The wedding party – I mean the occasion, not the people – was for Natalie, remember. Naomi's younger sister. Naomi and Natalie Wishart, like I said.'

'You've been doing your homework.'

'Too hot to sleep, isn't it?'

'Well, I'm going to put Mulholland on to sorting that out, if he can break away from being a media star for two minutes and get back to sitting in front of a keyboard without Elvie holding his hand.'

'Holding his foot, more like.'

'Costello, that's not PC.'

The look she gave him could have shattered bulletproof glass.

'Oh, here we go.' They both looked round as the front door of the house opened and DCI Allison, at the top of the steps, waved that they should come in. He held the black painted door, with its gleaming brass handle, and they walked into the hall: polished floorboards, Turkish carpet runner, the high window in the half landing catching the sun and spilling it down the stairway.

It was as beautiful as Anderson's house, but while the detective's was full of life, there was a sense that life had merely passed through here and had left the Clearwaters behind.

Bob Allison indicated that they should stay in the hall, as they heard quiet, respectful chatter coming from the room to their left, the front room that looked on to the bright patchwork of car roofs in the driveway.

'How are they?' asked Anderson.

'As you would expect. I can tell that Naomi dare not believe it's true. Nice lady, been to hell and back.' He placed his hands in his pockets, uncomfortable. 'There's a chance the sample was contaminated?'

Costello was impatient. 'Oh, for God's sake, Rachel Sinclair ended up with the DNA on her face, so somebody near her has contact with the boy. End of.'

'Why was Rachel killed?'

'We don't know,' Costello snapped.

'Why are you hanging round here, then?'

'Waiting for you to get out of the way. Have you explained to Naomi that she needs to keep her hopes in check?'

Allison dropped his head, giving a sideways jerk, indicating that was what was happening now. 'Not sure how much success he's going to have. Naomi has always believed that the way to find those responsible for taking Johnny was to keep him in the public eye. She's agreed to do a documentary on it.'

'We heard.'

The door opened and the three detectives turned to see Naomi Clearwater framed in the doorway, the light shining from behind her, emphasizing how frail she looked in the flesh.

Bob Allison stepped to the side to introduce the other two detectives, and Naomi shook their hands, her dry and cool palms clasping theirs, tight with a sense of desperation.

Behind her, in a room of polished floorboards, silk wallpaper and flower arrangements, sat Richard Clearwater on a wing-backed chair, his face as dark as the night. Anderson looked at the photographs of Johnny, his blonde curly hair, the big blue eyes, the reddened cracks in his skin. The room was a shrine to their lost son. Something about Johnny, the cheek in his grin, reminded Anderson of Moses.

He looked away.

TEN

'They don't seem to have been close?' said Costello to Doreen Sinclair, as they waited for the electronic lock to release on the door of the mortuary. 'Rachel and your husband.'

Doreen nodded, walking more slowly, allowing enough distance so that their apparently casual chat would not bridge the gap between them and Wyngate and Sinclair, who were walking ahead.

'Not close. They weren't brought up in the same home, so there wasn't an issue. Well . . .'

'So there was an issue?'

Doreen hesitated. 'I don't want to speak badly of the dead . . . but . . .'

'Don't let it bother you – anything that helps us colour in her life is helpful.'

'With Rachel, it was as if she got to about sixteen years old and got stuck. I don't think her passing came as any surprise to us. I thought she'd fall off a balcony drunk in Benidorm or break her neck while paragliding or parachuting, something like that. She liked a drink. A snort – that was her latest thing.'

'Did she take cocaine?'

'I know she did. She spoke to Rosie about it. We didn't want that near our daughter. David went nuts.'

'How old is Rosie?'

'Fifteen – difficult enough to keep them on the straight and narrow.'

'And your son?'

'Eight.'

'Is he your natural child?'

Doreen stopped walking and looked at Costello. 'No. He's adopted, but how did you know? Why, is that important?'

'It's not,' lied Costello. 'Rosie is yours, though?'

Doreen nodded.

'It's a routine question, sorry. We can get caught out by non-matching DNA so we ask it all the time.'

'Oh, I see. Couldn't have any more after Rosie.'

'That must have been hard. How did they take the news about their aunt?'

'The kids were devastated when we told them about Rachel. "Mercurial" was how somebody described her – up and down, all over the place – but she was one of a kind, definitely one of a kind.'

Costello held the door open for her. 'When was the last time you saw her?'

'Not for a while – a month or more. Maybe there was somebody special, but she wasn't around as much. But Auntie Rachel was lovely, funny, witty, always entertaining. She was one hundred miles an hour all the time.' She stopped walking. 'I never saw her living to a ripe old age. Some people shine so brightly that they burn themselves out, don't they?'

'Do you think she was seeing somebody? Her friends thought so.'

'Could have been, but it was difficult to tell with her. Changed her men as often as she changed her shoes. Usually somebody else's husband. But she did seem more settled.'

'Because?'

'A few things she said, talking longer term. No screaming hysterics, she was calmer. There was some change in her, as if she had found an anchor.' Doreen nodded. 'Yes, that was it, as if she was . . .'

'Happy?'

'Yes, happy.'

And Costello smiled, sensing a motive.

Rachel Elizabeth Sinclair looked like a supermodel – too tall, too lanky, too skinny to be normal. O'Hare seemed obsessed with her hands, picking them up by the wrist, then moving each finger in turn back and forth, seeing the short cut nails, the slightly rough skin on her fingertips as if she did something manual, worked with raw materials in some way but something so delicate she couldn't wear gloves to protect herself.

He looked closely at the scar on her left shoulder, the result of the car smash he had read about in her history. Then he picked up the legs and tested the loose play in her knee joints, her long elegant feet, each toe slim and finger-like. Standing back, he looked at her from top to toe, his eyes slightly closed, superimposing one image on top of another and trying to make sense of what he was seeing. She was bruised and punctured, injuries caused by the paramedics as they had tried to get her heart into some kind of rhythm, injecting adrenaline, anything that might have helped. Her clothes were torn; she still had little squares of adhesive on her skin where the plasters had already come away. The comment from both the paramedics, experienced men, was that no matter what they did, she was gone. Nothing they did could induce an electrical rhythm in her cardiac muscle, and they had tried. They had presumed that she was a young healthy woman, which intrinsically she was, so there was something else going on. Hearts tend to start, then struggle to maintain the activity; Rachel's heart failed to start.

He wondered, as he always did, what happened when they walked that tightrope between life and death. What made a living thing fall to one side or the other? She still had her make-up on – her eyes were smudged in black, the pink of her lipstick had been smeared down to her chin. He'd received a request from Mathilda McQueen over at the forensic lab to take another two sets of swabs from her face, as well as the set his own technician would take for their own use, and had done so when Rachel had arrived in the morgue. The sample had already been tested and the DNA sample repeated the results of the previous sample. It was up to him now to find any new evidence that Rachel might have.

O'Hare started on the chest cavity of the deceased, having noted the pectus excavatum, the abnormal indentation in the middle of her sternum, the hypermobile limbs. As soon as he saw the heart, he knew something was terribly wrong. The pericardial sac was distended, a blue-black colour rather than the normal subtle tan. When he pressed it with his gloved finger, he could feel the fluid underneath. Asking for a large-bore syringe, he slowly emptied the sac of the blood, measured it – 550 millilitres – and then placed his hand back in the chest cavity looking for the small tear that he knew was there. Now devoid of the fluid within, the little render was closed over, but it had been enough to kill her. For somebody with her condition, the cocaine on her nasal swab, the run, the excitement of the incident had been sufficient to raise her blood pressure enough to cause her aortic arch to tear. Then death was inevitable. The sac round the heart filled up with blood, and the heart muscle was compressed by the fluid on the outside, trying to contract with an increasingly erratic electric signal.

He knew that Rachel Sinclair's story involved a police hunt for the murder that had never happened. Anderson had tried to tell him the story, but O'Hare didn't want to hear it; he liked to do the PM without having any preconceived ideas lodged in his head. It left the question of who deposited the DNA of Johnny Clearwater on her face.

'Do you think anybody else has contributed to this death?' O'Hare asked of Dr Gibson, the second pathologist.

'Doubt it,' she said and looked at the mortuary assistant.

'The cocaine dealer might have something to answer to.'

O'Hare speculated. 'What if somebody was chasing her? Maybe attacking her? Or she thought she was going to be attacked? Surely that would put her blood pressure up?'

Gibson looked back at the body. 'But there's no sign that somebody attacked her, is there?'

'I think there's an eyewitness,' said O'Hare. 'With the insults on her body caused by the paramedics, it's not an issue I'd like to argue in court.'

The three of them looked at the body on the table, bright under the lights.

After an hour, he reported back to Costello that he had found no outward sign of any obvious injury – there was no stabbing, no broken bones that he could find, no sign of trauma that he couldn't put down to the attempts to resuscitate her.

'No punch in the face?'

'No evidence of any physical assault,' said O'Hare, sitting down across the desk from her, turning the computer monitor so she could see better. 'But that doesn't mean it didn't happen. But whatever you think about the death of Rachel, I do have to tell you that she was not murdered.'

'Not murdered? Fuck!' she hissed through her teeth. 'OK, so what happened to her?'

'Like many natural deaths, there was a chain of events. First, when she was lying on the table, I noticed her build. She was very tall, very long, slender toes, very long fingers, very supple.'

'Yes, she looked like a model.'

'And she had a dip on her chest wall over the sternum. Those signs lead to a suspicion that she was born with Marfan syndrome and there's nothing abnormal about that. It's a genetic condition and not generally life-threatening, but she was unfortunate. Her blood pressure went too high and damaged her aorta. It would have been quick and unavoidable, but not murder.'

Costello sighed and huffed.

'I'm sorry, but there it is.'

'Did she know she had this thing, this Marfan syndrome?'

'Oh, yes. She's known since she was eleven or so. She'd spoken to her GP about getting pregnant and if that would be a good idea.'

'Recently?'

'Within the last year,' answered O'Hare.

'She didn't say who she intended the father to be, did she? That would be something of interest.'

'There you go again, Pollyanna, thinking that life should be easy.'

'Is there any way that Mr Baseball could be responsible for what happened to her? He left Callaghan to pick up the pieces.'

'I doubt it. Her heart was double the size it should have been, so that's a sign that she's been suffering from high blood pressure for most of her life.' O'Hare swung on his chair a little. 'And on top of that, she has some irritation in her nasal passage; she has a perforation on her nasal septum, so probably some cocaine abuse. We'll know after the toxicology, but recent use will have caused the blood pressure and the heart rate to spike. The blood rushes into the aorta at high pressure and it rips; the tear appears, and once that happens, there was nothing anybody could do.'

'She was not murdered, but anything else?'

'Such as?'

'No pregnancy? Nothing like that?'

'No nothing like that.'

'No sign of a recent pregnancy or a termination?'

'Nope.'

'No sexual assault, no other body fluids that we could get the DNA of the guy from?'

'If only it was that easy. You look disappointed.'

'No, more confused about the minor concern over the

death of a young woman and the obsession with the disappearance of Johnny Clearwater. Am I right in thinking there was no unidentified sample on Rachel? So we have no sample from Mr Baseball?'

'Indeed, it's been checked four times now. And it's simple, Costello: who, in Rachel's life, deposited Johnny's DNA among the DNA soup that Mathilda lifted? That shouldn't be too hard.' O'Hare looked past Costello as if he had just noticed that she was on her own. 'Where's Colin?'

'Oh, the bold Anderson was in a meeting all afternoon; he said he couldn't stay up at night and run around like an idiot. He needs to go home. He missed the first two children growing up, and doesn't want to miss Moses achieving his milestones. They're waiting for his first word, apparently. After that, they'll be desperate for him to shut up, but home is where he wants to be. Johnny Clearwater doesn't crop up in his subconscious at all.'

O'Hare shook his head. 'I don't think that's true, Costello.'

'I told him I was coming here; he said that was because I didn't have anyone to go home to.'

'And what did you say?'

'I told him to go and fuck himself.'

'Oh, good. For a moment there, I thought there was something wrong between the two of you.'

Carol was looking at the low table where her TV sat. Directly opposite the settee where she tended to sit, and sometimes slept. Table, TV screen, a photograph of her mum and dad in a silver frame sitting at the back, a decorated pot full of pens, her two pomegranate and black pepper candles on either side of the screen, her stone carved pony and a dirty mug from her supper last night. Or was that this morning? Or during the night perhaps? She was losing track of time and she was losing track of herself. She had been asleep, she had been walking around, drinking tea, unable to get to sleep because of noises echoing through the wall; the geothermal heating, as Lulu had said. Carol sat back on the sofa, looking at the photograph. It was on the left side of the TV. She had put it on the right the first day when she had unpacked her personal stuff – her candles, her photographs, the stone pony that her granny had given her. She had placed them beside the two tall white candlesticks and the white ballerina figurine that had come with the flat.

She was sleepwalking again; she went to sleep on top of the bed and woke up underneath it. It was all the fault of that bloody programme about the Night Hunter and Eric Manson. She should never have watched it; it had exploded a thousand memories into her consciousness.

These bumps along the path to recovery had brought her down before, and she knew how to pick herself up, how to push the reset button. She got up and went upstairs to the bedroom, opened the top drawer in the bedside cabinet, carefully taking out the box of small dolls. She took them out, one by one and wrapped them up, slipping them into their own little bed, pulling the tiny blankets over them. Then she put the lid on the box, put the box in the drawer and closed the drawer. Keeping them safe.

Then she lay back on the top of the bed, enjoying the draught of air coming through the balcony doors. Music drifted in as well – somebody was playing soft gentle melody, so quiet that she had to listen to hear it. 'Summertime.' The living was easy. Was it really?

She closed her eyes, wanting sleep to come, concentrating her mind on the soft music, thinking of her fingers over the keys; she used to play when she was young. It was so hot, so sticky she thought about having another shower.

She must have fallen asleep, as she was woken up by her mobile ringing.

Anderson had intended to go home, but he had phoned the house from the car to see how everybody was. His daughter Claire had answered, excited about something; Moses had said a word: more than a word – he had actually tried to form a sentence. It had sounded like 'I want biscuit', which, of all the things that Moses was likely to say, was the most probable.

He felt a warm glow spread inside him, for his little Down's boy who had taken a great step forward and for his daughter who was thrilled at the progress of her wee brother. He said he'd be home as soon as possible but he might be a bit late. Claire said that Brenda had left his dinner on a plate in the microwave which was an improvement on it being in the bin or in the dog. Things were better all round.

He sat in the car, letting the heat ease the stress from his bones, ruminating on what he had said to Costello. It had been cruel and he had regretted it the minute the words were out of his mouth, but she had been a total pain in the arse lately, using up her energy in her work because she had nothing else to distract her. It was her refusal to admit it that was so wearing. And he was being truthful when he said he wanted to be around while Moses was little, although that phone call had proved what nice human beings Claire and Peter had grown up to be, in spite of his absence as a parent. Or maybe because of it.

What had Naomi and Richard gone through in the last four years? Despite Naomi's public proclamation, there must have been moments in the darkest hours when she admitted to herself that the most likely outcome was that her son was dead. Her face to the outside world might not have shown the internal narrative of black and totally wretched despair. They'd endured years of suspicion: if Naomi had been a better mother, if the family had been more attentive. Likewise, Richard had been scrutinized, which must have been painful for such an intensely private man, stern-faced and rarely showing emotion. And that suspicion sat so much worse with him, given his status and deep religious faith. Anderson wondered which way the new evidence would point. He'd yet to view the digital images from the wedding party.

Anderson wondered how many times conversations stopped dead at dinner parties when the guests remembered, how many heads turned when Naomi and Richard walked down the street, or walked into church, the focus of silent accusations in the eyes of strangers.

He wasn't wilfully going to let the Clearwaters suffer a minute longer, so he picked up his phone and called a number. Instead of heading home, he turned left, out towards the Maltman Green.

From what Costello had said, Anderson had expected Carol Holman to be much odder than she appeared to be. There were little subtleties, the way she had paused before opening the door, even though he had phoned her from the car, even though he had shown his ID. As he made his way through the kitchen, apologizing for the lateness of the hour, she had walked in front of him, wrapped in a scarlet dressing gown that drowned her, keeping her face turned towards him, as if she expected him to do something. She also looked as though she had been crying.

'Thank you for talking to me,' he said.

'If it's about the girl, I think I've already said what I saw. Then I saw the news on social media. The girl had been near a missing boy – is that why she was killed?'

Anderson picked up on that. Had she seen something that made her think Rachel had been killed? Costello's brief text had informed him otherwise.

'We are checking the possibility that the boy might be near here, which might explain why the DNA was left on the face of the dead girl. Had you seen her before? Rachel?' asked Anderson, showing her the photograph.

Carol Holman took a step closer while keeping as far away from him as she possibly could, almost circling him like a suspicious animal. She looked at the photo, then shook her head, backing away, moving like a much older woman, holding on to the furniture as she walked over to a chair that looked unused. Looking round the room, the big sofa had the direct line to see the TV, was dented and had a blanket crumpled up on it, showing Carol's habitual TV watching position.

'Do you live here on your own, Carol? It's a very nice flat.'

She stood beside the chair, her fingers digging into the cushion of the upright. 'Yes, I do.'

'And you haven't lived here long?'

'A month.'

'Where were you before?' He kept his tone casual, as if this was not why he was here. He was watching her think.

'I was in London before.'

'And before that? You're not from around here?'

'No, I'm from Trondheim, Norway, but my grandmother was Scottish.'

'Really, so you have not been to Glasgow before.'

She shook her head, looked at him, straight in the face.

He could swear he saw a flash of recognition. He smiled. 'You look familiar.'

'We've not met before.'

Anderson looked at her more closely. 'Are you sure?'

She shook her head, her chin sticking out, reminding him of

how Peter postured when he was lying. Carol was lying, too. He smiled at her, looking at the long, grey hair, frizzy at the bottom, the scarlet dressing gown hanging from her bony shoulders. There was something about her face, around her eyes, that he thought he recognized, and he wasn't often wrong.

'I'm sorry, you must remind me of somebody.' He sat down. 'Can you talk me through what you saw after the girl ran into the Green?'

'I've already said.'

'I'd like to hear it from you, in your own time. Better than reading it off a piece of paper.'

Carol sat down, pulling her dressing gown beneath her. 'I saw her come in, running like she was hiding from him, then she hid behind the hut thing. They have a special name for it.'

'The Loggia.'

'Yes, then the man with the hat came in. It looked like they were kissing. Then she looked up as if she was looking at the sky. She put her hand up to her throat. Then he raised his hand, as if to hit her.'

'Was she struggling or anything?'

'No,' Carol sat quietly. 'That was later when the other man came, the one with the white T-shirt. I think he hit her. I think he put his hand up and brought it down. Like he was striking her face. Then she fell and he stood still. I think that was when I passed out.'

'Did you see anybody else about?'

'No.' Carol looked out of the window, her eyes settling on the house opposite. 'Maybe Lulu saw something.'

'Pardon?'

'I get emails from Lulu. She lives across there, so maybe she saw something. She's like me, she doesn't sleep, so maybe . . .'

'Across where?'

'The Green, in the Halfhouse.'

'Have you met her?'

'No.'

He sat back on the sofa so she knew he wasn't going anywhere. 'Can you run through it again? One more time. What happened immediately after Rachel ran into the Green?'

The story didn't change much. The hit got a little more violent maybe, the run in a little more rushed, the hiding a little more dramatic, but the basic story stayed the same and it tended to confirm what Callaghan had said, except, according to Carol, Callaghan had hit Rachel, and that was why she fell to the ground. In his version, she was on the ground when he got there. Anderson asked for a small tour of the flat, including the bedroom balcony where she had witnessed the incident and, as Costello had done, he gauged her line of sight and looked across to the duplex above the dress shop. If Lulu had been at the far end, the opposite diagonal, she would have had a better line of sight than Carol. And he recalled that Louise Dawson, who probably called herself Lulu, had been indoors when the event took place.

He looked at his watch when he walked out of Carol's flat, wondering what would be the quickest way round two sides of the rectangle. He turned left at the door to the deli, deciding to go up Park Lane, past the front door of the Maltman House where the Swedish family lived. The building was impressive, looking on to the park. He wondered if this part had always been a dwelling house, or at least the offices, the board room of the marmalade factory, if Costello was to be believed. It certainly had a beautiful outlook over the park. The other three sides looked on to lawyer and accountant territory as the gentrification of Glasgow continued to spider outwards. After walking the breadth of the park, he turned left again, then the length of the clothes shop. Like the deli at the other end, there was an expanse of wall with high windows, the door and then the shop front. At the far end, nearly back on Brewer Street, was the door to the Halfhouse. He looked up. The lights were still on. If the flats were similar, Louise's kitchen, dining room and living room were up there, the open-plan arrangement running along the full length of the building.

He rang the doorbell. Nothing happened. He waited, then rang again, taking two steps back.

The lights went out.

So whatever Lulu saw that night, she was keeping it to herself.

SUNDAY 27TH JUNE

Something had happened. He was sure of that but had no idea
what. He kept almost catching a memory, something that he
could use to help him remember the life he once had, but his
memories were elusive. There was the juice, orange instead of the
usual apple. There was the tuna sandwich put down on the table.
He had felt familiar fingers run through his rough, curly hair, and
somebody was speaking words that didn't make any sense. That
woman had patted him on the back, called him a name he didn't
recognize. Then they were away again. He watched the door
swing shut, heard the other door close and the key turn in the
lock, and he was left alone again with the music for company.
His friend had been there last night up at the window. They had
had their usual silent conversation, waving to each other with
their code: thumbs and fingers; a sailor's salute was their sign-
off. Sometimes he couldn't remember the code, sometimes he
couldn't remember if his friend was there at all, but he went to
the window anyway.
He huffed his breath on the glass and then drew faces for his
friend's amusement. He always remembered to wipe the
window with the sleeve of his pyjamas. He had forgotten to do
that once and she had found out. There had been a fight and he
had bruised her face.
He wasn't going to forget again in a hurry.

ELEVEN

Anderson hadn't slept much. Moses had been coughing, and he and Brenda had been up and down during the night, then he had lain awake, listening to every sound. Glasgow seemed to be taken with midsummer madness; the city wasn't sleeping either. He checked on Moses again, then went downstairs to the kitchen and made himself a cup of tea. The family laptop was sitting in the middle of the table. He googled Carol Holman. A few people came up on the search but none of them bore any resemblance to the woman he had been chatting to a few hours before.

He then googled Louise Dawson, who came up on Facebook, the second one down. It looked as if she kept her profile quiet; she didn't post anything wild or indiscreet. There was no mention of her son, no mention of a husband. There was little you could garner from the photos apart from the fact she read a lot of literary fiction and made cakes, decorating them into cartoon characters for kids' birthdays. He wondered if there was a link there with the deli and Pauline's son, Joshua. Was there one link to all of them?

He scrolled down. Joe was never in the pictures. Louise was cautious. Joe had his own Facebook page – nothing on it for last three years. He had probably moved to Twitter, Instagram and WhatsApp for stuff he wouldn't want his granny to see.

He typed in Lulu Dawson; nobody there who had anything to do with the Maltman Green. Lulu must be short for Louise, surely. He could wait for her to say what she had to say, although the fact that she said one thing on email to Carol and something else in her statement to Costello, and her subsequent statement to Redding, was interesting. Maybe, like many people, she didn't want to be involved.

Anderson had sent Costello an email informing her that Carol Holman's story had changed, and that had put Martin Callaghan's story a little out of focus. There could be an unreliable memory in either case. Callaghan was stressed and Carol Holman was not the most credible witness. The truth probably lay somewhere in the middle. Did it matter any more now the results of the PM had come through?

Out of interest, he checked the local news. Callaghan was a hero, indeed. A nice new picture of him in a fresh uniform, friendly, helpful, brave. Like the Police Scotland motto, he was always vigilant; he was keeping Scotland safe. The few words of trite crap he spoke had obviously been penned by Elizabeth Davies.

Rachel had died of natural causes. It was a death that was going to happen at some time. It was sad and tragic – such a wild spirit walking around with a time bomb ticking away inside of her. How fragile life was. Was there even a case here to be investigated? He picked up his mobile phone and swiped his way through his photographs, pausing at his favourite one of Claire, Peter and Moses sitting in the garden with Nesbit, the old grey-faced Staffie in the middle. More of his children: two of them very healthy, but the third, he knew, could have issues. He tapped the phone against his chin, wondering about the last time a doctor had looked at Moses, the last time somebody had listened to his chest.

He felt a wet nose on his hand, Norma reminding him that she hadn't had her breakfast yet, but she decided to jump up on his knee and lick his face, sensing his disquiet about his son.

While stroking Norma's wiry coat, he put a note on his phone to organize an appointment as soon as possible, privately if that was quicker. Had Rachel ever had any warnings? Had she ignored them, thinking that she always had another chance, another day to see to it?

And Naomi and Richard – they thought they had a whole life-time with their son. Now there was a possibility that they might have him home and see him grow up, get married, have children of his own, live a happy life. Wasn't that what all parents wanted for their children?

By nine a.m., Anderson made himself comfortable at his desk with a mug of coffee and a piece of carrot cake for breakfast; he had spent ten minutes looking at the wall, scanning the photographs, the usual wedding type of folk smiling at the camera, group photos, a few candid shots. He recognized Naomi, Richard, Natalie and

a man he presumed was Niles Nascimento. A few constant faces
who were either family or close friends. On the timeline, there
were no pictures of Johnny after one thirty; the main buffet in the
marquee had started at one. Johnny, like many of the kids, had
been wearing a small kilt and a white shirt, which, at various times
was either tucked in neatly or hanging out, longer than the kilt
itself. He seemed a good kid, but Anderson couldn't help thinking
how sore his skin looked.

Then Warburton had called, having read O'Hare's report and
instructed him to keep the PM results as restricted information;
they wanted to use the investigation into Rachel as a channel for
Operation Taurus. And that was a direct order from upstairs, as
Warburton put it.

Anderson was now in possession of the enormous amount of
documentation from the original investigation into the disappearance of Johnny Clearwater. There was no way he could absorb it
all. He needed an overview of what was actually known, and not
what he had gleaned erroneously from social media and general
office gossip. He remembered rumours of a paedophile ring oper-
ating down the coast, some human trafficking of attractive blonde
children, but he needed to know if they had been definite lines of
enquiry or merely rumours flying around those not involved in the
investigation.

The wedding party had taken over the entire Stewart Hotel out
in Cellardyke, a small village on the east coast, ten miles south
of St Andrews. A hundred and twenty guests enjoyed the garden,
the buffet and the dancing to a live band. It was a summer afternoon affair. Natalie was later to marry than most brides; most of
her friends already had children so there were chocolate fountains,
street food, swings, a climbing frame, a small train, an ice-cream
van, a fort and a clown to keep the children amused. Anderson
looked at the images on the wall again – it looked like a dream-
scape for a four-year-old. The wedding celebration had been well
planned. Anderson could imagine, maybe not Moses who was
made of different stuff, but Claire and Peter as youngsters going
wild, tugging at his arm, keen to get away and explore the way
kids do. Then the heart-stopping chill when he might call them,
and they were nowhere to be seen.

The river at the end of the lawn had been the subject of debate at the time of the . . . abduction? He liked to think of it as such. The previous team had no evidence, no proof of life after the time that Johnny was last seen. Even then, Bob Allison had noted that the 'last seen', at twenty past two, was not that reliable. There was a lot of alcohol, many of the guests had booked to stay the night, so the drink flowed freely. That night and over the next few days the river and the area of trees behind had been searched by a party a hundred strong or more.

But what really happened? Anderson read the brief summary Allison had left him. Richard noticed first that Johnny was not where he should be. There would be no panic. Folk would start looking for him, expecting him to be in the toilets. Part of that garden was an old fort the kids could go and climb over. Imagine how long it would take them to look round that. Naomi wasn't particularly worried. Her husband was, though; he was worried right from the start.

Was he? Was that odd? Anderson knew that he'd panic before Brenda, but that was a result of his professional experience.

Most other couples, it would be the mother who'd have their panic alarm more sensitively set. Richard had wanted to sound the alarm sooner; Naomi thought Johnny was up to his old tricks.

His old tricks, the words marked in the file with an asterisk.

He scrolled on, finding another interview where Naomi clarified Johnny's habit of hiding so he could eat things he wasn't allowed to eat. Things that were bad for his eczema, like chocolate, bread and cheese.

He read on about Naomi Wishart. She had married into the Clearwater family, but there were slight suggestions she had never been totally accepted. She had a few romances before that, including one broken engagement to a local man called William Pimento when she had been seventeen. Ten years later, she married Clearwater. She had stopped working as a marketing consultant once Johnny had disappeared and had devoted herself to finding her own child, dead or alive. He scrolled through the photographs and scanned in cuttings which were of interest; at some point, she had been considered a suspect. Had she ever been totally discounted? He found an image of her shaking hands with a dark-haired woman whom Anderson recognized, although it took a while to place her with any certainty: Mary Parnell. What was

Mary Parnell – the woman who had employed Elvie McCulloch in the summer of the Night Hunter – doing shaking hands with Naomi Clearwater? Of course, Mary had set up a charity to help those lost and lonely to get home. The difference in the women was obvious from the picture. Mary's expression was set on her face, her eyes slightly narrowed. Naomi had her dazzling smile on display. She, like Mary Parnell before her, had decided to use her experience to help others who had been unfortunate enough to find themselves in the same situation. Anderson's mind jumped to the connection of the Maltman: Naomi's son's DNA had been found there, Elvie McCulloch had been standing in the Green as Vik was being filmed hours after Rachel's death. And Costello didn't trust either of those women.

Anderson took a minute to think about the coincidences. Were they that coincidental? The Night Hunter case and Manson had introduced Mulholland to Elvie. The TV programme had brought Vik and therefore Elvie to the Green. The common factor was Mulholland's cheekbones.

He looked up at the pictures. The Nascimento wedding had taken place overseas. The Stewart Hotel party was a big affair. Through the pictures of the kids playing on the riverbank, Anderson remembered a picture of an exhausted female police officer, leaning on the bridge, her head in her hands, maybe the photograph taken at that moment when she realized that they were no longer looking for a boy and they were looking instead for a body.

Allison had calculated that there could be a gap of an hour, more or less – between one thirty and two thirty p.m. – when nobody could be sure if they had seen the boy. Just another wee fair-haired child running around screaming, over-excited. Johnny had been playing down at the small river that ran at the bottom of the lawn of the hotel, wide but little more than ankle deep; strands of water flowing round and over large white stones, an easy strip of water to cross. The kids had been down there trying to dam it up earlier in the day while the adults danced and drank, eating an outside catered buffet that was housed in the large marquee – everything thought of, in case it rained, which it did later on in the proceedings.

Anderson looked at the map of the hotel and the floor plan on his computer screen. The hotel was more than a hundred years old, a large house built to face the magnificent view of the rolling hills. The car park was on the roadside; a narrow lane ran from the car park down the side of the hotel to the front and the stretch of green lawn where the marquee was. On the right of the plan as Anderson looked at it, there was a small bridge, wooden, ornamental, but it didn't look strong and it was far away in a dip in the land. Did that mean the noise of a screaming child would not be heard, or would it be assumed to be kids carrying on? Anderson knew that the sound of a child in real distress was something once heard, never forgotten. No way could you mistake that for kids larking around.

And he thought that Johnny Clearwater was a sensitive child, or maybe even a troubled child. He had terrible eczema – his face was red raw, with dark red lines bordering the damaged and the new skin. He'd stand out in a crowd. Naomi had gone on record since, saying that the usual treatments had not worked for him so she was trying alternative remedies – hence the very restricted diet. At the wedding, he'd been banned from the chocolate fountain, the ice-cream van, the celebration cake and definitely from any of the hot dogs and burgers that were on offer as the day went on. From the look of him in the pictures, the new regime had not had time to work; his skin was still red and angry.

Having the geography in his head, he looked back at the photographs: the patio that ran the length of the back of the house where the guests were sitting and drinking gin or standing around, eating canapés. All eyes would be drawn to the water, the natural focal point. If little Johnny had been taken from there, somebody would have seen something. The previous investigation team had moved from the logical to the improbable, and then to the downright bizarre.

He could remember seeing Bob Allison on the TV being asked all kinds of complex questions. If he wasn't careful, that would be him tomorrow. But he had a smaller pool of suspects who had been in such close contact with Rachel in that small window of time. And as Mathilda McQueen had said, skin-to-skin contact would pass some cells, the old 'every contact leaves a trace' standard. But for DNA on a cheek like that to remain, it would be more likely that somebody who had been kissed on the cheek by Johnny had then brushed their cheek against Rachel's face with some force. He could see the latter, tilting the head while doing CPR, trying to sense an outbreath on the skin of the cheek. He could see a situation where that would happen. How long did anybody leave a kiss from a loved one on the side of their cheek these days? Not long, he thought, so not the paramedics. More likely to be Mr Baseball as he had kissed her. Or Sven or Murdo. Or Martin Callaghan.

Johnny was up to his old tricks: hiding to eat food he wasn't allowed. Hiding. Anderson was still thinking about that when he heard footsteps along the corridor.

It was Costello, dumping her bag on her desk, raking her hair with the leg of her sunglasses. 'Are you getting anywhere with this?' She gestured to the wall of photographs.

'And good morning to you, too. No, I'm trying to establish some lines of investigation via Rachel rather than all this, trying to focus.'

Costello sat on the edge of his desk. 'Have you read Carol Holman's statement? Do you think she's a reliable witness?'

'Well, she gave me a statement last night that she saw the man in the T-shirt hit Rachel.'

'There was no sign of violence to her face. O'Hare said that. So Carol said both men hit her? Really?'

'Callaghan doesn't know what Carol has told us. If a police officer, Callaghan, goes about hitting women, I want to know about it.'

'But why would he?'

'Why did Carol say he did?'

Costello looked at the wall, her arms folded, thinking. 'So you didn't go straight home last night?' Her voice was accusatory.

'Yes, I spoke to Carol first, then went home. Sorry, are you my minder?'

Costello gave an irritated shake of her head. 'OK, so moving on. Who do you think would be most likely to have an affair with Rachel? Of those in the Green?'

'Sven or Murdo, maybe Bobby or Joshua, sexual orientation permitting.'

'I'd say either of the two older guys because of what she did, where she went. I think Rachel was going into his territory, if you like, with another man. When you were young and your girlfriend dumped you, did you not wish that she could see you out with a prettier girl than her?'

Anderson shrugged.

'Oh, don't tell me, you probably couldn't face up to the task of chucking somebody, so you behaved so badly that they dumped you.'

Anderson shrugged again and the thought of punching his long-term colleague passed slowly through his mind.

'What if he had decided to put an end to it? She didn't agree. She's sending him two messages. One, that she was still desired by another man. And two, she could make trouble for him. Both Murdo and Sven appear to be happily married; they have this happy house-living going on. I don't know how entrenched the wives are in the business, but you can see the potential for trouble if there was a divorce and one of the marriages broke up. Financially, the whole house of cards would come tumbling down. Imagine Rachel meets Mr Baseball, whom she knows from some-where, knows he likes women in uniform. She was up for a bit of a snog, leads the bloke on. You know, a bit of a laugh, some shenanigans. She takes him into the Green, lines herself up so she's facing the security camera, and snogs the guy, whatever. She looked up, her hand to her chest. Carol said that, but maybe that wasn't the pain – maybe she was showing him the rose pendant. She was sending a message to him. "I am here, I have the code, I could make trouble." Then she collapses. He does a runner. Not a nice thing to witness.'

'He doesn't hang around and help her?'

'If he's married, he wouldn't.'

'Must be good to think like a devious cow.'

'You're the one good at having affairs.'

Anderson didn't answer; Costello was staring at the wall, angry about something. He let the silence lie, watching her looking at the montage of photographs, the passage of time marked in quarter-hour slots in Wyngate's childish handwriting. Then she slid off the desk and walked up to the wall, studied it for a while, then stabbed one photograph with her pen.

'Look at this picture. This lady in the blue is gazing wistfully at this guy here.' She tapped the man in the picture. 'And he is looking back at her, smiling, so you can bet they aren't married.

The other two in the picture can't stand each other, so they probably are married. Rachel was acting like a lover, playful but covert. It's the only way she could have got in. She had the code from her lover? Murdo Wallace says that he always locks the door – it's his door, his responsibility. He was very clear about that. The shutter is part of the fortress that is the Maltman Green. He doesn't want anybody else coming through there, uninvited. When you see the value of what they have in the back garden, it's totally understandable.'

'Sven the Swede says that he has found Wallace's door unlocked on a few occasions,' said Anderson.

'It's not his door. How would he know?' said Costello, still looking at the photographs.

'I think this lot are capable of sleeping with each other's wives, never mind unlocking each other's doors. Sven owns it all, so it's his keypad and lock system. Might be something there, though, if the keypads are owned by Sven – do they all have the same code? A better question might be who turned off that security camera? All that noise outside, two dogs that don't bark, the security lights that didn't come on? It doesn't ring true. But she died of natural causes, so can I investigate now? Is it worth the money?'

Anderson nodded. 'Yes, we can, but only if it piggybacks on Operation Taurus. We use Rachel's death to locate Johnny, as you rightly said. Rachel was not murdered. What's your next move?'

'I'd like to sniff around Callaghan. Get Wyngate to dig a bit deeper on him, off the record. Find out if their son is indeed their son. But I think we can disregard the Sinclairs; they had not seen Rachel for a month or more, so no physical contact, no way for the DNA to transfer. Hang on a moment.'

Anderson looked at the crumpled papers Costello was emptying out of her handbag, throwing them at the wastepaper basket and missing. 'What the hell is that?' He pushed a few of them round with the toe of his shoe.

'It's a collection of Maisy Daisy ice cream wrappers. We keep having to go to the Maltman. The deli always seems to be open. And Ruby drags me in there and there's a lot of flavours to try. The spinach and ricotta bagels are to die for.'

Anderson picked up one of the wrappers, then opened it out. 'I've seen that logo before.'

'It's very popular.'

Anderson looked at the wall of photographs taken at the wedding celebration. He was waving his forefinger in the air, looking for one in particular, scanning the whole wall.

'What are we looking for?' asked Costello. 'The logo?'

'Somewhere on here. I know I saw it.'

Costello looked at the pictures of the hotel, then googled their website. 'Well, the restaurant at the hotel doesn't sell Maisy Daisy. Do you have the file on the caterers for the party?'

'It's on the desk.'

'They had a chocolate fountain, street food, burgers . . .' She opened the file and held it close to her face. 'And an ice-cream van.'

'Here.' Anderson stabbed a small picture before taking it off the wall. It showed two kids eating a cone, but down the right-hand edge was the side window of an ice-cream van, showing the serving hatch and logos for 99 Flakes and Maisy Daisy ice cream.

'Yes, that's an ice-cream van selling a bestselling ice cream,' said Costello, her voice rich with sarcasm.

'Sometimes I'd like to stab you,' Anderson replied sweetly.

Carol was sitting at her desk, looking at the transcript of the research paper but not really reading. Her editor had called again asking if she was OK. She was, wasn't she? She felt she had been walking around the flat all night, exhausting herself. The noises that she thought had been keeping her awake, the tap-tap-tap had turned into footfall in her nightmares, coming through the walls, through the ceiling.

And she had woken up, under the bed, her fingers bleeding where she had bitten and pulled on the skin with her teeth.

And the face of that woman with the spikey black hair had upset her. She was here in the Green. Carol had travelled thousands of miles, spent ten years trying to forget about it, and it seemed to have found her.

The guys from the deli had delivered her breakfast as usual, making sure that she was all right. She said she was fine. Joshua nodded as he handed over two salmon and cream cheese bagels, a large Americano and a small Danish. He didn't look as if he believed her. He looked at the mess of her hands. She didn't even sound convincing to herself.

The bagels were still in their bag, her hope of a working breakfast now evaporated. Half an hour later, she was sitting on her
bed, staring at the floor when she heard her laptop ping; if it was
her editor, she could take a hike.

Hi,

How are you doing, Carol? I've not seen you about on the
balcony recently. We have seen a few of the cops up at your
flat, looking down to the Green. Are they going to do a
re-enactment? Do you think we are going to be on the telly?
I saw the other detective, the really good-looking one doing
the filming, with that blonde lassie who does the crime
programme on a Thursday night.

It's so hot, isn't it? We are lucky that the big windows at
the front face north, so the flat stays cool. I guess if yours
are south-facing, you'll be like a Christmas turkey by noon
each day. They are saying that the weather will break soon.
We Scots can't do too much in the sunshine and Sven will
go mad if there's a hosepipe ban and he can't keep the grass
of the Maltman the right shade of green. He might need new
sunglasses to correct the colour – have you seen him in those
ridiculous blue ones? I think he should have given them up
about twenty years ago. Along with his stonewashed jeans.

When you moved in, did you receive a little notebook
about the history of the Maltman Green? About how it was
a brewery and all that. Well, that was true except they missed
the big bit from 1950 to the 1970s when it was a jam factory
or something totally mundane. That makes it a whole lot less
sexy, doesn't it?

I came across it the other day while looking for the lemon
squeezer. It says there is a ghost by the way, like you
suspected. Some poor bloke who fell in a vat of whisky and
drowned (what a way to die!). I think if I get a moment, I
will do some research on that as I bet it's as much tosh as
everything else about this place.

Do you ever hear anything at night like somebody moving
around? That might be Sven or Murdo. Obviously, with the
way the place was built originally, the first and second floors
are continuous round the whole quad. So through the wall

from me is one of the rooms where Sven runs his business. I think he must be up during the night. He looks like the sort who needs little sleep – he has a type of restless energy about him. Murdo collects all kind of weird stuff and stores it in the attic. Pauline told me he has a humidifier and everything.

Or it might be the noises of the spirit of the man who died in the vat of pure alcohol. However, sometimes when I am upstairs, looking out of the window the way you do when you can't sleep, I see a face at the window on the corner. Or maybe that's the gin. This is a weird place we live in.

I wish I could function better with less sleep, I'm knackered by ten o'clock these days, so much worse with the heat. I was thinking of going up and sleeping on the roof garden. It's there to offset the carbon dioxide footprint of the building. Have you ever been up there? I have never been up alone. Sven has taken me up twice, but he likes to keep the nice stuff of the Maltman in his control. But then why shouldn't he? He paid for most of it. And, let's face it, our rent is really cheap.

Oh yes, everybody's in awe of the Jonssons. They'd be easy to dislike, or to cast in some kind of Stepford Wives. They look as if they've been designed by the winner of a 'design the perfect family' competition. I mean, none of that was accidental, was it? Were they designed by a robot or bred from the bottom of a petri dish?

Like I said, he's not Swedish – well, the mum is, so the kids are fifty per cent, but Sven was born in Glasgow, plain Johnson, but he doesn't know that we know that. He even talks with a false Swedish accent – he's such a tosser. Inside my head I call him the peudoswede. It makes him appear a bit of a twat rather than the pompous git he appears to be. I wonder if he thinks it gives him some mystique. She, Sabina, was a language student, over here on work experience, a bit like you, I guess, though I think she's more acquainted with the bottom of a glass than the rest of them. I get the feeling that she's always a little bit drunk – she'd have to be, married to him. I suppose you clocked that he even called their dog after that Swedish detective's dog. They're not allowed to pee in the Green, the dogs. They used to have a wee area – pardon the pun – but now they've to be taken out to the park, no matter what time of day or night. Wonder if that's how the shutter was left open.

How are you doing?

Hope you are good, not too disturbed by it all.

Lulu

She read that line again, the bit about somebody moving around. She didn't hear it, but she sensed it, and maybe it was why she and Lulu bonded – another sleepless soul.

She walked down to the living room, checking that the photograph and the pony were where she had left them, then went back upstairs and pulled out the drawer where the dolls lived. The box was there, the lid was closed. She paused, sensing something was wrong. Picking them up, she tried to remember if she had tucked the box in at the left or the right-hand side of the drawer. She thought the right-hand side, as her medication tended to be on the left. The box was now on the left. She opened the lid.

Their little blankets were crumpled. Trembling, she lifted the cover of the first doll, the daddy doll, the one that was supposed to protect the others; his body was twisted and broken.

She sobbed, a deep, heartfelt, wrenching cry. She wouldn't have done this; she wiped the snot from her nose, the tears from her eyes, reconsidering. Of all the things she'd do, of all the things she'd forget, this was not one of them. She was not that person, not now, and never had been.

She needed to talk to somebody. Her mind drifted to the nice detective who had been there the night before. She picked up her mobile, scrolled through. Knowing that she had put his number in her contacts 'just in case'. Then she swiped her phone off. He wouldn't believe her.

She walked upstairs to the bedroom, opened the door on to the balcony, realizing that she had not dressed yet; she was still in her pyjamas with her scarlet dressing gown over the top, so she stayed against the wall, behind the curtain, looking through the thin muslin to see if there was anybody down on the Green today. It was eighty-five degrees. The air was stuffy and warm within the four walls of the quadrangle, unable to get out. The flowers were still, and even the fish seemed to be holding their breath. Uneasy. Disquieting.

She retreated a little, listening. Usually, there was music from somewhere or the noise of somebody's TV playing. Or the chatter of the Jonsson children, or Murdo Wallace sitting on the deck, or out on his balcony on his mobile phone talking business. Sven coming and going from the garage to the house, his golden retriever bouncing all over him. The Great Dane lying on the decking, chewing a bone noisily.

Yes, it was too quiet, as if the ghost of Rachel was still walking around the lawns, up the paths and over the small arched bridge at the Japanese pond, with her police cap under her arm, raising her arm, loosening her blonde hair, walking free, reborn.

Carol closed her eyes, feeling the cloth on her forehead, the coolness of the wall. When she opened her eyes, the ghost was gone. She looked across the Green to the house opposite, her eyes searching each of the windows for any sign of her new friend. Maybe an exchange of a friendly wave. It was a Sunday, so nobody should be at work. She hoped Lulu might be at home – after all, she must have been thinking about her to send her the email.

But she was nowhere to be seen. She saw the boy, Joe, take something out to the bin. He looked up, saw her, nodded to her dismissively and went back up the stairs at the rear of the property.

Carol closed the balcony door, blocking out the silence of the Green below, but she stayed on the seat looking out, not wanting to think about the broken dolls. How could she explain that to anybody, even to herself?

She must have fallen asleep, woken up by the roll of the steel shutters at the Jonsson gate. Then Sven came out of the back and walked over to his garage, opening the door and letting in four or five people; two of them, carrying equipment, a cameraman and a sound recorder. A woman came in; Carol recognized her from the TV the other night – Naomi Clearwater, the mother of the missing boy was here, where the DNA was found. She was talking to the blonde woman from the *Eyes and Ears* programme. The handsome policeman, the one who couldn't quite stand up properly on his own, was with them, and as before there was the figure, dressed in black, the short spikey hair shining in the sun. Again, she got a chair for the handsome detective to sit on before walking away in the direction of the Japanese pond, in search of shade. Sven sat down. They moved the seat, the camera, his position. The cameraman looked at the sun and indicated that he wanted the chair moved a little more to the right. Carol stopped watching and went back to looking at the figure dressed in black. She reopened the balcony doors, leaning on the upright to look over the garden, the beauty of it, these people having a good time in the sun. Sabina came out with iced drinks on a tray. Naomi hugged her, they both hugged Kathy. They moved around again.

It was too much for Carol. They looked round, then up when they heard her sobbing. It was the figure in black who started to move, jogging across the Green to get to the steel shutter, shouting up at Carol to open her door. Naomi and Kathy looked at each other and shrugged, then went back to sorting out who was going to stand where as they did their piece to camera, at the location where Johnny's DNA was found.

Sven Jonsson sat on the chair at his patio doors, undisturbed by the sobbing of his tenant, keeping his distance on the decking but listening to every word they said.

Carol pressed the buzzer and the screen lit up. She knew the face on the other side.

'Go away.'

'Are you OK? You looked upset.'

'Go away.'

'I don't think I should. I am a doctor. They are worried about you. Do you need any help?'

'Why are you here?'

'Because you're crying.'

'Why are you here in the Green?' Carol was almost screaming at her.

'Because I'm with the police. The police and a camera crew are in the Green.' There was a pause. 'I'm not going away until I know that you're OK.'

Carol slumped on to the floor, looking round at the mess, at her hands, the rough skin bloodied, the nails opening up like a budding flower. The woman was a doctor. She reached up to click the door open.

Elvie climbed up the steep stairs that smelled of fresh paint, coffee, bread and cinnamon.

When she got to the door, it was already open. Sitting on the floor was a woman with long grey hair, dressed in a scarlet dressing gown, her thin legs sticking out of the bottom, barefooted, the ends of her fingers bleeding. She looked too thin to stand up.

Elvie stopped. 'Are you OK?'

'I'm not sure.' Carol wiped the snot and tears from her face with her forearm.

'You seemed very upset.' Elvie took her time, looking at the woman sitting in front of her, imagining her younger. Her hair dark, her face thin and black-eyed. 'I know who you are. Not the name you are using; I would have recognized it. But I know who you are.'

'Please don't tell anybody,' she said, her voice melodious and tuneful, her blue eyes red-rimmed with purple shadows.

'I won't. Why would I? Can I help you up?'

Carol took the offered hand; it felt strong and cool as it grasped her own, firmly but kindly. She allowed herself to be lifted, then they walked together into the open-plan room, bright patterns of light flooding in from large windows that opened on to the Green. 'I can't believe that you are here. Why are you around the Maltman? It's to do with the death of that girl, isn't it? Do you follow that kind of thing around?'

'My partner was in the TV show, *Eyes and Ears*. I'm driving him around – he had part of his leg amputated, so can't drive himself.'

Carol sat down on the single chair, her eyes never leaving her companion's face. 'That must be difficult.' She swallowed. 'Did you break my dolls?'

'No. I don't know what you're talking about.'

'Sorry, of course you didn't. I'm upset.' Carol nodded. 'She died, didn't she, your sister?'

'Sophie, she was killed. Yes. But you're not Carol Holman. You were' – Elvie searched her memory for the right name – 'Carla Holmen. That was it.'

'Yes, I didn't want to bring that life back with me, so I anglicized it. I was never the same, after that.'

'Nobody would be. You were in a box, locked and . . . I don't remember seeing you at the enquiry.'

'No, I went home to Trondheim. But I need to say goodbye to it, I need closure.' Her blue eyes closed. 'So I came to London, then to Glasgow, and I hope one day to go up to Strachur and see where it happened. I feel as though I've never been there. All I remember is the dark, and the noise of the water running.'

'It's a very beautiful place. I'll take you there if you want to go. I know it very well.'

'You used to work up there?'

'In another lifetime.'

'Did you get over it?'

'Yes.'

'How did you do that?'

'My experience was not yours,' Elvie answered with her extreme logic.

'Now I can't go outside. I can't step across the front door.'

'Trauma'll do that to you. It'll follow you like a black shadow, then one day you'll look behind you and you will be alone.'

'You think?'

'I know.'

'You're very sure.'

'I'm a doctor. I know. The human brain is tougher than you think.'

'It's taking its time. Do you think it would help to go back up there? To Strachur, to the water clock?'

'When you're ready to poke the tiger. Not before then.'

'But you worked it out, the Manson thing?'

'Manson, yes; I had the right killer, but he didn't kill my sister. I was wrong in the one respect that mattered to me.'

Carol leaned forward, her voice urgent. 'I need your help. I think I am going crazy. I can't sleep, I can't eat. I put things down and they are not where I remember leaving them. I think I am losing my mind. Things are getting worse, not better.'

Elvie looked around the room, the half-unpacked boxes. 'Is that the only thing? You are not forgetting days? Dates? Names? Can you do your work OK? Keep to schedule?'

Carol nodded. 'I'm behind with my work but that's because I can't sleep. I can't get out. I feel like I'm in jail. And that's easy – I have food, I have work, I can earn money, I shop online and

I open the balcony windows to get fresh air. I know I'm very lucky. I think I might be going mad.'

'Just stuff being moved about?'

'I think so, and noises – noises at night.' She looked up. 'I can hear them in the other houses, the kids next door. And the woman across the way says that the place is haunted, so when I read that, I began to think that maybe there is something else going on.'

'Or maybe there is somebody coming into this flat and moving stuff around. That's logical if what you say is true.'

Carol looked around at the mess. 'It might be my imagination.'

'Yes, it probably is,' agreed Elvie, thinking that it was a very specific thing to imagine.

TWELVE

C ostello left, muttering about getting some clarity on what had happened in the minutes before Rachel died. She was planning a reconstruction of the events with a view to establishing the timing involved, after reading Carol's statement and comparing it to Callaghan's.

She left, closing the door behind her with a degree of force.

As soon as it closed, Anderson flicked her a V and sat back down, sitting for a minute or two in the peace and quiet before he pulled the computer mouse towards him and started to scroll, but his mind wasn't on it. His eyes fixed on the wall beyond, looking at the pictures of the wedding party, Naomi appearing young and carefree. The last four years had destroyed her. Her smile was dazzling, looking over to her right, to somebody off camera whom she was pleased to see. How big would that smile be when she saw her son?

Then he got up, standing close to the wall, starting to move the photographs by unpinning and pinning them, keeping them within their quarter-hour time bands but getting a better sense of time. He knew he was tracking Naomi. Most of the pictures were of Natalie and Niles, but he studied each one of Naomi and looked closer. Who was she talking to? Who was she looking at? Richard was in most of them, standing behind her, dressed in a good shirt and trousers, his hands behind his back as if he was walking behind the Queen. Naomi was dressed in a bright turquoise-blue dress – shapely, he would have called it. Her brown hair was longer then, wound up on top of her head. There was one picture, the four of them: Natalie, Naomi, Niles and Richard. Three of them were looking straight at the camera, Naomi looking past it, smiling. That picture was in the section from two fifteen to two thirty. He scanned the rest of them, looking to see if he could find a view from the other side. Naomi must have been looking at her son, surely, with that expression.

But if not? He scanned the photographs, pulling out the images of four men that Naomi seemed to smile at more than others. They could be close friends, but the man with the black hair down to his collar? He looked like one to watch. He put the photos on Vik's desk, the images of those of interest to be isolated, cleaned up and laminated.

At two o'clock, Costello parked across the road from the Quarterhouse Deli and called across to Wyngate and Redding to get her a tuna melt bagel and a tea. She then opened Google Maps and studied the streets around the Maltman, mentally placing where Callaghan, Rachel and Mr Baseball had come from, so she could claim it was a working lunch. After doing the run a few times, she bet Ruby would be up for the fudge and coconut Maisy Daisy.

While drinking his coffee, Wyngate explained that he wanted Costello to jog slowly, at the same speed that Rachel had used on the tape. Then Wyngate, acting Mr Baseball, was going to do the same thing on an eight-second delay, humming a tune he knew to keep pace. Ruby was playing Martin Callaghan. They knew to keep count so that they'd keep the right distance apart, and then see where they were when they reached the shutters.

They had already worked through Rachel's options, now not convinced she was in any danger, having viewed her face on the CCTV. She was smiling, so Costello thought she was right: Rachel ran into the Green because that was where she wanted to be. And she knew the code.

If she had felt threatened by Mr Baseball, she'd have screamed, stopped – there were people about – but she didn't. She jogged through them. Ruby, as Callaghan, was to bring up the rear, but keeping far enough back so that she'd be missed by the camera as Callaghan had been. Then they walked up Brewer Street, intent on coming back down at a certain speed.

Costello even paused, as Rachel had, for a single beat, but when they got to the alley, Wyngate was always too close to Costello for her to have even a remote chance of going up the alley without being seen and Costello being aware of that. So Rachel knew he was there, she knew he would follow, and that fitted with what Costello had been thinking. If she had wanted to stay safe, she would have stayed on Brewer Street; she would have run a bit further to the glass front of the deli. Or knocked on a door.

But she was having fun.

Who else was in on the joke?

'So what do you think? I think she knew him and enticed him in there for reasons of her own,' said Ruby.

'I agree,' said Costello carefully.

Wyngate pulled a face and did that head-rolling thing he did when he had an opinion but was too scared to voice it.

'Gordon?'

'I don't see how it worked. I don't see how Mr Baseball got away and Callaghan arrived. No matter how we do it, we run into each other.'

'They did.'

'He says they did. But if I'm Callaghan, I follow him in the alley, he comes out . . . we bump into each other. But there's a delay of Callaghan going into the Green, as Carol said.'

'I don't think she's the most reliable witness. She's well intentioned, but she was stressed, she was far away, and then she fainted.'

'But she said there was a delay; Carol has stated that quite clearly. There was a delay of a slow count of eight before he appears running – running, she said – into the square.'

'That's what I said.'

'No, actually,' said Costello, 'What we see is Mr Baseball going out, a gap of a few seconds, then Martin Callaghan coming in. What were they doing in the archway of the alley for a count of eight? Having a quick snog?'

'No,' thought Ruby. 'I think Mr Baseball threatened him, punched him, told him to mind his own business. That might explain why he's . . . well . . . unable to provide a good ID for one.'

'OK, back to that later. Ruby, while you're here, can you look at these four men?' Costello swiped the images of the four men from the wedding party across the phone. 'What do you think? Who would you marry? Who would you have an affair with?'

'Why do I not get asked?' moaned Wyngate.

Costello showed him the pictures as well.

'My wife would like him; he's got clean fingernails.'

Ruby did a magnificent eye roll. 'Yeah, I'd marry him, Mr Fingernails, but I'd not kick *him* out of bed.'

'The one with the long hair? Mr Pimento. Interesting.' Costello pulled her hair back from the sweat on her face. 'I need some water.'

Ruby looked up at the scorching sun. 'I need an ice cream.'

Wyngate nodded. 'I'm going to ask to use their toilet.'

Brenda was clearing up after a Sunday dinner where the main entertainment had been trying to get Moses to speak. He had steadfastly refused. Norma was going to speak before Moses did. Anderson took his coffee into his study, saying that he would be out in an hour. The rest of his family were going into the garden to enjoy the sun and eat some ice cream, which might be the second and third words his son would utter.

Costello had phoned to say that the result of their efforts was that Callaghan and Mr Baseball had spent some time together. Maybe they had a fight and Callaghan lost. Anderson said he'd review it later but he didn't see it helping to locate Johnny Clearwater and that was where their focus should be.

He scrolled through the files on his desktop, leaning back in the chair, sipping coffee, scrolling on the mouse. Naomi Clearwater was squeaky clean: a local girl who had married well. Richard, if anything, was even cleaner, although an occasional smile wouldn't hurt his public image. But Anderson couldn't make him fit with a man who would abduct his own son for any reason.

The girl who had the wedding party, Natalie, had one driving offence under her belt in Scotland before she went to the States and married an American called Niles Nascimento, a doctor who had gone through an acrimonious divorce to marry Natalie. They met when Natalie flew over to donate bone marrow to a four-year-old Californian boy who was suffering some rare kind of cancer. So there was a nasty divorce and then Natalie's wedding party got disrupted by the abduction of her four-year-old nephew. Those two avenues had been fully investigated and borne no fruit at all.

Naomi had no known enemies. Richard was a QC but dealt with mostly white-collar crime. Nobody had stood out there or Bob Allison would have clocked it.

Anderson had to make a decision: whether to go over old ground that had been gone over before with a huge team and a bigger budget or look elsewhere and find something that they had missed, which was unlikely.

There was a list of those who had been invited to the wedding party in Cellardyke on 24th June 2017. He looked through the names. Nothing rang a bell with him, no immediate connection with the Maltman, but the list had gone back for Wyngate and Mulholland to trace. There was a note that said it was a party, not a sit-down event, so the invitation list might not be complete; it wasn't that formal an affair. Four years had passed; something might bubble to the surface. It was almost impossible to keep a four-year-old child hidden, never mind an eight-year-old.

There was a huge amount of information, thousands of statements, hundreds of actions, but, again, experienced feet had walked this way and found nothing.

He went back to skim-reading Allison's reports, the actions and the results; his glasses on the top of his head, his pen noted down points from the electronic copy. He had a sense that Bob Allison was frustrated by the wall of money wrapped around the couple that often blocked or obfuscated or derailed the police investigation. He couldn't play the cards he wanted, follow the leads he wanted, because the Clearwaters' own private investigative team, Securiate, had come up with another lead: a man seen in the distance, a phone tip that said somebody knew something and asked how much it was worth, an uninvited guest at the party. Naomi wanted every lead Securiate came up with followed, regardless of the validity of the evidence; she never left the police to do their job properly. Allison had been running the entire investigation with one arm tied behind his back, as he was instructed to chase down every lead in case that was the 'one'. Anderson was not so hobbled; Warburton had made sure of that.

Naomi intrigued him. She'd had three TV programmes made about her and was in the process of filming another. She was an after-dinner speaker, a campaigner, but Anderson thought only to get her own child back, unlike the Mary Parnells of the world who had quietly used their money to get other people's children back.

With his political sway, Richard was also the head of a children's charity. Somebody had underlined that: a thought process that might have been picked up elsewhere in the actions of the investigation. He had no idea if it had.

But Naomi was clean. He read again about her younger sister's incident when she had been driving, not fast, not drunk, but on a dangerous road, early on a winter's morning. The young boy in a dark jacket had cycled across the road right in front of her and she had reacted a little too late, but the enquiry had said it was incredible that she had reacted at all.

So Anderson started googling the name of the boy, his parents who had lived in the same village as Natalie, the village where the Wishart sisters had grown up. Anderson drummed his fingers on the top of the desk. Was there anything in this? Did the mum of the child so badly hurt in the incident suddenly decide to take a child at the driver's wedding party and keep him in a basement for years? It read like a B-movie script.

But he felt there was something. Allison had already agreed an action on this line of enquiry; it had led nowhere.

The list went on for ages, a long reference number after each item. One caught his eye: the spiritualist, Una Parryman. He looked at his watch. She was ten minutes away. He thought about phoning her to say he was coming, but if she was any good at her job, she'd already know that.

Redding was sitting in interview room one, her black hair neatly in a chignon, looking as fresh and alert as ever, smiling at the young man across the table.

Costello was very irritated. 'Callaghan, stop it. Stop talking nonsense and digging a bigger hole for yourself. We've an eyewitness who saw you strike Rachel Sinclair. I'll do you the courtesy of telling you to think carefully before you open your mouth.'

'You don't have a witness because I didn't hit her. Why would I?'

'Well, that's something we've to get to the bottom of and then prepare a report for the Fiscal. And yes, we do have a witness. So what do you have to say?'

He dropped his head into his hands. 'This is becoming a bloody nightmare. It happened as I said it happened. Look, I thought she had passed out through drink, so I took her keys and threw them away, intending to pick them up later, but she died.'

Costello put her pen down on the table. 'OK, version three. Think clearly. Tell us as it happened.'

Callaghan nodded, relenting.

'I saw her walk past the garden of the Drunken Monkey. That's

why I got up and left. I did walk after her. It happened as I said
– the guy who came out did rattle me against the wall. I might
have taken longer to get over that than I thought. He did hit me
pretty hard. I might have looked down the street, trying to see
where he went. I couldn't see him, so I looked in, saw the woman
on the ground. I went in to help her, and, you know, she was really
beautiful, the way she looked, over my shoulder, up to the sky as
if, you know, she was posing for the camera somewhere.'

Costello and Redding exchanged a meaningful glance.

'Which shoulder was she looking over?'

'My left. I heard that she might have been on cocaine. Is that
relevant? Was it a drug thing? But then there was the outfit she
was wearing. Was she on cocaine?'

'It's the go-to drug of choice at the moment.'

'Her face became unfocused. Then she dropped to the ground,
she slid down the wall like a sack of potatoes. Then I started CPR.
Then the other two came out.'

'It's a strange story. I bet your wife won't believe it. She won't
believe that you were perfectly innocent in going into a secluded,
lovely place with a tall, gorgeous blonde and then saying you were
only there to do your civic duty. Would you believe that?' Costello
asked Redding.

She thought for a moment, long enough to be sarcastic. 'Nope.'

'Neither would I.'

'Shame,' muttered Redding.

'Look, I love Becs. She's the love of my life, but I'm doing all
the overtime I can get my hands on. It's been like that for three
years now. I'm tired of being tired.' Callaghan was on the verge
of tears.

'The cocaine contributed to her death, according to O'Hare.'

Callaghan let out a long sigh.

'You look relieved.'

'Of course I am. So you know I didn't do it. I tried to help her.
I didn't do anything to her.' Callaghan started to cry.

'Rachel had some genetic issue with her arteries. She had taken
some cocaine but the pathologist suspects there's another reason
why her blood pressure went up and why that blood vessel burst.
Something more than a run along the road. Maybe some sexual
activity?'

'Well, if it was, it wasn't with me.'

Costello nodded, got up and walked out of the room, Ruby Redding following her. 'Leave him to stew for a bit. He's still not telling us something.'

The boy is alive.

That was the message from the spiritualist Una Parryman after she had held a photograph of Johnny Clearwater in her bony, red hands. She had recreated this moment for the TV cameras at the time and found herself on every front page of every daily paper; her appointment diary was booked out for the entire year.

But it had the desired effect and Johnny Clearwater was still on the front of the papers months after he had been taken, if indeed he had been taken.

Now there was another ending to the story. All Anderson had to do was figure it out. Una Parryman should have lived in a small cottage somewhere on the side of a misty loch, with a lilting sky and low, angry clouds. The satnav had taken Anderson to a very modern block of flats that looked on to the motorway.

He was buzzed in and, after climbing the stairs, he knocked on the open door of flat 3B. A woman in her late fifties appeared in the hall, a knife in her hands. The apron tied tightly round her waist was splattered with either blood or tomatoes. Anderson held up his warrant card.

'Oh, how can I help you?' She flicked a look at the clock on the wall.

'I'd like to talk to you about Johnny Clearwater,' Anderson said, while pulling out the laminated script of the phone call that Una had made to the incident room in Edinburgh some three years before.

'You had better come in,' Una said, opening the door wider and pointing her way to the front room where the bright summer sunshine was highlighting a floral settee.

He walked over to the window to look out on to the motorway, noticing the triple glazing to keep the noise out. The radio in the kitchen was turned off, halting Marc Bolan mid-lyric. Una popped her head round the door and asked if he wanted a cup of tea. He declined.

Una nodded and then closed the door behind her, joining Anderson in the front room and taking the chair beside a fireplace filled with dried flowers and straw dollies. They reminded him of witchcraft. Una, in a flowery yellow skirt, light-blue T-shirt and white apron, offered Anderson a seat.

'So,' she said, 'Johnny Clearwater – you found some DNA?'

'Yes, we did.'

'Look, I don't have him, so stop making me nervous. You look so serious.'

Reluctantly, Anderson sat down and tried to rearrange his features so he did not look as if he was regretting this as a total waste of time. 'Can you tell me how you know this? How you knew the boy was alive? In 2018, you called the helpline.'

'Was I right?'

'I can't say.'

'I know I was. Three times I've had information about the whereabouts of a missing person. Three times I've been to the police. Three times I've been right. Each time I was ignored. Naomi didn't ignore me, and she didn't let Bob Allison ignore me either. So yes, I can tell you how it came about.' She looked up at the ceiling, searching for the next memory, or maybe checking that her lie was robust. 'I was watching the appeal that his mum made on the television, the one at the press conference on the first anniversary. They showed a bit of film of Naomi and Johnny – she's holding her son on her hip, swaying slightly back and forth as if she was rocking the child to sleep. The skin on his face and his hands was very raw . . .'

Anderson nodded. He recognized the description. So would anybody who read the news online.

'I got the feeling that my face was burning and sore, and I knew there was a connection. There was a photograph of them in that morning's newspaper, the *Express*, and I put my hand over it. I knew he hadn't moved over to spirit. Not at that point.'

They let that statement hang in the air like a bad smell.

'You don't believe me, but I don't care if you do or don't. It's what I felt. That and a feeling of height as if I was above, looking down, looking across, looking over water.' Una closed her eyes and inhaled deeply through her nose, as if smelling the gravy on a Sunday roast.

'So where is he? I mean if you can tell me that, why can't you tell me where he is?'

'It's not like that. I can't get him on speed dial, Mr Anderson.'

'What if we brought you something, his clothes or his teddy bear? Could you get a reading off that?'

Una shook her head. 'No, that only happens in films. What does help is if there's something in the public eye, then there's people talking about it and there's a buzz around. Then the messages seem to come through, as if the power of prayer, good thought or the collective conscious is a truly physical thing and it can channel whatever is out there in the ether.'

Anderson looked confused.

Una smiled. 'We can only say what we hear or what we feel, even if it makes no sense to us. And I feel that Johnny is here on this plane. He's not dead. And I think his skin has stopped burning.' She closed her eyes, nodding to herself. Then stood up. 'Yes. Excuse me.'

Anderson waited for her to give him some words from beyond the grave.

'I need to turn the gas off,' she said and vanished into the kitchen.

'How do you know he's alive?' Anderson asked, following her, his hands in the pocket of his trousers, rather fascinated by this woman, who was far too normal to be mystical in any way.

'It's a different feeling.'

'Confidentially, there are some things about Naomi that don't make sense.'

Una closed her eyes, tilted her head for a moment. 'You know, when I think of that kid, I think of his beating heart and that he's looked after. He's loved. My face is not burning the way it did before. He's not in danger.' She lifted her hands and looked at the palms. 'When I saw Naomi on that TV programme and when the phone number was running across the screen, I started to feel a bit uneasy.' She looked around at Anderson. 'I don't think they should have done that.'

'I'm sorry but I'm not getting this.'

'I would read into it that somebody saw that phone helpline, and they have the boy. The boy might be in danger simply because people are now looking for him. I see a cauldron with lots of swirling soup. Round and round. It's hot. There was a dog, wasn't there?'

'Where, with the boy?'

'Yes, when he went missing.'

'No.'

'There's a dog there now.'

'Or maybe his birthmark has changed into that of a dog.'

'Maybe.' She looked at him, smiling. 'And for some reason, I'm being shown a man in medieval armour, on a horse . . . Sometimes it's difficult to interpret what I see, but there is a sense of death around you – well, around somebody who is around you.'

'I do work on a serious crime unit, so murder is not that unusual for us.'

'It's around you. Deceit comes to my mind.'

'Very good. Death and deceit are my job.'

Una was standing very still, her eyes slightly closed, observing him, scrutinizing him.

'And I'm getting a name, I'm hearing a name.'

Despite himself, Anderson felt his body tense. He thought she was going to say Moses. And he was ready to believe her.

'Fred? Freddie? But there's deceit to that as well; I think when you meet somebody called Fred, Freddie, that'll not be their name. And it's not business – this is personal. Dark clouds are rolling in over somebody's head, very dark clouds.'

'And?'

'Usually, when I see that, it means that somebody is thinking of dying by their own hand.' She nipped the bridge of her nose with her forefinger and thumb, closing her eyes, as if she had been struck by a sudden headache. Then she opened her eyes and shook her head. 'Well, that's it. Somebody walked over my grave. Horrible feeling.'

Anderson was still shivering when he got into the car.

'What brings you round here at this time of night? I thought you'd be at home playing happy families and getting Moses to memorize the *Iliad* before his fourth birthday,' said Costello, stepping back to let him into her flat.

'Wanted to find out how you got on with Callaghan.' Anderson followed her in.

Costello started to walk down her hall, saying that they had kept it short and sweet, told him nothing. 'I think he panicked. So it was explainable, understandable, acting like a cop, except I don't believe him. And I don't believe that you're here to talk about that.'

'No, I wanted to run something past you.' He walked into the living room, saw the coffee table covered with photographs. 'Have I interrupted something?'

'No.' Costello hastily bent down to gather them in her hand. Two escaped, fluttering to rest on the blue carpet. Instinctively, Anderson picked them up, seeing, before she snatched them from his hand, that it was a photograph of a very young Costello, maybe aged five or six, with two women – her mother and her grandmother, he judged. The two women who had brought her up, after her dad had left, taking her brother with him, seeing early exactly what a monster her brother would grow up to be. The picture was taken of them sitting on a fence, the sea behind them.

Water.

Scary how two children, the same DNA, could play out so differently. Maybe not that different, just moulded in a different way. The age-old question: nature or nurture?

'What's this? Cleaning out a drawer or looking at old memories?'

'Neither. I'm looking for something. So what can I help you with? Do you want a cup of tea? I've no milk. Or tea.'

'Have you anything cold? It's still bloody hot out there. The car was like a greenhouse even with the windows open. Do you have a cold drink?'

'Water? The tap will have water in it.' She folded her arms over. Not like her, this staccato conversation.

'If it's a bad time, I can go and . . .'

'No. What was it you wanted? You've a file under your arm. It must be about something.'

Anderson shrugged. 'I've two years of evidence to review in a matter of hours; I've days to solve a case that took a full team four years to get nowhere.'

'So you've got to look somewhere else.' Costello folded herself up on the settee, knees up to her chest, cradling her legs, but her eyes were full of thought. 'I guess you've to look at something more sideways.'

'OK. I need your honest opinion.'

'As if I'd ever give you anything else.'

'There are lots of leads here, hundreds of them, all tracked down, most of them about Naomi and Richard.'

'It was their son who was taken,' answered Costello logically.

'Do you think it could have been about ruining Natalie's day? She's home for a celebration of a wedding that took place three thousand miles away. Family, friends, everybody who was important to her was there. And that day will be remembered as the day her nephew was abducted.'

'Steal a child because you didn't get an invite to the wedding?' asked Costello.

'What about taking a child because the bride was involved in an accident that injured your child?'

Costello narrowed her eyes. 'And?'

'The boy, a Daniel McIntosh, was left disabled. The file doesn't say how badly. The inquest said there was no blame and asked for a barrier to go on the bike path. It was November, early morning, bad light, bad bend, bad weather, and the boy dressed in dark clothes on a dark bike came out of a path on to the road right in front of her. There was no way she could have missed him.'

'To some, that could sound like she got away with it.' Costello craned her neck at the ceiling, bending it from side to side until it cracked loudly. Anderson winced. 'And you want to know – because he's a disabled child, and you have a disabled child – if you're making connections, if you're seeing something that isn't there.'

'I was actually wanting to know if it's worth ruining a wedding party for. But yes, the Moses thing had crossed my mind.' Anderson looked out on the river. The view from his colleague's flat really was something. He walked over to the window and looked down. 'Is that Elvie out for a run?'

'Sure is. She runs all the time – must do a marathon a week. She gets on my nerves. She's like Ruby. Endless appetite, endless energy.'

'They probably have food in their cupboard. Do they speak to you at all? Vik and Elvie?'

'Nope. I see him at work and that's that. Are you going out to speak to this McIntosh boy? Did the original investigation action that?'

'Yes, they did. His parents had a good alibi. As an avenue of investigation, it stopped as soon as it started.'

'You think you'll get somewhere?'

'There was four years between the accident and the abduction. Is that too long to hold a grudge?'

'Danny got a life sentence. The man that boy'll not grow up to be, the children he'll not have.'

'Tell me about it.' He looked out of the window, Elvie a diminishing figure on the Clyde walkway.

'But it's tugging at you because of Moses?'

'I think so. It's like an itch I can't really get at.'

'So go out and see them. Where are they?'

'Killenwood.'

'Well, that's not far. It's a tiny place, isn't it? Three houses, a pub and a dog kennel.'

'Yeah.' Anderson looked across the cityscape, slowly cooling from a day of boiling in the harsh heat of the sun. Even now, shards of bright light flashed off the glass of the high-rise. Looking at the sky, the bright blue rolled on for ever.

'Did Natalie grow up in Killenwood?'

Anderson turned to look at her. 'Yes.'

'If one sister grew up there, then so did the other. Maybe there is something way back in the past of Naomi that might be common knowledge round the village – you know, childhood sweetheart, paganism, witches, dogging, Satanism, sabotaging each other's courgettes for the flower show. You know what the wee villages in the west are like. Why not go out and sound out the dad for what he knows in the wider sense. Are the sisters close in age?'

'Four years apart – Natalie's younger.'

'So go out, scratch your itch, but get a sense of what these girls were like when they were younger; might give you some insight as to what kind of people they grew up into.'

'Naomi married her Bible-thumping lawyer and lives her best life campaigning for the return of her son. Natalie married her doctor and lives in California somewhere, having gone there in the first instance to donate bone marrow to save a wee guy's life. We know what kind of people they grew up into.'

'Did Natalie come back for Naomi's wedding? She must have got married around then, doing the maths. Four months later?'

'I'll check,' said Anderson. 'All four are high flyers now, and those on high pedestals have further to fall.'

Costello picked up the picture of herself as a child. 'You never know . . . believe me, you never know what kind of adult a child might grow into.'

Anderson looked out, over the river, watching it roll out to the west coast. 'What were you called in those days, when you were wee?'

'Why?'

'I'm curious. I'm sure your mum didn't call you Costello.'

'I was called Winifred, Winifred Prudence after my grand-mothers. Why?'

'So you get called Winifred? Winnie? Pru?'

'Too much of a tomboy. I got called Freddie.'

The queue at the deli was shorter than usual; the smell of espresso and fresh salmon seemed to drift across the street to the lone jogger doing his fourth circuit of the park. He slowed a little as Joshua Wallace keyed the security number into Carol's keypad and pressed the button, knowing it would ring up in the duplex and alert her that her ricotta bagels and coffee were ready for delivery. The runner crossed the road, dashing between the traffic, in a hurry now. He had paused as the man stopped at Carol's door, hand on his stomach, slightly bent over as if he had a stitch. He already had the first four numbers, running past as he always did at this time, with his baseball cap and his vest top and dark glasses hiding his eyes. He caught the final two numbers in the sequence, and then ran on. It was a common sight around these parts. Nobody would think twice, nobody would recognize him, so with the six-digit code lodged in his memory, he ran on round the block and headed for home, repeating the numbers over and over to himself so they got burned into his memory. There was no hurry now. He knew that he could come back at any time.

Carol was eating her second tuna bagel. She felt better today, calmer for some reason. She had bathed her fingertips and dressed them with plasters. Elvie McCulloch hadn't laughed at her. Her dolls were back in their beds, all was good, and she had managed to do some work in the relative coolness of the evening, the first time she felt she had achieved something useful for ages. For a brief moment, she was tempted to go down the back stairs to the Green, for a minute or two, to see how it felt to be in the open air.

Maybe not. She nibbled round the edges of her bagel. Better to stay inside where she knew she was safe. Her demons were inside her head. There was no way she could leave them behind.

A message appeared on her laptop screen, an email coming in.

Hi Carol,

How are you surviving this heat? I think I am going to melt. I'm having about four showers a day, and even then the minute I leave for work, my hair is soaking again, and I think I'm stinking. The forecasts keep saying that the weather is going to break, but I wish it would hurry up and rain. I confess that I went outside at about midnight. The Green was very quiet, nobody around. Somebody was playing soft music somewhere, one of the Swedish girls, I think, Sam probably. It was so lovely to sit and take a breath – you know, if I had found the switch for the sprinklers, I'd have put them on. It's a very peaceful place at night. I had never noticed how much scent the herb garden gives off; it was basil and mint yesterday, really lovely. And then guess what happened? The sprinklers came on! They go on overnight on a timer. I think I might have known that, but if they ever told me, I forgot. They can't put the water on the grass in the heat of the day because it then burns the leaves seemingly. Who knows these things?

Did you know the Green is a sensory garden? It hadn't dawned on me, but there's a lot to see, to smell, to hear, to touch, and if you are into eating grass, I suppose it should be tasty. I wouldn't eat it, though – you never know where those dogs have peed when Sven's not looking.

I see you had a visitor the other day, that tall dark-haired woman – told you I can sound stalkery! She was there the night they did that bit of filming. Is she with the folk on the television? You can tell I'm bored, can't you?

How are you doing anyway? I'm covering for maternity

at work, so it's long hours and I'm really tired. Can't wait
for the weather to cool down a bit. I see you are too hot to
be bothered getting dressed these days. I like the colour of
your dressing gown but I think that shade would be a little
too close a match for my red and bleary eyes.
    Cheers,
    Lulu

Carol stood in the hot shower for a long time. The solar panels
meant that the water was very hot and there was always a lot of
it. The bathroom steamed up easily, cloaking the room in scented
fog. When she finally, finally felt relaxed, she turned on the cold
tap, spiralling the control round and round, keeping under the flow
of water, letting the cold jets needle her skin. She closed her eyes,
enjoying the cold on her face. It reminded her of home: the rain,
the chill in the air, the refreshing bite of zero degrees.

The temperature had been climbing each day since she had
arrived in Scotland: unprecedented, burning heat. She longed for
some rain, plain old rain. And puddles.

She tried to calm down. Had Lulu been spying on her? *I like
the colour of your dressing gown.*

And how was she doing that? She must have a telescope or
something looking across the full length of the Green to see what
she was wearing. No, it was a comment, just the way it was
phrased. Lulu was no more her stalker than she herself was stalking
the Jonssons. It was the set-up of the Green.

She pulled a towel round her, fastened it at the front, pulled
another smaller towel through her hair and turned to the mirror,
wiping the condensation from it with her free hand. Then screamed.

The face that looked back at her was not her own.

She jumped back, screamed again, pulling the towel closer to
her, reversing into the corner. Then she looked again. Of course
it was her own reflection, distorted by the steam in the room, the
moisture on the mirror.

She put the light out and got dressed in the dark, then hid in
the corner before she climbed under the bed.

Where she thought she was safe.

MONDAY 28TH JUNE

He didn't like looking out of the window when his friend
wasn't at the other side, when the kids were indoors and the
dog was out for his walk.

He liked to look out when the children were playing; he liked
the sounds they made. The adults, too, when they had too much
to drink and started raising their voices.

He had seen his best friend, lifting his hand up to his face,
spanning his fingers before he placed his palm on the window
pane in the darkness of the night.

His friend did the same. Then they had placed their cheeks to
the cold glass, and looked at each other across the Green. His
friend had drifted from one window to another, a long white
dress floating behind them. They were an angel, the way they
looked, the way they floated through the walls.

He couldn't seem to reach the window today. There was a way,
but he couldn't remember what it was he had to do. So he
walked back across the thick carpet, his bare feet sinking a little
into the soft pile. It was always a jolt when he stepped on to
the cold laminate in the hall on his way to the toilet. Today, he
walked past the toilet door, into the darkness beyond. Running
his fingers along the wall, he felt the change from the plaster to
wood, and then the cold metal of the handle. He gripped hard
with all the strength his little fingers could manage and pushed
down hard.

It didn't move.

It was locked.

It always was.

THIRTEEN

'Hi, Mr McIntosh.' Anderson offered his hand. 'DCI Colin Anderson.'

The receiving hand had desperation in its grasp.

'Hello. A DCI? Is this being reinvestigated?' McIntosh asked with some suspicion, as he walked along the slightly damp hall. The navy-blue carpet was wrinkled, the wallpaper raised as if it had blistered in the heat. He stopped and held out his hand, indicating that Anderson should go into the living room, where there was the noise of a familiar property TV programme – somebody trying to buy a house abroad. Then Mr McIntosh dropped his arm. 'But I guess you're here to see Danny? So maybe you'd be better coming in.' He turned and walked away, a man so slim he looked as if he hardly had the strength to hold himself up. His shirt looked too big, clean but not ironed; it hung round him like a smock. His socks were mismatched under the cuff of his joggy bottoms. Everything was very clean, Anderson could smell disinfectant or a lemon-scented bleach, maybe chlorine and the sharp tang of salt.

The door, which had been brilliant white when first painted, was now cream, the area round the handle dull and stained. McIntosh placed his hand on the brass knob, then stopped. 'They say that he's not aware of anything, but he is, so please don't say something that would upset him. He can hear, he can understand. He's not stupid.' He went to turn the handle down, but Anderson stopped him, feeling awful giving hope to somebody where there was none. This was going nowhere. He was here because he was nosy and because he didn't like Naomi Clearwater. What excuse was that to come here and upset this man?

'I'm not here officially. I don't want you getting the wrong end of the stick.'

'No?' McIntosh looked straight ahead for the moment, through him and out of the door. Anderson thought he was going to tell him where to go. 'You here for some ghoulish look at the little handicapped boy?'

'No, not that.'

'So why are you here?'

Anderson looked into his eyes, saw a flicker of humour, or at least intrigue. 'Honestly? I read the file and got angry.'

'Angry. That's an interesting word.' He nodded. 'Fair enough, come through and say hello to Danny.'

He opened the door and walked into a different world: the oak flooring, the large bed, the plasma TV screen on the wall, a chair at the log-filled fireplace. There were pictures of some footballers that Anderson couldn't identify; framed and hung with a sense of order. On the other wall was a heart-breaking montage of the family as they used to be. Mum and dad, then Danny. The last picture showed him astride his new bike, taken on the street outside, both his thumbs up, pleased with the new present. From the look of it, the accident was a week later.

The accident.

The back wall had been converted to large patio doors that were now open. The garden beyond, in the bright sunlight, was full of red and yellow snapdragons and gnomes, an aviary of birds in full song and a pond with goldfish, netted against the attention of herons. There was a busyness of dragonflies; he could see the flashing irradiances of blue and green, rainbow tinted. It was a beautiful garden, rich with sights and smells and sounds. A large chair – more than a wheelchair, more like a hospital bed on wheels – stood within the shade of the patio doors. The top of the chair was raised so that the occupant was almost sitting, able to see the garden, watch the birds, protected from the sun but getting full benefit of the fresh air.

'He'll be asleep probably,' said McIntosh. 'Come and sit out in the garden. We can chat there.'

Anderson stepped past the chair, pausing beside it. The occupant looked much older than he had expected: a young man really. He could have been in his early twenties, but was skeletally thin, with sunken cheeks, eyes deep in their sockets, pinched nose. His long fringe had fallen over his forehead. His dad flicked it back, smoothing the stray hairs down, patting his son on the head like the proud father he was. There was an oxygen tube going from the boy's nose to a tank somewhere. His head was turned to the side, looking down slightly, supported by the large cuff on the back of the chair. Anderson could see tiny shoulders through the thin material of his T-shirt, visible above the thin blanket that covered his body. He wore a set of straps that crossed in front of him, a complicated seatbelt arrangement to keep Danny and his blanket in place as he dozed during the day.

Anderson couldn't bear to think that this boy was the same age as his daughter.

'Hello, Danny,' Anderson said awkwardly, with no idea what he was to say next. 'Sorry to disturb you.'

McIntosh nodded. 'Do you want a cup of tea?'

They settled on a glass of lemonade each, and sat sipping it in the sun, listening to the birds and chatting. Apart from the Maltman Green being huge and surrounded by its own red and yellow bricks, and this garden being tiny and surrounded by the walls of its neighbours, Anderson was struck by the similar feel to the place.

'Have you always lived here?'

'Yes, Danny knows where he is. We swapped bedrooms, of course, so that he could have the big one. When Sharon left, I had no need for the bigger room. Why are you here, exactly?'

Anderson looked round the lovely garden, trying to think of something to say. 'I have a boy with Down's. Moses. It resonated with me when I was reading through the case file.'

'About Danny?'

'I suppose about Danny, but more about Natalie Wishart.'

'Ah, yes, she went to America somewhere? Natalie Nascimento as she is now, I believe.'

So he had been keeping tabs on her. 'California,' Anderson said. 'She's flying back now that we have found Johnny's DNA – you know, in case we do track him down.' He watched McIntosh for a response.

McIntosh shook his head. 'God knows how you live with that. At least I've still got Danny – well, a version of Danny, but he's still our boy.'

He noted the 'our'. 'What happened to your wife?'

'Sharon?' McIntosh shrugged his shoulders. 'Well, it's not true what it said in the papers – salacious nonsense that she ran away with the milkman, not able to cope with Danny. Load of crap. Sharon did find it difficult – she really couldn't cope with looking after him. We had a discussion about what would make her happy.'

'And what did make her happy?'

'She wanted her career back. She earns. I look after Danny. She looks after us. She and her new man come to look after Danny any time I want a break. They pay for everything and they visit all the time. It's not true that she abandoned us. Sharon got the offer of a promotion down south; it made sense for her to go, so she went, and she went with my blessing. When it happened, when Danny was hit by that car, we became very different people. It killed our marriage – victims left, right and centre. But as to the present set-up, nobody would blink an eye if it was a man who had the career and the woman was left at home looking after the kid. Funny the attitudes that still prevail in a so-called modern society. But overall, we're fine.'

'And what about you, Stephen? Are you fine?'

'Ninety per cent of the time. The other ten is pretty crap, but thank God it's not the other way round. Some folk say that we should put him in a home, but then I'd worry if he was OK and if they were looking after him properly. When he's here with me, I know that he is doing fine.'

'I totally understand that. Do you get any help?'

'We have a private nurse come in once a week, to check that he's well, or she comes whenever I call. I have to watch his temperature, as he can get too hot or too cold easily.'

'If you don't mind me asking, how do you afford that? Sharon?'

'Like I said, Sharon's got a very good job. Do you want a top-up?'

So they sat in the garden talking about football, Danny, Moses, passing the time of day as if they were on holiday. Anderson had asked him about the inquest.

McIntosh shrugged his shoulders; it was what it was. Nothing was going to bring Danny back, not the Danny that he was. Every so often, he would get up, wipe Danny's mouth with a damp cloth, offer him a drink from a cup with a straw, then check his son's forehead with the back of his hand. He once applied some sunscreen.

He was a good dad. He toddled off to get something and left Anderson and Danny alone in the garden. Anderson stood up and walked to the pond, talking to Danny, saying how lovely it was and the mess his dog made of his own garden, getting a little tearful at the memory of Nesbit digging up the lawn. Norma was too lazy. He realized he was talking out loud, then realized that Danny's eyes were open, watching him. Danny's brown eyes looked directly at him, then dropped, then raised, as if taking full measure of the man in front of him. He knew it was fanciful that the boy was trying to tell him something, but he found the intelligence in those brown eyes unnerving.

McIntosh came back, with his mobile phone, wanting a picture of them together so it could go on the wall. Anderson happily obliged and took a selfie with Danny.

Everybody was smiling.

Becs Stewart was getting frustrated at the kids. She'd a lot to do that day, and the kids were playing up, moving cornflakes around and refusing to eat them. The main thought, apart from her anger at Martin who was either at the pub or at work and had spent last night on the couch, was to pack her bags and leave. What was the point of staying? When Martin was home, he was either shouting at the kids or slamming doors.

Then the doorbell rang: a delivery from Amazon. Yet another pair of trainers for her useless other half. Reebok Nano X – another hundred quid down the drain. She dumped them down in the hall, and the small dish on the narrow table caught her eye. She picked up the set of car keys with the flashy glittering R nestled in between the key and the remote lock, a couple of keys that looked like house keys. Keys to a house that was not hers.

Pulling his clothes from the wardrobe, she checked his pockets. When she found the small red box, she picked up her mobile and dialled the young policeman, the nice one whose ears stuck out and who had made her a cup of tea. The one who spoke about his wife as if he still loved her, the one who wouldn't cheat on the mother of his children with a tall skinny blonde; he wouldn't have bought her a fucking ring. Now the kids were screaming and the breakfast was all over the floor. Her mother was on her way to look after the children and she was going out, a bag over her arms, the contents of which would end her relationship. Well, Martin had managed to do most of that by himself with no help from her.

Bastard.

Total and utter bastard.

'There's a Mrs Rebecca Stewart downstairs wanting to talk to somebody on the team?'

'Who?' asked Costello. 'Actually, I don't care who. She'll be another bloody journalist and we are too busy to be bothered with them right now. Fob her off with Betty Davies at Media Liaison.'

There was silence on the phone and then the voice came back. 'It's actually Wyngate she wants to speak to, I think, judging from the description of a tall, skinny bloke with big ears.'

'That's Gordon right enough.'

Costello looked across at her colleague. 'Rebecca Stewart? Mean anything?'

Wyngate looked confused, which was a minor change from his usual expression of slight bemusement. He shrugged, then enlightenment crossed his face. 'That's Martin Callaghan's missus.'

'OK, shall we talk to her together, DC Wyngate? It could be important.'

Wyngate nodded. He was never too confident being trusted with 'important'.

He did the introductions once they were sitting in the comfortable, cool interview room.

They had let Becs speak for five minutes without interruption. They had had little option.

'I mean, it's one thing when you suspect they are having an affair. Finding out is a different thing, isn't it?'

'I suppose it is. Are you OK?'

'Better now that I know. I found these car keys. They belong to her, don't they? The dead lassie?'

Wyngate reached out and pulled them over towards him with the point of his pen. 'They could belong to the victim.' He couldn't meet Costello's eyes. They both knew they were Rachel's car keys.

'And this.' She slid a small red box across the table, her fingers trembling. 'He bought her a fucking ring – can you believe that? Little Mr I've-never-seen-her-before-in-my-life actually bought her a ring. What a piece of shit.'

They waited until Becs had calmed down, her anger turning to tears. 'Did he hurt her?'

'What do you mean by that?' asked Costello gently, opening the box and looking at the silver ring, a quick flash of it to Wyngate before she closed the lid.

'Did he do anything to that woman? She did die, didn't she?'

'We are still looking into that, but there's no real evidence that he did anything to her. Certainly, there was no violence. Why would that trouble you?'

'Is he a danger to my kids? Did he . . .?'

'There was no evidence of violence. No evidence of any sexual contact.'

Becs gave a little snort. 'I've gone from happy families to my kids have a serial killer for a dad, an adulterous serial killer, in the space of a few days.'

'Really?'

'Well, they are trophies, aren't they? They take them from their victims and then hide them, so they can relive it all, don't they?'

'Look, we have no evidence that any of that is true; it could be a chain of circumstances. Serial killers do not leave their trophies in the hall for their partners to find. The deceased's car keys were removed from the scene, we think because Martin picked them up and put them in his pocket – an instinctive thing to do. He thought she was drunk and she was intending to drive home. He was acting like a cop.'

'Was he now? It's time he acted like a grown-up.'

'Becs, can we ask how old your children are? Marty, Emily, Vanessa?'

'Eight, four and six. Why?'

'And if you don't mind me asking, are they yours – yours and Martin's?'

'Yeah, poor bastards.'

'All three pregnancies went well?'

'Aye. What's that got to do with the price of cheese?'

'Nothing, it's a lot – three kids so close together. Wears you out.'

'Wears me out, you mean. That shit of a father of theirs can't be arsed. So are we finished with the family history because my question to you is this: if he's such a good cop, what about these?' She dumped a bag on the table, a half-full carrier bag from Lidl. 'The jeans you were asking about.'

'Thank you,' said Wyngate, a little stunned.

'And the trainers, the T-shirt, the shirt. And his good watch. He only wears that on special occasions, so meeting that blonde bird must have been special for him. It's all yours. I don't want any of it, or him, back.'

Elvie rang the doorbell and waited, then rang again, looking at the keypad and the small screen as if Carol's face would appear out of the wall, ready to greet her. They had arranged to meet as a welfare check, and Carol admitted that she never went out, so why was she not answering the door? She must be asleep. So Elvie called her on the mobile. No answer.

She popped into the deli and asked if anybody had seen Carol from upstairs. Joshua came out from behind the counter and nodded at the newspaper, the coffee and the bagel that were sitting in its paper bag with the name *Carol Upstairs* scrawled on it in big black felt pen.

So she hadn't opened the door to them either, and that had only happened twice before, and each of those times, she had phoned the minute she had woken up to say that she was up and ready for something to eat. She'd take the cold coffee and heat it up in her microwave.

Joshua tried calling on his mobile. No answer. They both then walked round the corner to the first door in the quadrangle they came to. Pauline Wallace, Joshua's mum, would let them through. Joshua called into the entry system and told her it was probably nothing, but Carol Holman was not opening her door.

Pauline came to the door, breathless and rushing, and raised her eyebrows in surprise to see the two oddly matched people standing in front of her. She stood for a moment, slightly confused, rubbing her upper arms as if she was cold. 'Sorry, Joshua, I thought it was the police.'

'Mum? Can we get access to the Green? We can't seem to get Carol to open her door.'

'Carol?' Pauline momentarily looked confused, then said, 'Oh, yes, of course, come through.' She stood back to let them in through to the patio doors at the back. The Great Dane was out sleeping on the lawn in the sunshine. He looked up lazily and got up to greet Joshua, who called the dog a 'stupid great galloot'.

The three of them walked out and stood looking up at the balcony thirty feet up, where the muslin curtains at the open French doors were waving, white seaweed drifting in a slow tide.

'Do you think she's OK?' asked Pauline, looking over her shoulder at the folded trampoline, thinking about Rachel. She felt a cold shiver run through her despite the heat of the day and the cauldron effect of the quadrangle on the stuffy air. 'Do you think she's OK?' she repeated.

'Don't worry. Maybe she had a bad night and didn't want to be disturbed. No need to panic. Don't worry about it,' said Joshua.

Elvie creased her eyes, thinking of what Carol had said about things going missing. She had been scared, scared that she was imagining it. Maybe she should have been more scared that it was real. 'We need to be sure,' she said. 'Do you have ladders?' She eyed the wall, the height of the balcony. 'I could climb up there and get in.'

'Are you sure? It's very high,' Pauline said doubtfully. Joshua simply turned back to Elvie, not being the heroic type.

'Yes, I can climb up there, no bother.'

Pauline showed them where the ladders were kept safely stowed, locked and secured at the side of the garage.

Joshua retrieved them and laid them against the wall, stood back to look. 'You'll never get on that balcony from the top of the ladder – it's too far.'

'No, it's fine,' said Elvie, her hand over her eyes to shield them from the sun as she got a good look. 'Yes, I can do that.'

Elvie tucked her phone in her pocket and dropped her rucksack at the foot of the ladder and started on up, after checking that it was leaning on the wall securely. The metal ladder clanged with every step of her trek boots. Pauline watched as she climbed, the palm of her hand over her chest with concern. She didn't have a good head for heights and couldn't understand those that had no issue with being far off the ground.

'I think she's done this before,' said Joshua as Elvie rattled up the rungs.

'She's not a police officer, though?' asked Pauline, her voice quiet.

'No, I don't think she is, but she knows the police.'

'Do you think we should call them and let them know? I mean, we don't know her from Adam. Is this technically breaking and entering?'

'Well, entering, but I'm not sure about breaking. I think she's a friend of Carol's,' said Joshua.

'The woman who lives up in the Quarterhouse doesn't have friends. I'm going to ask Murdo to phone that cop, that Costello. She'll know what's going on.' She pulled out her mobile, rubbing her upper arm as if it pained her.

'I don't think she'll get in there anyway,' said Joshua as he watched Elvie move to the side of the ladder. She was at the same height as the balcony, almost at the top rung. She didn't climb any higher. While still on the ladder, she dropped back down and reached out with her arm, her fingers catching the lower part of the nearest rail. She gripped hard and swung herself across on one hand, then lifted one foot up until it had a purchase on the small ledge on the outside of the balcony. She moved her hand up to grasp one of the ornate wrought-iron bars and swung the other leg over.

Pauline gasped and Elvie turned, giving them a little sign that she was OK. She pulled back the white curtain and stood. From the ground, they saw her pause and then step into the relative darkness of the bedroom, where she disappeared from their sight.

Carol Holman was lying on the settee, dressed in her scarlet dressing gown, stained darker round the neck with the blood seeping from her head wound. The TV screen was on but paused with the image of a shoal of multicoloured fish, caught like a mosaic behind the glass. Her eyes looked as though she had been watching it before the blow that had splattered the settee and the cushions with blood, lacerated her scalp and exposed her skull. Elvie felt for a pulse at the side of her neck and closed her eyes, concentrating on what she was feeling. She didn't pray, she didn't hope; there was no point. Carol was either still alive or she was dead. She could only help if there was a chance that medical intervention may be of some benefit; if not, no help on this earth was going to bring her back. She began to feel a flicker of a pulse under her finger: faint but it was there, however weak it was. She pulled out her phone from her pocket and called an ambulance, describing the head injury succinctly. This was not a subtle crime; somebody had picked up a heavy, blunt object and battered Carol Holman over the head, repeatedly. She could see shards of bone through the dark hair, among the clotting blood, and small fringes of skin, white and already dying. Two blows, maybe three, from what she could see. She looked round: there was the figurine of the white ballerina still in its place at the side of the TV, with two candles and two white candlesticks. Plus an ominous-looking dust-free circle where something else had stood.

She went back out to the balcony and shouted down that Carol had been attacked and that she was going down to open the front door for the paramedics. Could they make their way round? Joshua responded immediately, running for the patio doors, and made his way out on to the street. Pauline stood very still, her mouth open, looking around the quadrangle, from the Quarterhouse to the Maltman House itself, the Halfhouse and then to her own house. She looked worried, standing alone in the silence of the Maltman Green, rubbing the bruise that was blossoming on her upper arm, making the skin quiver. Something evil had invaded their paradise.

They sat in the incident room, cooler now with the movement of air. They had stolen three fans from the outer office, and so far the others hadn't noticed.

Mulholland had done the ground work – he had been sitting closely with Ruby Redding, going through three documents and comparing the contents to whatever was on screen. Ruby would tap on the screen with her pen, reciting something as Mulholland ran his hands down the contents of a beige file.

'OK, so we didn't find any connection with Sven, Sabina, Pauline or Murdo, but we did find a connection with' – she tapped the board under the picture of Sven Jonsson – 'John Stuart Andrew Johnson as he was born, before he had a very nasty divorce and changed his name.'

'Are you sure he's not Swedish? Have you got the right guy? He talks with a slight accent,' said Anderson, pressing send on a document for the printer.

'An affectation for realism. His ex-wife took most of the money from his business, so he closed that one down and set up Trappa with Wallace, and decided it might help the image of the company if he was Swedish. Then he married a Swede, the second wife, to complete the picture. Or maybe that happened the other way round.'

'OK,' said Costello.

'I've found something interesting. I think it might be a connection – it's tenuous, but I kept running the computer program and it has come up with a very slight connection between Sven and the Clearwaters, but not with Naomi – it's with Richard,' said Ruby.

The temperature in the room changed.

'Are you sure?'

'Well, I think so. I got to thinking divorce, lawyers. This was a long time ago. Clearwater is an unusual name; he was a family lawyer before, from a family of wealthy lawyers. There's a divorce certificate that we need to look at more closely, but it was his company that dealt with the divorce.'

'Clearwater's company?'

'Yes.'

'OK, but lots of folk get divorced. They were a big company in the west of Scotland. It's hardly a cast-iron connection,' said Costello. 'Did Richard deal with any of it himself?'

'Not that I can find. But there's a birth certificate for a son, John Angus Johnson, who we can't locate.'

'We can't find the son.'

'He must be with the mother; it's four girls he has with Sabina.'

'What about Sven?'

'John,' corrected Ruby.

'Where's he from? That's in the notes.'

'Motherwell.'

'God, no wonder he pretends to be Swedish.'

'Why would they, whoever they are, take the boy, though? Why do that to somebody? To anybody?'

'To ruin the wedding party? To get revenge? To let Richard know what it's like to grow up without the one you love the most?' suggested Ruby.

'OK,' said Anderson, 'I might go along with that as motive. What about the means? And where the hell is he, the kid?' He turned as the printer spat out the single sheet of A4 paper, and walked over to pin it in the middle of the board. 'Daniel McIntosh. Age nine. Hit by a car driven by Natalie Wishart in November

2011, the eighth, at quarter to nine in the morning. Six years later, Natalie's wedding celebration was ruined by the abduction of her nephew.' Anderson nodded at them. 'There might be something there.'

Anderson printed out the original report from the road traffic incident and the report of the enquiry that followed. It seemed to tie up the loose ends. Natalie had hit Danny when driving back from walking Oliver, her dog, something she did early every morning. There was a car park at the top of the brae. She drove up, let the dog out, had a walk and a run around, drove back home, had a shower and went to work, so on this occasion, the dog was still in the back of the Vitara when the police arrived. Natalie had been distraught; she had been taken back to her house, less than a mile down the brae. It was still early, before nine in the morning. Her sister Naomi had stayed the previous night and was still upstairs asleep. Naomi had been drunk and hadn't driven home. Natalie, knowing she had work in the morning, had been easy on the drink. They had been planning Naomi's wedding to Richard the next April and were having a good girly time of it. Natalie had been both breathalyzed at the scene and blood-tested later. She had no alcohol in her system.

Naomi was still in her bed when Natalie was taken back to the house by police car; she was badly hungover and spent the rest of the morning making tea and comforting her younger sister.

Anderson was thinking how that played out. It hadn't been Natalie's fault; it was a dreadful situation. He made a note to investigate who represented Natalie at the enquiry. He was still thinking about it when he sensed Costello coming up behind him, to see his screen and the image of Danny McIntosh in his chair, cheek to cheek with his dad, both smiling.

'You are going to pursue this, aren't you?'

'I'm going to keep going until I get to the bottom of it. Or until Warburton takes me off it. Naomi has been in a hell since Johnny was taken; I think she deserves our best game, doesn't she?'

'There's an accident enquiry at the time. Then it was examined by Operation Aries. Two teams of professionals were satisfied. What do you think you're going to achieve? If I didn't know you better, I might think that you were looking for an excuse to go out to Killenwood again and befriend that isolated dad and his boy.'

'If it's relevant to the case, why shouldn't I?'

'Is it relevant to the case?'

'I doubt it. Anyway, something has happened at the Green.'

'Really?'

'I'll go. Mathilda wants to see us. Maybe she has reviewed some of the evidence from the wedding party in Cellardyke. Why was the bloody wedding thing out there in any case? Why east coast when they were from the west?'

'Who knows? Maybe Natalie was scared somebody was going to kidnap her nephew,' said Costello with extreme sarcasm.

'Don't think I haven't thought of that.'

FOURTEEN

'Two attacks on women in the same place. Do you think they are connected?' asked Ruby.

'The first one was not an attack,' said Costello, looking at the blood on the sofa and hoping that O'Hare had not made some terrible mistake. It would be the first time she had known it to happen, but there was a first time for everything. She threw up silent thanks that they had not made the results of Rachel Sinclair's post-mortem public. 'What's the news from the hospital?'

'Fractured skull, a small brain bleed. It was fortuitous that she was found sooner rather than later.'

'By Elvie McCulloch.'

'You don't trust her, do you?'

'She's not human. I'm worried that the two things are connected. Why was Elvie McCulloch in here, anyway? She has a nose for getting herself into bad situations, but thank God she did. Otherwise, we might be here looking at murder.' She turned and looked round the room.

Mathilda and her team were doing tests. Mathilda reminded Costello that she had left two messages for her, Costello replied that she hadn't got either of them. They talked over the noise of the camera flash going off every so often, the quiet whirr of the video. It was sunny in the living room of the flat, which looked on to the Green. The white walls were spattered with blood, a nasty stain on the white sofa, some marks that looked like bloodied palm prints. She had been struck where she was sitting.

'Any news?'

'They think that she'll be OK, but from the look of her bathroom cabinet, she wasn't OK before the attack. She has a busload of anti-depressants and anti-anxiety meds.'

'Do we have any idea who was here?' she asked Ruby.

'We spoke to the guys in the deli – they saw somebody come in yesterday, wearing a baseball cap. The Green residents are all talking about it. They think it's connected.'

'Of course they would. Mr Baseball. Who the hell is he?'

Costello was going to respond but somebody shouted for her.

'You need to see this.' A uniform was looking at Carol's laptop. 'This was open, she was working on something before the doorbell rang or whatever it was that interrupted her. I think you need to read these emails.'

'The email from Lulu – they think that there is somebody else in the house. Listen to this. "Sometimes when I am upstairs, looking out the window the way you do when you can't sleep, I see a face at the window on the corner." End quote.'

'I wouldn't put too much store by what the victim says. I think she might have a history of being troubled.'

'Yes, but this is from the neighbour who sounds quite sane.'

'Lulu?'

'Is that Louise? She says she's Joe's mum?'

'Do we know what Carol was hit with? That wee sculpture of a ballerina? It looks heavy.'

'Nope, it's too clean. On an initial look about, I think whoever hit her took it with him.'

'Or her. Carol thought that things were going missing, and that sometimes she was not alone in here.'

Mathilda raised an eyebrow at Costello.

'Or she was sleepwalking and had no idea what she was doing.'

The Halfhouse was the first house in the Maltman that Costello had been into that smelled like a home that was actually lived in. Louise and her son Joe lived together in this house. The dad, the ex-husband, had remarried and gone to live in New Zealand. Louise did accounts for a company, working long hours. Costello wondered how much the rent was; Louise looked stressed and overworked. She pulled at her hair, then would catch herself doing it and snatch her fingers away, a very childlike gesture.

She had looked worried when they had knocked on her door, then relieved when she recognized who they were. The set-up of the duplex was similar to Carol's but bigger, being deeper from back to front. She showed them upstairs to the front of the lounge so they were looking on to the Green, less peaceful and life-affirming, suddenly walled in and oppressive.

They sat on the sofa, a pale-blue one from IKEA. The light

wooden floor went all the way to the window, and the decking beyond.

'I heard about the girl across the way – is she OK?' Louise looked frightened, a thin, triangular, bland face, loose cardigan over a skirt, dry curly hair that looked as if it had a slight pink tinge to it, irregularly applied. The dye made it look a bit splotchy. In contrast to Ruby, who still looked neat and cool, and very self-possessed.

'She's in hospital. Can we ask how you know her?'

Louise shrugged. 'I'm not sure that I do know her.' She sat down, carefully pulling her skirt underneath her. 'There's something going on around here, isn't there? The blonde girl who ran into the Green – Sven said she passed away of natural causes. But if the girl from the Quarterhouse has been attacked, too . . .' She put her hand up to her neck.

'But you've been emailing her?'

'Who?'

'You've been emailing Carol Holman.'

'No, I haven't. I couldn't even tell you her name.'

'So you're not Lulu?'

'Lulu who?'

Costello and Ruby went back round the outside of the building. It felt huge, like a fortress, enclosed and impregnable.

'When I first saw this place, I really thought it was heaven, but there is a sense of repression and control, isn't there? I mean, you can't go outside and eat a crisp sandwich, can you? Not without the style Nazis coming forward and offering you artisan bread and hummus.'

'That's not what I mean. I mean, it's not all lived in, is it? They have so much space – why only four houses? I know there're offices but it's still a lot of space.'

'I don't know. Four daughters might mean four bathrooms. And I think Murdo Wallace collects things. Or because they are a couple of selfish bastards. One or the other.'

Ruby looked up, thinking of how Elvie had climbed up that ladder on to the railing, her eyes tracking round to the roof gardens, the leaves overhanging the wall, down on to the third floor of the Maltman.

'If there's a link between Sven and Richard – i.e. the lawyer represented Sven's wife – that might be a reason for him to have taken Richard's boy. And we know from the emails that Carol and the elusive Lulu were talking – well, thinking – about somebody walking around here at night.'

'Or it might be the noises of the ultra-efficient green heating system in an old brick building.'

Ruby thought for a minute. 'We need to get back to the DNA, back into that house. Costello, we need to know if the boy is in there, and it might be useful to get another view of the Maltman.'

'What do you mean, Ruby? We can't go near it. We have applied for the plans of the building, but from the look of the ones I saw, they are difficult to understand when we have such little knowledge of the inside. A walk through would be good, but we think Sven has told the rest of them to resist letting us into any of the properties. But yes, another viewing would be helpful, although I am heartened by the fact that he's not allowing it. That must mean something.'

'My boyfriend has a drone. What if he flew the drone over, recorded it, you know? Then we could . . .'

'. . . get slapped for privacy invasion. It'd mean any action we took on the basis of it would be inadmissible. I think Sven has made it clear it's private property. So good thinking, but we need to find a lawful way in,' said Costello. 'I suppose the first thing to do would be to ask nicely.'

'What would you say if I treated my senior officer to an ice cream from the deli and we sat in your car with the windows open and compared notes on the emails?'

'I would say that was a good way to promotion, PC Redding.'

They returned to the car, Ruby with a caramel crunch tub and Costello with a spinach and salmon bagel. They compared notes, one reading from the iPad, the other listening, concentrating while the wind carried the noise of the street through the open windows of the hot car.

'Did you notice that comment about the dogs barking? I don't think Lulu is anywhere near this place.' Costello scrolled. 'OK, the dogs did not bark. And I think I was at the door talking to Louise when this was being emailed. We never went in and had a cup of tea. I don't think she's covering for maternity leave. It's

like it's written from somebody outside the Green, imagining what
was going on.'

'The emails are a silent conversation to Carol. Somebody trying
to build a relationship. Somebody who feels they can't speak out.'

'Sven's daughter? The older girl? The voice in the email sounds
young. Maybe one of them was looking out of the window when
Rachel died and Sven has told them to be quiet. Sabina came out
that night, didn't she?'

'She did indeed. And this person sees somebody's face at night.
On the corner, so where would that be?' mused Ruby.

'Could be bloody anywhere; it's a rectangle.' Costello looked
out, thinking. 'You stay here, pick over those emails. I'm going
to walk up to the Drunken Monkey. I'll be back in fifteen minutes.'

Once back at the station, Costello dragged a reluctant Anderson
away from his desk, out of earshot of the others.

'I think I might have worked it out,' she said, slipping her jacket
from her shoulders.

'What?'

'A scenario that might make some kind of sense of what
happened in the Maltman Green. The mistake we made was sending
Ruby Redding to interview the landlord of the Drunken Monkey.'

'Well, that was a mistake you made, I'm glad to say.' But he
made sure he was smiling when he said it – if he hadn't said
something, she would have recognized that he was being
condescending.

'So I sent Ruby to the Drunken Monkey. I had assumed wrongly
that Martin Callaghan was a regular in there, because he told me
so. So I went back myself and had a word with a few folk. Turns
out that Thursday night was the first time Callaghan had been in.
Only two of the staff remembered him. Ruby asked the landlord
what Callaghan was wearing, which was what she had been asked
to do, but I found the barmaid who had served him. I asked her
what he was wearing and got the same answer that Ruby had
received: T-shirt and jeans, as he was when he appeared in the
Green. It was a hot evening, and Martin Callaghan was sitting
outside. But I then asked if he had anything else with him.'

Anderson saw where she was going with this. 'And?'

'The barmaid thought for a while and then said Martin Callaghan almost walked away and left his shirt on the table where he had been sitting. There had been a pile of clothes on the table, the hat on top. He nearly walked away without them.'

'What kind of hat?'

'Just a normal skip cap, baseball cap type of thing.' She pulled her phone out, swiping between two images. 'Martin Callaghan, Mr Baseball. One and the same. And he has an eight-year-old son. I know Becs said that the boy was theirs but . . .'

Anderson took a deep breath. 'Get proof before we present it to him. We don't want to ruin his career for nothing.'

'OK.'

'If you were that sure, we wouldn't be having this conversation in a corner.'

TUESDAY 29TH JUNE

It was still sunny outside. Would the lady in the white dress take him out to play sometimes? He liked her company. He stayed at the window having conversations with her, even though they had never spoken. Sometimes she would sit at her window, her long, black hair draped over her shoulders, staying there for hours during the night. They'd look at each other, thinking their own thoughts, both trapped, both looking across their beautiful prison.

Nobody was about today, so he sat on his chair and stared at the blank TV screen for a while, then looked at the wall, at the framed photographs hung in a group, creating a triangle of images. Sometimes he could recognize these people, sometimes he recognized nobody. Sometimes he couldn't recognize himself but knew he was up there somewhere. Today, he couldn't remember who he was now.

Or who he had been.

FIFTEEN

Mathilda McQueen was drinking a huge cup of frothy coffee, so large she could have taken a bath in it. She was sitting on a tall stool, her lab coat round her neck like a duvet; she was partially hidden behind three brown paper bags.

Anderson and Costello sat at the other side, preparing to be amazed.

'So we have the trainers, relatively common trainers from Reebok that anybody can wear to a gym or while out chasing blonde ladies in stockings into swanky premises. It might be that kind of thing.'

'You're of no help, Mathilda,' said Costello, knowing that better was to come.

'Here we've Callaghan's jeans – common jeans from Marks and Spencer. Now the thing about jeans is that they last a long time; they become like fingerprints in their wear pattern, so they are individual to their owner.'

'Can we get there? I have a birthday sometime this year,' snapped Costello, but Mathilda, used to explaining complex science to cops, refused to be hurried.

'So we have this sorted by our guy who was enlarging the side view of Mr Baseball from the camera image.'

'He had his cap down over his face, too far for the high camera to see any features. I checked,' said Costello.

'Of his face, yes, but of the lower half of his jeans? That we have.' All three leaned forward. 'Look at this image at high res. You see here, where the side seam meets the hem, there's a U-shaped area of fading or rub; the right arm of the U is taller than the left. And there, at a point seven centimetres along, there's a V-shape. Then this zigzag pattern in white which is almost frayed. Do you see that a few threads are sticking out there?' She dabbed the screen with her pen.

'I'll take your word for it.'

'Well, have a look here.' Mathilda, the cuffs of her lab coat turned up three times at her wrists, took four sheets of A4, with a coloured photograph of the bottom hem of a blue jeans leg in each one. 'Four images of four different pairs of jeans, three belonging to men in this lab, one belonging to Mr Baseball. A, B, C and D. Can you pick out which one? Go on. No starters for ten, I know you are in a hurry, Costello.'

After looking at the screen and the photographs, both Anderson and Costello pointed to B.

'Both correct, so you agree it's as identifiable as a fingerprint.'

'Will it stand up in court?'

'Do what I did to you; let them make their own mind up. Do you both agree that these here are the exact same jeans?' She pulled out a brown paper bag with a clear cellophane window at the front, through which they could see the side seam and the hem.

Anderson nodded. 'I'd say so. Where did these come from?'

'These were handed to DI Costello and DC Wyngate by Rebecca Stewart.'

'Callaghan's jeans?'

'Indeed. Martin Callaghan was Mr Baseball.' Mathilda folded her arms with a look of smug satisfaction that quickly faded. 'You two don't look as impressed as I would like you to, or shocked or surprised.'

'More disappointed.'

'We had our suspicions, but it's nice to have it confirmed.'

'So what did he actually do?' Mathilda asked.

'In the light of O'Hare's post-mortem findings, kind of nothing, but maybe something. I think he . . .'

'Got into something that was way over his head, and I don't think he managed to find his way out. But we needed this for Complaints; we had to cover every argument that he had.'

'So he's caught between Gruppenführer at Complaints or the bold Becs. I don't fancy his chances either way.'

'If I were him, I'd leave the country,' said Costello.

'Might be better to leave the planet. Poor bastard.'

'But I do think the correct procedure at this point might be to refer Martin Callaghan over to Complaints, right now,' Mathilda said, her voice rather stern. 'We've been through the DNA at Carol Holman's flat, multiple samples as you would expect. Sven, Murdo and unknown female, but also Martin Callaghan. His DNA was at her flat. So regardless of what trouble he's been in before, he's in bigger trouble now.'

Anderson pulled the Beamer into the parking place of Windy Hill Community Woodland, a nice little gravelled space, fenced in. A pond with a slatted wooden bridge across it bordered the car park on the far side. There were three cars in the parking area, but nobody around. From here you could walk for twenty or thirty miles and never be near a car, yet he was so close to the village he could hear somebody's radio blaring in the distance, though he was unable to pin down exactly what direction it was coming from. He could picture the neighbours sitting out in their back gardens enjoying the sun, but it was difficult for him to imagine that dark early November morning, rain pissing down, the trees bare. Taking his iPad and a bottle of water, he climbed up the slope that allowed him a better view of the village below; he could see the red roof of the primary school that Danny had attended. It was closed for the summer holidays at the moment, but there was something going on in the small playground: kids running around in a very ordered way – a summer school for football, he guessed. They looked like older primary kids, ten or eleven years old. The age Danny would have been when he met the car, about twenty feet from where he was standing now. Anderson walked back to the road; the entrance to the car park was the last straight, level section before it descended on its twisting path to the village.

As he stood there, he heard a car and, looking behind him, saw nothing on the road. The vehicle came from below, heading up over the brae, the lie of the land echoing the sound around in different directions, confusing and disorientating. The car, a white Kia, went past him at speed, forcing him to step up on to the grass verge for safety; he clocked the plate as it vanished from view. The verge itself was uneven, raised so far that the arrowed pattern of dried mud was evidence that wet weather produced a small river down the road. He wondered if that was significant. Opening his iPad, he looked at the road traffic incident photographs of the scene at Killenwood, moving into the shade of the trees to get the picture clearer on the screen. Danny's bike had been thrown clear; the original investigation thought it had been catapulted by the force and angle of the impact, given it had landed so far away. The bushes had their full summer leaves now, but even in the midst of winter and with the branches bare, the bike was so far in that it was hidden from anybody on the road. Natalie had been walking the dog, a very pale retriever called Oliver. She had driven her Vitara out of the car park and turned right to come down to the village. She'd indicated appropriately and was on the correct side of the road. It was flat here – the descent didn't start until after the location of the collision with Danny's bike. How did she manage to be going so fast that she could knock a bike so far into the undergrowth? The damage to the boy, as the enquiry decided, was totally accidental. It was a tragic combination of factors. If the car had merely nudged him, he could still have hit his head that way. A delay in getting help had caused much of the brain damage.

A delay in getting help. Carol was lucky she was found quickly according to the medics.

The bike being so far away.

He looked at the path that ran on to the opposite side of the road. It came right across the two feet of verge down to the tarmac, with small stones and debris where the water ran thick and fast to a drain at the bottom. It was dry today and had been for weeks. That November morning had been very wet; the rain hadn't stopped all night. Very wet, cold, very dark. He looked again at the pictures. The side of the road had a good deal of water pouring off the land.

The accident investigators had written much about the combined force and the distance the bike had been thrown.

He got back in his car, sitting for a moment, wondering why the hell he was even here. This wasn't part of the case, but there was something, a wrong that could be corrected. He kept thinking that he could see it, then the picture would fade and disappear into the shadows, leaving the screen black. He swiped the screen closed, drummed his fingers along the steering wheel, trying to think. He jumped when he heard a car door slam, then an engine starting up. A car pulled past him, two spaniels in the back, dancing around, steaming up the windows. Happy, dirty dogs.

He opened his iPad again and swiped through the photographs at the scene. It took a while to get to the one he was looking for, the one that showed Oliver the white retriever standing beside the car, tied to a fence, wagging his tail and panting, even though he was soaked by the rain.

Natalie had lived at the foot of the hill, in one of the streets that bordered the bottom of the brae. He fired up the iPad again and got the address off the file, then put it into his satnav. It was less than five minutes away.

He pulled forward, following the other car out, down the road, winding to the left and to the right, the tunnel of trees meeting overhead, then down past the field with the Highland cattle glowing russet in the sunshine. The satnav told him to take the first right, then right again, and he had reached his destination. Number twenty-four, Ivanhoe Drive. The family home of the Wishart family. It was a very modest house.

He got out, thinking about having a stroll up and down this perfectly normal, isolated street of neat terraced houses, each with a driveway at the front. These would be two-bedroomed houses for young families who'd then move to another part of the village once the second kiddie arrived. He walked slowly, looking at number twenty-four with a vague idea trying to crystallize in his mind; he had to give it time. The answer was here. Natalie Wishart left the country quickly; she had already gone to the States and had to return for the inquest about the car accident. She left the country, the gossip and the speculation. She had left her beloved Oliver behind, to donate her bone marrow to a child she did not know, and she had never come back until her own wedding party.

At the time, Natalie said she got out of the car, had checked on the boy and then phoned emergency services. Anderson had heard the call – Natalie's voice started off calm, then became frantic.

He heard a door open. An elderly man in shirt and braces appeared and asked him if he could help, in that way that meant, 'What are you doing standing outside my house?'

'Hello,' Anderson said. 'Number twenty-four was where Natalie Wishart lived, wasn't it?'

'If you're a reporter, you can piss off.'

He pulled out his warrant card. 'No, I'm really here looking for some background information on what happened that morning. When Danny McIntosh was injured.'

The man shook his head, but stepped out from his doorway. 'That was a terrible thing.' He pointed to the house next door. 'The Wisharts lived there: the two girls, mum and dad.'

Anderson nodded. 'Do you remember much about that morning?'

'Aye, terrible weather. I had an early start at the airport so I was up at the back of five and took Jasper out. Natalie was already out. She often was up in the hills early. She loved that Oliver, big daft lump that he was.'

Anderson nodded, waiting, knowing there was more to come.

'Strange that she left the dog when she went to the States.' The old man sucked on his teeth.

'You went out at five and she was already away? So she was out with the dog for two hours or so?'

'Not so unusual.'

'In that weather? What makes you say she wasn't at home?'

'The car wasn't there. Where else would she be at that time in the morning?'

Anderson nodded and pulled four photographs from his pocket. 'Do you recognize any of these men?' He walked up the driveway a little, holding the images, fanned out in his hand.

The old man took them, his arm trembling, tilting his head slightly to look through the lower part of his bifocals. He tapped the second one, laughing slightly. 'That's Billy, Billy Pimento. He lives up there but I've never seen him dressed up like that before. He might have got his bloody hair cut if he was going to wear a suit like that. And that one, well, he is that chap that married Claire, er, yes, Claire Whyte she became. She was a village girl. I'm sorry, I don't know the other two.'

They stood for a moment, enjoying the sunshine and the birdsong.

'Are you looking for the wee lad now?'

'Yes, we are. I'm really just getting a feel for the family and a few folk Natalie invited to the wedding party.'

'I was there.' The neighbour walked down his driveway a little. 'They were a nice family, all of them. Nancy Graham taught them both at school; she still plays the piano at the church. Alan Knight, he was the one who saw it, and then there was Mary – she lives over there.' He pointed across the road. 'I think she came over, made Natalie a cup of tea. She was in a terrible state.'

'Was Naomi not in the house?'

'Oh, yes, but she was too busy calming down Natalie. All that wedding stuff they were planning and that tragedy happened right among it. We'd been campaigning to get a barrier on that road, on the bad bend.'

'It looks like it could do with it.' Anderson took a deep breath and asked, 'Did you say there was an eyewitness to the accident?'

'Aye, Alan. Alan Knight. He was spoken to at the time – four or five times, I think.' The neighbour nodded as if this was common knowledge.

Anderson felt his phone vibrate. 'Thank you. Here's my card if you recall anything.'

It was Costello. 'You still got that pic of Danny and his dad on your phone?'

'Yes.'

'You have your iPad with you? Blow that picture up, look down to the right. We have the connection we've been looking for.'

Sabina smiled and nodded, then lifted up her phone and had a conversation – in English, Costello noticed – agreeing that the two detectives could be shown through to the Trappa offices. They had been standing in the kitchen with its elongated brick walls. The cream floor was spotless, despite a dog and four kids living here. There were some pictures pinned neatly on to the front of the fridge. Even Jussi had her paws tucked into her dog bed. Everything was tidy and in its place.

Costello and Redding were guided to an internal door that led out of the kitchen, Sabina knocked and walked into another hall, along a frosted glass wall. Costello could see Sven on the phone, his grey hair swept off his high forehead, his glasses dangling from his forefinger as he illustrated a point by waving them in the air. He was leaning back on a modern take of a director's chair. On seeing them, he rippled his fingers in acknowledgement and indicated that he'd be off the phone in two minutes.

The three women walked through, the two cops walking slowly to admire the large framed posters on the wall. It took Costello a while to realize that they were of buildings before and after, refurbishments carried out by Trappa; the work of these two architects did make the world a more beautiful place to live in.

Sven occupied the big office to the front of the building; the windows to the street on Plantation were frosted. Costello had never noticed the lettering on the top part of the window: *Trappa Architects*. The door to the office at the back opened, and Murdo Wallace came out, beautifully dressed in a pale-blue shirt, his tie relaxed round his neck. For a couple of men who had been in the stifling office all morning, they both looked very fresh.

Sabina introduced them; Murdo nodded and said that he recognized them from the night of the incident. He rubbed his hands together like an estate agent desperate to seal the deal.

'Well,' he said, 'what can we do for you? We've a meeting room in here if you want to come in and have a seat. Do you want some tea, coffee or we have iced water in the machine? And we have some lovely fresh Danish pastries from the deli.' He opened the door in front of them, on to a surprisingly large room, lit only by the glass panels than ran round three sides. Most of the room was taken up by a large table, seats along the entire wall, a water cooler in the corner, a small cabinet with tea and coffee in pods and bags, and a small coffee machine. There was a pile of biscuits, neatly wrapped, two to a packet, ready for the next meeting and a small bundle in a white wrapper. The smell of fresh pastry floated round the room. Costello heard somebody's stomach rumble. 'We have a lot of work on. The incident has kept us back so we are working an all-nighter tonight. Deadlines are deadlines!'

'Oh my goodness, look at this!' said Ruby, looking down at the table.

Costello walked over to see what she was looking at.

'It is rather impressive, isn't it?' said Murdo. 'We actually made it ourselves.'

Costello looked at the table, glass-topped like a display case. Under the glass was a large-scale model of the Maltman, with the Green, the patios, the decking, the wildlife and Japanese garden ponds. When she looked really closely, she could even see minuscule koi swimming around under the wooden bridge.

'It's amazing. How long did that take you?'

'All in all, a couple of years – almost as long as the actual refurb took. Please take a seat. Do you want to talk to me or to Sven?'

'Well, both of you really, so as you're here, maybe we should start with you.'

The three of them sat down. Sabina had disappeared, so quietly that nobody had noticed she had gone.

'How is Miss Holman? I heard she had an accident last night,' asked Murdo.

'She's recovering in hospital. We're still not sure what happened or if it's related to the events of Thursday night.' Costello leaned forward in her seat, hands clasped on the spotless glass table. 'Is there anybody else living here? One of the others says that they hear noises at night. I mean, I suspect the sound-proofing in this place is pretty solid, so I'm wondering if there's anything else going on.'

'Like what? We've four noisy girls – it might be them they are hearing?' said Sven, sitting down to join them, which made Costello rethink the conversation.

'From both sides of the house?'

'It's a strange house – sounds can echo around. It's warm air convection; there are connecting channels for air. That might be it. I think Louise used to complain – no, not complain. It bothered her at first, but once she got used to it, she was fine. Does that make sense to you?' said Murdo happily.

'I suppose it does. Can we have a look around the house? The model is wonderful, but it would be good to experience it for ourselves.'

'If you have a good legal reason and a search warrant, of course, but it is our home and our workspace, so I need to refuse what I would see as an intrusion.' The eyes stilled to a slightly colder blue.

'Does the name Daniel McIntosh mean anything to either of you?'

They looked at each other. 'Daniel McIntosh? It sounds familiar. Is he a client?' asked Sven.

Murdo screwed his eyes up. 'We designed a sensory garden for a McIntosh. That was out west.'

Sven said, 'I'd remember if I saw the garden, but I'm not good with names.'

Costello slid the picture of Danny's garden over the top of the table. 'Do you recognize this?'

'Yes, it's one of ours. It was a charity we do some work with. We supply the goods at cost, volunteers plant the flowers and build the furniture to our design spec,' said Sven.

'There're a few of us on a register who offer our services – an annual donation for children who might benefit from sensory calming.'

'When was this one?'

'Years ago. Pauline'll check the records if you want. We'll have the paperwork somewhere. Our logo will be on the furniture.'

Costello was upbeat. 'Can we chat about a related issue?'

'About what happened on Thursday night?'

'Maybe we can chat in private, Mr Jonsson?'

'Of course.'

'Well, I'll get out of your way. Don't confess to anything, Sven,' said Murdo, ever the joker.

Costello waited until the office door was closed, then said quietly, 'And can I call you Mr Johnson?' She didn't think she'd ever seen a look of such pure hatred in the eyes of another human being, but she stared right back at him and refused to blink. 'It's not an offence, Mr Johnson. I'm curious.'

'Jonsson works better with the design we do, as you can see around you. Anything Scandinavian is very now; it matches our style.'

'How long have you been divorced?'

'Too long to count the days. My life is here and now.'

'How long has it been since you have seen your son?' She saw that flicker in his eyes. 'If you don't mind me asking.'

'John? Far too long. He's on the other side of the world, but he'll be at an age soon when he'll want to know about his dad. He'll see there's two sides to a story.'

'And the truth is somewhere in the middle?'

'Indeed.'

'You denied that you knew Rachel.'

'I did deny it. I've never met the woman. And that's all I have to say without a lawyer present. And while you're here, we were aware of a drone flying over our property last night, and we'll be taking legal action about that. So if you don't mind, I'm asking you to leave.'

They left, without sampling the Danish.

They walked in silence back to the car.

'I suppose now's not the best time to try another flavour of ice cream?' asked Ruby.

Costello let out a long slow breath of frustration. 'Believe me, you can't afford it. You might be out of a job soon. Bloody drone – you went ahead and did it!'

Mr McIntosh opened the door into a room that used to be a spare room, the walls covered with pictures of his son – pictures of Danny from before . . .

Anderson didn't say anything, walked round, looking at the pictures showing a wee kid growing up. The same photographs that a hundred parents all over the world take of their children. Loads of them, bordering on the obsessional. Obsessional enough to take somebody else's child?

'Why so many?' Anderson cursed his clumsiness. 'I mean, how did you get so many? I absolutely understand why.'

'There's precious few of Danny afterwards. They're all from before. It was the wife's idea, to keep a wall. Maybe we'll get him back to the person he used to be.'

'I hope so; they make medical advances all the time. Where's Sharon now?'

'Amsterdam today, I think. She always calls so I can tell Danny where she is and what she's doing. She sends us a picture of what she's about to eat. Just a wee joke between us.' McIntosh pulled his hands over his face, tired. 'It was after the event. Sharon's sister, Miranda, gave us some pictures of Danny that were on her phone. I think that was the first one.' He unpinned a small informal photograph of Danny, smiling, eating a huge spoonful of trifle, pulling a face, his eyes wide and cheeky: the boy that got the cream. There was a small elbow at either side, their owners cut off, so the focus was on Danny and just Danny. 'That picture started a trend. People started sending in videos they had of him, photographs of him. It's the way things are nowadays: every movement is documented by pixels.' McIntosh stroked the picture with his forefinger, remembering his son the way he was.

'Does that not make it worse?'

'Maybe. It would be much worse if we didn't.' He pinned the trifle picture back up. 'And there's always the hope that one day they'll be able to rebuild him and we'll get our boy back.' His eyes welled up, as if, as the years passed, he had come to terms with the fact that it might not happen. 'You think that's daft?'

'Not at all. Moses is only three and I'm already worrying about what would happen to him if something happened to Brenda and me. I've two other children. Would they look after him? Is it fair that I want them to look after their wee brother? And who knows – Moses may well be capable of independent life. We don't know yet.' He looked over the photographs of Danny. 'They aren't disabled, are they? They'll just live a different life.'

'Your other two children?'

'My daughter's a remarkable human being. My son's a typical teen – not sure what he's going to do with himself. But I have Brenda, always at home, always tying the ends together.'

'Sharon's never stopped caring for Danny.'

Anderson kept quiet, his instinct telling him that there was something else to be said about Sharon McIntosh, but her husband changed the subject.

'Where's Danny?'

'In the sensory room. I'll show you.'

Danny was lying in a large plastic tank of blue water, in T-shirt and shorts, floating face up, watching the ceiling, which was a slow-moving kaleidoscope of geometrical patterns, drifting back and forth. There were quiet, gentle sounds from a speaker some-where. Anderson thought it might be whale song. A hoist was folded neatly at the side. The air was warm yet smelled fresh. He could hear a low murmur like the motor of a filter or a purifier – this was the source of the salty smell Anderson had noticed when he had first walked through the front door.

'I don't understand how it works, but it soothes frayed nerves. I feel like climbing in myself sometimes.' McIntosh closed the door, leaving Danny to his peace.

'Can I ask you to look at these photographs?'

'Yes, of course.' McIntosh flicked through them. 'That's Malkie Whyte – he's put on a lot of weight since then. The other one is Billy Pimento. He's always been a ladies man. He has a farm up the brae.' He gave a little chuckle. 'Is this at the Wishart girl's wedding?'

'Yes.'

'Well, I hope they had a good time.'

'The boy was abducted there,' Anderson pointed out.

'Yes, of course. Of course he was.'

*   *   *

Costello took a long time in the toilets, washing her face, rubbing some cream into her cheeks, brushing her teeth, trying to stop the panic. She needed to concentrate on the interview with Callaghan, no more the nice young cop who wandered into a situation too big for him; he could be a potential murderer. Ten minutes later, she was in the interview room, Wyngate at her side. Callaghan had waived his rights to legal or Federation representation which suited Costello fine as she was sick to the back teeth with him.

'Why did you do that stuff with the baseball cap and the shirt? That makes me think that you know you did something to Rachel and that you knew it brought about her death.'

'I didn't.'

'So why did you run away, then?'

'I panicked. I'm guilty of being stupid but not of murder. I saw her when I came out of the pub. I thought it was a coincidence . . . but I don't know how it got to this.'

'So tell us. Slowly.'

'I met Rachel at a craft fair at Christmas. Becs was there. She'd remember her. Becs said that she loved her silverware, especially the Celtic rings. I wanted to get Becs a Celtic twist ring for our anniversary so I took Rachel's card and called her later. In fact, she slid her business card across the table to me, right under Becs' nose. We met up, talked about the design.' Martin Callaghan shrugged.

'And?' asked Costello, knowing there was more to come.

'And she was a lot friendlier than I had expected. I liked her, I really did – as a person, I mean.'

'Did you have an affair with her?'

Martin Callaghan shook his head, 'No. But she had a problem. She wanted somebody to talk to.'

'Problem?'

'Ill, addicted or broken-hearted.'

'Did she say she was?'

'Not in so many words.' He thought for a moment.

'What happened on Thursday? The truth.'

'I saw her. The cop thing was a joke. She wanted me to follow her. She was supposed to be handing over the ring.'

'Follow her? Why?'

'No idea. But I did. She went up round the corner, into the Green. I followed her and saw she was off her tits on something.

I got angry, I admit that. She was dangling the ring in front of me and I snatched it from her. Then I took her car keys as well – I actually don't recall doing that, but I told her she was getting a taxi home. I never hit her.'

'Yes. You forgot to take your watch off. But still very quick thinking for a man who had just seen somebody die. So there was no point in stuffing the cap in your pocket and . . . what did you do with the shirt? Did you stick it in the fire pit or in the chiminea or something?'

He shook his head. 'No, I folded it into a roll and wrapped it round my waist. It's what we used to do with extra clothes as students when we wanted to avoid paying for extra baggage on a cheap flight. But I didn't kill her, I took her car keys out of her hand and she was reaching up trying to get them, then she started kind of smiling and being all Marilyn Monroe, for no reason. She was looking up, over my shoulder,' Callaghan went on. 'The whole police uniform thing was one of her little jokes for me. One minute she was laughing and, you know, teasing me – she was even a bit cruel about it, but I know it was the drugs talking.'

'You ran away. You could have kept running. We'd be none the wiser.'

'I thought about it. I got out of the Green, on to the corner – that bit that isn't on the street. I couldn't leave her but I realized I was hidden between the two buildings. I pulled my hat off, undid my shirt, tied it round my waist under my T-shirt and jeans, and pulled my T-shirt out of the waistband of my trousers. I went back round and started CPR. I shouted. The woman was out, with the wee kid. The kid started screaming, the woman started crying. The two guys came running out.'

'Jonsson and Wallace?'

'Yes, they obviously looked at me a little oddly and I made up the story of seeing the other bloke run out. I had to tell you the same story. Sorry.'

Costello closed her eyes, let out a long deep sigh and then nodded at Callaghan to continue.

'Rachel and I got together a few times to discuss the ring. I helped to design it. Once Becs sees that, she'll realize that the engravings on it could only mean her. If I ever get the chance to tell her that.'

'How many times did you meet Rachel?'

'Six, maybe seven. I was trying to get her to get help. But she never admitted that there was a problem. But sometimes I got the feeling she was seeing me so she could tell somebody else that she was out dating a guy, if that makes sense. She'd take a phone call and say, "I can't talk to you right now, I'm out at the pub having a great time."' He paused. 'I might be wrong, but it was a feeling I got.'

'So we have the facts as they stand. They establish the nature of the relationship between you and Rachel. Somebody took her laptop and her phone.'

'Not me. I swear.'

'We are content that the cause of death, in the strictest sense, was from natural causes, but the circumstances of that death do not sit right with us. I hope you understand that.'

He nodded.

'So how well do you know Carol Holman?'

'Not at all.'

'Did you go to see her yesterday?'

'No.'

'Try again. How did you get into her flat?'

'Why would she open the door to me? She didn't to you.'

'Well, we know you were there and that you showed her your warrant card, PC Callaghan, or otherwise she would never have let you in. I don't want to think how you gained her trust. Do you want to tell us why your DNA was in Carol Holman's flat?'

He went very pale, then muttered, 'Oh, Christ.'

'No, it's Costello. But we need the truth now, please.'

'Because I'd been to see her.'

'Yes, but why?'

'Because I wanted to know why she was lying about me?'

'Lying about you?'

'She had reported to you that I had punched Rachel. I hadn't done anything of the sort. I wanted to see for myself how much she could have seen from that window because whatever it was she saw, it wasn't what she thought she saw.'

'How do you know what she saw?'

'Because Ruby told me. I was furious.'

Costello tried not to roll her eyes at that statement and made a note on the pad in front of her: another black mark against the young cop. She probably didn't even realize what she had said, but the consequences of that statement, if Carol didn't pull through, could be far-reaching for all concerned. Just as they would be if Sven complained about the drone – he wouldn't need to try too hard to prove it had something to do with the police presence. They could lose access to the Green, maybe lose the chance of finding the boy there.

'Are you telling me that she opened the door to you? A woman as nervous as that, as wary as that, opened her door to the man she thought had punched a woman and that punch had resulted in a fatality. Guess what, Callaghan? I don't believe you.'

He folded his arms and slumped slightly in the seat. 'She didn't know it was me she had accused of punching Rachel. We had a conversation on the intercom. I said I wanted to talk to her, told her DCI Anderson had sent me out, showed her my warrant card. She let me in.'

'How was the conversation after you had gained entry under false pretences?'

'She was OK. I explained that I didn't hurt Rachel, that I wasn't sure what she saw. She saw me pulling my arm back and up. Carol demonstrated it and I realized that was when I snatched Rachel's car keys from her. Rachel was intoxicated and she was determined to get in the car and drive. I am a police officer, you know.'

Costello shook her head and closed her notebook.

'And what happened when you left?'

'Nothing.'

'Why did you attack her?'

Martin leaned forward, his eyes screwed up in disbelief. 'I didn't.'

'She's in hospital with a nasty head wound and your DNA was in her flat, so we now need to move this on to a more official footing, I'm sure you understand.'

'I didn't touch her.'

'Don't believe you. What have you done with Rachel's laptop?'

'I don't know anything about her laptop.'

'Her phone?'

'I don't know anything.'

'OK, you keep lying. We'll need to escalate this. If you think

I'm bad, wait until you meet the woman at Complaints. She'll have your testicles for earrings, mate.'

'Hi. How did it go with Callaghan?'

'I don't think he can open his mouth without lying about something. What are you doing?' Costello looked at the pile of files on top of Anderson's normally clear desk. There was a mountain of them, two dusty boxes and a small pile on the floor that had toppled over to spread like a fan.

Costello plonked her handbag on his desk and knelt down to pick them up, her knees cracking loudly. 'What are you looking for?'

'Oh, something that's not here. Something has been misfiled. A statement by a Mr Knight. With a K. You know, a guy on a horse, like Parryman said.' The significance just dawned on him.

'What are you talking about?' asked Costello. 'Has the heat got to you?' She looked at the pile and then at her watch. 'Tell me what it is you are looking for and I'll give you a hand.'

'No point, Costello. Brenda and Claire are going to some do tonight at the Botanics, and I promised I'd be home to watch Moses.'

'So what? You've made promises like that all your professional life and never made it home. Come on, I'll go to the machine and get a couple of sandwiches and we can get stuck in.'

'No, Costello, I'm going home. I got the ID of three of our likely lads, so if you want to make something of that, fill your boots. Details are on the desk.'

'But what are you looking for?'

'A statement from Mr Knight. It could be important.'

Costello pursed her lips slightly; he could see her mind working, trying to come up with the argument that would make him stay. She knew him well enough to get it right first time.

'So what is it you are looking for? Something to do with Johnny or something to do with Danny. It's Danny, isn't it?'

'Something Natalie's neighbour said, and McIntosh confirmed, about a witness statement that was made to the police the day of the accident. I can't find it here; I can't find it in the log. Somebody, nearly, very nearly, was an eyewitness.'

'You can't *nearly* be an eyewitness. You either see it or you don't.'

'Thick forest, early morning, bad visibility. He heard it rather than saw it.'

'So interview him again.'

'He was buried thirteen months ago.'

'OK, so get Una Parryman to interview him, then. You need to think outside the box.'

Costello watched the door close and let out a long sigh. Everybody had gone home, except maybe Wyngate whose car was still in the car park, but it wouldn't be the first time that somebody had dropped him off back at his house on a day when he had driven to work.

She dug through her handbag, looking for something to eat, wishing she'd stopped at the deli for a nice sandwich to keep her going, but she was keen to get out of Ruby's company. The atmosphere in the car had been tense on the drive back. She could always go home, of course. To do what? Sit in silence, looking at the world outside her window? Thinking about the date? She hated thinking about the shitshow her life had been at points, but sometimes it came up and hit her. The date. End of June. This year would be a terrible anniversary.

She dug around until she found a Twix with an ice-cream wrapper stuck to it. Maisy Daisy. Unwrapping the Twix, she walked over to the wall, locating the photo with the ice-cream van, the logo obvious now she recognized it.

Johnny wasn't allowed ice cream. That was part of his regime. Johnny was up to his old tricks, hiding as well as eating stuff he shouldn't. What did that mean for a four-year-old boy?

She looked at the wall, holding the Maisy Daisy wrapper in one hand, a cup of tea in the other. There was a clear picture of one ice-cream van in the middle distance, a 17 plate. She looked closely, trying to recognize the young man leaning forward as he served through the hatch; his face was too blurred. She went back in time, her hand with the Maisy Daisy wrapper moving over each image slowly. When she found nothing, she moved forward again. She found it: a picture taken later in the day. The registration was not as clear as the other photograph; the camera, or phone, had been further away, and the rest of the plate was obscured by the leg of the man posing at the wedding party with his girlfriend.

Costello got out a magnifying glass that did not help much, but there was no way she could make the second digit a seven; it looked like a five. Had there been two different ice-cream vans? It took her ten minutes to find the vehicle log of the incident on the system. There was only one ice-cream van, the second one, logged as going in and out. Allison's team were far too savvy to make a mistake like that. She checked the pictures again, looking closely. As far as she could see, the vehicle was positioned in the same place, parked in their spot on the lane at the side of the hotel. It was facing the lawn so the serving hatch was at the public side. If it reversed, even the length of itself, it would be hidden behind the side of the building. All they had to do was reverse to the car park at the front, and they'd be on the main road. At that time, the guests would be at the rear lawn, in the marquee, eating. Was there a replacement vehicle waiting to take its place, the 15 plate? Again she looked at the windscreens, the slight variance in the positioning of the Maisy Daisy logo, the 99 Flakes sticker. They were not the same van. The exchange must have happened earlier in the day. Johnny must have been seen afterwards; otherwise, it would have been in the log and investigated. Or it might have been a simple mistake. But the driver of the second vehicle had not admitted that there had been two on the site.

And Johnny was not allowed ice cream.

Or was he getting up to his old tricks? Eating ice cream. And hiding.

So who was in the van? She googled the company, the Seahorse Café; they had closed for business during the pandemic and never reopened. After another five minutes searching around for suppliers of Maisy Daisy, she found the name Robert Connaught. Who the hell was that? And where had she heard or seen that name recently? Her eyes fell on the Maisy Daisy logo. The deli at the Maltman. Her heart was thumping as she googled the owners of the Quarterhouse Deli. Joshua Wallace and Bobby Connaught. There it was. The connection: east to west, across the country.

Pauline had said to her that Bobby had a family business in St Andrews. She smacked herself on the forehead, annoyed. She knew she had heard something somewhere.

She needed to think this through.

*   *   *

Costello pushed the keyboard away. She needed somebody to talk to. She needed to place the events in the right chronological order. Maybe her new colleague could redeem herself, so she called Ruby's mobile. It was switched off. She called the landline and spoke to Ruby's boyfriend, Jeff, who immediately apologized, misunderstanding the reason for her call. He said he had used the drone for footage of the roof of 'that place' and he had shown it to Ruby on their laptop. He said that she had watched it over and over, and got quite excited, saying something about the toys on the roof – boys' toys. He had got bored and gone out for a takeaway. The queue had been long and he had met somebody he knew and got chatting. When he came back, Ruby had gone and he had not seen her since. Her dinner had burned in the oven. He was a bit ratty about that. It wasn't like her.

Costello asked if she could see the footage the drone had taken. At that point he had faltered and said that Ruby had deleted it, including the original copy. She said it would be helpful if he didn't record anything else on the micro card in case they needed to retrieve it later.

He said he already had.

She tried Ruby's phone again. Still turned off.

She called Wyngate who was over with the guys at the tech section trying to trace the internet provider address on the emails from the elusive Lulu, who, more than anyone, seemed to know what was going on in the Maltman building. They had narrowed the address to somewhere within the range of the Dawsons' Wi-Fi signal, but they had no idea whose fingers were on that keyboard.

Wyngate had said on day one that the building was odd, that the residents didn't seem to live in it all. When he arrived, she talked him through her thought process from the ice-cream van, to the Maltman, Bobby and Sven, or John as he was really called, or Murdo. But Lulu had said there was somebody up at the window, somebody she didn't know. Ruby had now seen toys on the roof. Jeff had said boys' toys.

'Sven has two girls who still might play with toys.'

'Ruby's too intelligent to get excited by girls' toys, and why on the roof? Their toys would be in the Green, surely.'

'Maybe Ruby's less gender-specific than you. Maybe Sven doesn't like the wee kids ruining his grass.'

'We need to get in the building. Do we need a search warrant if we think a child is in danger? I'll phone Anderson.'

'He won't do anything.'

Wyngate was right.

Anderson was trying to keep the irritation from his voice. 'I hear what you're saying, but we can't go in there all guns blazing, can we? I mean, where do we think Johnny is? I can't believe we are even having this conversation.'

Costello could imagine Anderson dragging his fingers through his hair.

'What do you want us to do, Costello? Go round and ask to see in every room because we like the décor? Get some concrete evidence, something to work with, but nothing from the drone footage.'

'Look, boss, we know the DNA's there. Johnny's alive and he's somewhere . . .'

It crossed Anderson's mind what Una had said: high up and looking over water. It could mean the Maltman Green; it could mean the sewage works.

'Have you looked into Martin's kid? He could have left the DNA; they could be hiding in plain sight, among a family, other kids?'

'There are wives and other kids in the Maltman Green. They're controlled. They have driving licences but are not on the insurance. The place is as clean as a lab. The premises are big – there's all sorts in there. And we have Lulu.'

'No, we don't.'

'But we know what she knows. Imagine Louise. She's on the outside. She's intimidated but she has found out what's going on and then found an ally, the new tenant in the block. Lulu was drip-feeding information to Carol – the incident with Rachel was common knowledge, then the information with the DNA came out – and maybe Lulu, whoever she is, is trying to let us know what she knows. Noises, toilet flushing at night, somebody walking around in a house that's supposed to have super-duper insulation for heat and sound. What about up in the attic? Nobody ever goes up there, and Lulu said that's where the face was.'

'And she could be playing us, Costello, and pissing herself laughing. You do what your instinct tells you is right, but nothing

you do has been sanctioned by me. You're on your own. I need
to go, it's bath time. Good luck.'

Costello looked at the phone as she ended the call. 'Arsehole.'
She tapped her mobile against her chin, then looked at Wyngate.
'Are you doing anything tonight, Gordon?'

'Pauline – she's the most approachable. It'll be interesting to see
if she asks for a search warrant. She might be glad if we turn up
– for all we know, she might be Lulu.'

Wyngate remained unconvinced.

'We'll play it by ear. Murdo and Sven, or John or whatever his
bloody name is, will still be at work across the quad. Do your
puppy-dog act, Wyngate. Let's see what we can see.' Costello
knocked on the door.

'Mrs Wallace, we are investigating a very serious crime and we
think you ought to welcome the opportunity to come clean about
what really goes on in this house.'

Pauline pursed her lips, slightly screwing up her face; she winced
at the pain in the deep bruising around her left eye.

'Did you walk into a door, Pauline?' Costello asked.

'No. How can I help you?' she said curtly.

'We've looked at the original plans of this house, and there does
seem to be an entire floor upstairs that you never use. Could we
see round your house? To get our bearings, you know. Get to see
the Green from a higher angle?'

'Why?'

'New line of enquiry.'

'Do you have a search warrant?'

'No, but we could get one,' said Costello. 'It's just that it's
dragging on a bit and we really do want our ducks in a row.
Otherwise' – she laughed slightly – 'my boss is going to be hanging
around here forever.'

'Oh, right.' But still Pauline Wallace didn't move. She looked
terrified.

Costello, standing on the doorstep, the sun behind her, took one
step closer. 'We know who we're looking for, Pauline, and we're
not going to go away. Life is like that – one thing leads to another
to another.'

Pauline stepped back. 'I knew we would be found out one day. Oh my God.' She covered her face with the palms of her hands. Wyngate thought she was going to start weeping. 'We did our best, you know.'

'Of course you did.' Costello stepped inside the house. Pauline looked as if she was going to faint. Costello gave her a minute to recover. 'Why don't you show us?' she said kindly.

Pauline nodded, opening the door out of the kitchen into another hall, her hands shaking, her face now drained of colour. Costello and Wyngate exchanged a glance as they moved through the original hall at the front of the house, then upstairs, past a bedroom and a room that might have been a craft room, then an office. The large sliding door opened right to left, the door behind that slid left to right, leading them into a small square hall, then another set of stairs that led to a door, the lock on it large and strong.

Pauline slid a key from a hook. 'You might want to take a step back.'

Wyngate threw Costello a look, his eyes slightly confused. How much trouble could a boy that age be, cut off from society, kept alone in an attic, away from his friends and family. How much human development had he missed out on?

Johnny might be feral by now.

The door open, warm air drifted out, filled with the faint scent of scrambled eggs and cheesy toast. Costello felt her stomach rumble. She heard music, something she recognized from *Singin' in the Rain*. It got louder as they walked along the laminated floor of a long hall, the walls decorated with paintings of flowers and landscapes, photographs of the Green: pictures of the great outside.

Pauline Wallace opened the final door, into a large room lit by the long, thin windows, eyes in the top of the building, the ones Costello had presumed were Velux windows for the loft. Lying in a big chair, covered by a blanket, his red-slippered foot tapping gently to the music in his sleep, was a very old man, his face bristly with white hair. The Great Dane lying on the rug slowly lifted his huge black head, still dozy despite the interruption.

Both Wyngate and Costello stopped in their tracks.

Wyngate recovered himself first. 'Sorry,' he said, 'sorry to disturb you.'

The old man woke, turned his head and smiled at his guests, before telling them to fuck off.

*   *   *

Pauline was sitting at the kitchen table, crying her eyes out, apologizing over and over, talking to herself, while Wyngate boiled the kettle and Costello stood beside him, whispering.

'We need to get a doctor to look at him. What's going on here?'

'She was keeping her dad locked in the attic, that's what.'

'Who does that? What reason can there be?'

'He looks well cared for. He had the dog, his soft toys, he's well fed.' Wyngate looked at Costello. 'Has there been a crime committed? Do you want me to see if there's a social work record?'

'Yes, and have a good look around that room upstairs – see what you can see. I'm going to talk to her.'

'Here?'

'Yes, here. I don't think I need to drag her back to the station. But does it answer the questions we had? I was actually hoping that we'd find the boy; in fact, I was kind of banking on it.'

'I think Anderson will lecture you on the perils of doing that.'

'Oh, thanks, Wyngate – the world loves a smartarse.'

Pauline's story was not an unfamiliar one. Her dad had a slow kind of dementia; the onset had been five years before he needed care. 'When he was unable to live on his own, my sister decided that he should be put in a care home. She wanted to get the house closed up and sold. Dad had signed it over to our ownership, so when Mum died, any proceeds from the sale of the house would be ours.' At that point, Pauline started to cry. The two police officers sipped their tea and waited.

'Then my sister moved abroad. She wasn't doing the visiting, wasn't seeing the deterioration he went through in the home; he lost weight, his confusion was getting worse, he was becoming aggressive through lack of sleep. They couldn't medicate him properly because by that time he could not give his consent.'

'Did you complain to the care home?'

'They were doing their best. We could see the pressure they were under. They didn't have the time. Dad always liked his own company; he hated the fact that he was jammed in with these folk talking nonsense around the dinner table and repeating the same stories over and over. They tried to give him his favourite food and encourage him to eat, but they have a lot of people to look after, so . . . we decided to take him out the care home.'

'And put him in the attic?'

'We spoke to Sven. The upper part of this building was never really used, so he put a bathroom up there, and another door. He levelled off the floor so it would be suitable for the wheelchair. My dad was always a loner, happiest in his own company or with just the dog. He liked to eat alone, with his books, listen to his music, so that's the life he lives now.'

'But he's locked away?'

'Yes. Otherwise, he'd be down the street at four in the morning. And after the pandemic, those care home deaths, I didn't want to put him back in, so he stayed here. He's more secure with us than he ever was when he was in the home. Here he gets bathed and showered, he gets his medication. His living space is clean and tidy; we can visit him for hours at a time if he's having a good day. If he's on a bad day, we leave him the food and we let him get on with it. If I hang around when he's having a bad day, he has been known to lash out.' She pointed at the bruised skin around her eye, the purple pattern on the top of her arm. 'He has a good life, Mr Wyngate. He's my father and I wouldn't let anything bad happen to him. He was slowly dying in that home.'

'But he never goes out,' said Costello.

'He wasn't allowed out in the home – the doors were locked. We do what society thinks is best, but that's not really true for each and every one of us. Get your doctor to look at Dad, and they'll tell you that he's heavier and happier than he ever was in the home.'

'Can you not let him come down into the house? Surely you can keep an eye on him doing that?'

'We did at the start – I mean, before he went into the home – but it unsettled him. He hated it. He likes being up there in his cocoon, like a wee kid in his den.'

Wyngate thought how true that was of his middle boy. He liked his own space, liked to know his surroundings.

'Despite his age, he's very strong.' She rubbed the top of her shoulder, recalling the injury again. 'He feels secure up there; we see him on the camera. He's loved, he's fed, watered and warm; he loves Hamlet, he loves his Bob Bear. What more can he want?'

WEDNESDAY 30TH JUNE

He thought it was very good. His daughter had come in
yesterday. He didn't recognize her. She was smaller than he
recalled and had brought her husband to visit him. His ears
stuck out. He didn't like the look of him so he told them both
to fuck off.
They hadn't stayed for a cup of tea or to watch a film.
He thought she said she was a police officer. She had never told
him that. Funny.
He climbed up to the window and sat looking out. There was
nobody there tonight.
He climbed back down again.

SIXTEEN

'How much of a mess could you actually make of this?' Warburton looked from Anderson to Costello and back again. 'Her bloody father!'

'Her bloody father indeed,' agreed Costello. 'I thought the boy was there.'

'Because you wanted to believe that he was there. There was no real evidence,' argued Anderson.

'We had evidence of somebody being there. It was just the wrong person. Wrong for the DNA we've found.'

'Yes,' said Warburton. 'But the issue still stands: you invaded their privacy twice – the drone.'

'I forbade Ruby to . . .'

'Yes, send PC Redding to me when she decides to come back, but you are banned from the Maltman. The kids are getting upset.'

'We haven't been near the kids, any of them,' argued Costello.

'Can they ban us from Louise's and Carol's places? They're tenants, and the latter is a crime scene.'

'Don't wind me up. Keep away.'

'Rachel died in the Green.'

'Of natural causes. There's no crime. Callaghan might be a stupid, adulterous, lying bastard, but if that was the criterion for kicking folk out the police, we'd have nobody working here, would we?'

'We don't know about Carol,' said Costello.

'Time will tell on that one. What was it I wanted to talk to you about before Costello went off on her private mission to embarrass Police Scotland? Oh, yes.' He clicked on his screen and read an email. 'Fuck,' he said quietly. 'So you know there was nothing on the file about the ice-cream vans changing over.'

'I presumed that was because the boy was seen after that. After one fifteen?' asked Anderson.

'He's not on any of the photographs after the second van appears at about quarter past one,' snapped Costello.

'Allison has statements that Johnny was seen after one fifteen.' Warburton took a deep breath. 'But Naomi had caught Johnny eating a Maisy Daisy and was furious at him. Really lost her rag. Richard had to pull her off him and calm her down – there was an actual physical assault on the child. Johnny ran off in tears and disappeared soon after that.'

'So he was upset when he legged it?' asked Anderson softly.

'He was. Very.'

'Tarnishes the memory of it a little, all that lovey-dovey, mumsy stuff,' said Costello. 'Why's that not in the case notes? It puts a very different spin on things.'

Warburton put his pen down. 'Off the record. I think Allison was getting too close to Naomi, too close for his own good. The Securiate firm came up with the intel that Johnny had run off because his mum had hit him. That wasn't as bad as Bob Allison's theory that there had been some drug abuse at the party, and that Johnny may have stumbled across a stash of something at some point. It wouldn't take much heroin for a wee boy like that to swallow, thinking it was sherbet. It would have depressed parts of the brain that keep respiration going. He might have taken some and passed away, and the theory was that his parents, both or either of them, may have found him curled up dead in a corner some-where and had to make an instant decision: admit it or say he had disappeared. Allison couldn't prove it; then, as time passed, Naomi and Bob started getting close, lines were blurred. I think he started believing everything she said.'

The three officers sat quietly for a moment, then Costello said, 'Naomi was engaged to William Pimento. Do we know anything about him that's not in the file?'

'Low-level supplier of cocaine for the well-heeled recre-ational user – nothing more than that. With him being at the party, you can see why Allison thought the boy might have taken something.'

'Pimento's certainly got that bad-boy vibe about him, compared to all the other stuffed shirts at the wedding party. How reliable are those eyewitnesses, the ones who saw Johnny after two o'clock?' asked Costello. 'Like I say, he's not in any of the pictures.'

'Maybe you should take that as a positive line of enquiry.

Congratulations. I think you're getting somewhere. Close the door as you leave.'

'Mr Callaghan, how are you?'

Callaghan looked from Costello to Wyngate and back again, trying to judge the mood of the meeting. A colleague had already phoned him to tell him about the debacle at the Maltman the previous day, but he thought better of mentioning it, knowing it might make a bad situation worse.

'OK, so the hospital have phoned today, and we've sent one of the uniforms up to speak to Carol Holman. I've been updated with the results of that interview.'

'Did she say that I hit her? Because I didn't.'

'Her brain injury is such that she has no memory of what happened immediately before the attack.'

Callaghan shook his head. 'I don't believe this.'

'So she can't recall who did it. She has no memory of it at all. Seemingly, a bump on the head like that can mean the memory fails to form. Her brain didn't get far enough in processing it before she passed out. Fortunately for you, she has a very clear memory of thumping you in the chest. And if she has a clear memory of that, then you didn't attack her.'

Callaghan looked from one to the other, sensing a trap and not quite quick enough to follow the logic of what they were saying.

'And also, if you had injured her in that way, then her brain bleed would have been much more advanced than it was. So she was attacked shortly before she was found and that was a good few hours after she threw you out.'

'OK.' Callaghan nodded slowly. 'Is she going to be all right?'

'We hope so, but it'll be a while.'

Callaghan dropped his head into his hands and started sobbing, relief flooding over him. Costello and Wyngate let him regain his composure, leaving him to pick up the conversation when he was ready.

'I kind of miss Rachel, you know; she was a fun person. I've three kids at home who never stop crying. I work all the overtime I can get. I don't think that I have had a good night's sleep for about nine years. Becs is tired out. I . . .' He shrugged, tired out, stressed out.

'Your wife found this, and rather than talk to you about it, she phoned us.' Costello let Wyngate put the box in front of Callaghan while she folded her arms and sighed. 'That speaks volumes about the state of your relationship. Well, it does to me. What does it say to you, Constable Wyngate?'

'I dunno. If my wife found me with a ring that had the initials of another woman, a woman I had been up a back alley with, then, yes, I think I'd call the police. Especially if that woman had been found dead.'

'I guess I have no need for that ring now.' Martin Callaghan looked at the small circle of silver lying on the table in between them; its gleaming shine and the red velvet box showed how dirty the table surface was, an island of glamour in a sea of grime.

'That's the ring Rachel made for our anniversary.'

'But the initials? They are Rachel Sinclair's initials, not . . .' Costello stopped. 'You call her Becs, but her name is Rebecca . . . Rebecca Stewart. So that does make her RS?'

'Of course.'

'And the date?' asked Costello.

'I got the ring to celebrate the tenth anniversary of being together. That's why I asked Rachel to make me the ring.'

Ten minutes later, Costello was sitting on Anderson's seat in the office with a cup of tea, a chicken sandwich and a packet of Cool Doritos. She had sent Callaghan off to the canteen. The Fiscal, HR and Complaints were going to have to decide what to do with him; she had no ideas. And it would give Elizabeth Davies a headache, having built him up as a hero. The Rachel incident had sparked off a chain of events that had taken them close to finding Johnny Clearwater but had ended in a PR disaster. The papers were full of it today. Rubbish, of course, saying they had bullied and stormed into the Grainhouse, without a warrant, disturbing an eighty-four-year-old man with dementia who had then needed medical assistance. Wallace and Jonsson were lodging some very serious complaints.

Yet the other evidence, such as it was, still stood: the undeniable DNA.

Costello thought she'd like to talk to the old man, but that was a non-starter now with the debacle of the previous day. He might be a lot more compos mentis than his daughter made out. She had felt a great deal of empathy with Pauline Wallace, a daughter who was doing her best, and Costello knew she was in no position to make any moral judgement. It was admirable, but she couldn't quite shake that sense of complete control, from Murdo, from Sven, from somewhere. It hung like a cloud over the Maltman, a strong but subtle oppression that had nothing to do with the heat.

Anderson came in, swearing. 'It takes us bloody nowhere, that great piece of work on the ice-cream van, my valued assistant,' he said.

'Your face says otherwise.'

'They knew the vans were changed over an hour before Johnny's last sighting. They had run out of ice cream.'

'Really?'

'You are thinking it's too sweet. The coincidence, I mean, not the ice cream.'

'You agree.'

'I do.'

'I think Johnny was upset. He ran away from the hotel, towards the ice-cream man, to the nice young man who sold him the ice cream. I think we need to visit the deli, talk to Bobby. Find out what happened,' said Costello.

'And I want to know who Naomi is looking at. This picture here at two thirty. If we are right, then Johnny hasn't been around for what, maybe ninety minutes, maybe a bit less. She's gazing, adoringly if you like, at somebody. Not Richard – he's standing behind her as he always does.'

'OK, do you want us to reconstruct the celebration, call everybody in? Natalie and Niles are both in Scotland,' asked Anderson, his stomach falling.

'No. I want to set it up on the desk here so we can see who was looking where.' She started taking plastic cups from the drinking fountain, drawing eyes and writing names on them. Then she placed them on the top of the desk and started moving them around like Daleks. Anderson took the orientation from a single photograph for reference, before going through each one, moving the players around, all fifteen of them, making sure they were looking in the right direction. They did it twice; twice they got the same result.

Costello sat down on the desk and folded her arms. 'Told you. It points, literally, at one man. Billy Pimento, the chap Naomi used to be engaged to.'

'The one Ruby said she wouldn't kick out of bed? The bad boy.'

'The very one.'

Anderson looked at the set-up, then sat down at his own desk. 'OK, so I knocked on the door of the last known address of Mr Alan Knight, the man who had been first on the scene when Danny was hit by the car.'

'You're obsessed with that boy,' muttered Costello, twirling the plastic cup named Billy Pimento in her hand.

'A boy being hurt. A boy going missing. Eighty-four miles and six, seven years apart, but it's a coincidence too far. Can I have a bit of your sandwich? I'm hungry and I want to think. Has anybody seen Ruby?'

'Nope. I think she'll call in sick. She's not answering her phone.'

'Not like her.' Anderson looked at the desk, the upturned plastic cups, the piles of folders. 'All I can find is a note that says the testimony of Mr Knight can be discounted due to his ongoing medical condition.'

'Pissed?'

'Do you want to help me look for it?'

'Through all this? Why? Because I have nothing better to do?' Costello snapped.

Anderson looked at her. 'Because it's important.'

It took them forty minutes. Costello found it, folded over twice. It wasn't well-thumbed the way a document of importance should be. She passed it over to her boss.

'Well, his statement's clear. He'd been in the woods, walking his dog. He'd seen Danny on his new bike – he actually says that, *a new bike*, so he knew the family well – on the path through the trees, then he heard a noise, a bang and a yelp. He heard the car continue down the hill, thought somebody had hit a deer . . .' Anderson stopped.

'He heard it continue? You mean, it didn't stop?'

'That's what he says. He resumes his walk, and when he reaches the road, he saw the car stopped.'

'So it did stop? That's what the accident investigation report said.'

'In the car, Natalie Wishart was crying her eyes out, trying to call an ambulance on her mobile and not succeeding. It was then he realized that there was a bike lying in the hedgerow and a couple of school books, open on the road, pages dirty, a shredded rucksack, and he thought that maybe she hadn't hit a deer after all.'

Costello drummed her fingers against the desktop, trying to think what was unreliable about that. What was there about that statement that was not to be believed? She didn't know Windy Hill but she could imagine it; sound travels and bounces around. She called it up on Google Maps, seeing the road zigzag down the hill, the car park at the top where, she presumed, Natalie had taken her dog before work – hence why she was out so early. Anderson had already looked out the photographs of the incident scene, a few of them showing two bored dogs, Natalie's and Knight's, tied to the fence in the rain.

What was the significance of any of it? Natalie Wishart had put Danny in the state he was in now. At her wedding celebration, her nephew was abducted. How close had she been to Johnny? Close enough to hurt? Or did someone do it to ruin her day? How did the sisters get on after that? Naomi was here, doing her thing, married to Richard. Natalie was in California, but back in Scotland now that the DNA had been found.

'Do you think Natalie might have another reason to come back?' asked Costello. 'She didn't come back for Naomi's wedding. For two sisters so close, that must have hurt. And there must be a reason for it.'

'I'm tired, Costello, I'm tired of it all. I'm going home.' Anderson lifted his jacket, slung it over his shoulder and said goodbye. He was already on the phone to Brenda before he was out of the door.

Costello leant back in the seat, swinging it from side to side, pushing against the floor, and looked round the empty office, the second hand of the clock jerking round, making its way past the display for the day and the date. Anderson was going home to Moses. Wyngate would be at home with his ever-growing brood. Mulholland and Elvie McCulloch would be having a film night, eating a takeaway, watching a movie, while Vik planned the next stage of his TV career.

She needed to move the situation on, but her eyes drifted back to the date on the clock, a dry sinking feeling in front of her. Slumping down on the desk, she rested her face against the surface and wished the hands of the clock to hurry on their way.

Colin Anderson was out with Norma, thinking about the case, trying to tie together those little ends that he couldn't quite get to meet. His wiry wee dog was trotting along in front of him on a long lead, happy with her lot and her tail high in the air. He almost didn't notice the two women walking toward him. Once he was closer, he saw it was Elvie McCulloch, saturnine and sulky. He wondered if he had ever seen her smile. He glanced at her companion, Mary Parnell. The former was employed as a nanny by the latter in the year she was out of medical school and looking for her sister, Sophie, the one missing woman who had not been a victim of the Night Hunter, Eric Manson.

'Hello,' he said. 'Lovely to see you, Mary. How are you?'

She had the same shy smile: an abused woman who was obviously still fighting to find herself. 'I'm doing well, thank you.' She hesitated briefly. 'Do you mind if we walk with you a little?' Elvie had already gone slightly ahead, making a fuss of the dog, trying to wrench the ball out from Norma's clenched teeth.

'Of course you can.'

'It's something or nothing, but I was telling Elvie and she said I should speak to you.'

'You can speak freely, Mary. I'm not on duty.'

'I was reading in the paper about Rachel Sinclair – where she was found.'

'Hmm, the Maltman Green.'

'Off Brewer Street.'

'Correct.'

'You know, after that business, I set up a charity to trace missing people, to help them get home, financially really.'

'Yes, it's doing very well, I hear. I saw a picture of you recently with Naomi Clearwater.'

'Yes, I've met her a few times – I wish I had her energy – but what I was saying to Elvie was that we once looked for a missing woman and none of the agencies involved, here or in Europe, could find her.'

Anderson stopped walking.

'Her last known address was the Maltman Green.'

Costello lay on her bed, looking at the night sky outside her window, the single sheet pulled down round her feet. The air was hot and stifling. She had already got up and had a shower to cool herself down, had a cup of tea, then stood in front of the fridge to get a draught of cool air. Nothing had worked. Even the normally cool spare bedroom was too hot to sleep in. She was bored thinking about the case. Where was Johnny? Where could he have been all this time? And Carol? There was something very odd about her, not criminally odd but a few things that did not fit. And the Maltman Green was so lovely, so cultured, and everybody was so well behaved. Apart from the one who had the matching part of the necklace. Costello thought about what both Martin and Carol had said, about the way Rachel had looked up. It struck her that she might have been showboating, showing her neck and her rose pendant to the camera, making a point. But the camera had been switched off, and that indicated Sven. Mr Control. An affair with Rachel might have upset their beautiful lives. Sven had been in the Green; he could have picked up her phone. He could have gone round to her flat to get her laptop. The neighbours might not have noticed him, though Costello thought that Sven was a rather noticeable man. She checked back. The statement was that the only person seen around Rachel's villa was a cleaner. Costello thought about that for a while, then called Doreen and had a short conversation. She then spent a very long time waiting for British Airways to answer her call. While listening to the 'Flower Duet' for the seventh time, she found herself thinking about what they were doing across the hall – Vik and Elvie, the odd couple.

Eventually, as her mind was filling with depressing thoughts, BA answered, then gave her another number to call. Costello cursed loudly, then texted Mulholland and told him to get on to it. He was texting her back when her phone pinged, an email from Anderson: *Look up Maria Padua*. It took her a moment to understand it, less than a minute to track it on Google. And then a search on Interpol. Padua was a mature student, Spanish, had left the Maltman to go back to Barcelona. Her plan was to travel first by train to the south coast, then ferry to Calais and then use her student railcard to go to Paris before going home to Barcelona. She never made her way back to her family.

She was traced as far as boarding the ferry. Then nothing.

Her 'last known' was the Quarterhouse flat at the Maltman Green.

And now Ruby was missing. Her boyfriend had called in; she hadn't come home. She hadn't turned up at work, either. Costello called the boyfriend back and confirmed that he'd phoned round her friends to make sure she wasn't there. Ruby Redding had watched the drone film over and over, saw something on the roof and nipped out when her boyfriend went to collect the curry.

And Ruby knew the code to get into Carol's flat. It was on her file. Costello had a very bad feeling about where Ruby might have gone; the young cop was hungry for success, for a career break, something to make her name, something to redeem herself after the drone incident.

Costello picked the phone back up and called Anderson. He said that he was busy with the wee guy and asked her what she wanted. She should call out uniform if she thought that Ruby might be in trouble. That could end Ruby's career, if she hadn't managed to do that already.

Then she called Wyngate, but the phone rang out. She thought about phoning Mulholland to bounce the idea off him. Then decided it might be better to call Elvie McCulloch. She wasn't a police officer so they couldn't do that much to her. They only lived across the landing. Why not knock on her door? Costello checked the weather. It was a clear night, still a dull glow round the edges of the horizon. Pulling on a light jacket and her trail boots, she closed her own door behind her and tapped on the door opposite.

The Maltman Green had changed character with the weather: dull, dark, gloomy and foreboding. Costello had put the code for the entry system of Carol's flat in her phone but needn't have bothered. Elvie had memorized the number. They went up the stairs, Elvie first, Costello following, her truncheon out. She had come armed, but knew Elvie could look after herself.

'Why did you go up to see Carol? I'm surprised she let you in,' Costello asked quietly as they paused on the top landing.

'We'd met before,' said Elvie.

'Really?' Costello couldn't imagine any circumstances where those two could be friends.

'Life's full of surprises.'

In silence, Costello walked round the living room, foot covers on, aware of the chemical smell left by the scene of crime guys. It was quiet, very quiet. The street below was busy, but there was no sound of the traffic now that the triple-glazed window was closed. This part of the duplex was open plan; the kitchen and the dining table were at the road side of the flat, directly above the café part of the deli below. The living area, with the big sofa and fire, looked out on to the Green and had the small balcony with its round table and a couple of seats. From the style of them, and the clean minimalist lines of the rest of the furniture in the flat, they belonged to the Green and not the tenant. Costello went up to the window, crouching down, getting an idea of what Carol could see from up here, while remaining relatively hidden. It was one floor up, close to the evergreen tree perfectly placed in the corner of the garden. It was a little creepy.

She walked round the living space, then the utility room, looking in the airing cupboard. The flat was very high-tech, the heating stuff that she didn't understand, but there was nothing suspicious. She went back to the small hall at the top of the stairs. According to Callaghan, he had got in here simply by watching the guys from the café deliver the coffee. He had showed his warrant card, lied about being sent by Anderson to gain entry. Carol's attacker might have got the code the same way, but why did Carol let him in through the second door? Did she recognize him, or her, on the camera? Surely, after everything that she had been through, she'd not let a relative stranger into her sanctuary. Or had they lied their way in as well?

They walked round the duplex; nothing had been touched, nothing searched. The kitchen/living/dining room was in the usual state that Carol lived in; throws lying over the settee. Books everywhere. The TV was still there, her candles, her photographs, the two tall white candlesticks, the pot of pencils and the figurine of the white ballerina that had come with the flat.

Elvie pointed at a clean circle in the dust. 'There was a dark ornament there – a horse carved from stone. It's missing. If we find that, I think we might have found our weapon.'

*   *   *

Upstairs, Costello went into the bedroom, which was a total mess – a room where somebody had been unpacking, then got distracted. There was a case on the wooden floor kicked into the corner, stuffed with woolly jumpers; a wicker basket full of dirty laundry on the floor and next to that she saw a small shining object. As she got closer, she recognized it as the fob from a key ring. Ruby's silver key ring.

'Ruby was here.' She held up the tiny striped figure.

'Maybe she left it?' asked Elvie. 'Maybe she just dropped it.'

'She's also not answering her phone. I think she dropped it here for us to find.'

'Maybe she just dropped it,' Elvie repeated blankly.

'Elvie, I know that you are the most logical person on the face of the planet, but try to think like Ruby. An ambitious young cop, she's smart, she knows the shitshow we're in at the moment – some of it caused by her. She wouldn't come here, have a meeting with a person or persons unknown and then leave without reporting back to me.'

'She came here without your knowledge.'

'Because I wouldn't, didn't, listen to her about the drone footage. It would be inadmissible as evidence so we couldn't use it, so there was no point. I'm suspecting that she hasn't reported back to me because she didn't leave here.'

'OK, but I'm more convinced by this.' Elvie nodded at a small blood spatter pattern on the skirting board, then cocked her head slightly, her mouth still open. Her dark brown eyes tracked over the ceiling above them, listening. Then she pointed up as she started talking about Ruby. 'Have you known her long?' She made opening and closing gestures with her hand, indicating that Costello should start talking, as Elvie herself crept across the room while listening to something above her head.

Costello tried to sound like herself, talking unnaturally, Elvie answering, a bit of chit-chat going back and forth, as they listened to the sounds above them. Somebody was tracking their movements. Elvie moved very slowly to the bedroom fireplace, listening as if she was hearing something up the chimney.

Costello started talking again. 'So I'll tell you what, I'll show you where Carol was when she saw Rachel Sinclair come into the Green.' And so they both went back to the window, then silently

Costello followed Elvie out across the hall and into the spare bedroom. The fitted wardrobe door was slightly open. Costello pointed to the inside of the wardrobe door – black scuff marks, a couple of marks on the carpet, a few smears of blood.

'Drag marks?' whispered Costello, then saw more blood stains, teardrops on the wall of the empty wardrobe; the clothes that should occupy the space were still in the boxes strewn across the floor. She pointed. 'Slow dripping blood?' she mouthed.

Elvie nodded, then began to palpate the ceiling with her fingers. Eventually, a panel lifted up an inch and she held it there over her head without lifting it up any higher. They both listened, trying to make out what they were hearing . . . two dull thuds and a dragging sound; something soft being pulled over something hard; a pause and it moved again.

A chill ran through Costello's veins. Elvie put her hand through the hole and withdrew it, streaked and damp with blood.

'I'll call it in,' said Costello very quietly, reaching for her phone.

Elvie wagged her finger, whispering, 'She could be up there, bleeding to death.' She shook her head, looking at the blood on her hands, and tapped the back of her wrist, indicating that they might not have time. She nudged the ceiling panel gently with the flat of her palm, hoisted herself through, then was gone.

Suddenly, Costello heard the grinding metallic click of a steel shutter slowly rising. She went to the window to look down on to the Green. Sven walked out, looking over his shoulder, and closed the boot of his Volvo, running around to get into the driver's seat. The cool guy was in a hurry . . .

He was taking Ruby.

Costello bolted from the bedroom. He was going to get away with it. She ran as fast as she could down the stairs, out of the flat door and on to the street, then headed down Brewer Street and along Park Lane to the far side of the Maltman. She ran quicker, imagining Ruby rolled up in the boot, probably bound and gagged, bleeding and terrified. Images of Maria Padua having suffered the same fate. How many before, how many in between, how many women from this house of horror were ghosted away? She ran on, bouncing off people enjoying an evening stroll in the sun, shouting apologies, ignoring the pain in her chest, the stabbing in her knees as her flat boots struck the pavement. On she sprinted, not stopping when she got to the corner, too late to see the nose of the Volvo emerge from the alley, the car already travelling at speed.

Costello felt the blow against her hip, heard her skull crack and saw the world go black.

Elvie eased herself up into the attic space, finding herself in a narrow walkway, wide enough for her to walk through as long as she moved sideways. She could see marks of blood here and there, scraping on the plasterboard walls on either side. Light was coming in on the Green side of the walkway, yet she knew she was moving towards the Brewer Street/Park Lane junction. Then she saw a large glass panel with a small lever at the side. Placing her hands on it, the lever lowered gently; mirrored glass fell back and she was looking into what she presumed was Carol's en-suite. Somebody had been spying on the residents.

Pervert. It was the same in the en-suite in the spare room and then the spare bedroom itself. Above each glass pane was a narrow panel of mirror that ran the width of the window. Elvie turned the lever, flicking the mechanism up and down; somebody standing here was able to change the angle to what, or who, they wanted to spy on in the bedroom. And whatever they wanted to see, they had a good view. Had Carol discovered her peeping Tom and some struggle had occurred between them?

The shit. Elvie moved quickly along the narrow passage, her hands against the walls, to an end of sorts, a shaft that went straight down with a ladder flat against the side. There was a smell of cool fresh air, sparkles of sunlight filtering through the vents. The shaft went upwards.

Should she go up there? Go back or go down? She was on the third floor. She was guessing that this might take her up to the attic space which Costello suspected was not as unused as the residents might lead them to believe. She climbed quickly. The metal ladder was fixed to the wall with new bolts. Once on the next floor, she stood to get her bearings, sensing the air was not as dusty as it should be; the air here was cool and smelled as if the space was well ventilated. With silent footfall, she made her way along a plain plaster-boarded corridor to a wooden door – an old, panelled door with warped wood and a deep patina. The handle turned easily. She placed the palm of her hand flat on the painted surface and pushed gently.

Elvie was in a museum. She stood for a moment, not really taking in what she was seeing, apart from weird arrangements of metal and wood that were not in any shape or structure that she could recognize easily. They were bits of apparatus of some kind, with small wooden nameplates and dates in front of them – the scavenger's daughter, a burning fork, a man catcher and Austrian boot – and others unnamed. A metal box sat in the corner, the dials registering moisture.

Costello had mentioned the old man kept in a room up here. She thought she must be diagonally opposite that now; this part was above Carol's bedroom. Elvie turned round, thinking she heard the squeak of an old door opening, and she thought she caught a flash of white, something moving fast along the narrow passageway. It looked like a woman, a girl maybe, dressed in white, half turning before vanishing round the corner. Elvie moved forward, then jumped back at a movement beside her, holding her chest as her heart thumped. Then swore when she realized it was a mirror. She was supposed to be alert; she shouldn't be caught out like that. Elvie slumped against the wall, getting her breath, her feet against the opposite wall. She needed to think. The woman had gone, vanished like a rabbit down the hole, there was no noise, just a disturbance in the air. All she needed to do was follow, so she got up and walked to the end of the corridor but couldn't see anywhere the girl might have gone.

These passages were hardly wide enough for a human being to move through. Above her, lining the ceiling, were three insulated pipes, so these passageways might appear on the drawings as service corridors or conduits, wires and pipes running along the walls. Vik had said something about the place being a state-of-the-art eco-friendly build. At the end, through some plastic strip curtains, the flooring turned from old rough floorboards to white vinyl. A door was sitting open. This was a place people walked with some regularity, scuffing the flooring. The vinyl ran along for twenty feet or so to meet the top of a single flight of stairs heading down. The air smelled different here – fresh, of family, of cooking, of life – unlike the cold, stale, dusty air of the service corridor she had just left. She saw a door, a double door closed over with bolts top and bottom. Both bolts were drawn back, so she pushed the doors open slowly, surprised that they moved so smoothly. Climbing the four steps on the other side, the warm air of the night rushed in to greet her as she stepped out on to the roof garden, using her arms to pull her through, taking a moment to get her bearings, seeing the plants, the raised beds, the basketball ring and a small football goal. In the dim light, she saw a white figure at the far end of the roof garden. Elvie was about to shout when she heard squealing behind her. She turned expecting to see a guinea pig or a rabbit, but instead, sitting on the ground, with her back against the wall, between two large flower pots, was a very shaken, and bleeding, Ruby Redding.

Elvie had crouched down to make sure she was OK when she heard an ambulance below. Ruby's brown eyes looked at hers, the same *Don't leave me* message that she had seen once before. She gripped Ruby by the arm, lifting her up.

THURSDAY 1ST JULY

It was getting too much for him. He was too tired to get out of
bed today. The bed was soft and warm. He could hear the birds
chirping outside as they hopped between the stalks of the taller
plants on the roof garden.
It was a nice place and he was glad to be here. He couldn't
quite remember why he was glad to be here but he was content
to be in his bed. During the night, his feet had got very cold,
and now he couldn't feel them at all. This morning, his hands
had started to go the same way. Looking down now, he could
see his fingertips had gone blue, turning to black.
He was content and he knew that he was slipping away.
Then he remembered why he was content, as he looked at
Bob Bear on the pillow beside him.
He remembered that he was loved.
He closed his eyes.

SEVENTEEN

Costello looked in the mirror. She was a state. The left side of her face was bruised and battered, a nasty laceration above her left eye, one more scar to add to the one already on her forehead. The Volvo had caught her on her hip. Sven said that she rolled up on to the bonnet and slid off again as he slammed the brakes on, dumping her on the pavement. Both impacts, on the car and on the ground, had thrown her heavily on to her left side. Her elbow, shoulder, pelvis and head had been X-rayed and revealed no fractures. She had been given painkillers and a bed for the night at the Queen Elizabeth Hospital, then allowed to go home. The nurse wanted her to wait until somebody came to collect her.

Knowing there was nobody to come and pick her up, Costello said she had made arrangements and she'd go downstairs to wait at the patient pick-up area. Then she got a taxi back to work, her left hip grinding, as if bone was hitting bone with every step. It took her a long time to walk along the top corridor into the investigation room. When she got there, it was empty.

Anderson sat in the interview room, thinking. He had asked Natalie Wishart Nascimento to come in for an informal chat, knowing that she'd want to give all the assistance she could to the investigation of Johnny Clearwater, her nephew, who had been abducted at her own wedding celebration. She was always going to turn up. She had no option.

Anderson had been woken up in the middle of the night by a call, asking him to come in early as Costello had been hit by Sven's car, but was largely unhurt, and Ruby had been found on the Maltman roof, badly concussed, suffering a broken arm, cuts and bruises, but otherwise OK.

'Where did Costello find her?'

'She didn't. Elvie McCulloch found her. You need to come in. We're having a planning meeting,' said Warburton.

'I have an interview prearranged. I don't want to cancel it, but it won't take long. She'll walk before it gets interesting.'

The tall, slim woman was well dressed: expensive jeans, a neat white summer jacket over a navy top, a single gold chain round her neck. Her fingers played with her wedding ring, twisting it round and round her finger. She was deeply tanned, the skin around her eyes starting to crinkle, making her look a little older than her thirty-one years.

Anderson was polite, chatty. He had made sure that Natalie Nascimento had a fresh coffee and was comfortable in her seat, that the draught from the open window was not annoying her.

He had started with the questions that she would be expecting, talking through the events at her wedding party, placing new pictures in front of her, asking her who was this person or that. Natalie was open, happy to talk. She identified the people in the four photographs; two were husbands of friends of hers, one was the guy who ran the pub where she had grown up and the other, Billy Pimento, was also somebody she had grown up with, the guy with the long hair. If Anderson hadn't been looking for it, he might have missed the slight rush as she went through the pictures; she wanted it over with. As well she might. It had been four years. She had a child of her own now, a baby girl whom she had left in California.

She asked if Anderson knew where Johnny was.

He shook his head. 'But we'll get to the bottom of it.'

Natalie closed her eyes, tilted her head to look at the ceiling, and let out a long slow sigh. 'I hope to God you find him and bring him home.' She was more relaxed now, confident that she was here to clear up a few loose ends about who had been at the party.

Anderson took a twist on the truth. 'We have a colleague in hospital with a head injury, just like Danny.'

'Please don't go there. I've been through it so many times.' Natalie almost lifted her bum from the seat, ready to go.

'One of the reasons why our colleague will be OK is that she was discovered very quickly, no time for the brain to be damaged by the internal bleeding, no time for the pressure build-up. It's the pressure that does the damage, you see.'

'Yes I know that. I sat through the enquiry and I'm married to a doctor. And the enquiry said . . . well, you know what it said. It was a terrible accident.'

'I don't doubt that, but can you tell me what happened, Natalie? Tell us in your own words. The complete truth, please.'

She sighed again, this time in frustration. 'Do I need to?'

'Your decision. I'm only asking.'

'For the hundredth time, I normally walked Oliver every morning up Windy Hill. That was my routine. I was driving back down the hill and I either hit the boy, or he cycled into me, one or the other or fifty-fifty. It was the weather, it was terrible.' She regained her composure.

He put the photograph in front of her. She looked at it, smiling at Oliver, the dog she had left behind.

'He was a big dog, Oliver?'

She nodded.

'Needed a lot of exercise, I'm sure, especially if you were at work all day – you wanted him exhausted.'

Natalie's eyes flicked around the room.

'How long did you normally walk him for? It says in the records it was an hour.'

'That was about right.'

'The weather that morning, as we both know, was terrible. There had been so much rain that the surface of the road was like a river. You walked a blonde, almost white, dog through that mud.' He pointed to the dog in the picture. 'Bloody clean paws. So what were you doing up there, Natalie?'

'I think it's time I left.' This time she pushed her seat right back and stood up, swinging her bag over her shoulder.

'I can't stop you, but you'll be back.' He held the door open for her, smiling.

Warburton stood in the middle of the room, enjoying his moment out from behind a desk, feeling the power of being operational, in charge of a twenty-strong search team.

'Right, only going to say this once. We are going to go through the Maltman Green with a fine-tooth comb. We have an eyewitness statement from Elvie McCulloch; she was on the roof last night, confirming what PC Redding had verbally reported from the drone footage. There are signs on the roof garden of a child playing, a male child. There's a whole adventure garden up there. We have a search warrant. McCulloch tells us that for every room, there's a very narrow corridor running round it. There's a warren of service passages, evidence of two-way mirrors, hidden mirrors – there's voyeur activity and that's why we are here. And there's the disappearance of Maria Padua, which may have nothing to do with this case, or it might be tangential. Or it could be central. And, in case you have not heard, DI Costello was hit by Sven Jonsson's car yesterday, slow impact, no long-term damage done. He says that she ran out in front of his car as he was coming out of his garage on his way to pick up his girls from swimming. She's OK, a bit sore, but she's determined not to miss out on this. She's waiting downstairs.

'We have to be polite but forceful, and we have two joiners with us in case we need to do some structural alterations. We start on the ground floor and work up. We are looking for these secret spaces. James Black, Pauline Wallace's father, was taken to hospital this morning, so that apartment is available to us. We are looking for signs that Johnny Clearwater was there, at any time, and, of course, for any sign of what happened to Ruby Redding as she has no memory at all of who hit her or where the assault took place.'

The search was well organized. Sabina and Louise were in the living room of the main house; a very tearful Pauline had gone with her dad to the hospital. Murdo Wallace and Sven Jonsson were nowhere to be seen. The two women were joined by the children, including Joe from the Halfhouse. The adults sat apart, drinking coffee, both of them caught up in their own thoughts, each playing with their own anxiety and what they had to lose. The girls, and Joe, congregated round the long dining table, sitting on the bar stools, playing with laptops. They seemed to be totally unaware, and strangely incurious, as to what was going on in the rest of the Maltman, as if they already knew or had been expecting it.

Outside, the search teams had been divided up. The Quarterhouse was still under the control of the crime scene techs. Warburton, standing in the middle of the Green, directed officers into the other properties. Elvie McCulloch sat at a table outside, the architects' drawings open in front of her, showing where and how she had got on to the roof. Ruby, bruised and with a cast on her right arm, sat beside her, helping out with any little bits of information she could supply from her fractured memory. All the officers involved had been asked to stay in pairs, strictly for corroboration, as they were aware that this was going to court, and it was going to be messy. And they had been warned to stay vigilant. Jonsson and Wallace could be anywhere in the building. If they felt they could not get out, they could prove to be dangerous. Although, Warburton had thought, reasoning it out to himself, Jonsson could have killed Costello with his car if he had wanted. Carol and Ruby could both have been killed. But they had not. They had been incapacitated. Ruby had been attacked from behind and, from the state of her fist, she had managed to land a blow on her attacker before she lost consciousness. Then she told some story of being rescued by a ghost in a long white dress, which Warburton had put down to the clonk on the head. Until Elvie, who he had heard referred to as the most logical person on the face of the planet, told exactly the same story. So he added that to the list of the things and persons to look for. Was there another elderly person loose on the upper floor of the building? Costello and Anderson exchanged glances when they heard the figure in the white dress had run away from Elvie. Not many old people could move so nimbly through the narrow passages.

It may have looked as if Louise and Sabina had been allowed some comfort while the Maltman House was being searched, but a look out of the window on to the park, or a walk to the shuttered doors, the gates over the deli and the dress shop, would have shown them the tight police presence round the building. The fortress of the Maltman Green was now under siege.

Warburton had allowed Anderson to pair up with Costello, on the basis that he would keep her out of trouble. They were to head up to the roof using the route that Elvie had followed, then work their way back down, using the most obvious route. From what Elvie had said, there were parts of the house that looked little more than service passageways between the rooms, while others were decorated and carpeted. That gelled with what Costello and Wyngate had said about the apartment the old man lived in, high up on the third floor. The scenes of crime had collected a wealth of blood samples from the wall and the fingermarks from the handle of the two-way mirror. Warburton had carefully noted everything Elvie, Ruby and Costello had said. At the end of the search, he wanted somebody under arrest for voyeurism, child abduction, assault on a police officer, serious assault – maybe an attempted murder – and maybe murder; Costello's thoughts about Maria Padua had not passed him by. His DI had placed a photo of Maria in front of him, next to a picture of Pauline Wallace: the same hair, the same type. As was Carol Holman.

Warburton was sure that meant something. He hoped he wasn't going to justify digging up the Green on a whim.

'Are you OK?' Anderson asked Costello, looking at the bruising on her face. He had walked with her, slowly as she was limping badly, from the car, past the closed deli and into the Green. Passers-by in the street looked at her, then glared at him, the words 'wife batterer' writ large on their faces. 'You don't look very comfortable walking.'

'I'm not. We're here to find the boy, so let's get upstairs after him. I'm also looking for half a necklace, a laptop and a phone. These smug bastards aren't going to get away with it.'

'With what?'

'Any of it!'

They walked to the decking of the Maltman, Anderson lifting a hand to the two women sitting separately on the couches round the open fire pit. Nobody was talking.

'Are you sure you'll manage the ladder?' Anderson asked. He thought he heard her reply, 'Fuck off', but he might have been mistaken. 'They have already found stairs so let's go up that way.'

Costello mumbled that she could have managed it fine, then struggled to get up the normal stairs to the bedrooms, pulling herself up on the handrail, her raspy breathing testament to the effort it was taking. The uniformed branch had already uncovered the door, behind the sliding doors of a wardrobe that was not used, in a room that was occupied by a rowing machine that had not yet been assembled. This looked a more common route to the roof, rather than the ladder Elvie had climbed. Anderson stepped through nimbly, then put his hand out for Costello so that they were in the small hall beyond, floored with white vinyl as Elvie had described when she was explaining how she got off the roof. They went up a single flight of wide stairs that turned at a tall narrow window facing the park, and headed back towards the centre of the house. At the top, Anderson turned left, heading towards the Halfhouse, where a door was slightly open, light spilling out. He pulled out his phone and pressed video. He needed to record this, whatever it was they were about to discover. Standing to one side, he let Costello past, so she opened the door further, revealing an empty room that showed signs of recent use. A cushion, a laptop and an opened can of Diet Coke grouped against the wall, a simple but comfortable workplace. The opposite wall had the same type of sliding-door wardrobe, with a few dresses hanging neatly on hangers. On the far right was a long, white dress, just as Elvie had described.

'So, not Johnny,' said Anderson, turning off the recording on his phone.

'No, not Johnny.'

'Is that the laptop you are looking for?'

'I doubt it, but I'll get it bagged just in case. I think this is Lulu's lair.'

'So who is Lulu?'

'At the moment, I think they are downstairs in the Maltman House,' said Costello thoughtfully, then wincing as she turned round at the sound of footsteps of the search team behind them. 'Hi, guys, can you bag up everything in here – the clothes as well, the few things on the rail there. Maintain the evidentiary chain as this could be important. Very important.'

'Now I know how you felt when you were looking for Johnny and found Pauline's dad,' admitted Anderson.

'But we're not finished yet. If this place is symmetrical, then all this is replicated on the other side.' Costello squeezed past him, limping onwards, the uneven sound of her footfall echoing along the hall.

They came to a carpeted area, a long, narrow passageway. Costello put her hand out, listening. They could hear faint noises coming from other parts of the house, reverberating from areas they knew were exterior walls, the search going on elsewhere. But she listened, and then Anderson heard it, too. Voices.

Anderson listened. 'That's a cartoon. That's *Pingu*.'

Costello nodded. 'You go. I'll film.' She switched her mobile on to video and followed her boss along the thick red carpet, until they came to a door that was firmly closed.

They opened the door and walked into a small hall, through another door, the air tinged with the scent of salt and vinegar crisps. Into a sunny living room with large windows, a cream rug on an oak floor. In the corner was a large sofa. On it, watching the television, was a small boy with brown hair. He looked up with steady eyes at the two detectives. Then he went back to eating his crisps as the man with a ponytail who had been dozing on the easy chair beside him startled, awakened from his sleep.

'Sven?' said Anderson.

The man opened his eyes and looked from one to the other, his face expressionless, and then his features settled in concern, warning the detectives to be careful.

He gestured that they should sit down and join them to watch *Pingu*. Anderson had watched it many times, the bright colours and the lack of language held Moses' attention longer than most things did.

Sven said, 'He likes *Pingu*. It'll be finished in a couple of minutes; maybe we can sort things out after that.' And with that he moved from his seat across to the settee and sat with his arm round the boy, smoothing his hair, kissing him on the top of his head. As he lifted the dark fringe from his forehead, Anderson clearly saw the likeness. Older, fuller-faced, taller, thinner, the chubby-cheeked wee boy had grown by four years, but it was unmistakably Johnny Clearwater.

So they sat down and watched the cartoon, Sven and Anderson chatting, even laughing as the cheeky wee penguin urinated outside the igloo, while Costello quietly messaged Warburton on her mobile.

They had split up the spoils of their success. Warburton himself was talking to Pauline Wallace about her husband and Maria Padua, while being assured that her father was being kept comfortable. Pauline admitted to leaving the country on Maria's passport and coming back on her own. She had no idea what had happened to the woman, but Murdo had asked her to make the journey. So she did. She didn't need to add what might have happened to her or her dad if she ever did not do what Murdo wanted. Warburton was already sure he knew the answer to that one, as there was only one set of fingerprints on the mirror handle; Murdoch Wallace.

Sven was being interviewed by Bob Allison and Vik Mulholland about the abduction of Johnny Clearwater. The boy was being kept by social services and had been taken to the hospital to be checked over. Naomi had been told and was making plans to be reunited with her son.

With the activity in the Green, the police had closed the deli and the clothes shop. Costello and Anderson were sitting in the kitchen of the former, talking to Bobby before they took Joshua to the hospital to see his grandpa.

'So, take us back to the wedding party, Cellardyke, four years ago. The day you abducted Johnny Clearwater,' asked Costello, the idea floating around her head now. 'And tell us about the Maisy Daisy ice-cream van.'

Bobby looked sideways at Joshua, wiping the inside of a cup, round and round with a clean cloth.

'You need to tell them Bobby. It wasn't your fault.'

Bobby was upset, tears rolling down his face. He sniffled as he spoke. 'I knew the boy. I knew Naomi and Richard – they used to come in on their holidays when we owned the Seahorse Café in St Andrews.'

'Family business,' added Joshua helpfully.

'The wee guy, Johnny, had been up to the van, at the wedding, for ice cream. I had given him a cone and his mum found out and went mental. I think Naomi and Richard were having a slight disagreement about what he was and wasn't allowed to eat; Johnny was really upset when he came back to me. I had run out of ice cream; the second van was on its way, so I offered him a wee run. That's all it was. A wee shot in the front seat of the ice-cream van.

'Nobody noticed he was gone for an hour. More than an hour. I thought they knew. I had my phone out waiting for a call to say he's had his fun, bring him back. I never knew what was going on.' He shrugged.

'So you're in the van. And didn't think to mention the boy was there as well?' asked Costello, incredulous.

'It got complicated.' Bobby looked at Joshua.

'Have you found my dad yet?' Joshua asked.

Anderson shook his head. 'Mr Wallace remains elusive, I'm afraid. His passport has gone. We need to draw our own conclusions from that. We are obviously keen to talk to him about Maria Padua and the assaults on the woman you know as Carol Holman, and Ruby Redding. We need to stick with this for now. Tell the truth, Bobby.'

'I am. Like I said, we ran a café in St Andrews; my family had been making ice cream for years. We were asked to provide a van for the wedding party. It was a hot day and our stock was being consumed quickly. So I phoned Joshua and asked him to load up another van and come out.'

'When was that?'

Bobby shrugged. 'The changeover was after one o'clock. I reversed out, the other van drove in. I doubt anybody noticed. The buffet had arrived, so most guests were in the marquee.'

'And where was Johnny Clearwater?'

'He had climbed in the van, to help us – you know the way kids do, but they just get in the way. He was still there when we swapped vehicles.'

'So he was simply driven out?'

'Yes, it was over ninety minutes before anybody noticed he was missing. And then my dad got involved and Sven. Nobody asked us where he was. But he was happier, and we simply failed to give him back.' Bobby smiled a weak, watery-eyed smile.

Anderson gave him a long, steady stare. 'Nice try, Bobby, but not good enough. We can link from Danny to Natalie to Johnny. We know about the charity Richard is on the board of and the fact it sponsored Danny's sensory garden, which in turn was designed by Trappa, which squares the circle. And somewhere in there, I don't know, maybe you had reported how unhappy the boy was when you saw him in the café in St Andrews, or maybe Sven asked about him outright once he heard Danny's story, but the "the abduction all happened by accident" story just doesn't cut it. And it won't in front of a jury.'

'I always knew it would come to this.' Bobby put his arms out to Joshua and they hugged for a long time.

*   *   *

Costello watched the news on her phone. The second story was
the reunion of the Clearwater family. Naomi had wanted it to be
a public affair and there were rumours that there was a five-figure
deal in the offing from one of the glossy picture magazines.
The *Eyes and Ears* programme was ready to film the reunion,
which was planned for the doorstep of the house out in Drymen.
The local cops were out in force, trying to keep the media back
so that Kathy Lamont and her programme got the exclusive.

Costello had left Vik back at the station, either writing up reports
for the Fiscal as requested or doing his own script for the inevitable
Eyes and Ears: The Clearwaters Reunited special. Her phone told
her that the car with Johnny was ten minutes away, so she parked
up the road and limped back, cutting down the driveway to the
rear of the house where she showed her warrant card to the cop
standing on duty.

In the hall, Richard was pacing, his arms folded. 'She's in the
bathroom,' he snapped.

Costello nodded and started to climb the stairs. Naomi was
sobbing, sitting on the wooden floor of the bathroom, her back
against the roll-top bath, her arms wrapped round her knees.

'Come on. Johnny will be arriving soon. They are waiting for
you, Naomi. Time to put your face on. Do you need a bit of time?'

Naomi murmured something.

'Pardon?'

'I don't want him back. He'll hate me.'

Costello sighed, tired and wanting the drama to be over. 'No,
he won't. You're his mum. Of course he'll want to get back to
you. Back home. Come on. Get up. Wash your face or you will
frighten him.'

Five minutes later, the Clearwaters were on their front steps,
arm in arm, putting on a united front; those present put the puffi-
ness around Naomi's eyes down to emotion. Costello was in the
front room with the dried flowers and the sideboard covered with
photographs of Johnny, watching out of the bay window. She saw
the small crowd in the street separate. A very clean BMW indicated
and slowly turned into the driveway, obviously stage-managed so
the cameras would get the best view possible.

The back door opened and the child care officer climbed out,
holding Johnny by the hand. The boy had no interest in going

anywhere near his biological parents, although his eyes flitted from one to the other.

There was a stand-off.

Nobody moved.

Naomi took a step forward.

Johnny took a step back.

That image was recorded a hundred times and sent a flurry of activity through social media.

He took one look at his mum and started to cry, horrible tears. Costello looked away.

Naomi gave a little laugh and took a step forward, held out her hand. Johnny pulled his hand away. A hundred camera shutters clicked.

Costello closed her eyes. It was too painful to watch.

'Why do I feel so awful?' asked Anderson. 'I feel like I have committed a crime, not solved one.'

The rest of the room stayed quiet, knowing that the question was rhetorical.

'The thing I can't get my head round is how well that boy looked. He looked really upset when we said that he was going home to his mum and dad. Poor wee sod.'

'I think he was just wheeled out for the photo opportunity. After that, there'll be counselling, all kinds of psychological support. He's been torn away from the family he's known for, what, four years, really the only people he has known for those years, so no wonder he's bamboozled by it all. Twitter has gone mad, questioning how long it takes a child to forget its parents and speculating on brainwashing, physical abuse, sexual abuse, drug abuse. The coverage was harrowing, but through it all Johnny looked calm, you must admit that.'

'Yes, the doc reported Johnny spoke very well, but all he really said was "Where's Sven?" and "When can I go home?"' said Costello. 'He's a bright lad, well educated, polite. He knows his stuff, seems well adjusted. It's interesting that his skin was perfect when he was found and now it's terrible again. There were almost tears in his eyes when he looked at Sven, John or whatever his bloody name is. He looked at him, son to father. It was quite touching.'

'He's not his father, though. That's the whole point.'

'So how did it come about?'

'At some point there was a conversation about how to get revenge for what happened to Danny. It was the Trappa company that designed the sensory garden so it is as stimulating as it can be for Danny, as it really is the limit of his entire world. It's all he inhabits. On balance, it looks like Johnny got the better deal.'

'And Sven wanted a son after four girls. After losing his son, John, in the divorce. So he took one, or the boys took one for him, when they got the chance. When the charitable foundation Richard Clearwater runs said that Danny McIntosh was to receive a garden, those guys at Trappa were all over it. Imagine the relative of the woman who crippled your son being so magnanimous as to give him a cage to keep birds in and some flowers to smell. Danny lost his future, and his parents lost the thing most precious to them. Talk about rubbing your face in it. They took the thing most precious to the Clearwaters: Johnny. How culpable Bobby was, I'm not convinced. I think he knew all along that they were taking him, however well-meaning it was. It was still kidnapping, child abduction.'

'It would have worked if Rachel hadn't gone into the Maltman House to show somebody that she was still desirable. She went there to make somebody jealous.'

'Sven? He was the one who had turned off the security cameras.'

'He wasn't the only one who had access to the security system,' said Mulholland.

'And he was very clear. He said he'd never met the woman. He could have said they were acquainted, or she was stalking him, but he didn't. He said he'd never met her.' Costello said, 'I've been looking at the person who was upset when Rachel died. Who had the other part of the necklace? Who got cheap flights on Rachel's buddy ticket? Only one person had the chance to pick up Rachel's mobile. The "cleaner" who went to retrieve the laptop. Three out of the four didn't seem to care less when Rachel died, but Sabina was very upset when she realized who it was. Sabina was the one who had the opportunity to pick up the phone when her youngest daughter was running around – remember it was Sabina who came out to get her. She lied when she said that she only saw the man through the window. I thought it was just the stress of the situation, but it was maybe more than that. She was right there.'

'Sabina?'

'Yes, they all had something. Did they all have a pact about their little secrets? Sven had Johnny. Sabina had Rachel. Pauline had her dad and then, well, Murdo? What are we thinking? Pervert for sure. Collecting weird torture paraphernalia?'

'Sabina, though?' asked Anderson again. 'Not Sven?'

'Sabina used British Airways to fly back and forth to Stockholm when her mother was ill, I've checked. Sabina and Rachel or Sven, Sabina and Rachel flew together quite a few times. I think Rachel wanted to be part of this. You know, the Maltman Green looks idyllic, but everybody is in their little boxes, segregated. Everybody knows their place. It was OK when Rachel was outside, when their affair and togetherness was something outwith the Green and Trappa. But when Rachel was made redundant, Sabina paid for her flat, then maybe she tried to distance herself a little, just as Rachel wanted to up the ante. As Sabina was thinking about ways to drop Rachel quietly, Rachel used Martin Callaghan to show Sabina just what damage she could do.'

'So what was he doing, then, Callaghan?' asked Wyngate.

'Just look at Rachel – she was stunning. I think, despite what he says, he fancied his chances with her. He must have thought all his holidays had come at once when she agreed to meet to design the ring.'

'So he followed her into the Green. She knew he would be in the pub that night as they had arranged to pass the ring over. But Rachel did her uniform thing not because Martin had a thing about women in uniform, but because Sabina did.'

'OK, as you have been so active online, have you traced who Lulu is yet?'

'Was she the lady in white that Elvie saw? I have no idea,' said Mulholland.

'I think I know,' said Anderson. 'Very few folk in the Maltman could outrun Elvie McCulloch in a short sprint. I can think of only one.'

'Louise?'

'Yes.'

'Can we come in please?'

'Why?'

'It's about Joe. Can we speak to him?' asked Costello.

'Why, what's he done?'

'Just let's have a chat.' Costello thought that the door was going to close, but Louise nodded and they found themselves walking up a similar stairway to that in Carol's house, directly across the Green.

'Is he in trouble?'

'No, not at all. We were wondering about his welfare.'

'OK.' Louise sat down, pensive.

Costello got the feeling that the other woman knew exactly what she was going to say. She told her briefly about the emails to Carol and the laptop in the room in the attic, working off the Wi-Fi of the office below. 'I'm sure he was clever enough to use the password that the Swedish girls used to get on the network when they were out in the Green.'

Louise nodded. 'Yes. Joe likes computers.'

'Do you know anybody called Lulu? Does he?'

'No.' She shook her head. 'Not really.'

'He either knows somebody called Lulu or he doesn't. Do you mean he knows of her but doesn't know her personally?' asked Costello, acting more confused than she actually was.

Louise bit her lower lip, then said very quietly, 'I think Lulu might exist, but only in Joe's head.'

'We need to speak to him.'

'He's not done anything wrong,' Louise blurted.

'Of course he hasn't. But we do want to talk to him. We actually want to thank him.'

Louise stared at the carpet for a long time, then took a deep breath. 'All I want is for my son to be happy. But he's not.' She wiped tears from her eyes. 'I work all the time because it's easier than being here with him. Conversations that he starts and I can't finish. Things he wants to do with his life that I don't understand. We don't have that kind of relationship now. We live in the same house but . . .' She shrugged. 'I don't know why we don't. I don't know who he is anymore.'

'Well,' said Anderson, 'I can tell you who he is: a very brave and intelligent young person, maybe at a crossroads in his life.

If you can't have a conversation, then just listen to him. I'm sure he'll have it set out in his head – he doesn't want you to show him the way, he wants you to be there. By his side. He'll want to hold your hand. His other hand will be in your wallet if he's a typical teen like mine. None of them are any different; they are all on a spectrum of something.'

Louise smiled. 'His fingers in my purse – yes, I guess you are right. A typical teen indeed.'

Anderson nodded. 'And nobody gets a guidebook on how to be a parent. You work hard. Joe has a good life. He's a bright, bright boy, he's brave and compassionate. He knew there was something going on in this building, and when he realized what he was up against, he thought of another way of getting the truth out. He's a child to be proud of, very proud.'

EIGHTEEN

'So why did Rachel do it, dressing up and acting like a hooker?' asked Ruby, sitting in the incident room, trying to tidy up the piles of paperwork and documentation that were strewn round the room, using only her left arm and making more of a mess than she was clearing up.

'She was having a laugh with Martin. They liked each other, they were good mates.'

'Weird thing to do with a mate.'

'Elton John streaked naked through the studio while they were recording "Don't Go Breaking My Heart", just to cheer Kiki Dee up,' said Costello.

'Who?' asked Ruby.

'Never mind. Rachel did it for a laugh and was hoping that the security footage would be seen by Sabina, just to make her jealous and show Sabina that Rachel could make a bit of trouble for her after all. I think Rachel had left BA to be closer to Sabina. The affair had been going on for a while – Sabina was her buddy flight named person for three years. I wonder if Rachel thought that she was going to move into the Quarterhouse. When Sven moved Carol in, she realized that her time with Sabina was over at most, or at least it was never going to progress further. If you look at the corridors in that house, secret passageways, unoccupied floor, it would have been easy for the two women to be together. They could almost be living together and nobody would be any the wiser.'

'What did Sven say about that, Sabina with another woman?'

'John, you mean? He didn't care. They don't live as a married couple. He had Johnny to educate and to care for, up on the roof playing football, being a dad. There's absolutely no sign of any sexual abuse, nothing. Johnny was loved, educated and well fed.'

'The whole situation is bloody odd.'

'John's – Sven's – ex-wife is selling her story to the tabloids. She sounds a right bitch. Even I felt sorry for him for about ten minutes, but I got over it. Four kids and every one of them a daughter, the one kid he didn't see was the son he adored. It's weird but I do get the psychology.'

'It's all being packed off to the Fiscal.'

'God help them trying to make sense of it.'

'I don't care who her legal representative is, bring her back in,' said Anderson.

'It's Richard Clearwater.'

'Oh, old stony-face himself. So he has got his son back after four years and he's already returned to work.'

'Naomi insisted that Richard represents Natalie. She's getting the family to pull together.'

'Aye, and I believe that pigs will fly and there'll be no last-minute penalty for Rangers. Where are they?'

'In the interview room. The nice interview room.'

Natalie had changed her suit as well as her demeanour; Anderson could smell the anxiety from her. He was pissed off at her, and he was even more pissed off when he saw the patronizing face of Richard Clearwater, informing him that Natalie was going to review her story in light of the other evidence that had been uncovered. His tone was condescending.

Anderson wanted to ask him if they were keeping an eye on Johnny now they had him back, but instead he smiled sweetly and said, 'Natalie? You wish to review your statement.'

'Yes, I do.' She coughed, rehearsing it in her head. 'I drove up to the car park as usual, but I decided it was too wet to walk Oliver, so he ran round the car park a few times. I cleaned his feet before I let him back into the car.'

'It took you twenty-four hours to think that up?' asked Anderson, sounding disappointed.

'My client is trying to be as helpful as she can,' said Richard.

'So the dog ran around the car park for a couple of hours, three hours. Four maybe?' Anderson tapped the desk with the tip of his pen.

Natalie didn't answer immediately. 'No, it wasn't for that long.'

'Really? From our calculations, that leaves a lot of time unaccounted for.'

'On what are you basing these . . . calculations?' asked Clearwater, his voice dripping sarcasm.

'Evidence,' answered Anderson. 'Want to try again, Natalie?'

Natalie Nascimento glared at him, then continued. 'When I left the car park, I wasn't aware that I had hit something. I heard a bang; I thought it was from under the car, something mechanical, so I drove on. I think that was what Alan Knight heard. I made a U-turn at the edge of the village and drove back to check, right back up to the car park, and came down again to retrace my steps, so to speak. I didn't see the boy, or any trace of him on the way up.' Her eyes clouded slightly. 'There was nothing to suggest I had hit the child.'

'Not even his school books in tatters over the road?'

'I didn't see them. I had my lights on, but no, I didn't. You know sometimes something doesn't register, until you are past it and you realize what you've seen. The boy . . .'

'Danny.'

'Wasn't there. He had been knocked into the hedgerow. The road was dark, he was wearing dark clothes, the light was poor. I drove back down really slowly, thinking I'd see a bit of my car or a dead deer. Then I saw Danny lying in the ditch at the side, but there was no sign of the bike. I saw the books at that point – the headlights caught them on the full beam. So I phoned the ambulance.'

'You admitted that you did it?'

'Yes, of course. The car had marks on it. The damage was examined at the enquiry.'

'Oh, I agree that it was your car that did it, Natalie.' Anderson looked from her to Richard Clearwater. 'But who was driving?'

Natalie remained silent. Then murmured, 'Me.'

'Who was driving the car?' he repeated.

'I was.'

'You do talk a load of twaddle, Natalie. Who is this man?' He showed her the picture of Billy Pimento. 'Just remind me?'

The deep inhale of breath didn't come from Natalie but from Richard.

'OK. No answer to that, so let's go back a bit. The car hit Danny with such force that he ended up in the ditch, but you didn't notice, then you drove away, until you came to your senses and went back up the hill, did a U-turn and came back down again? You expect me to believe that explanation of the delay?'

'There was no delay. Mr Knight was an old drunk.'

'I'm not sure that was true. He was an old man, he liked a drink, but it was early morning. He was out with his dog, Major. He often met you and Oliver, and you often walked together. He knew you, he knew you well. On that morning, he had already spoken to two other people and they both said that he was perfectly sober. You kind of wrote the script for that one yourself. To what end? To disprove that you drove away and came back? Because that was enough of a delay to cause long-term issues for Danny – his brain damage, the build-up of pressure. It would have taken less than ten minutes for an ambulance to get there over the back road. He wouldn't be in the mess he's in now. You took a very long time to do that U-turn and drive back up again.'

'I must protest,' interrupted Richard.

'Oh, you can protest all you want. You have Johnny back and you can't even tell the truth as to what happened in that incident at Killenwood.'

'She has told you what happened,' said Richard.

'No, she hasn't.'

Natalie was quiet, her eyes searching round the room. 'Too much time has passed.'

'Too much time passed for him, his little brain being squashed. Well, who did it? Was it Naomi? Was she driving your car?'

'Oh, don't be ridiculous! Naomi was back at the house . . .' Even as Richard said it, Anderson saw a flash of doubt cross his face as his eyes glanced down at the photograph of Pimento.

'It was me driving,' insisted Natalie.

'You do surprise me. Do you want to see this picture? It's from a newspaper, tabloid, taken at the house you lived in. The local press were quick on the scene, and they snapped this picture of you and Naomi, upset, at your front door. You can see Naomi's face. We blew that picture up; her face is streaked with make-up, as if she'd been out all night.'

Natalie stared straight ahead. Richard Clearwater opened his mouth to complain and then closed it.

'And we listened to your call to the emergency services. You say, "A boy has been hit." Not "I have hit a boy."'

'Hardly relevant. She was under stress,' said Richard, but

Anderson heard the uncertainty in his voice as a whole new interpretation of events was already forming in his mind.

Anderson looked at Natalie and let the silence lie.

'Who was driving?'

She turned away and looked at the wall.

'If it's not enough that she has told you that it was her, she was young and she . . .'

'And now she has a child of her own, don't you, Natalie? I think the McIntoshes deserve the truth.'

There was a long silence broken by a door banging, a laugh in the distance.

Then Natalie turned to Richard. 'I'm so, so sorry. It was Naomi. It's always bloody Naomi. She spent the night with that bloody man. I had to go through that utter shite because she didn't want you to find out, Richard. She didn't want you to find out about Billy, that she was still pissed when she was driving back that morning. She was so drunk. She didn't want you to know, so close to your wedding . . .'

'Billy Pimento?' asked Richard, logic dawning on his face. 'Well, I guess that's nothing new. She's never stopped sleeping with Billy Pimento.'

Anderson and Costello walked into the house at Drymen. Even in the heat of the day, the house was cold now. There was only one car in the driveway; after hearing the confirmation of Naomi's infidelity, Richard had packed his bags and left without a single word and without Johnny.

Anderson knocked quietly on the door of the living room. A thin voice invited them in. Naomi was standing at the window, as still as a statue, a sliver of silhouette against the light.

'Richard has gone. I hope you two are happy.'

'Doing our job,' said Anderson.

Naomi turned. 'I was devastated when Johnny was taken. You know, when there was a chance that he might not have been killed or some harm come to him, there was hope to cling on to. They never found a body, and then there was the thing with that spiritualist woman. I knew he was alive and that gave me a reason to be on the earth.'

'You were his mum. You had all the reasons you could want,' said Anderson. 'He was your child.'

'This is going to sound terrible, but it was easier when he was missing. Now he's back, I have to cope with the reality of the situation. Richard won't talk to me, Billy won't talk to me. For the last four years, I was something of a celebrity, and I thought I was doing some good. But now, I am being treated like a criminal.'

'We have three witnesses who will swear you were still drunk the morning you hit Danny when you were driving Natalie's car. We are treating you like a criminal because you are one.'

'I suppose so. One bad decision in a lifetime of bad decisions. What do you think is going to happen now? What are you going to do?'

'It's being handed over to the Fiscal. All of it. It's up to them to decide, but you were guilty of a hit-and-run that proved nearly fatal.'

'Yeah,' Naomi said, and turned back to the window.

The case was closed. There was going to be the usual party, but nobody felt like celebrating. Johnny Clearwater was very unhappy about being away from the four people that had been his life for the last few years. He was crying himself to sleep without Jussi. He kept talking about his friend at the window.

James Black had passed away in the Queen Elizabeth Hospital, two days after he was taken out of the Maltman House in an ambulance. His daughter Pauline and grandson Joshua stayed at the hospital by his side.

Anderson was thinking his way through the different stories of Martin Callaghan. What did he think he was doing when it started off? Just buying a ring for the tenth anniversary of the day he had met his partner; that had descended into a caper that had nearly led to a break-up. Martin seemed to have learned his lesson, a few hours in casualty after Becs had smacked him in the face with her elbow. But in deference to their ten years together and the unusual precursor to the situation, Martin had decided not to press charges.

In case Becs hit him again.

The team had handed all reports and documentation to the Fiscal; he'd work out who was being prosecuted with what. Anderson didn't envy them that task. Murdoch Wallace was nowhere to be found. The cops, between them, believed that

Wallace had seen this coming, and that he had put things in place well in advance. He was the type not to get caught out. It wasn't easy to disappear, but he had managed it.

'How are you Ruby?'

'I'm good, healing well.'

'Murdo Wallace should have known better than to attack a young fit police officer. You injured him, he bled, and because of that it's a clear-cut case. But overall, did you enjoy your experience with us on the case? Apart from being attacked? If "enjoy" is the right word?' asked Anderson, sipping a Diet Coke, glad that the young police officer had joined them, still a bit woozy, bruised, with her arm in a cast and a dressing on her forehead.

'You do need to have a different sort of heart, though, to be in MIT, don't you, and I think you run a slightly different team – compact, all opinions count, everybody has their voice.' She smiled at him. She really had the most amazing eyes: deep, deep brown velvet. 'But my other half thinks it's too dangerous.'

'Only when you run off with a good idea and don't tell anybody.'

'I thought Costello would be here, but I guess she's not coming.'

'It looks that way.' Anderson took a sip of Coke, enjoying the bubbles on his tongue. 'So, Ruby, usually when somebody makes a comment about having a voice in the police, it's normally an opening to start on about feminism or marginalism. What are you going to do me for – racism?'

She smiled. 'No, sir. I'm not.'

'No need to call me sir.'

'It's Costello.'

'Well, you can't complain about Costello being racist – she'll be as rude to you as she is to the rest of us, so there's nothing racist about it. She's just rude, full stop. But complain if you wish, I won't stop you. There's not much can be done. God knows, we've tried to rein her in a bit.'

'No, sir, that's not what I mean. I think you should read this – just something that I've put together in my free time, while I was in the hospital, bored.'

He took the envelope she offered reluctantly. He liked Ruby; he hoped she wasn't going to turn out to be a player. 'I'll open it back in the office.'

'Please open it now.' Ruby smiled again, picked up her drink and wandered off to see what the good joke in the corner had been. Anderson had a quick chat with Bob Allison who was floating around the room, both men acting with great bonhomie to show that there were no hard feelings on either side, but the envelope was burning his curiosity. As soon as he could, he slipped into his own office, took the single sheet out the envelope and read. The contents were a list of four bullet points and then a very bad photocopy of a newspaper article. He scanned over it, recognizing the names, filling in the blanks for himself. He pulled out his phone and checked the date.

'Fuck.'

Anderson found Costello down at the river; she was standing very still, looking over the water, watching it roll past. He stopped for a moment; the idea floated across his mind that his colleague of twenty years was thinking about jumping. But she wasn't the type. Then he thought how many people realized their friend was exactly the type when it was too late.

Her light-blue shirt, worn like a jacket, was blowing in the breeze coming up off the river. The energy in the tail of the shirt showed how very still she was standing, totally motionless, very deep in thought.

'Hi,' he said, walking up to her while keeping his distance, giving her space.

She didn't turn round. 'Was the party that boring?'

'Warburton was about to appear and give us one of his hearty talks, so I thought I'd leave them to it.'

'That'll be the sausage rolls gone.'

'I think Wyngate is responsible for that. Don't think he gets fed much at home, poor lad.'

'Why did you leave?'

'I've an excuse. I've got the wee guy to see to.'

'Did you follow me because you think I've got nobody at home?'

'No, you're used to that. You've not been yourself lately and Ruby Redding is a good cop. She got hold of a few newspaper reports about your mother and then . . . well, then she noticed the date. It can't be easy.' He took a couple of steps forward, moving to stand alongside her, looking into the Clyde, flowing fast and glinting in the evening sun. 'Nice here, isn't it?' He looked down to the Glenlee, the Rigger, a black silhouette on the cityscape. 'It looks rather cosmopolitan, rather beautiful. We could be anywhere.' He breathed in a lungful of fresh air. The city was cooling down at last. 'A thought struck me when I heard you'd been hit by that car. If you get killed on duty, I'll be the only one crying at your funeral. The rest of the squad, obviously, will have disco lights on top of your headstone so they can dance on your grave.'

'Better have a big lair, then. What did Ruby tell you?'

'She condensed it to one page of highlights and slipped it to me. She didn't say anything to anybody else.'

Costello looked at her watch, at the date, the time. 'It would be about now. I'd been studying at the library. The house was always noisy with Mum in it; she'd be clattering and banging around, singing badly.'

'Was it today?'

'Yes, and I'm the same age now as she was when she died.'

'I knew she had died young, but you never said how. I know she liked a drink.' Anderson's phone went. 'It's Brenda, do you mind if I . . .'

'Go ahead, it's a free world.'

Anderson answered his phone, listened, then said light-heartedly, 'Well, at least that's a start. Look, something's come up. I might be a bit late.' He ended the call. 'Moses has just spoken his first word.'

'What was it? Mama or Dada?'

'Neither. It was Norma.'

'Ungrateful wee shite.' Costello smirked, turning to look at him. She felt the cold wind catch the blonde hairs of her fringe, lifting it, biting the new wound, revealing the old scar on her forehead. It was the first time she'd felt the chill of the wind in days. She looked at her watch again: it was twenty-five past seven on the first of July. That was the day she walked into the house. The smell hit her. There was a long, long dark hall, with a carpet runner down the middle that used to ruffle up behind the front door. It struck her how similar the layout of the house she grew up in was to the flat she lived in now. But that smell drifted into her memory that day and it had never really found its way back out.

She had opened the front door and she knew.

There was a song playing on the radio, 'Unchained Melody',

the version by those two blokes off the television. She had walked into the kitchen and turned the radio off, then she'd gone into the bathroom and there was her mother, in the bath, with the iron, an empty glass of whisky still on the side, balanced carefully. Her mum's eyes were open; her lips retracted, baring her teeth, so she didn't really look like her mother at all. Costello closed the door and went to put the kettle on.

For years her mother had been trying, and failing, to kill herself with drink. So all she did was bring the process forward.

'Did you have anything to eat at the party?' asked Anderson. 'You left pretty early.'

'Yes, I did. Felt queasy, too much of that posh Maisy Daisy ice cream and ricotta bagels. I could murder a Greggs' steak bake.' Costello sighed.

'To be honest, the sausage rolls were cold, so come on, let's go to Greggs and get something decent to eat.'

'Arse.' Costello turned back to the river, the surface chopping slightly as the wind picked up. 'My mum used to say that with my attitude, I'd get nowhere. I think those were the last words I heard her say.'

'Was that just before she passed away?'

'No, it was a long time before that. That was when I stopped listening.'

EPILOGUE

Friday 9th July

Elvie had hired a Land Rover, knowing that there was no point in asking Vik for a loan of the Audi as it would never manage the road up to the top of the glen, on to the moor to the water clock, where she hoped her companion would find some peace. Or at least she would realize that the peace she sought was buried deep inside her and not on a Scottish hillside.

They had set off early. The sky was full of low rumbling clouds, the long, seemingly endless stream of sunny days now a distant memory. The drive north took them through the sleepy city, along the loch side and then up to Strachur before the Land Rover turned up the rocky track.

There had been silence most of the way, Carol making the odd comment about the scenery, asking Elvie about the weather and how long did she think it was going to take. Elvie replied that it would take as long as it would take, and then Carol fell silent again, her head leaning against the side window as the vehicle climbed and wound its way round the upper part of the glen.

'I recall this noise,' she said, keeping her eyes closed. 'I recall the noise of the engine moving up this way. He drove one of these, didn't he?'

'Yes, it was a much older one than this, but they all sound the same,' replied Elvie.

Carol had her eyes open now, watching the moor, watching the sky, a cool, dark sky coming down on them. They seemed to be driving up to the clouds.

'Can you stop here?'

Elvie stopped the Land Rover, turned the engine off. She had seen this sight many times before, at the crest of the hill where the road ran down to the camp built by the Italian prisoners of war. There was a much fainter track, largely overgrown now, its course still visible by the different shades of green.

Carol put her hand on the door handle, looking out of the front, then the side, then towards Elvie, who stayed looking ahead.

The glen was a wide open space that went on forever. Carol saw a couple of deer high on the hill in the distance. A tear rolled down her cheek, knowing what had happened here. Lorna, the one who ran across this moor in the middle of the night and crashed on to the roof of the car. She had nearly made it but had died in Elvie's arms.

Carol put her hand out and touched her companion's hand. 'You were only looking for your sister. You weren't interested in me.'

'I wasn't particularly, but the man who put you in that box would have known I was there if I had let you out. So I didn't. It was the only way I could get out to get help. It might have seemed harsh at the time but it was logical.'

'I thought I was going to die.'

'You had been thinking that for weeks.'

'Did you really try to save me?'

'I got out and got help. If I hadn't, you'd have died of septicaemia or hunger. I came to see you in hospital. I saw your mum visit you. I spoke to her.'

Carol looked back at the deer. 'I'd forgotten you were there when Lorna died.'

'I was. She fell and broke her neck.'

'Yes, she did.'

'Are you OK?'

'I'm going to go out here. Try to walk down to the water clock.'

'Good.'

'Do you think I can make it?'

'You can do anything you want to do. It's a free world now.'

'It's not a free world for me.'

'It is. Of course it is. You see that coffin lid over your face everywhere you go, but it's in your head, nowhere else.'

'You are very direct.'

'I'm not the one who can't go outside because they are scared of something that isn't there.'

'Is that the house?' Carol asked.

'It is indeed. That circle in the front – that's what's left of the water clock.'

'The water clock. All those closed doors, the water pressure rising and falling.' Carol fought back the tears.

'Yes, I ran through those tunnels a few times. I got very wet trying to get under the door before the slab came down and crushed me.'

'You were looking for me.'

'No, I was looking for Sophie.'

'But you found me.'

'I didn't find her.'

Carol slumped back in the seat as if the conversation had exhausted her. 'I do need to walk down there. I need to walk out again on my own two feet, not carried out on a stretcher. I remember the daylight. And the body bags.'

'Survivor's guilt, as an emotion, is useless. So go. I'll wait here.'

And Carol walked. She turned for a moment and waved back at Elvie, smiling through her tears, resuming her journey to a confident new life.

Elvie gave her the thumbs up. A thousand words spoken in a silent conversation.